Welcome to THE W[barcode obscured] W9-APR-651

Praise for:

From the Two Rivers and *To the Blight*
Parts One and Two of
The Eye of the World

VOYA Outstanding Books of the Year

American Library Association
Best Book for Young Adults

"A major piece of fantasy." —*Chicago Sun-Times*

"This richly detailed fantasy presents a fully realized complex adventure which will appeal to fans of classic quests. Recommended." —*Library Journal*

"This exciting fantasy adventure tale chronicles the coming of age of Rand. Jordan's fantasy world is well presented, the characterizations are precise, and the action is fast paced with a great many hairbreadth escapes." —*KLIATT*

"An excitiing story. The reader is drawn in early and kept there until the last page. There is adventure and mystery and dark things that move in the night—a combination of Robin Hood and Stephen King that is hard to resist."
—*Milwaukee Sentinel*

"A powerful novel. A fantasy epic. As the novel progresses, the young heros develop new talents, a different one for each." —*Locus*

THE WHEEL OF TIME
by Robert Jordan

To the Blight

Part Two of
The Eye of the World

The Beginning of
The Wheel of Time

Robert Jordan

STARSCAPE

A TOM DOHERTY ASSOCIATES BOOK
NEW YORK

Note: If you purchased this book without a cover you should be aware that this book is stolen property. It was reported as "unsold and destroyed" to the publisher, and neither the author nor the publisher has received any payment for this "stripped book."

This is a work of fiction. All the characters and events portrayed in this novel are either fictitious or are used fictitiously.

TO THE BLIGHT: The Eye of the World, Part 2

Copyright © 1990 Robert Jordan.
Glossary copyright © 2002 by Bandersnatch Group, Inc.

All rights reserved, including the right to reproduce this book, or portions thereof, in any form.

Maps by Ellisa Mitchell
Interior Illustrations used with permission by Wizards of the Coast, Inc.
Copyright © 2001 Wizards of the Coast, Inc
Additional interior illustrations by Sally Wern Comport
Interior ornament art by Matthew C. Nielson
Cover art by Charles Keegan

A Starscape Book
Published by Tom Doherty Associates, LLC
175 Fifth Avenue
New York, NY 10010

www.starscapebooks.com

ISBN: 0-765-34221-9

First Starscape edition: January 2002

Printed in the United States of America

0 9 8 7 6 5 4 3 2 1

To Harriet
Heart of my heart,
Light of my life,
Forever.

CONTENTS

And the Shadow fell upon the Land, and the World was riven stone from stone. The oceans fled, and the mountains were swallowed up, and the nations were scattered to the eight corners of the World. The moon was as blood, and the sun was as ashes. The seas boiled, and the living envied the dead. All was shattered, and all but memory lost, and one memory above all others, of him who brought the Shadow and the Breaking of the World. And him they named Dragon.

> (from *Aleth nin Taerin alta Camora,*
> *The Breaking of the World.*
> Author unknown, the Fourth Age)

And it came to pass in those days, as it had come before and would come again, that the Dark lay heavy on the land and weighed down the hearts of men, and the green things failed, and hope died. And men cried out to the Creator, saying, O Light of the Heavens, Light of the World, let the Promised One be born of the mountain, according to the prophecies, as he was in ages past and will be in ages to come. Let the Prince of the Morning sing to the land that green things will grow and the valleys give forth lambs. Let the arm of the Lord of the Dawn shelter us from the Dark, and the great sword of justice defend us. Let the Dragon ride again on the winds of time.

> (from *Charal Drianaan te Calamon,*
> *The Cycle of the Dragon.*
> Author unknown, the Fourth Age)

To the Blight

CHAPTER
24

Flight Down the Arinelle

Water dripped in the distance, hollow splashes echoing and reechoing, losing their source forever. There were stone bridges and railless ramps everywhere, all sprouting off from broad, flat-topped stone spires, all polished and smooth and streaked with red and gold. Level on level, the maze stretched up and down through the murk, without any apparent beginning or end. Every bridge led to a spire, every ramp to another spire, other bridges. Whatever direction Rand looked, as far as his eye could make out in the dimness it was the same, above as well as below. There was not enough light to see clearly, and he was almost glad of it. Some of those ramps led to platforms that had to be directly above the ones below. He could not see the base of any of them. He pressed, seeking freedom, knowing it was an illusion. Everything was illusion.

He knew the illusion; he had followed it too many times not to know. However far he went, up or down or in any direction, there was only the shiny stone. Stone, but the dankness of deep, fresh-turned earth permeated the air, and the sickly sweetness of decay. The smell of a grave opened out of its time. He tried not to breathe, but the smell filled his nostrils. It clung to his skin like oil.

A flicker of motion caught his eye, and he froze where he was, half crouched against the polished guardwall around one of the spire tops. It was no hiding place. From a thousand places a watcher could have seen him. Shadow filled the air, but there were no deeper shadows in which to hide. The light did not come from lamps, or lanterns, or torches; it was simply there, such as it was, as if it seeped out of the air. Enough by which to see, after a fashion; enough by which to be seen. But stillness gave a little protection.

The movement came again, and now it was clear. A man striding up a distant ramp, careless of the lack of railings and the drop to nothing below. The man's cloak rippled with his stately haste, and his head turned, searching, searching. The distance was too far for Rand to see more than the shape in the murk, but he did not need to be closer to know the cloak was the red of fresh blood, that the searching eyes blazed like two furnaces.

He tried tracing the maze with his eyes, to see how many connections Ba'alzamon needed before reaching him, then gave it up as useless. Distances were deceiving here, another lesson he had learned. What seemed far away might be reached by turning a corner; what appeared close could be out of reach altogether. The only thing to do, as it had been from the beginning, was to keep moving. Keep moving, and not think. Thinking was dangerous, he knew.

Yet, as he turned away from Ba'alzamon's distant form, he could not help wondering about Mat. Was Mat somewhere in this maze? *Or are there two mazes, two Ba'alzamons?* His mind skittered away from that; it was too dreadful to dwell on. *Is this like Baerlon? Then why can't he find me?* That was a little better. A small comfort. *Comfort? Blood and ashes, where's the comfort in it?*

There had been two or three close brushes, though he could not remember them clearly, but for a long, long time—how long?—he had run while Ba'alzamon vainly pursued. Was this like Baerlon, or was it only a nightmare, only a dream like other men's dreams?

For an instant, then—just for the length of time it took to take a breath—he knew why it was dangerous to think, what it was dangerous to think about. As it had before, every time he allowed himself to think of what surrounded him as a dream, the air shimmered, clouding his eyes. It turned to jell, holding him. Just for an instant.

The gritty heat prickled his skin, and his throat had long since gone dry as he trotted down the thorn-hedge maze. How long had it been now? His sweat evaporated before it had a chance to bead, and his eyes burned. Overhead—and not too far overhead, at that—boiled furious, steely clouds streaked with black, but not a breath of air stirred in the maze. For a moment he thought it had been different, but the thought evaporated in the heat. He had been here a long time. It was dangerous to think, he knew that.

Smooth stones, pale and rounded, made a sketchy pavement, half buried in the bone-dry dust that rose in puffs at even his lightest step. It tickled his nose, threatening a sneeze that might give him away; when he tried to breathe through his mouth, dust clogged his throat until he choked.

This was a dangerous place; he knew that, too. Ahead of him he could see three openings in the high wall of thorns, then the way curved out of sight. Ba'alzamon could be approaching any one of those corners at that very moment. There had been two or three encounters already, though he could not remember much beyond that they had happened and he had escaped . . . somehow. Dangerous to think too much.

Panting in the heat, he stopped to examine the maze wall. Thickly woven thorn bushes, brown and dead-looking, with cruel black thorns like inch-long hooks. Too tall to see over, too dense to see through. Gingerly he touched the wall, and gasped. Despite all his care, a thorn pierced his finger, burning like a hot needle. He stumbled back, his heels catching on the stones, shaking his hand and scattering thick drops of blood. The burn began to subside, but his whole hand throbbed.

Abruptly he forgot the pain. His heel had overturned one of the smooth stones, kicked it out of the dry ground. He stared at it, and empty eye sockets stared back. A skull. A human skull. He looked along the pathway at all the smooth, pale stones, all exactly alike. He shifted his feet hastily, but he could not move without walking on them, and he could not stay still without standing on them. A stray thought took vague shape, that things might not be what they seemed, but he pushed it down ruthlessly. Thinking was dangerous here.

He took a shaky hold on himself. Staying in one place was dangerous, too. That was one of the things he knew dimly but

with certainty. The flow of blood from his finger had dwindled
to a slow drip, and the throb was almost gone. Sucking his fingertip, he started down the path in the direction he happened
to be facing. One way was as good as another in here.

Now he remembered hearing once that you could get out of a
maze by always turning in the same direction. At the first opening in the wall of thorns he turned right, then right again at the
next. And found himself face-to-face with Ba'alzamon.

Surprise flitted across Ba'alzamon's face, and his blood-red
cloak settled as he stopped short. Flames soared in his eyes, but
in the heat of the maze Rand barely felt them.

"How long do you think you can evade me, boy? How long
do you think you can evade your fate? You are mine!"

Stumbling back, Rand wondered why he was fumbling at his
belt, as if for a sword. "Light help me," he muttered. "Light
help me." He could not remember what it meant.

"The Light will not help you, boy, and the Eye of the World
will not serve you. You are my hound, and if you will not
course at my command, I will strangle you with the corpse of
the Great Serpent!"

Ba'alzamon stretched out his hand, and suddenly Rand knew
a way to escape, a misty, half-formed memory that screamed
danger, but nothing to the danger of being touched by the Dark
One.

"A dream!" Rand shouted. "This is a dream!"

Ba'alzamon's eyes began to widen, in surprise or anger or
both, then the air shimmered, and his features blurred, and
faded.

Rand turned about in one spot, staring. Staring at his own
image thrown back at him a thousandfold. Ten thousandfold.
Above was blackness, and blackness below, but all around him
stood mirrors, mirrors set at every angle, mirrors as far as he
could see, all showing him, crouched and turning, staring wide-
eyed and frightened.

A red blur drifted across the mirrors. He spun, trying to
catch it, but in every mirror it drifted behind his own image and
vanished. Then it was back again, but not as a blur. Ba'alzamon strode across the mirrors, ten thousand Ba'alzamons,
searching, crossing and recrossing the silvery mirrors.

He found himself staring at the reflection of his own face,

pale and shivering in the knife-edge cold. Ba'alzamon's image
grew behind his, staring at him; not seeing, but staring still. In
every mirror, the flames of Ba'alzamon's face raged behind
him, enveloping, consuming, merging. He wanted to scream,
but his throat was frozen. There was only one face in those
endless mirrors. His own face. Ba'alzamon's face. One face.

Rand jerked, and opened his eyes. Darkness, lessened only
slightly by a pale light. Barely breathing, he moved nothing
except his eyes. A rough wool blanket covered him to his
shoulders, and his head was cradled on his arms. He could feel
smooth wooden planks under his hands. Deck planks. Rigging
creaked in the night. He let out a long breath. He was on the
Spray. It was over . . . for another night, at least.

Without thinking he put his finger in his mouth. At the taste
of blood, he stopped breathing. Slowly he put his hand close to
his face, to where he could see in the dim moonlight, to where
he could watch the bead of blood form on his fingertip. Blood
from the prick of a thorn.

The *Spray* made haste slowly down the Arinelle. The wind
came strong, but from directions that made the sails useless.
With all Captain Domon's demand for speed, the vessel crept
along. By night a man in the bows cast a tallowed lead by lantern light, calling back the depth to the steersman, while the
current carried her downriver against the wind with the sweeps
pulled in. There were no rocks to fear in the Arinelle, but shal-
lows and shoals there were aplenty, where a boat could go hard
aground to remain, bows and more dug into the mud, until help
came. If it was help that came first. By day the sweeps worked
from sunrise to sunset, but the wind fought them as if it wanted
to push the boat back upriver.

They did not put in to shore, neither by day nor by night.
Bayle Domon drove boat and crew alike hard, railing at the
contrary winds, cursing the slow pace. He blistered the crew for
sluggards at the oars and flayed them with his tongue for every
mishandled line, his low, hard voice painting Trollocs ten feet
tall among them on the deck, ripping out their throats. For two
days that was enough to send every man leaping. Then the
shock of the Trolloc attack began to fade, and men began to

mutter about an hour to stretch their legs ashore, and about the dangers of running downriver in the dark.

The crew kept their grumbles quiet, watching out of the corners of their eyes to make sure Captain Domon was not close enough to hear, but he seemed to hear everything said on his boat. Each time the grumblings began, he silently brought out the long, scythe-like sword and cruelly hooked axe that had been found on the deck after the attack. He would hang them on the mast for an hour, and those who had been wounded would finger their bandages, and the mutterings quieted . . . for a day or so, at least, until one or another of the crew began thinking once more that surely they had left the Trollocs far behind by now, and the cycle began yet again.

Rand noticed that Thom Merrilin stayed clear of the crew when they began whispering together and frowning, though usually he was slapping backs and telling jokes and exchanging banter in a way that put a grin on even the hardest-working man. Thom watched those secretive mutters with a wary eye while appearing to be absorbed in lighting his long-stemmed pipe, or tuning his harp, or almost anything except paying any mind at all to the crew. Rand did not understand why. It was not the three who had come aboard chased by Trollocs whom the crew seemed to blame, but rather Floran Gelb.

For the first day or two Gelb's wiry figure could almost always be found addressing any crewman he could corner, telling his version of the night Rand and the others came on board. Gelb's manner slid from bluster to whines and back again, and his lip always curled when he pointed to Thom or Mat, or especially Rand, trying to lay the blame on them.

"They're strangers," Gelb pleaded, quietly and with an eye out for the captain. "What do we know of them? The Trollocs came with them, that's what we know. They're in league."

"Fortune, Gelb, stow it," growled a man with his hair in a pigtail and a small blue star tattooed on his cheek. He did not look at Gelb as he coiled a line on deck, working it in with his bare toes. All the sailors went barefoot despite the cold; boots could slip on a wet deck. "You'd call your mother Darkfriend if it'd let you slack. Get away from me!" He spat on Gelb's foot and went back to the line.

All the crew remembered the watch Gelb had not kept, and

the pigtailed man's was the politest response he got. No one even wanted to work with him. Gelb found himself relegated to solitary tasks, all of them filthy, such as scrubbing the galley's greasy pots, or crawling into the bilges on his belly to search for leaks among years of slime. Soon he stopped talking to anyone. His shoulders took on a defensive hunch, and injured silence became his stance—the more people watching, the more injured, though it earned him no more than a grunt. When Gelb's eyes fell on Rand, however, or on Mat or Thom, murder flashed across his long-nosed face.

When Rand mentioned to Mat that Gelb would cause them trouble sooner or later, Mat looked around the boat, saying, "Can we trust any of them? Any at all?" Then he went off to find a place where he could be alone, or as alone as he could get on a boat less than thirty paces from its raised bow to the sternpost where the steering oars were mounted. Mat had spent too much time alone since the night at Shadar Logoth; brooding, as Rand saw it.

Thom said, "Trouble won't come from Gelb, boy, if it comes. Not yet, at least. None of the crew will back him, and he hasn't the nerve to try anything alone. But the others, now . . . ? Domon almost seems to think the Trollocs are chasing him, personally, but the rest are beginning to think the danger is past. They might just decide they have had enough. They're on the edge of it, as it is." He hitched his patch-covered cloak, and Rand had the feeling he was checking his hidden knives—his second-best set. "If they mutiny, boy, they won't leave passengers behind to tell the tale. The Queen's Writ might not have much force this far from Caemlyn, but even a village mayor will do something about that." That was when Rand, too, began trying not to be noticed when he watched the crewmen.

Thom did his part in diverting the crew from thoughts of mutiny. He told stories, with all the flourishes, every morning and every night, and in between he played any song they requested. To support the notion that Rand and Mat wanted to be apprentice gleemen, he set aside a time each day for lessons, and that was an entertainment for the crew, as well. He would not let either of them touch his harp, of course, and their sessions with the flute produced pained winces, in the beginning, at least, and laughter from the crew even while they were covering their ears.

He taught the boys some of the easier stories, a little simple tumbling, and, of course, juggling. Mat complained about what Thom demanded of them, but Thom blew out his mustaches and glared right back.

"I don't know how to play at teaching, boy. I either teach a thing, or I don't. Now! Even a country bumpkin ought to be able to do a simple handstand. Up you go."

Crewmen who were not working always gathered, squatting in a circle around the three. Some even tried their hand at the lessons Thom taught, laughing at their own fumblings. Gelb stood alone and watched it all darkly, hating them all.

A good part of each day Rand spent leaning on the railing, staring at the shore. It was not that he really expected to see Egwene or any of the others suddenly appear on the riverbank, but the boat traveled so slowly that he sometimes hoped for it. They could catch up without riding too hard. If they had escaped. If they were still alive.

The river rolled on without any sign of life, nor any boat to be seen except the *Spray*. But that was not to say there was nothing to see, and wonder at. In the middle of the first day, the Arinelle ran between high bluffs that stretched for half a mile on either side. For that whole length the stone had been cut into figures, men and women a hundred feet tall, with crowns proclaiming them kings and queens. No two were alike in that royal procession, and long years separated the first from the last. Wind and rain had worn those at the north end smooth and almost featureless, with faces and details becoming more distinct as they went south. The river lapped around the statues' feet, feet washed to smooth nubs, those that were not gone completely. *How long have they stood there*, Rand wondered. *How long for the river to wear away so much stone?* None of the crew so much as looked up from their work, they had seen the ancient carvings so many times before.

Another time, when the eastward shore had become flat grassland again, broken only occasionally by thickets, the sun glinted off something in the distance. "What can that be?" Rand wondered aloud. "It looks like metal."

Captain Domon was walking by, and he paused, squinting

toward the glint. "It do be metal," he said. His words still ran together, but Rand had come to understand without having to puzzle it out. "A tower of metal. I have seen it close up, and I know. River traders use it as a marker. We be ten days from Whitebridge at the rate we go."

"A metal tower?" Rand said, and Mat, sitting cross-legged with his back against a barrel, roused from his brooding to listen.

The captain nodded. "Aye. Shining steel, by the look and feel of it, but no a spot of rust. Two hundred feet high, it be, as big around as a house, with no a mark on it and never an opening to be found."

"I'll bet there's treasure inside," Mat said. He stood up and stared toward the far tower as the river carried the *Spray* beyond it. "A thing like that must have been made to protect something valuable."

"Mayhap, lad," the captain rumbled. "There be stranger things in the world than this, though. On Tremalking, one of the Sea Folk's isles, there be a stone hand fifty feet high sticking out of a hill, clutching a crystal sphere as big as this vessel. There be treasure under that hill if there be treasure anywhere, but the island people want no part of digging there, and the Sea Folk care for naught but sailing their ships and searching for the Coramoor, their Chosen One."

"I'd dig," Mat said. "How far is this . . . Tremalking?" A clump of trees slid in front of the shining tower, but he stared as if he could see it yet.

Captain Domon shook his head. "No, lad, it no be the treasure that makes for seeing the world. If you find yourself a fistful of gold, or some dead king's jewels, all well and good, but it be the strangeness you see that pulls you to the next horizon. In Tanchico—that be a port on the Aryth Ocean—part of the Panarch's Palace were built in the Age of Legends, so it be said. There be a wall there with a frieze showing animals no man living has ever seen."

"Any child can draw an animal nobody's ever seen," Rand said, and the captain chuckled.

"Aye, lad, so they can. But can a child make the bones of those animals? In Tanchico they have them, all fastened together like the animal was. They stand in a part of the Pan-

arch's Palace where any can enter and see. The Breaking left a
thousand wonders behind, and there been half a dozen empires
or more since, some rivaling Artur Hawkwing's, every one
leaving things to see and find. Lightsticks and razorlace and
heartstone. A crystal lattice covering an island, and it hums
when the moon is up. A mountain hollowed into a bowl, and in
its center, a silver spike a hundred spans high, and any who
comes within a mile of it, dies. Rusted ruins, and broken bits,
and things found on the bottom of the sea, things not even the
oldest books know the meaning of. I've gathered a few, myself.
Things you never dreamed of, in more places than you can see
in ten lifetimes. That be the strangeness that will draw you on."

"We used to dig up bones in the Sand Hills," Rand said
slowly. "Strange bones. There was part of a fish—I think it was
a fish—as big as this boat, once. Some said it was bad luck,
digging in the hills."

The captain eyed him shrewdly. "You thinking about home
already, lad, and you just set out in the world? The world will
put a hook in your mouth. You'll set off chasing the sunset, you
wait and see . . . and if you ever go back, your village'll no be
big enough to hold you."

"No!" He gave a start. How long had it been since he had
thought of home, of Emond's Field? And what of Tam? It had
to be days. It felt like months. "I will go home, one day, when
I can. I'll raise sheep, like . . . like my father, and if I never
leave again it will be too soon. Isn't that right, Mat? As soon as
we can we're going home and forget all this even exists."

With a visible effort Mat pulled away from staring upriver
after the vanished tower. "What? Oh. Yes, of course. We'll go
home. Of course." As he turned to go, Rand heard him muttering under his breath. "I'll bet he just doesn't want anybody
else going after the treasure." He did not seem to realize he
had spoken aloud.

Four days into their trip downriver found Rand atop the
mast, sitting on the blunt end with his legs wrapped in the
stays. The *Spray* rolled gently on the river, but fifty feet above
the water that easy roll made the top of the mast sway back and
forth through wide arcs. He threw back his head and laughed
into the wind that blew in his face.

The oars were out, and from here the boat looked like some

twelve-legged spider creeping down the Arinelle. He had been as high as this before, in trees back in the Two Rivers, but this time there were no branches to block his view. Everything on deck, the sailors at the sweeps, men on their knees scrubbing the deck with smoothstones, men doing things with lines and hatchcovers, looked so odd when seen from right overhead, all squat and foreshortened, that he had spent an hour just staring at them and chuckling.

He still chuckled whenever he looked down at them, but now he was staring at the riverbanks flowing by. That was the way it seemed, as if he were still—except for the swaying back and forth, of course—and the banks slid slowly by, trees and hills marching along to either side. He was still, and the whole world moved past him.

On sudden impulse he unwrapped his legs from the stays bracing the mast and held his arms and legs out to either side, balancing against the sway. For three complete arcs he kept his balance like that, then suddenly it was gone. Arms and legs windmilling, he toppled forward and grabbed the forestay. Legs splayed to either side of the mast, nothing holding him to his precarious perch but his two hands on the stay, he laughed. Gulping huge breaths of the fresh, cold wind, he laughed with the exhilaration of it.

"Lad," came Thom's hoarse voice. "Lad, if you're trying to break your fool neck, don't do it by falling on me."

Rand looked down. Thom clung to the ratlines just below him, staring up the last few feet grimly. Like Rand, the gleeman had left his cloak below. "Thom," he said delightedly. "Thom, when did you come up here?"

"When you wouldn't pay any attention to people shouting at you. Burn me, boy, you've got everybody thinking you've gone mad."

He looked down and was surprised to see all the faces staring up at him. Only Mat, sitting cross-legged up in the bows with his back to the mast, was not looking at him. Even the men at the oars had their eyes raised, letting their stroke go ragged. And no one was berating them for it. Rand twisted his head around to look under his arm at the stern. Captain Domon stood by the steering oar, ham-like fists on his hips, glaring at him atop the mast. He turned back to grin at Thom. "You want me to come down, then?"

Thom nodded vigorously. "I would appreciate it greatly."

"All right." Shifting his grip on the forestay, he sprang forward off the mast top. He heard Thom bite off an oath as his fall was cut short and he dangled from the forestay by his hands. The gleeman scowled at him, one hand half stretched out to catch him. He grinned at Thom again. "I'm going down now."

Swinging his legs up, he hooked one knee over the thick line that ran from the mast to the bow, then caught it in the crook of his elbow and let go with his hands. Slowly, then with increasing speed, he slid down. Just short of the bow he dropped to his feet on the deck right in front of Mat, took one step to catch his balance, and turned to face the boat with arms spread wide, the way Thom did after a tumbling trick.

Scattered clapping rose from the crew, but he was looking down at Mat in surprise, and at what Mat held, hidden from everyone else by his body. A curved dagger with a gold scabbard worked in strange symbols. Fine gold wire wrapped the hilt, which was capped by a ruby as big as Rand's thumbnail, and the quillons were golden-scaled serpents baring their fangs.

Mat continued to slide the dagger in and out of its sheath for a moment. Still playing with the dagger he raised his head slowly; his eyes had a faraway look. Suddenly they focused on Rand, and he gave a start and stuffed the dagger under his coat.

Rand squatted on his heels, with his arms crossed on his knees. "Where did you get that?" Mat said nothing, looking quickly to see if anyone else was close by. They were alone, for a wonder. "You didn't take it from Shadar Logoth, did you?"

Mat stared at him. "It's your fault. Yours and Perrin's. The two of you pulled me away from the treasure, and I had it in my hand. Mordeth didn't give it to me. I took it, so Moiraine's warnings about his gifts don't count. You won't tell anybody, Rand. They might try to steal it."

"I won't tell anybody," Rand said. "I think Captain Domon is honest, but I wouldn't put anything past the rest of them, especially Gelb."

"Not anybody," Mat insisted. "Not Domon, not Thom, not anybody. We're the only two left from Emond's Field, Rand. We can't afford to trust anybody else."

"They're alive, Mat. Egwene, and Perrin. I know they're alive." Mat looked ashamed. "I'll keep your secret, though. Just the two of us. At least we don't have to worry about money now. We can sell it for enough to travel to Tar Valon like kings."

"Of course," Mat said after a minute. "If we have to. Just don't tell anybody until I say so."

"I said I wouldn't. Listen, have you had any more dreams since we came on the boat? Like in Baerlon? This is the first chance I've had to ask without six people listening."

Mat turned his head away, giving him a sidelong look. "Maybe."

"What do you mean, maybe? Either you have or you haven't."

"All right, all right, I have. I don't want to talk about it. I don't even want to think about it. It doesn't do any good."

Before either of them could say more Thom came striding up the deck, his cloak over his arm. The wind whipped his white hair about, and his long mustaches seemed to bristle. "I managed to convince the captain you aren't crazy," he announced, "that it was part of your training." He caught hold of the forestay and shook it. "That fool stunt of yours, sliding down the rope, helped, but you are lucky you didn't break your fool neck."

Rand's eyes went to the forestay and followed it up to the top of the mast, and as they did his mouth dropped open. He *had* slid down that. And he had been sitting on top of. . . .

Suddenly he could see himself up there, arms and legs spread wide. He sat down hard, and barely caught himself short of ending up flat on his back. Thom was looking at him thoughtfully.

"I didn't know you had such a good head for heights, lad. We might be able to play in Illian, or Ebou Dar, or even Tear. People in the big cities in the south like tightrope walkers and slackwire artists."

"We're going to—" At the last minute Rand remembered to look around for anyone close enough to overhear. Several of the crew were watching them, including Gelb, glaring as usual, but none could hear what he was saying. "To Tar Valon," he finished. Mat shrugged as if it were all the same to him where they went.

"At the moment, lad," Thom said, settling down beside them, "but tomorrow . . . who knows? That's the way with a gleeman's life." He took a handful of colored balls from one of his wide sleeves. "Since I have you down out of the air, we'll work on the triple crossover."

Rand's gaze drifted to the top of the mast, and he shivered. *What's happening to me? Light, what?* He had to find out. He had to get to Tar Valon before he really did go mad.

Thom Merrilin

CHAPTER
25

The Traveling People

B ela walked along placidly under the weak sun as if the three wolves trotting not far off were only village dogs, but the way she rolled her eyes at them from time to time, showing white all the way around, indicated she felt nothing of the sort. Egwene, on the mare's back, was just as bad. She watched the wolves constantly from the corner of her eye, and sometimes she twisted in the saddle to look around. Perrin was sure she was hunting for the rest of the pack, though she denied it angrily when he suggested as much, denied being afraid of the wolves that paced them, denied worrying about the rest of the pack or what it was up to. She denied, and went right on looking, tight-eyed and wetting her lips uneasily.

The rest of the pack was far distant; he could have told her that. *What good, even if she believed me? Especially if she did.* He was of no mind to open that basket of snakes until he had to. He did not want to think about *how* he knew. The fur-clad man loped ahead of them, sometimes looking almost like a wolf himself, and he never looked around when Dapple, Hopper, and Wind appeared, but he knew, too.

The Emond's Fielders had wakened at dawn that first morning to find Elyas cooking more rabbit and watching them over his full beard without much expression. Except for Dapple, Hopper, and Wind, no wolves were to be seen. In the pale, early daylight, deep shade still lingered under the big oak, and the bare trees beyond looked like fingers stripped to the bone.

"They're around," Elyas answered when Egwene asked
where the rest of the pack had gone. "Close enough to help, if
need be. Far enough off to avoid any human trouble we get
into. Sooner or later there's always trouble when there's two
humans together. If we need them, they'll be there."

Something tickled the back of Perrin's mind as he ripped free
a bite of roast rabbit. A direction, vaguely sensed. *Of course!
That's where they.* . . . The hot juices in his mouth abruptly lost
all taste. He picked at the tubers Elyas had cooked in the
coals—they tasted something like turnips—but his appetite was
gone.

When they had started out Egwene insisted that everyone
take a turn riding, and Perrin did not even bother to argue.

"First turn is yours," he told her.

She nodded. "And then you, Elyas."

"My own legs are good enough for me," Elyas said. He
looked at Bela, and the mare rolled her eyes as if he were one
of the wolves. "Besides, I don't think she wants me riding her."

"That's nonsense," Egwene replied firmly: "There is no
point in being stubborn about it. The sensible thing is for everybody to ride sometimes. According to you we have a long way
still to go."

"I said no, girl."

She took a deep breath, and Perrin was wondering if she
would succeed in bullying Elyas the way she did him, when he
realized she was standing there with her mouth open, not saying a word. Elyas was looking at her, just looking, with those
yellow wolf's eyes. Egwene stepped back from the raw-boned
man, and licked her lips, and stepped back again. Before Elyas
turned away, she had backed all the way to Bela and scrambled
up onto the mare's back. As the man turned to lead them
south, Perrin thought his grin was a good deal like a wolf's,
too.

For three days they traveled in that manner, walking and riding south and east all day, stopping only when twilight
thickened. Elyas seemed to scorn the haste of city men, but he
did not believe in wasting time when there was somewhere to
go.

The three wolves were seldom seen. Each night they came to
the fire for a time, and sometimes in the day they showed them-

selves briefly, appearing close at hand when least expected and vanishing in the same manner. Perrin knew they were out there, though, and where. He knew when they were scouting the path ahead and when they were watching the backtrail. He knew when they left the pack's usual hunting grounds, and Dapple sent the pack back to wait for her. Sometimes the three that remained faded from his mind, but long before they were close enough to see again, he was aware of them returning. Even when the trees dwindled to wide-scattered groves separated by great swathes of winter-dead grass, they were as ghosts when they did not want to be seen, but he could have pointed a finger straight at them at any time. He did not know how he knew, and he tried to convince himself that it was just his imagination playing tricks, but it did no good. Just as Elyas knew, he knew.

He tried not thinking about wolves, but they crept into his thoughts all the same. He had not dreamed about Ba'alzamon since meeting Elyas and the wolves. His dreams, as much as he remembered of them on waking, were of everyday things, just as he might have dreamed at home . . . before Baerlon . . . before Winternight. Normal dreams—with one addition. In every dream he remembered there was a point where he straightened from Master Luhhan's forge to wipe the sweat from his face, or turned from dancing with the village girls on the Green, or lifted his head from a book in front of the fireplace, and whether he was outside or under a roof, there was a wolf close to hand. Always the wolf's back was to him, and always he knew—in the dreams it seemed the normal course of things, even at Alsbet Luhhan's dinner table—that the wolf's yellow eyes were watching for what might come, guarding against what might come. Only when he was awake did the dreams seem strange.

Three days they journeyed, with Dapple, Hopper, and Wind bringing them rabbits and squirrels, and Elyas pointing out plants, few of which Perrin recognized, as good to eat. Once a rabbit burst out almost from under Bela's hooves; before Perrin could get a stone in his sling, Elyas skewered it with his long knife at twenty paces. Another time Elyas brought down a fat pheasant, on the wing, with his bow. They ate far better than they had when on their own, but Perrin would as soon have gone back on short rations if it had meant different company. He was not sure how Egwene felt, but he would have been willing to go hungry if he could do it without the wolves. Three days, into the afternoon.

A stand of trees lay ahead, larger than most they had seen, a good four miles across. The sun sat low in the western sky, pushing slanted shadows off to their right, and the wind was picking up. Perrin felt the wolves give over quartering behind them and start forward, not hurrying. They had smelled and seen nothing dangerous. Egwene was taking her turn on Bela. It was time to start looking for a camp for the night, and the big copse would serve the purpose well.

As they came close to the trees, three mastiffs burst from cover, broad-muzzled dogs as tall as the wolves and even heavier, teeth bared in loud, rumbling snarls. They stopped short as soon as they were in the open, but no more than thirty feet separated them from the three people, and their dark eyes kindled with a killing light.

Bela, already on edge from the wolves, whinnied and almost unseated Egwene, but Perrin had his sling whirling around his head in an instant. No need to use the axe on dogs; a stone in the ribs would send the worst dog running.

Elyas waved a hand at him without taking his eyes from the stiff-legged dogs. "Hssst! None of that now!"

Perrin gave him a puzzled frown, but let the sling slow its spin and finally fall to his side. Egwene managed to get Bela under control; she and the mare both watched the dogs warily.

The mastiffs' hackles stood stiff, and their ears were laid back, and their growls sounded like earthquakes. Abruptly Elyas raised one finger shoulder high and whistled, a long, shrill whistle that rose higher and higher and did not end. The growls cut off raggedly. The dogs stepped back, whining and turning their heads as if they wanted to go but were held. Their eyes remained locked to Elyas's finger.

Slowly Elyas lowered his hand, and the pitch of his whistle lowered with it. The dogs followed, until they lay flat on the ground, tongues lolling from their mouths. Three tails wagged.

"See," Elyas said, walking to the dogs. "There's no need for weapons." The mastiffs licked his hands, and he scratched their broad heads and fondled their ears. "They look meaner 'than they are. They meant to frighten us off, and they wouldn't have bitten unless we tried to go into the trees. Anyway, there's no worry of that, now. We can make the next thicket before full dark."

When Perrin looked at Egwene, her mouth was hanging open. He shut his own mouth with a click of teeth.

Still patting the dogs, Elyas studied the stand of trees. "There'll be Tuatha'an here. The Traveling People." They stared at him blankly, and he added, "Tinkers."

"Tinkers?" Perrin exclaimed. "I've always wanted to see the Tinkers. They camp across the river from Taren Ferry sometimes, but they don't come down into the Two Rivers, as far as I know. I don't know why not."

Egwene sniffed. "Probably because the Taren Ferry folk are as great thieves as the Tinkers. They'd no doubt end up stealing each other blind. Master Elyas, if there really are Tinkers close by, shouldn't we go on? We don't want Bela stolen, and . . . well, we do not have much else, but everybody knows Tinkers will steal anything."

"Including infants?" Elyas asked dryly. "Kidnap children, and all that?" He spat, and she blushed. Those stories about babies were told sometimes, but most often by Cenn Buie or one of the Coplins or Congars. The other tales, everybody knew. "The Tinkers make me sick sometimes, but they don't steal any more than most folks. A good bit less than some I know."

"It will be getting dark soon, Elyas," Perrin said. "We have to camp somewhere. Why not with them, if they'll have us?" Mistress Luhhan had a Tinker-mended pot that she claimed was better than new. Master Luhhan was not too happy about his wife's praise of the Tinker work, but Perrin wanted to see how it was done. Yet there was a reluctance about Elyas that he did not understand. "Is there some reason we shouldn't?"

Elyas shook his head, but the reluctance was still there, in the set of his shoulders and the tightness of his mouth. "May as well. Just don't pay any mind to what they say. Lot of foolishness. Most times the Traveling People do things any which way, but there's times they set a store by formality, so you do what I do. And keep your secrets. No need to tell the world everything."

The dogs trailed along beside them, wagging their tails, as Elyas led the way into the trees. Perrin felt the wolves slow, and knew they would not enter. They were not afraid of the dogs—they were contemptuous of dogs, who had given up freedom to sleep by a fire—but people they avoided.

Elyas walked surely, as if he knew the way, and near the center of the stand the Tinkers' wagons appeared, scattered among the oak and ash.

Like everyone else in Emond's Field, Perrin had heard a good deal about the Tinkers even if he had never seen any, and the camp was just what he expected. Their wagons were small houses on wheels, tall wooden boxes lacquered and painted in bright colors, reds and blues and yellows and greens and some hues to which he could not put a name. The Traveling People were going about work that was disappointingly everyday, cooking, sewing, tending children, mending harness, but their clothes were even more colorful than the wagons—and seemingly chosen at random; sometimes coat and breeches, or dress and shawl, went together in a way that hurt his eyes. They looked like butterflies in a field of wildflowers.

Four or five men in different places around the camp played fiddles and flutes, and a few people danced like rainbow-hued hummingbirds. Children and dogs ran playing among the cook-fires. The dogs were mastiffs just like those that had confronted the travelers, but the children tugged at their ears and tails and climbed on their backs, and the massive dogs accepted it all placidly. The three with Elyas, tongues hanging out, looked up at the bearded man as if he were their best friend. Perrin shook his head. They were still big enough to reach a man's throat while barely getting their front feet off the ground.

Abruptly the music stopped, and he realized all the Tinkers were looking at him and his companions. Even the children and dogs stood still and watched, warily, as if on the point of flight.

For a moment there was no sound at all, then a wiry man, gray-haired and short, stepped forward and bowed gravely to Elyas. He wore a high-collared red coat, and baggy, bright green trousers tucked into knee boots. "You are welcome to our fires. Do you know the song?"

Elyas bowed in the same way, both hands pressed to his

chest. "Your welcome warms my spirit, Mahdi, as your fires warm the flesh, but I do not know the song."

"Then we seek still," the gray-haired man intoned. "As it was, so shall it be, if we but remember, seek, and find." He swept an arm toward the fires with a smile, and his voice took on a cheerful lightness. "The meal is almost ready. Join us, please."

As if that had been a signal the music sprang up again, and the children took up their laughter and ran with the dogs. Everyone in the camp went back to what they had been doing just as though the newcomers were long-accepted friends.

The gray-haired man hesitated, though, and looked at Elyas. "Your . . . other friends? They will stay away? They frighten the poor dogs so."

"They'll stay away, Raen." Elyas's headshake had a touch of scorn. "You should know that by now."

The gray-haired man spread his hands as if to say nothing was ever certain. As he turned to lead them into the camp, Egwene dismounted and moved close to Elyas. "You two are friends?" A smiling Tinker appeared to take Bela; Egwene gave the reins up reluctantly, after a wry snort from Elyas.

"We know each other," the fur-clad man replied curtly.

"His name is Mahdi?" Perrin said.

Elyas growled something under his breath. "His name's Raen. Mahdi's his title. Seeker. He's the leader of this band. You can call him Seeker if the other sounds odd. He won't mind."

"What was that about a song?" Egwene asked.

"That's why they travel," Elyas said, "or so they say. They're looking for a song. That's what the Mahdi seeks. They say they lost it during the Breaking of the World, and if they can find it again, the paradise of the Age of Legends will return." He ran his eye around the camp and snorted. "They don't even know what the song is; they claim they'll know it when they find it. They don't know how it's supposed to bring paradise, either, but they've been looking near to three thousand years, ever since the Breaking. I expect they'll be looking until the Wheel stops turning."

They reached Raen's fire, then, in the middle of the camp. The Seeker's wagon was yellow trimmed in red, and the spokes of its tall, red-rimmed wheels alternated red and yellow. A plump woman, as gray as Raen but smooth-cheeked still, came out of the wagon and paused on the steps at its back end, straightening a blue-fringed shawl on her shoulders. Her blouse was yellow and her skirt red, both bright. The combination made Perrin blink, and Egwene made a strangled sound.

When she saw the people following Raen, the woman came down with a welcoming smile. She was Ila, Raen's wife, a head taller than her husband, and she soon made Perrin forget about the colors of her clothes. She had a motherliness that reminded him of Mistress al'Vere and had him feeling welcome from her first smile.

Ila greeted Elyas as an old acquaintance, but with a distance that seemed to pain Raen. Elyas gave her a dry grin and a nod. Perrin and Egwene introduced themselves, and she clasped their hands in both of hers with much more warmth than she had shown Elyas, even hugging Egwene.

"Why, you're lovely, child," she said, cupping Egwene's chin and smiling. "And chilled to the bone, too, I expect. You sit close to the fire, Egwene. All of you sit. Supper is almost ready."

Fallen logs had been pulled around the fire for sitting. Elyas refused even that concession to civilization. He lounged on the ground, instead. Iron tripods held two small kettles over the flames, and an oven rested in the edge of the coals. Ila tended them.

As Perrin and the others were taking their places, a slender young man wearing green stripes strolled up to the fire. He gave Raen a hug and Ila a kiss, and ran a cool eye over Elyas and the Emond's Fielders. He was about the same age as Perrin, and he moved as if he were about to begin dancing with his next step.

"Well, Aram"—Ila smiled fondly—"you have decided to eat with your old grandparents for a change, have you?" Her smile slid over to Egwene as she bent to stir a kettle hanging over the cookfire. "I wonder why?"

Aram settled to an easy crouch with his arms crossed on his knees, across the fire from Egwene. "I am Aram," he told her in a low, confident voice. He no longer seemed aware that anyone was there except her. "I have waited for the first rose of spring, and now I find it at my grandfather's fire."

Perrin waited for Egwene to snicker, then saw that she was staring back at Aram. He looked at the young Tinker again. Aram had more than his share of good looks, he admitted. After a minute Perrin knew who the fellow reminded him of. Wil al'Seen, who had all the girls staring and whispering behind his back whenever he came up from Deven Ride to Emond's Field. Wil courted every girl in sight, and managed to convince every one of them that he was just being polite to all the others.

"Those dogs of yours," Perrin said loudly, and Egwene gave a start, "look as big as bears. I'm surprised you let the children play with them."

Aram's smile slipped, but when he looked at Perrin it came back again, even more sure than before. "They will not harm you. They make a show to frighten away danger, and warn us, but they are trained according to the Way of the Leaf."

"The Way of the Leaf?" Egwene said. "What is that?"

Aram gestured to the trees, his eyes fastened intently on hers. "The leaf lives its appointed time, and does not struggle against the wind that carries it away. The leaf does no harm, and finally falls to nourish new leaves. So it should be with all men. And women." Egwene stared back at him, a faint blush rising in her cheeks.

"But what does that mean?" Perrin said. Aram gave him an irritated glance, but it was Raen who answered.

"It means that no man should harm another for any reason whatsoever." The Seeker's eyes flickered to Elyas. "There is no excuse for violence. None. Not ever."

"What if somebody attacks you?" Perrin insisted. "What if somebody hits you, or tries to rob you, or kill you?"

Raen sighed, a patient sigh, as if Perrin was just not seeing what was so clear to him. "If a man hit me, I would ask him why he wanted to do such a thing. If he still wanted to hit me, I would run away, as I would if he wanted to rob or kill me. Much better that I let him take what he wanted, even my life, than that I should do violence. And I would hope that he was not harmed too greatly."

"But you said you wouldn't hurt him," Perrin said.

"I would not, but violence harms the one who does it as much as the one who receives it." Perrin looked doubtful. "You could cut down a tree with your axe," Raen said. "The axe does violence to the tree, and escapes unharmed. Is that how you see it? Wood is soft compared to steel, but the sharp steel is dulled as it chops, and the sap of the tree will rust and pit it. The mighty axe does violence to the helpless tree, and is harmed by it. So it is with men, though the harm is in the spirit."

"But—"

"Enough," Elyas growled, cutting Perrin off. "Raen, it's bad enough you trying to convert village younglings to that nonsense—it gets you in trouble almost everywhere you go, doesn't it?—but I didn't bring this lot here for you to work on them. Leave over."

"And leave them to you?" Ila said, grinding herbs between her palms and letting them trickle into one of the kettles. Her voice was calm, but her hands rubbed the herbs furiously. "Will you teach them your way, to kill or die? Will you lead them to the fate you seek for yourself, dying alone with only the ravens and your . . . your friends to squabble over your body?"

"Be at peace, Ila," Raen said gently, as if he had heard this all and more a hundred times. "He has been welcomed to our fire, my wife."

Ila subsided, but Perrin noticed that she made no apology. Instead she looked at Elyas and shook her head sadly, then dusted her hands and began taking spoons and pottery bowls from a red chest on the side of the wagon.

Raen turned back to Elyas. "My old friend, how many times must I tell you that we do not try to convert anyone. When village people are curious about our ways, we answer their questions. It is most often the young who ask, true, and sometimes one of them will come with us when we journey on, but it is of their own free will."

"You try telling that to some farm wife who's just found out her son or daughter has run off with you Tinkers," Elyas said wryly. "That's why the bigger towns won't even let you camp nearby. Villages put up with you for your mending things, but the cities don't need it, and they don't like you talking their young folks into running off."

"I would not know what the cities allow." Raen's patience seemed inexhaustible. He certainly did not appear to be getting angry at all. "There are always violent men in cities. In any case, I do not think the song could be found in a city."

"I don't mean to offend you, Seeker," Perrin said slowly, "but. . . . Well, I don't look for violence. I don't think I've even wrestled anybody in years, except for feastday games. But if somebody hit me, I'd hit him back. If I didn't, I would just be encouraging him to think he could hit me whenever he wanted to. Some people think they can take advantage of others, and if you don't let them know they can't, they'll just go around bullying anybody weaker than they are."

"Some people," Aram said with a heavy sadness, "can never overcome their baser instincts." He said it with a look at Perrin that made it clear he was not talking about the bullies Perrin spoke of.

"I'll bet you get to run away a lot," Perrin said, and the young Tinker's face tightened in a way that had nothing to do with the Way of the Leaf.

"I think it is interesting," Egwene said, glaring at Perrin, "to meet someone who doesn't believe his muscles can solve every problem."

Aram's good spirits returned, and he stood, offering her his hands with a smile. "Let me show you our camp. There is dancing."

"I would like that." She smiled back.

Ila straightened from taking loaves of bread from the small iron oven. "But supper is ready, Aram."

"I'll eat with mother," Aram said over his shoulder as he drew Egwene away from the wagon by her hand. "We will both eat with mother." He flashed a triumphant smile at Perrin. Egwene was laughing as they ran.

Perrin got to his feet, then stopped. It was not as if she could come to any harm, not if the camp followed this Way of the Leaf as Raen said. Looking at Raen and Ila, both staring dejectedly after their grandson, he said, "I'm sorry. I am a guest, and I shouldn't have—"

"Don't be foolish," Ila said soothingly. "It was his fault, not yours. Sit down and eat."

"Aram is a troubled young man," Raen added sadly. "He is

a good boy, but sometimes I think he finds the Way of the Leaf a hard way. Some do, I fear. Please. My fire is yours. Please?"

Perrin sat back down slowly, still feeling awkward. "What happens to somebody who can't follow the Way?" he asked. "A Tinker, I mean."

Raen and Ila exchanged a worried look, and Raen said, "They leave us. The Lost go to live in the villages."

Ila stared in the direction her grandson had gone. "The Lost cannot be happy." She sighed, but her face was placid again when she handed out the bowls and spoons.

Perrin stared at the ground, wishing he had not asked, and there was no more talk while Ila filled their bowls with a thick vegetable stew and handed out thick slices of her crusty bread, nor while they ate. The stew was delicious, and Perrin finished three bowls before he stopped. Elyas, he noted with a grin, emptied four.

After the meal Raen filled his pipe, and Elyas produced his own and stuffed it from Raen's oilskin pouch. When the lighting and tamping and relighting were done, they settled back in silence. Ila took out a bundle of knitting. The sun was only a blaze of red above the treetops to the west. The camp had settled in for the night, but the bustle did not slow, only changed. The musicians who had been playing when they entered the camp had been replaced by others, and even more people than before danced in the light of the fires, their shadows leaping against the wagons. Somewhere in the camp a chorus of male voices rose. Perrin slid down in front of the log and soon felt himself dozing.

After a time Raen said, "Have you visited any of the Tuatha'an, Elyas, since you were with us last spring?"

Perrin's eyes drifted open and half shut again.

"No," Elyas replied around his pipestem. "I don't like being around too many people at once."

Raen chuckled. "Especially people who live in a way so opposite to your own, eh? No, my old friend, don't worry. I gave up years ago hoping you would come to the Way. But I have heard a story since last we met, and if you have not heard it yet, it might interest you. It interests me, and I have heard it again and again, every time we meet others of the People."

"I'll listen."

"It begins in the spring two years ago, with a band of the People who were crossing the Waste by the northern route."

Perrin's eyes shot open. "The Waste? The Aiel Waste? They were crossing the Aiel Waste?"

"Some people can enter the Waste without being bothered," Elyas said. "Gleemen. Peddlers, if they're honest. The Tuatha'an cross the Waste all the time. Merchants from Cairhien used to, before the Tree, and the Aiel War."

"The Aielmen avoid us," Raen said sadly, "though many of us have tried to speak with them. They watch us from a distance, but they will not come near us, nor let us come near them. Sometimes I worry that they might know the song, though I suppose it isn't likely. Among Aiel, men do not sing, you know. Isn't that strange? From the time an Aiel boy becomes a man he will not sing anything but battle chants, or their dirge for the slain. I have heard them singing over their dead, and over those they have killed. That song is one to make the stones weep." Ila, listening, nodded agreement over her knitting.

Perrin did some quick rethinking. He had thought the Tinkers must be afraid all the time, with all this talk of running away, but no one who was afraid would even think of crossing the Aiel Waste. From what he had heard, no one who was sane would try crossing the Waste.

"If this is some story about a song," Elyas began, but Raen shook his head.

"No, my old friend, not a song. I am not sure I know what it is about." He turned his attention to Perrin. "Young Aiel often travel into the Blight. Some of the young men go alone, thinking for some reason that they have been called to kill the Dark One. Most go in small groups. To hunt Trollocs." Raen shook his head sadly, and when he went on his voice was heavy. "Two years ago a band of the People crossing the Waste about a hundred miles south of the Blight found one of these groups."

"Young women," Ila put in, as sorrowful as her husband. "Little more than girls."

Perrin made a surprised sound, and Elyas grinned at him wryly.

"Aiel girls don't have to tend house and cook if they don't want to, boy. The ones who want to be warriors, instead, join one of the warrior societies, *Far Dareis Mai*, the Maidens of the Spear, and fight right alongside the men."

Perrin shook his head. Elyas chuckled at his expression.

Raen took up the story again, distaste and perplexity mingled in his voice. "The young women were all dead except one, and she was dying. She crawled to the wagons. It was clear she knew they were Tuatha'an. Her loathing outweighed her pain, but she had a message so important to her that she must pass it on to someone, even us, before she died. Men went to see if they could help any of the others—there was a trail of her blood to follow—but all were dead, and so were three times their number in Trollocs."

Elyas sat up, his pipe almost falling from between his teeth. "A hundred miles into the Waste? Impossible! *Djevik K'Shar*, that's what Trollocs call the Waste. The Dying Ground. They wouldn't go a hundred miles into the Waste if all the Myrddraal in the Blight were driving them."

"You know an awful lot about Trollocs, Elyas," Perrin said.

"Go on with your story," Elyas told Raen gruffly.

"From trophies the Aiel carried, it was obvious they were coming back from the Blight. The Trollocs had followed, but by the tracks only a few lived to return after killing the Aiel. As for the girl, she would not let anyone touch her, even to tend her wounds. But she seized the Seeker of that band by his coat, and this is what she said, word for word. 'Leafblighter means to blind the Eye of the World, Lost One. He means to slay the Great Serpent. Warn the People, Lost One. Sightburner comes. Tell them to stand ready for He Who Comes With the Dawn. Tell them. . . .' And then she died. Leafblighter and Sightburner," Raen added to Perrin, "are Aiel names for the Dark One, but I don't understand another word of it. Yet she thought it important enough to approach those she obviously despised, to pass it on with her last breath. But to who? We are ourselves, the People, but I hardly think she meant it for us. The Aiel? They would not let us tell them if we tried." He sighed heavily. "She called *us* the Lost. I never knew before how much they loathe us." Ila set her knitting in her lap and touched his head gently.

"Something they learned in the Blight," Elyas mused. "But none of it makes sense. Slay the Great Serpent? Kill time itself? And blind the Eye of the World? As well say he's going to starve a rock. Maybe she was babbling, Raen. Wounded, dying, she could have lost her grip on what was real. Maybe she didn't even know who those Tuatha'an were."

"She knew what she was saying, and to whom she was saying it. Something more important to her than her own life, and we cannot even understand it. When I saw you walking into our camp, I thought perhaps we would find the answer at last, since you were"—Elyas made a quick motion with his hand, and Raen changed what he had been going to say—"are a friend, and know many strange things."

"Not about this," Elyas said in a tone that put an end to talk. The silence around the campfire was broken only by the music and laughter drifting from other parts of the night-shrouded camp.

Lying with his shoulders propped on one of the logs around the fire, Perrin tried puzzling out the Aiel woman's message, but it made no more sense to him than it had to Raen or Elyas. The Eye of the World. That had been in his dreams, more than once, but he did not want to think about those dreams. Elyas, now. There was a question there he would like answered. What had Raen been about to say about the bearded man, and why had Elyas cut him off? He had no luck with that, either. He was trying to imagine what Aiel girls were like—going into the Blight, where only Warders went that he had ever heard; fighting Trollocs—when he heard Egwene coming back, singing to herself.

Scrambling to his feet, he went to meet her at the edge of the firelight. She stopped short, looking at him with her head tilted to one side. In the dark he could not read her expression.

"You've been gone a long time," he said. "Did you have fun?"

"We ate with his mother," she answered. "And then we danced . . . and laughed. It seems like forever since I danced."

"He reminds me of Wil al'Seen. You always had sense enough not to let Wil put you in his pocket."

"Aram is a gentle boy who is fun to be with," she said in a tight voice. "He makes me laugh."

Perrin sighed. "I'm sorry. I'm glad you had fun dancing."

Abruptly she flung her arms around him, weeping on his

shirt. Awkwardly he patted her hair. *Rand would know what to do,* he thought. Rand had an easy way with girls. Not like him, who never knew what to do or say. "I told you I'm sorry, Egwene. I really am glad you had fun dancing. Really."

"Tell me they're alive," she mumbled into his chest.

"What?"

She pushed back to arm's length, her hands on his arms, and looked up at him in the darkness. "Rand and Mat. The others. Tell me they are alive."

He took a deep breath and looked around uncertainly. "They are alive," he said finally.

"Good." She scrubbed at her cheeks with quick fingers. "That is what I wanted to hear. Good night, Perrin. Sleep well." Standing on tiptoe, she brushed a kiss across his cheek and hurried past him before he could speak.

He turned to watch her. Ila rose to meet her, and the two women went into the wagon talking quietly. *Rand might understand it,* he thought, *but I don't.*

In the distant night the wolves howled the first thin sliver of the new moon toward the horizon, and he shivered. Tomorrow would be time enough to worry about the wolves again. He was wrong. They were waiting to greet him in his dreams.

CHAPTER
26

Whitebridge

The last unsteady note of what had been barely recognizable as "The Wind That Shakes the Willow" faded mercifully away, and Mat lowered Thom's gold-and-silver-chased flute. Rand took his hands from his ears. A sailor coiling a line on the deck nearby heaved a loud sigh of relief. For a moment the only sounds were the water slapping against the hull, the rhythmic creak of the oars, and now and again the hum of rigging strummed by the wind. The wind blew dead on to the *Spray*'s bow, and the useless sails were furled.

"I suppose I should thank you," Thom Merrilin muttered finally, "for teaching me how true the old saying is. Teach him how you will, a pig will never play the flute." The sailor burst out laughing, and Mat raised the flute as if to throw it at him. Deftly, Thom snagged the instrument from Mat's fist and fitted it into its hard leather case. "I thought all you shepherds whiled away the time with the flock playing the pipes or the flute. That will show me to trust what I don't know firsthand."

"Rand's the shepherd," Mat grumbled. "He plays the pipes, not me."

"Yes, well, he does have a little aptitude. Perhaps we had better work on juggling, boy. At least you show some talent for that."

"Thom," Rand said, "I don't know why you're trying so hard." He glanced at the sailor and lowered his voice. "After all, we aren't really trying to become gleemen. It's only something to hide behind until we find Moiraine and the others."

Thom tugged at an end of his mustache and seemed to be studying the smooth, dark brown leather of the flute case on his knees. "What if you don't find them, boy? There's nothing to say they're even still alive."

"They're alive," Rand said firmly. He turned to Mat for support, but Mat's eyebrows were pinched down on his nose, and his mouth was a thin line, and his eyes were fixed on the deck. "Well, speak up," Rand told him. "You can't be that mad over not being able to play the flute. I can't either, not very well. You never wanted to play the flute before."

Mat looked up, still frowning. "What if they are dead?" he said softly. "We have to accept facts, right?"

At that moment the lookout in the bow sang out, "Whitebridge! Whitebridge ahead!"

For a long minute, unwilling to believe that Mat could say something like that so casually, Rand held his friend's gaze amid the scramble of sailors preparing to put in. Mat glowered at him with his head pulled down between his shoulders. There was so much Rand wanted to say, but he could not manage to get it all into words. They had to believe the others were alive. They had to. *Why?* nagged a voice in the back of his head. *So it will all turn out like one of Thom's stories? The heroes find the treasure and defeat the villain and live happily ever after? Some of his stories don't end that way. Sometimes even heroes die. Are you a hero, Rand al'Thor? Are you a hero, sheepherder?*

Abruptly Mat flushed and pulled his eyes away. Freed from his thoughts, Rand jumped up to move through the hurly-burly to the rail. Mat came after him slowly, not even making an effort to dodge the sailors who ran across his path.

Men dashed about the boat, bare feet thumping the deck, hauling on ropes, tying off some lines and untying others. Some brought up big oilskin bags stuffed almost to bursting with wool, while others readied cables as thick as Rand's wrist. Despite their haste, they moved with the assurance of men who had done it all a thousand times before, but Captain Domon stumped up and down the deck shouting orders and cursing those who did not move fast enough to suit him.

Rand's attention was all for what lay ahead, coming plainly
into sight as they rounded a slight bend of the Arinelle. He had
heard of it, in song and story and peddlers' tales, but now he
would actually see the legend.

The White Bridge arched high over the wide waters, twice as
high as the *Spray*'s mast and more, and from end to end it
gleamed milky white in the sunlight, gathering the light until it
seemed to glow. Spidery piers of the same stuff plunged into
the strong currents, appearing too frail to support the weight
and width of the bridge. It looked all of one piece, as if it had
been carved from a single stone or molded by a giant's hand,
broad and tall, leaping the river with an airy grace that almost
made the eye forget its size. All in all it dwarfed the town that
sprawled about its foot on the east bank, though Whitebridge
was larger by far than Emond's Field, with houses of stone and
brick as tall as those in Taren Ferry and wooden docks like thin
fingers sticking out into the river. Small boats dotted the
Arinelle thickly, fishermen hauling their nets. And over it all
the White Bridge towered and shone.

"It looks like glass," Rand said to no one in particular.

Captain Domon paused behind him and tucked his thumbs
behind his broad belt. "Nay, lad. Whatever it be, it no be glass.
Never so hard the rains come, it no be slippery, and the best
chisel and the strongest arm no make a mark on it."

"A remnant from the Age of Legends," Thom said. "I have
always thought it must be."

The captain gave a dour grunt. "Mayhap. But still useful despite. Could be someone else built it. Does no *have* to be Aes
Sedai work, Fortune prick me. It no has to be so old as all that.
Put your back into it, you bloody fool!" He hurried off down
the deck.

Rand stared even more wonderingly. *From the Age of Legends.* Made by Aes Sedai, then. That was why Captain Domon
felt the way he did, for all his talk about the wonder and
strangeness of the world. Aes Sedai work. One thing to hear
about it, another to see it, and touch it. *You know that, don't
you?* For an instant it seemed to Rand that a shadow rippled
through the milk-white structure. He pulled his eyes away, to
the docks coming nearer, but the bridge still loomed in the corner of his vision.

"We made it, Thom," he said, then forced a laugh. "And no mutiny."

The gleeman only harrumphed and blew out his mustaches, but two sailors readying a cable nearby gave Rand a sharp glance, then bent quickly back to their work. He stopped laughing and tried not to look at the two for the rest of the approach to Whitebridge.

The *Spray* curved smoothly in beside the first dock, thick timbers sitting on heavy, tar-coated pilings, and stopped with a backing of oars that swirled the water to froth around the blades. As the oars were drawn in, sailors tossed cables to men on the dock, who fastened them off with a flourish, while other crewmen slung the bags of wool over the side to protect the hull from the dock pilings.

Before the boat was even pulled snug against the dock, carriages appeared at the end of the dock, tall and lacquered shiny black, each one with a name painted on the door in large letters, gold or scarlet. The carriages' passengers hurried up the gangplank as soon as it dropped in place, smooth-faced men in long velvet coats and silk-lined cloaks and cloth slippers, each followed by a plainly dressed servant carrying his iron-bound moneybox.

They approached Captain Domon with painted smiles that slipped when he abruptly roared in their faces. "You!" He thrust a thick finger past them, stopping Floran Gelb in his tracks at the length of the boat. The bruise on Gelb's forehead from Rand's boot had faded away, but he still fingered the spot from time to time as if to remind himself. "You've slept on watch for the last time on my vessel! Or on any vessel, if I have my way of it. Choose your own side—the dock or the river—but off my vessel *now*!"

Gelb hunched his shoulders, and his eyes glittered hate at Rand and his friends, at Rand especially, a poisonous glare. The wiry man looked around the deck for support, but there was little hope in that look. One by one, every man in the crew straightened from what he was doing and stared back coldly. Gelb wilted visibly, but then his glare returned, twice as strong as it had been. With a muttered curse he darted below to the crew's quarters. Domon sent two men after him to see he did no mischief and dismissed him with a grunt. When the captain turned back to them, the merchants took up their smiles and bows as if they had never been interrupted.

At a word from Thom, Mat and Rand began gathering their things together. There was not much aside from the clothes on their backs, not for any of them. Rand had his blanketroll and saddlebags, and his father's sword. He held the sword for a minute, and homesickness rolled over him so strongly that his eyes stung. He wondered if he would ever see Tam again. Or home? Home. *Going to spend the rest of your life running, running and afraid of your own dreams.* With a shuddering sigh he slipped the belt around his waist over his coat.

Gelb came back on deck, followed by his twin shadows. He looked straight ahead, but Rand could still feel hatred coming off him in waves. Back rigid and face dark, Gelb walked stiff-legged down the gangplank and pushed roughly into the thin crowd on the dock. In a minute he was gone from sight, vanished beyond the merchants' carriages.

There were not a great many people on the dock, and those were a plainly dressed mix of workmen, fishermen mending nets, and a few townspeople who had come out to see the first boat of the year to come downriver from Saldaea. None of the girls was Egwene and no one looked the least bit like Moiraine, or Lan, or anyone else Rand was hoping to see.

"Maybe they didn't come down to the dock," he said.

"Maybe," Thom replied curtly. He settled his instrument cases on his back with care. "You two keep an eye out for Gelb. He will make trouble if he can. We want to pass through Whitebridge so softly that nobody remembers we were here five minutes after we're gone."

Their cloaks flapped in the wind as they walked to the gangplank. Mat carried his bow crossed in front on his chest. Even after all their days on the boat, it still got a few looks from the crewmen; their bows were short affairs.

Captain Domon left the merchants to intercept Thom at the gangplank.

"You be leaving me now, gleeman? Can I no talk you into continuing on? I be going all the way down to Illian, where folk have a proper regard for gleemen. There be no finer place in the world for your art. I'd get you there in good time for the

Feast of Sefan. The competitions, you know. A hundred gold
marks for the best telling of *The Great Hunt of the Horn*."

"A great prize, Captain," Thom replied with an elaborate
bow and a flourish of his cloak that set the patches to fluttering,
"and great competitions, which rightly draw gleemen from the
whole world over. But," he added dryly, "I fear we could not
afford the fare at the rates you charge."

"Aye, well, as to that. . . ." The captain produced a leather
purse from his coat pocket and tossed it to Thom. It clinked
when Thom caught it. "Your fares back, and a bit more besides. The damage was no so bad as I thought, and you've
worked your way and more with your tales and your harp. I
could maybe manage as much again if you stay aboard to the
Sea of Storms. And I would set you ashore in Illian. A good
gleeman can make his fortune there, even aside from the competitions."

Thom hesitated, weighing the purse on his palm, but Rand
spoke up. "We're meeting friends here, Captain, and going on
to Caemlyn together. We'll have to see Illian another time."

Thom's mouth twisted wryly, then he blew out his long mustaches and tucked the purse into his pocket. "Perhaps if the
people we are to meet are not here, Captain."

"Aye," Domon said sourly. "You think on it. Too bad I can
no keep Gelb aboard to take the others' anger, but I do what I
say I will do. I suppose I must ease up now, even if it means
taking three times as long to reach Illian as I should. Well,
mayhap those Trollocs *were* after you three."

Rand blinked but kept silent, but Mat was not so cautious.
"Why do you think they weren't?" he demanded. "They
were after the same treasure we were hunting."

"Mayhap," the captain grunted, sounding unconvinced. He
combed thick fingers through his beard, then pointed at the
pocket where Thom had put the purse. "Twice that if you come
back to keep the men's minds off how hard I work them. Think
on it. I sail with the first light on the morrow." He turned on
his heel and strode back to the merchants, arms spreading wide
as he began an apology for keeping them waiting.

Thom still hesitated, but Rand hustled him down the gangplank without giving him a chance to argue, and the gleeman

let himself be herded. A murmur passed through the people on the dock as they saw Thom's patch-covered cloak, and some called out to discover where he would be performing. *So much for not being noticed,* Rand thought, dismayed. By sundown it would be all over Whitebridge that there was a gleeman in town. He hurried Thom along, though, and Thom, wrapped in sulky silence, did not even try to slow down enough to preen under the attention.

The carriage drivers looked down at Thom with interest from their high perches, but apparently the dignity of their positions forbade shouting. With no idea of where to go exactly, Rand turned up the street that ran along the river and under the bridge.

"We need to find Moiraine and the others," he said. "And fast. We should have thought of changing Thom's cloak."

Thom suddenly shook himself and stopped dead. "An innkeeper will be able to tell us if they're here, or if they've passed through. The right innkeeper. Innkeepers have all the news and gossip. If they aren't here. . . ." He looked back and forth from Rand to Mat. "We have to talk, we three." Cloak swirling around his ankles, he set off into the town, away from the river. Rand and Mat had to step quickly to keep up.

The broad, milk-white arch that gave the town its name dominated Whitebridge as much close up as it did from afar, but once Rand was in the streets he realized that the town was every bit as big as Baerlon, though not so crowded with people. A few carts moved in the streets, pulled by horse or ox or donkey or man, but no carriages. Those most likely all belonged to the merchants and were clustered down at the dock.

Shops of every description lined the streets, and many of the tradesmen worked in front of their establishments, under the signs swinging in the wind. They passed a man mending pots, and a tailor holding folds of cloth up to the light for a customer. A shoemaker, sitting in his doorway, tapped his hammer on the heel of a boot. Hawkers cried their services at sharpening knives and scissors, or tried to interest the passersby in their skimpy trays of fruit or vegetables, but none was getting much interest. Shops selling food had the same pitiful displays of produce Rand remembered from Baerlon. Even the fishmongers displayed only small piles of small fish, for all the boats on the

river. Times were not really hard yet, but everyone could see
what was coming if the weather did not change soon, and those
faces that were not fixed into worried frowns seemed to stare at
something unseen, something unpleasant.

Where the White Bridge came down in the center of the
town was a big square, paved with stones worn by generations
of feet and wagon wheels. Inns surrounded the square, and
shops, and tall, red brick houses with signs out front bearing
the same names Rand had seen on the carriages at the dock. It
was into one of those inns, seemingly chosen at random, that
Thom ducked. The sign over the door, swinging in the wind,
had a striding man with a bundle on his back on one side and
the same man with his head on a pillow on the other, and pro-
claimed The Wayfarers' Rest.

The common room stood empty except for the fat innkeeper
drawing ale from a barrel and two men in rough workman's
clothes staring glumly into their mugs at a table in the back.
Only the innkeeper looked up when they came in. A shoulder-
high wall split the room in two from front to back, with tables
and a blazing fireplace on each side. Rand wondered idly if all
innkeepers were fat and losing their hair.

Rubbing his hands together briskly, Thom commented to the
innkeeper on the late cold and ordered hot spiced wine, then
added quietly, "Is there somewhere my friends and I could talk
without being disturbed?"

The innkeeper nodded to the low wall. "The other side that's
as best I've got unless you want to take a room. For when sailors come up from the river. Seems like half the crews got
grudges against the other half. I won't have my place broke up
by fights, so I keep them apart." He had been eyeing Thom's
cloak the whole while, and now he cocked his head to one side,
a sly look in his eyes. "You staying? Haven't had a gleeman
here in some time. Folks would pay real good for something as
would take their minds off things. I'd even take some off on
your room and meals."

Unnoticed, Rand thought glumly.

"You are too generous," Thom said with a smooth bow.
"Perhaps I will take up your offer. But for now, a little pri-
vacy."

"I'll bring your wine. Good money here for a gleeman."

The tables on the far side of the wall were all empty, but Thom chose one right in the middle of the space. "So no one can listen without us knowing," he explained. "Did you hear that fellow? He'll take some off. Why, I'd double his custom just by sitting here. Any honest innkeeper gives a gleeman room and board and a good bit besides."

The bare table was none too clean, and the floor had not been swept in days if not weeks. Rand looked around and grimaced. Master al'Vere would not have let his inn get that dirty if he had had to climb out of a sickbed to see to it. "We're only after information. Remember?"

"Why here?" Mat demanded. "We passed other inns that looked cleaner."

"Straight on from the bridge," Thom said, "is the road to Caemlyn. Anyone passing through Whitebridge comes through this square, unless they're going by river, and we know your friends aren't doing that. If there is no word of them here, it doesn't exist. Let me do the talking. This has to be done carefully."

Just then the innkeeper appeared, three battered pewter mugs gripped in one fist by the handles. The fat man flicked at the table with a towel, set the mugs down, and took Thom's money. "If you stay, you won't have to pay for your drinks. Good wine, here."

Thom's smile touched only his mouth. "I will think on it, innkeeper. What news is there? We have been away from hearing things."

"Big news, that's what. Big news."

The innkeeper draped the towel over his shoulder and pulled up a chair. He crossed his arms on the table, took root with a long sigh, saying what a comfort it was to get off his feet. His name was Bartim, and he went on about his feet in detail, about corns and bunions and how much time he spent standing and what he soaked them in, until Thom mentioned the news again, and then he shifted over with hardly a pause.

The news was just as big as he said it was. Logain, the false Dragon, had been captured after a big battle near Lugard while he was trying to move his army from Ghealdan to Tear. The Prophecies, they understood? Thom nodded, and Bartim went on. The roads in the south were packed with people, the lucky ones with what they could carry on their backs. Thousands fleeing in all directions.

"None"—Bartim chuckled wryly—"supported Logain, of course. Oh, no, you won't find many to admit to that, not now. Just refugees trying to find a safe place during the troubles."

Aes Sedai had been involved in taking Logain, of course. Bartim spat on the floor when he said that, and again when he said they were taking the false Dragon north to Tar Valon. Bartim was a decent man, he said, a respectable man, and Aes Sedai could all go back to the Blight where they came from and take Tar Valon with them, as far as he was concerned. He would get no closer to an Aes Sedai than a thousand miles, if he had his way. Of course, they were stopping at every village and town on the way north to display Logain, so he had heard. To show people that the false Dragon had been taken and the world was safe again. He would have liked to see that, even if it did mean getting close to Aes Sedai. He was halfway tempted to go to Caemlyn.

"They'll be taking him there to show to Queen Morgase." The innkeeper touched his forehead respectfully. "I've never seen the Queen. Man ought to see his own Queen, don't you think?"

Logain could do "things," and the way Bartim's eyes shifted and his tongue darted across his lips made it clear what he meant. He had seen the last false Dragon, two years ago, when he was paraded through the countryside, but that was just some fellow who thought he could make himself a king. There had been no need for Aes Sedai, that time. Soldiers had had him chained up on a wagon. A sullen-looking fellow who moaned in the middle of the wagonbed, covering his head with his arms whenever people threw stones or poked him with sticks. There had been a lot of that, and the soldiers had done nothing to stop it, as long as they did not kill the fellow. Best to let the people see he was nothing special after all. He could not do "things." This Logain would be something to see, though. Something for Bartim to tell his grandchildren about. If only the inn would let him get away.

Rand listened with an interest that did not have to be faked. When Padan Fain had brought word to Emond's Field of a false Dragon, a man actually wielding the Power, it had been the biggest news to come into the Two Rivers in years. What had happened since had pushed it to the back of his mind, but it was still the sort of thing people would be talking about for years, and telling their grandchildren about, too. Bartim would probably tell his that he had seen Logain whether he did or not. Nobody would ever think what happened to some village folk from the Two Rivers was worth talking about, not unless they were Two Rivers people themselves.

"That," Thom said, "would be something to make a story of, a story they'd tell for a thousand years. I wish I had been there." He sounded as if it was the simple truth, and Rand thought it really was. "I might try to see him anyway. You didn't say what route they were taking. Perhaps there are some other travelers around? They might have heard the route."

Bartim waved a grubby hand dismissively. "North, that's all anybody knows around here. You want to see him, go to Caemlyn. That's all I know, and if there's anything to know in Whitebridge, I know it."

"No doubt you do," Thom said smoothly. "I expect a lot of strangers passing through stop here. Your sign caught my eye from the foot of the White Bridge."

"Not just from the west, I'll have you know. Two days ago there was a fellow in here, an Illianer, with a proclamation all done up with seals and ribbons. Read it right out there in the square. Said he's taking it all the way to the Mountains of Mist, maybe even to the Aryth Ocean, if the passes are open. Said they've sent men to read it in every land in the world." The innkeeper shook his head. "The Mountains of Mist. I hear they're covered with fog all the year round, and there's things in the fog will strip the flesh off your bones before you can run." Mat snickered, earning a sharp look from Bartim.

Thom leaned forward intently. "What did the proclamation say?"

"Why, the hunt for the Horn, of course," Bartim exclaimed. "Didn't I say that? The Illianers are calling on everybody as will swear their lives to the hunt to gather in Illian. Can you imagine that? Swearing your life to a legend? I suppose they'll find some fools. There's always fools around. This fellow claimed the end of the world is coming. The last battle with the Dark One." He chuckled, but it had a hollow sound, a man

laughing to convince himself something really was worth laughing at. "Guess they think the Horn of Valere has to be found
before it happens. Now what do you think of that?" He chewed
a knuckle pensively for a minute. "Course, I don't know as I
could argue with them after this winter. The winter, and this
fellow Logain, and those other two before, as well. Why all
these fellows the last few years claiming to be the Dragon? And
the winter. Must mean something. What do you think?"

Thom did not seem to hear him. In a soft voice the gleeman
began to recite to himself.

> *"In the last, lorn fight*
> *'gainst the fall of long night,*
> *the mountains stand guard,*
> *and the dead shall be ward,*
> *for the grave is no bar to my call."*

"That's it." Bartim grinned as if he could already see the
crowds handing him their money while they listened to Thom.
"That's it. *The Great Hunt of the Horn.* You tell that one, and
they'll be hanging from the rafters in here. Everybody's heard
about the proclamation."

Thom still seemed to be a thousand miles away, so Rand
said, "We're looking for some friends who were coming this
way. From the west. Have there been many strangers passing
through in the last week or two?"

"Some," Bartim said slowly. "There's always some, from
east and west both." He looked at each of them in turn, suddenly wary. "What do they look like, these friends of yours?"

Rand opened his mouth, but Thom, abruptly back from
wherever he had been, gave him a sharp, silencing look. With
an exasperated sigh the gleeman turned to the innkeeper. "Two
men and three women," he said reluctantly. "They may be together, or maybe not." He gave thumbnail sketches, painting
each one in just a few words, enough for anyone who had seen
them to recognize without giving away anything about who they
were.

Bartim rubbed one hand over his head, disarranging his thinning hair, and stood up slowly. "Forget about performing here,

gleeman. In fact, I'd appreciate it if you drank your wine and left. Leave Whitebridge, if you're smart."

"Someone else has been asking after them?" Thom took a drink, as if the answer were the least important thing in the world, and raised an eyebrow at the innkeeper. "Who would that be?"

Bartim scrubbed his hand through his hair again and shifted his feet on the point of walking away, then nodded to himself. "About a week ago, as near as I can say, a weaselly fellow came over the bridge. Crazy, everybody thought. Always talking to himself, never stopped moving even when he was standing still. Asked about the same people . . . some of them. He asked like it was important, then acted like he didn't care what the answer was. Half the time he was saying as he had to wait here for them, and the other half as he had to go on, he was in a hurry. One minute he was whining and begging, the next making demands like a king. Near got himself a thrashing a time or two, crazy or not. The Watch almost took him in custody for his own safety. He went off toward Caemlyn that same day, talking to himself and crying. Crazy, like I said."

Rand looked at Thom and Mat questioningly, and they both shook their heads. If this weaselly fellow was looking for them, he was still nobody they recognized.

"Are you sure it was the same people he wanted?" Rand asked.

"Some of them. The fighting man, and the woman in silk. But it wasn't them as he cared about. It was three country boys." His eyes slid across Rand and Mat and away again so fast that Rand was not sure if he had really seen the look or imagined it. "He was desperate to find them. But crazy, like I said."

Rand shivered, and wondered who the crazy man could be, and why he was looking for them. *A Darkfriend? Would Ba'al-zamon use a madman?*

"He was crazy, but the other one. . . ." Bartim's eyes shifted uneasily, and his tongue ran over his lips as if he could not find enough spit to moisten them. "Next day . . . next day the other one came for the first time." He fell silent.

"The other one?" Thom prompted finally.

Bartim looked around, although their side of the divided

room was still empty except for them. He even raised up on his toes and looked over the low wall. When he finally spoke, it was in a whispered rush.

"All in black he is. Keeps the hood of his cloak pulled up so you can't see his face, but you can feel him looking at you, feel it like an icicle shoved into your spine. He . . . he spoke to me." He flinched and stopped to chew at his lip before going on. "Sounded like a snake crawling through dead leaves. Fair turned my stomach to ice. Every time as he comes back, he asks the same questions. Same questions the crazy man asked. Nobody ever sees him coming—he's just there all of a sudden, day or night, freezing you where you stand. People are starting to look over their shoulders. Worst of it is, the gatetenders claim as he's never passed through any of the gates, coming or going."

Rand worked at keeping his face blank; he clenched his jaw until his teeth ached. Mat scowled, and Thom studied his wine. The word none of them wanted to say hung in the air between them. Myrddraal.

"I think I'd remember if I ever met anyone like that," Thom said after a minute.

Bartim's head bobbed furiously. "Burn me, but you would. Light's truth, you would. He . . . he wants the same lot as the crazy man, only he says as there's a girl with them. And"—he glanced sideways at Thom—"and a white-haired gleeman."

Thom's eyebrows shot up in what Rand was sure was unfeigned surprise. "A white-haired gleeman? Well, I'm hardly the only gleeman in the world with a little age on him. I assure you, I don't know this fellow, and he can have no reason to be looking for me."

"That's as may be," Bartim said glumly. "He didn't say it in so many words, but I got the impression as he would be very displeased with anyone as tried to help these people, or tried to hide them from him. Anyway, I'll tell you what I told him. I haven't seen any of them, nor heard tell of them, and that's the truth. Not any of them," he finished pointedly. Abruptly he slapped Thom's money down on the table. "Just finish your wine and go. All right? All right?" And he trundled away as fast as he could, looking over his shoulder.

"A Fade," Mat breathed when the innkeeper was gone. "I should have known they'd be looking for us here."

"And he'll be back," Thom said, leaning across the table and lowering his voice. "I say we sneak back to the boat and take Captain Domon up on his offer. The hunt will center on the road to Caemlyn while we're on our way to Illian, a thousand miles from where the Myrddraal expect us."

"No," Rand said firmly. "We wait for Moiraine and the others in Whitebridge, or we go on to Caemlyn. One or the other, Thom. That's what we decided."

"That's crazed, boy. Things have changed. You listen to me. No matter what this innkeeper says, when a Myrddraal stares at him, he'll tell all about us down to what we had to drink and how much dust we had on our boots." Rand shivered, remembering the Fade's eyeless stare. "As for Caemlyn. . . . You think the Halfmen don't know you want to get to Tar Valon? It's a good time to be on a boat headed south."

"No, Thom." Rand had to force the words out, thinking of being a thousand miles from where the Fades were looking, but he took a deep breath and managed to firm his voice. "No."

"Think, boy. Illian! There isn't a grander city on the face of the earth. And the Great Hunt of the Horn! There hasn't been a Hunt of the Horn in near four hundred years. A whole new cycle of stories waiting to be made. Just think. You never dreamed of anything like it. By the time the Myrddraal figure out where you've gone to, you'll be old and gray and so tired of watching your grandchildren you won't care if they do find you."

Rand's face took on a stubborn set. "How many times do I have to say no? They'll find us wherever we go. There'd be Fades waiting in Illian, too. And how do we escape the dreams? I want to know what's happening to me, Thom, and why. I'm going to Tar Valon. With Moiraine if I can; without her if I have to. Alone, if I have to. I need to know."

"But Illian, boy! And a safe way out, downriver while they're looking for you in another direction. Blood and ashes, a dream can't hurt you."

Rand kept silent. *A dream can't hurt? Do dream thorns draw real blood?* He almost wished he had told Thom about that dream, too. *Do you dare tell anybody? Ba'alzamon is in your*

*dreams, but what's between dreaming and waking, now? Who
do you dare to tell that the Dark One is touching you?*

Thom seemed to understand. The gleeman's face softened.
"Even *those* dreams, lad. They are still just dreams, aren't
they? For the Light's sake, Mat, talk to him. I know you don't
want to go to Tar Valon, at least."

Mat's face reddened, half embarrassment and half anger. He
avoided looking at Rand and scowled at Thom instead. "Why
are you going to all this fuss and bother? You want to go back
to the boat? Go back to the boat. We'll take care of ourselves."

The gleeman's thin shoulders shook with silent laughter, but
his voice was anger tight. "You think you know enough about
Myrddraal to escape by yourself, do you? You're ready to walk
into Tar Valon alone and hand yourself over to the Amyrlin
Seat? Can you even tell one Ajah from another? The Light
burn me, boy, if you think you can even get to Tar Valon
alone, you tell me to go."

"Go," Mat growled, sliding a hand under his cloak. Rand
realized with a shock that he was gripping the dagger from
Shadar Logoth, maybe even ready to use it.

Raucous laughter broke out on the other side of the low wall
dividing the room, and a scornful voice spoke up loudly.

"Trollocs? Put on a gleeman's cloak, man! You're drunk!
Trollocs! Borderland fables!"

The words doused anger like a pot of cold water. Even Mat
half turned to the wall, eyes widening.

Rand stood just enough to see over the wall, then ducked
back down again with a sinking feeling in his stomach. Floran
Gelb sat on the other side of the wall, at the table in the back
with the two men who had been there when they came in. They
were laughing at him, but they were listening. Bartim was wiping a table that badly needed it, not looking at Gelb and the
two men, but he was listening, too, scrubbing one spot over
and over with his towel and leaning toward them until he
seemed almost ready to fall over.

"Gelb," Rand whispered as he dropped back into his chair,
and the others tensed. Thom swiftly studied their side of the
room.

On the other side of the wall the second man's voice chimed

in. "No, no, there used to be Trollocs. But they killed them all in the Trolloc Wars."

"Borderland fables!" the first man repeated.

"It's true, I tell you," Gelb protested loudly. "I've been in the Borderlands. I've seen Trollocs, and these were Trollocs as sure as I'm sitting here. Those three claimed the Trollocs were chasing them, but I know better. That's why I wouldn't stay on the *Spray*. I've had my suspicions about Bayle Domon for some time, but those three are Darkfriends for sure. I tell you. . . ."

Laughter and coarse jokes drowned out the rest of what Gelb had to say.

How long, Rand wondered, before the innkeeper heard a description of "those three"? If he had not already. If he did not just leap to the three strangers he had already seen. The only door from their half of the common room would take them right past Gelb's table.

"Maybe the boat isn't such a bad idea," Mat muttered, but Thom shook his head.

"Not anymore." The gleeman spoke softly and fast. He pulled out the leather purse Captain Domon had given him and hastily divided the money into three piles. "That story will be all through the town in an hour, whether anybody believes it or not, and the Halfman could hear any time. Domon isn't sailing until tomorrow morning. At best he'll have Trollocs chasing him all the way to Illian. Well, he's half expecting it for some reason, but that won't do us any good. There's nothing for it but to run, and run hard."

Mat quickly stuffed the coins Thom shoved in front of him into his pocket. Rand picked his pile up more slowly. The coin Moiraine had given him was not among them. Domon had given an equal weight of silver, but Rand, for some reason he could not fathom, wished he had the Aes Sedai's coin instead. Stuffing the money in his pocket, he looked a question at the gleeman.

"In case we're separated," Thom explained. "We probably won't be, but if it does happen . . . well, you two will make out all right by yourselves. You're good lads. Just keep clear of Aes Sedai, for your lives."

"I thought you were staying with us," Rand said.

"I am, boy. I am. But they're getting close, now, and the

Light only knows. Well, no matter. It isn't likely anything will happen." Thom paused, looking at Mat. "I hope you no longer mind me staying with you," he said dryly.

Mat shrugged. He eyed each of them, then shrugged again. "I'm just on edge. 1 can't seem to get rid of it. Every time we stop for a breath, they're there, hunting us. I feel like somebody's staring at the back of my head all the time. What are we going to do?"

The laughter erupted on the other side of the wall, broken again by Gelb, trying loudly to convince the two men that he was telling the truth. How much longer, Rand wondered. Sooner or later Bartim had to put together Gelb's three and the three of them.

Thom eased his chair and rose, but kept his height crouched. No one looking casually toward the wall from the other side could see him. He motioned for them to follow, whispering, "Be very quiet."

The windows on either side of the fireplace on their side of the wall looked out into an alleyway. Thom studied one of the windows carefully before drawing it up just enough for them to squeeze through. It barely made a sound, nothing that could have been heard three feet away over the laughing argument on the other side of the low wall.

Once in the alley, Mat started for the street right away, but Thom caught his arm. "Not so fast," the gleeman told him. "Not till we know what we're doing." Thom lowered the window again as much as he could from outside, and turned to study the alley.

Rand followed Thom's eyes. Except for half a dozen rain barrels against the inn and the next building, a tailor shop, the alley was empty, the hard-packed dirt dry and dusty.

"Why are you doing this?" Mat demanded again. "You'd be safer if you left us. Why are you staying with us?"

Thom stared at him for a long moment. "I had a nephew, Owyn," he said wearily, shrugging out of his cloak. He made a pile with his blanket-roll as he talked, carefully setting his cased instruments on top. "My brother's only son, my only living kin. He got in trouble with the Aes Sedai, but I was too busy with . . . other things. I don't know what I could have done, but when I finally tried, it was too late. Owyn died a few years

later. You could say Aes Sedai killed him." He straightened
up, not looking at them. His voice was still level, but Rand
glimpsed tears in his eyes as he turned his head away. "If I can
keep you two free of Tar Valon, maybe I can stop thinking
about Owyn. Wait here." Still avoiding their eyes, he hurried
to the mouth of the alley, slowing before he reached it. After
one quick look around, he strolled casually into the street and
out of sight.

Mat half rose to follow, then settled back. "He won't leave
these," he said, touching the leather instrument cases. "You
believe that story?"

Rand squatted patiently beside the rain barrels. "What's the
matter with you, Mat? You aren't like this. I haven't heard you
laugh in days."

"I don't like being hunted like a rabbit," Mat snapped. He
sighed, letting his head fall back against the brick wall of the
inn. Even like that he seemed tense. His eyes shifted warily.
"Sorry. It's the running, and all these strangers, and . . . and
just everything. It makes me jumpy. I look at somebody, and I
can't help wondering if he's going to tell the Fades about us, or
cheat us, or rob us, or. . . . Light, Rand, doesn't it make you
nervous?"

Rand laughed, a quick bark in the back of his throat. "I'm
too scared to be nervous."

"What do you think the Aes Sedai did to his nephew?"

"I don't know," Rand said uneasily. There was only one kind
of trouble that he knew of for a man to get into with Aes Sedai.
"Not like us, I guess."

"No. Not like us."

For a time they leaned against the wall, not talking. Rand
was not sure how long they waited. A few minutes, probably,
but it felt like an hour, waiting for Thom to come back, waiting
for Bartim and Gelb to open the window and denounce them
for Darkfriends. Then a man turned in at the mouth of the
alley, a tall man with the hood of his cloak pulled up to hide his
face, a cloak black as night against the light of the street.

Rand scrambled to his feet, one hand wrapped around the
hilt of Tam's sword so hard that his knuckles hurt. His mouth
went dry, and no amount of swallowing helped. Mat rose to a
crouch with one hand under his cloak.

The man came closer, and Rand's throat grew tighter with every step. Abruptly the man stopped and tossed back his cowl. Rand's knees almost gave way. It was Thom.

"Well, if you don't recognize me"—the gleeman grinned—"I guess it's a good enough disguise for the gates."

Thom pushed past them and began transferring things from his patch-covered cloak to his new one so nimbly that Rand could not make out any of them. The new cloak was dark brown, Rand saw now. He drew a deep, ragged breath; his throat still felt as if it were clutched in a fist. Brown, not black. Mat still had his hand under his cloak, and he stared at Thom's back as if he were thinking of using the hidden dagger.

Thom glanced up at them, then gave them a sharper look. "This is no time to get skittish." Deftly he began folding his old cloak into a bundle around his instrument cases, inside out so the patches were hidden. "We'll walk out of here one at a time, just close enough to keep each other in sight. Shouldn't be remembered especially, that way. Can't you slouch?" he added to Rand. "That height of yours is as bad as a banner." He slung the bundle across his back and stood, drawing his hood back up. He looked nothing like a white-haired gleeman. He was just another traveler, a man too poor to afford a horse, much less a carriage. "Let's go. We've wasted too much time already."

Rand agreed fervently, but even so he hesitated before stepping out of the alley into the square. None of the sparse scattering of people gave them a second look—most did not look at them at all—but his shoulders knotted, waiting for the cry of Darkfriend that could turn ordinary people into a mob bent on murder. He ran his eyes across the open area, over people moving about on their daily business, and when he brought them back a Myrddraal was halfway across the square.

Where the Fade had come from, he could not begin to guess, but it strode toward the three of them with a slow deadliness, a predator with the prey under its gaze. People shied away from the black-cloaked shape, avoided looking at it. The square began to empty out as people decided they were needed elsewhere.

The black cowl froze Rand where he stood. He tried to summon up the void, but it was like fumbling after smoke. The

Fade's hidden gaze knifed to his bones and turned his marrow to icicles.

"Don't look at its face," Thom muttered. His voice shook and cracked, and it sounded as if he were forcing the words out. "The Light burn you, don't look at its face!"

Rand tore his eyes away—he almost groaned; it felt like tearing a leech off of his face—but even staring at the stones of the square he could still see the Myrddraal coming, a cat playing with mice, amused at their feeble efforts to escape, until finally the jaws snapped shut. The Fade had halved the distance. "Are we just going to stand here?" he mumbled. "We have to run . . . get away." But he could not make his feet move.

Mat had the ruby-hilted dagger out at last, in a trembling hand. His lips were drawn back from his teeth, a snarl and a rictus of fear.

"Think. . . ." Thom stopped to swallow, and went on hoarsely. "Think you can outrun it, do you, boy?" He began to mutter to himself; the only word Rand could make out was "Owyn." Abruptly Thom growled, "I never should have gotten mixed up with you boys. Should never have." He shrugged the bundled gleeman's cloak off of his back and thrust it into Rand's arms. "Take care of that. When I say run, you run and don't stop until you get to Caemlyn. The Queen's Blessing. An inn. Remember that, in case. . . . Just remember it."

"I don't understand," Rand said. The Myrddraal was not twenty paces away, now. His feet felt like lead weights.

"Just remember it!" Thom snarled. "The Queen's Blessing. Now. RUN!"

He gave them a push, one hand on the shoulder of each of them, to get them started, and Rand stumbled away in a lurching run with Mat at his side.

"RUN!" Thom sprang into motion, too, with a long, wordless roar. Not after them, but toward the Myrddraal. His hands flourished as if he were performing at his best, and daggers appeared. Rand stopped, but Mat pulled him along.

The Fade was just as startled. Its leisurely pace faltered in mid-stride. Its hand swept toward the hilt of the black sword hanging at its waist, but the gleeman's long legs covered the distance quickly. Thom crashed into the Myrddraal before the black blade was half drawn, and both went down in a thrashing heap. The few people still in the square fled.

"RUN!" The air in the square flashed an eye-searing blue, and Thom began to scream, but even in the middle of the scream he managed a word. *"RUN!"*

Rand obeyed. The gleeman's screams pursued him.

Clutching Thom's bundle to his chest, he ran as hard as he could. Panic spread from the square out through the town as Rand and Mat fled on the crest of a wave of fear. Shopkeepers abandoned their goods as the boys passed. Shutters banged down over storefronts, and frightened faces appeared in the windows of houses, then vanished. People who had not been close enough to see ran through the streets wildly, paying no heed. They bumped into one another, and those who were knocked down scrambled to their feet or were trampled. Whitebridge roiled like a kicked anthill.

As he and Mat pounded toward the gates, Rand abruptly remembered what Thom had said about his height. Without slowing down, he crouched as best he could without looking as if he was crouching. But the gates themselves, thick wood bound with black iron straps, stood open. The two gatetenders, in steel caps and mail tunics worn over cheap-looking red coats with white collars, fingered their halberds and stared uneasily into the town. One of them glanced at Rand and Mat, but they were not the only ones running out of the gates. A steady stream boiled through, panting men clutching wives, weeping women carrying babes and dragging crying children, pale-faced craftsmen still in their aprons, still heedlessly gripping their tools.

There would be no one who could tell which way they had gone, Rand thought as he ran, dazed. *Thom. Oh, Light save me, Thom.*

Mat staggered beside him, caught his balance, and they ran until the last of the fleeing people had fallen away, ran until the town and the White Bridge were far out of sight behind them.

Finally Rand fell to his knees in the dust, pulling air raggedly into his raw throat with great gulps. The road behind stretched empty until it was lost to sight among bare trees. Mat plucked at him.

"Come on. Come on." Mat panted the words. Sweat and dust streaked his face, and he looked ready to collapse. "We have to keep going."

"Thom," Rand said. He tightened his arms around the bundle of Thom's cloak; the instrument cases were hard lumps inside. "Thom."

"He's dead. You saw. You heard. Light, Rand, he's dead!"

"You think Egwene and Moiraine and the rest are dead, too. If they're dead, why are the Myrddraal still hunting them? Answer me that?"

Mat dropped to his knees in the dust beside him. "All right. Maybe they are alive. But Thom— You saw! Blood and ashes, Rand, the same thing can happen to us."

Rand nodded slowly. The road behind them was still empty. He had been halfway expecting—hoping, at least—to see Thom appear, striding along, blowing out his mustaches to tell them how much trouble they were. The Queen's Blessing in Caemlyn. He struggled to his feet and slung Thom's bundle on his back alongside his blanketroll. Mat stared up at him, narrow-eyed and wary.

"Let's go," Rand said, and started down the road toward Caemlyn. He heard Mat muttering, and after a moment he caught up to Rand.

They trudged along the dusty road, heads down and not talking The wind spawned dustdevils that whirled across their path. Sometimes Rand looked back, but the road behind was always empty.

CHAPTER
27

Shelter From the Storm

Perrin fretted over the days spent with the Tuatha'an, traveling south and east in a leisurely fashion. The Traveling People saw no need to hurry; they never did. The colorful wagons did not roll out of a morning until the sun was well above the horizon, and they stopped as early as midafternoon if they came across a congenial spot. The dogs trotted easily alongside the wagons, and often the children did, too. They had no difficulty in keeping up. Any suggestion that they might go further, or more quickly, was met with laughter, or perhaps, "Ah, but would you make the poor horses work so hard?"

He was surprised that Elyas did not share his feelings. Elyas would not ride on the wagons—he preferred to walk, sometimes loping along at the head of the column—but he never suggested leaving, or pressing on ahead.

. The strange bearded man in his strange skin clothes was so different from the gentle Tuatha'an that he stood out wherever he went among the wagons. Even from across the camp there was no mistaking Elyas for one of the People, and not just because of clothes. Elyas moved with the lazy grace of a wolf, only emphasized by his skins and his fur hat, radiating danger as naturally as a fire radiated heat, and the contrast with the Traveling People was sharp. Young and old, the People were joyful on their feet. There was no danger in their grace, only delight. Their children darted about filled with the pure zest of moving, of course, but among the Tuatha'an, graybeards and grandmothers, too, still stepped lightly, their walk a stately dance no less exuberant for its dignity. All the People seemed on the point of dancing, even when standing still, even during the rare times when there was no music in the camp. Fiddles and flutes, dulcimers and zithers and drums spun harmony and counterpoint around the wagons at almost any hour, in camp or on the move. Joyous songs, merry songs, laughing songs, sad songs; if someone was awake in the camp there was usually music.

Elyas met friendly nods and smiles at every wagon he passed, and a cheerful word at any fire where he paused. This must be the face the People always showed to outsiders—open, smiling faces. But Perrin had learned that hidden beneath the surface was the wariness of a half-tame deer. Something deep lay behind the smiles directed at the Emond's Fielders, something that wondered if they were safe, something that faded only slightly over the days. With Elyas the wariness was strong, like deep summer heat shimmering in the air, and it did not fade. When he was not looking they watched him openly as if unsure what he was going to do. When he walked across the camp, feet ready for dancing seemed ready for flight, as well.

Elyas was certainly no more comfortable with their Way of the Leaf than they were with him. His mouth wore a permanent twist when he was around the Tuatha'an. It was not quite condescension and certainly not contempt, but looked as though he would rather be elsewhere than where he was, almost anywhere else. Yet whenever Perrin brought up leaving, Elyas made soothing noises about resting, just for a few days.

"You had hard days before you met me," Elyas said, the third or fourth time he asked, "and you'll have harder still ahead, with Trollocs and Halfmen after you, and Aes Sedai for friends." He grinned around a mouthful of Ila's dried-apple pie. Perrin still found his yellow-eyed gaze disconcerting, even when he was smiling. Perhaps even more when he was smiling; smiles seldom touched those hunter's eyes. Elyas lounged beside Raen's fire, as usual refusing to sit on the logs drawn up for the purpose. "Don't be in such a bloody hurry to put yourself in Aes Sedai hands."

"What if the Fades find us? What's to keep them from it if

we just sit here, waiting? Three wolves can't hold them off, and the Traveling People won't be any help. They won't even defend themselves. The Trollocs will butcher them, and it will be our fault. Anyway, we have to leave them sooner or later. It might as well be sooner."

"Something tells me to wait. Just a few days."

"Something!"

"Relax, lad. Take life as it comes. Run when you have to, fight when you must, rest when you can."

"What are you talking about, something?"

"Have some of this pie. Ila doesn't like me, but she surely feeds me well when I visit. Always good food in the People's camps."

"What 'something'?" Perrin demanded. "If you know something you aren't telling the rest of us. . . ."

Elyas frowned at the piece of pie in his hand, then set it down and dusted his hands together. "Something," he said finally, with a shrug of his shoulders as if he did not understand it completely himself. "Something tells me it's important to wait. A few more days. I don't get feelings like this often, but when I do, I've learned to trust them. They've saved my life in the past. This time it's different, somehow, but it's important. That's clear. You want to run on, then run on. Not me."

That was all he would say, no matter how many times Perrin asked. He lay about, talking with Raen, eating, napping with his hat over his eyes, and refused to discuss leaving. Something told him to wait. Something told him it was important. He would know when it was time to go. Have some pie, lad. Don't lather yourself. Try some of this stew. Relax.

Perrin could not make himself relax. At night he wandered among the rainbow wagons worrying, as much because no one else seemed to see anything to worry about as for any other reason. The Tuatha'an sang and danced, cooked and ate around their campfires—fruits and nuts, berries and vegetables; they ate no meat—and went about a myriad domestic chores as if they had not a care in the world. The children ran and played everywhere, hide-and-seek among the wagons, climbing in the trees around the camp, laughing and rolling on the ground with the dogs. Not a care in the world, for anyone.

Watching them, he itched to get away. *Go, before we bring*

*the hunters down on them. They took us in, and we repay their
kindness by endangering them. At least they have reason to be
lighthearted. Nothing is hunting them. But the rest of us. . . .*

It was hard to get a word with Egwene. Either she was talking with Ila, their heads together in a way that said no men
were welcome, or she was dancing with Aram, swinging round
and round to the flutes and fiddles and drums, to tunes the
Tuatha'an had gathered from all over the world, or to the
sharp, trilling songs of the Traveling People themselves, sharp
whether they were quick or slow. They knew many songs, some
he recognized from home, though often under different names
than they were called in the Two Rivers. "Three Girls in the
Meadow," for instance, the Tinkers named "Pretty Maids
Dancing," and they said "The Wind From the North" was
called "Hard Rain Falling" in some lands and "Berin's Re-
treat" in others. When he asked, not thinking, for "The Tinker
Has My Pots," they fell all over themselves laughing. They
knew it, but as "Toss the Feathers."

He could understand wanting to dance to the People's songs.
Back in Emond's Field no one considered him more than an
adequate dancer, but these songs tugged at his feet, and he
thought he had never danced so long, or so hard, or so well in
his life. Hypnotic, they made his blood pound in rhythm to the
drums.

It was the second evening when for the first time Perrin saw
women dance to some of the slow songs. The fires burned low,
and the night hung close around the wagons, and fingers tapped
a slow rhythm on the drums. First one drum, then another,
until every drum in the camp kept the same low, insistent beat.
There was silence except for the drums. A girl in a red dress
swayed into the light, loosening her shawl. Strings of beads
hung in her hair, and she had kicked off her shoes. A flute
began the melody, wailing softly, and the girl danced. Outstretched arms spread her shawl behind her; her hips undulated
as her bare feet shuffled to the beat of the drums. The girl's
dark eyes fastened on Perrin, and her smile was as slow as her
dance. She turned in small circles, smiling over her shoulder at
him.

He swallowed hard. The heat in his face was not from the
fire. A second girl joined the first, the fringe on their shawls

shaking in time to the drums and the slow rotation of their hips. They smiled at him, and he cleared his throat hoarsely. He was afraid to look around; his face was as red as a beet, and anyone who was not watching the dancers was probably laughing at him. He was sure of it.

As casually as he could manage, he slid off the log as if he were just getting comfortable, but he carefully ended up looking away from the fire, away from the dancers. There was nothing like that in Emond's Field. Dancing with the girls on the Green on a feastday did not even come close. For once he wished that the wind would pick up, to cool him off.

The girls danced into his field of view again, only now they were three. One gave him a sly wink. His eyes darted frantically. *Light,* he thought. *What do I do now? What would Rand do? He knows about girls.*

The dancing girls laughed softly; beads clicked as they tossed their long hair on their shoulders, and he thought his face would burn up. Then a slightly older woman joined the girls, to show them how it was done. With a groan, he gave up altogether and shut his eyes. Even behind his eyelids their laughter taunted and tickled. Even behind his eyelids he could still see them. Sweat beaded on his forehead, and he wished for the wind.

According to Raen the girls did not dance that dance often, and the women rarely did, and according to Elyas it was thanks to Perrin's blushes that they did so every night thereafter.

"I have to thank you," Elyas told him, his tone sober and solemn. "It's different with you young fellows, but at my age it takes more than a fire to warm my bones." Perrin scowled. There was something about Elyas's back as he walked away that said even if nothing showed, he was laughing inside.

Perrin soon learned better than to look away from the dancing women and girls, though the winks and smiles still made him wish he could. One would have been all right, maybe—but five or six, with everyone watching. . . . He never did entirely conquer his blushes.

Then Egwene began learning the dance. Two of the girls who had danced that first night taught her, clapping the rhythm while she repeated the shuffling steps with a borrowed shawl swaying behind her. Perrin started to say something, then decided it was wiser not to crack his teeth. When the girls added the hip movements Egwene started laughing, and the three girls fell giggling into one another's arms. But Egwene persevered, with her eyes glistening and bright spots of color in her cheeks.

Aram watched her dancing with a hot, hungry gaze. The handsome young Tuatha'an had given her a string of blue beads that she wore all the time. Worried frowns now replaced the smiles Ila had worn when she first noticed her grandson's interest in Egwene. Perrin resolved to keep a close eye on young Master Aram.

Once he managed to get Egwene alone, beside a wagon painted in green and yellow. "Enjoying yourself, aren't you?" he said.

"Why shouldn't I?" She fingered the blue beads around her neck, smiling at them. "We don't all have to work at being miserable, the way you do. Don't we deserve a little chance to enjoy ourselves?"

Aram stood not far off—he never got far from Egwene— with his arms folded across his chest, a little smile on his face, half smugness and half challenge. Perrin lowered his voice. "I thought you wanted to get to Tar Valon. You won't learn to be an Aes Sedai here."

Egwene tossed her head. "And I thought you didn't like me wanting to become an Aes Sedai," she said, too sweetly.

"Blood and ashes, do you believe we're safe here? Are these people safe with us here? A Fade could find us anytime."

Her hand trembled on the beads. She lowered it and took a deep breath. "Whatever is going to happen will happen whether we leave today or next week. That's what I believe now. Enjoy yourself, Perrin. It might be the last chance we have."

She brushed his cheek sadly with her fingers. Then Aram held out his hand to her, and she darted to him, already laughing again. As they ran away to where fiddles sang, Aram flashed a triumphant grin over his shoulder at Perrin as if to say, *she is not yours, but she will be mine.*

They were all falling too much under the spell of the People, Perrin thought. *Elyas is right. They don't have to try to convert you to the Way of the Leaf. It seeps into you.*

Ila had taken one look at him huddling out of the wind, then

produced a thick wool cloak out of her wagon; a dark green
cloak, he was pleased to see, after all the reds and yellows. As
he swung it round his shoulders, thinking what a wonder it was
that the cloak was big enough for him, Ila said primly, "It could
fit better." She glanced at the axe at his belt, and when she
looked up at him her eyes were sad above her smile. "It could
fit much better."

All the Tinkers did that. Their smiles never slipped, there
was never any hesitation in their invitations to join them for a
drink or to listen to the music, but their eyes always touched
the axe, and he could feel what they thought. A tool of violence. There is never any excuse for violence to another human
being. The Way of the Leaf.

Sometimes he wanted to shout at them. There were Trollocs
in the world, and Fades. There were those who would cut down
every leaf. The Dark One was out there, and the Way of the
Leaf would burn in Ba'alzamon's eyes. Stubbornly he continued to wear the axe. He took to keeping his cloak thrown back,
even when it was windy, so the half-moon blade was never hidden. Now and again Elyas looked quizzically at the weapon
hanging heavy at his side and grinned at him, those yellow eyes
seeming to read his mind. That almost made him cover the axe.
Almost.

If the Tuatha'an camp was a source of constant irritation, at
least his dreams were normal there. Sometimes he woke up
sweating from a dream of Trollocs and Fades storming into the
camp, rainbow-colored wagons turning to bonfires from hurled
torches, people falling in pools of blood, men and women and
children who ran and screamed and died but made no effort to
defend themselves against slashing scythe-like swords. Night
after night he bolted upright in the dark, panting and reaching
for his axe before he realized the wagons were not in flames,
that no bloody-muzzled shapes snarled over torn and twisted
bodies littering the ground. But those were ordinary nightmares, and oddly comforting in their way. If there was ever a
place for the Dark One to be in his dreams, it was in those, but
he was not. No Ba'alzamon. Just ordinary nightmares.

He was aware of the wolves, though, when he was awake.
They kept their dista e from the camps, and from the caravan
on the move, but he always knew where they were. He could

feel their contempt for the dogs guarding the Tuatha'an. Noisy beasts who had forgotten what their jaws were for, had forgotten the taste of warm blood; they might frighten humans, but they would slink away on their bellies if the pack ever came. Each day his awareness was sharper, more clear.

Dapple grew more impatient with every sunset. That Elyas wanted to do this thing of taking the humans south made it worth doing, but if it must be done, then let it be done. Let this slow travel end. Wolves were meant to roam, and she did not like being away from the pack so long. Impatience burned in Wind, too. Hunting was worse than poor here, and he despised living on field mice, something for cubs to stalk while learning to hunt, fit food for the old, no longer able to pull down a deer or hamstring a wild ox. Sometimes Wind thought that Burn had been right; leave human troubles to humans. But he was wary of such thoughts when Dapple was around, and even more so around Hopper. Hopper was a scarred and grizzled fighter, impassive with the knowledge of years, with guile that more than made up for anything of which age might have robbed him. For humans he cared nothing, but Dapple wished this thing done, and Hopper would wait as she waited and run as she ran. Wolf or man, bull or bear, whatever challenged Dapple would find Hopper's jaws waiting to send him to the long sleep. That was the whole of life for Hopper, and that kept Wind cautious, and Dapple seemed to ignore the thoughts of both.

All of it was clear in Perrin's mind. Fervently he wished for Caemlyn, for Moiraine and Tar Valon. Even if there were no answers, there could be an end to it. Elyas looked at him, and he was sure the yellow-eyed man knew. *Please, let there be an end.*

The dream began more pleasantly than most he had of late. He·was at Alsbet Luhhan's kitchen table, sharpening his axe with a stone. Mistress Luhhan never allowed forge work, or anything that smacked of it, to be brought into the house. Master Luhhan even had to take her knives outside to sharpen them. But she tended her cooking and never said a word about the axe. She did not even say anything when a wolf entered from deeper in the house and curled up between Perrin and the door to the yard. Perrin went on sharpening; it would be time to use it, soon.

Abruptly the wolf rose, rumbling deep in its throat, the thick ruff of fur on its neck rising. Ba'alzamon stepped into the kitchen from the yard. Mistress Luhhan went on with her cooking.

Perrin scrambled to his feet, raising the axe, but Ba'alzamon ignored the weapon, concentrating on the wolf, instead. Flames danced where his eyes should be. "Is this what you have to protect you? Well, I have faced this before. Many times before."

He crooked a finger, and the wolf howled as fire burst out of its eyes and ears and mouth, out of its skin. The stench of burning meat and hair filled the kitchen. Alsbet Luhhan lifted the lid on a pot and stirred with a wooden spoon.

Perrin dropped the axe and jumped forward, trying to beat out the flames with his hands. The wolf crumpled to black ash between his palms. Staring at the shapeless pile of char on Mistress Luhhan's clean-swept floor, he backed away. He wished he could wipe the greasy soot from his hands, but the thought of scrubbing it off on his clothes turned his stomach. He snatched up the axe, gripping the haft until his knuckles cracked.

"Leave me alone!" he shouted. Mistress Luhhan tapped the spoon on the rim of the pot and replaced the lid, humming to herself.

"You cannot run from me," Ba'alzamon said. "You cannot hide from me. If you are the one, you are mine." The heat from the fires of his face forced Perrin across the kitchen until his back came up against the wall. Mistress Luhhan opened the oven to check her bread. "The Eye of the World will consume you," Ba'alzamon said. "I mark you mine!" He flung out his clenched hand as if throwing something; when his fingers opened, a raven streaked at Perrin's face.

Perrin screamed as the black beak pierced his left eye . . .

. . . and sat up, clutching his face, surrounded by the sleeping wagons of the Traveling People. Slowly he lowered his hands. There was no pain, no blood. But he could remember it, remember the stabbing agony.

He shuddered, and suddenly Elyas was squatting beside him in the predawn, one hand outstretched as if to shake him awake. Beyond the trees where the wagons lay, the wolves howled, one sharp cry from three throats. He shared their sensations. *Fire. Pain. Fire. Hate. Hate! Kill!*

"Yes," Elyas said softly. "It is time. Get up, boy. It's time for us to go."

Perrin scrambled out of his blankets. While he was still bundling his blanketroll, Raen came out of his wagon, rubbing sleep from his eyes. The Seeker glanced at the sky and froze halfway down the steps, his hands still raised to his face. Only his eyes moved as he studied the sky intently, though Perrin could not understand what he was looking at. A few clouds hung in the east, undersides streaked with pink from the sun yet to rise, but there was nothing else to see. Raen seemed to listen, as well, and smell the air, but there was no sound except the wind in the trees and no smell but the faint smoky remnant of last night's campfires.

Elyas returned with his own scanty belongings, and Raen came the rest of the way down. "We must change the direction we travel, my old friend." The Seeker looked uneasily at the sky again. "We go another way this day. Will you be coming with us?" Elyas shook his head, and Raen nodded as if he had known all along. "Well, take care, my old friend. There is something about today. . . ." He started to look up once more, but pulled his eyes back down before they rose above the wagon tops. "I think the wagons will go east. Perhaps all the way to the Spine of the World. Perhaps we'll find a *stedding*, and stay there awhile."

"Trouble never enters the *stedding*," Elyas agreed. "But the Ogier are none too open to strangers."

"Everyone is open to the Traveling People," Raen said, and grinned. "Besides, even Ogier have pots and things to mend. Come, let us have some breakfast, and we'll talk about it."

"No time," Elyas said. "We move on today, too. As soon as possible. It's a day for moving, it seems."

Raen tried to convince him to at least stay long enough for food, and when Ila appeared from the wagon with Egwene, she added her arguments, though not as strenuously as her husband. She said all of the right words, but her politeness was stiff, and it was plain she would be glad to see Elyas's back, if not Egwene's.

Egwene did not notice the regretful, sidelong looks Ila gave

her. She asked what was going on, and Perrin prepared himself
for her to say she wanted to stay with the Tuatha'an, but when
Elyas explained she only nodded thoughtfully and hurried back
into the wagon to gather her things.

Finally Raen threw up his hands. "All right. I don't know
that I have ever let a visitor leave this camp without a farewell
feast, but. . . ." Uncertainly, his eyes raised toward the sky
again. "Well, we need an early start ourselves, I think. Perhaps
we will eat as we journey. But at least let everyone say good-
bye."

Elyas started to protest, but Raen was already hurrying from
wagon to wagon, pounding on the doors where there was no
one awake. By the time a Tinker came, leading Bela, the whole
camp had turned out in their finest and brightest, a mass of
color that made Raen and Ila's red-and-yellow wagon seem almost plain. The big dogs strolled through the crowd with their
tongues lolling out of their mouths, looking for someone to
scratch their ears, while Perrin and the others endured handshake after handshake and hug after hug. The girls who had
danced every night would not be content with shaking hands,
and their hugs made Perrin suddenly wish he was not leaving
after all—until he remembered how many others were watching, and then his face almost matched the Seeker's wagon.

Aram drew Egwene a little aside. Perrin could not hear what
he had to say to her over the noise of goodbyes, but she kept
shaking her head, slowly at first, then more firmly as he began
to gesture pleadingly. His face shifted from pleading to arguing,
but she continued to shake her head stubbornly until Ila res-
cued her with a few sharp words to her grandson. Scowling,
Aram pushed away through the crowd, abandoning the rest of
the farewell. Ila watched him go, hesitating on the point of calling him back. *She's relieved, too,* Perrin thought. *Relieved he
doesn't want to go with us—with Egwene.*

When he had shaken every hand in the camp at least once
and hugged every girl at least twice, the crowd moved back,
opening a little space around Raen and Ila, and the three vis-
itors.

"You came in peace," Raen intoned, bowing formally, hands
on his chest. "Depart now in peace. Always will our fires welcome you, in peace. The Way of the Leaf is peace."

"Peace be on you always," Elyas replied, "and on all the People." He hesitated, then added, "I will find the song, or another will find the song, but the song will be sung, this year or in a year to come. As it once was, so shall it be again, world without end."

Raen blinked in surprise, and Ila looked completely flabbergasted, but all the other Tuatha'an murmured in reply, "World without end. World and time without end." Raen and his wife hurriedly said the same after everyone else.

Then it really was time to go. A few last farewells, a few last admonitions to take care, a few last smiles and winks, and they were making their way out of the camp. Raen accompanied them as far as the edge of the trees, a pair of the dogs cavorting by his side.

"Truly, my old friend, you must take great care. This day. . . . There is wickedness loose in the world, I fear, and whatever you pretend, you are not so wicked that it will not gobble you up."

"Peace be on you," Elyas said.

"And on you," Raen said sadly.

When Raen was gone, Elyas scowled at finding the other two looking at him. "So I don't believe in their fool song," he growled. "No need to make them feel bad by messing up their ceremony, was there? I told you they set a store by ceremony sometimes."

"Of course," Egwene said gently. "No need at all." Elyas turned away muttering to himself.

Dapple, Wind, and Hopper came to greet Elyas, not frolicking as the dogs had done, but a dignified meeting of equals. Perrin caught what passed between them. *Fire eyes. Pain. Heartfang. Death. Heartfang.* Perrin knew what they meant. The Dark One. They were telling about his dream. Their dream.

He shivered as the wolves ranged out ahead, scouting the way. It was Egwene's turn to ride Bela, and he walked beside her. Elyas led, as usual, a steady, ground-eating pace.

Perrin did not want to think about his dream. He had thought that the wolves made them safe. *Not complete. Accept. Full heart. Full mind. You still struggle. Only complete when you accept.*

He forced the wolves out of his head, and blinked in surprise. He had not known he could do that. He determined not to let them back in again. *Even in dreams?* He was not sure if the thought was his or theirs.

Egwene still wore the string of blue beads Aram had given her, and a little sprig of something with tiny, bright red leaves in her hair, another gift from the young Tuatha'an. That Aram had tried to talk her into staying with the Traveling People, Perrin was sure. He was glad she had not given in, but he wished she did not finger the beads so fondly.

Finally he said, "What did you spend so much time talking about with Ila? If you weren't dancing with that long-legged fellow, you were talking to her like it was some kind of secret."

"Ila was giving me advice on being a woman," Egwene replied absently. He began laughing, and she gave him a hooded, dangerous look that he failed to see.

"Advice! Nobody tells us how to be men. We just are."

"That," Egwene said, "is probably why you make such a bad job of it." Up ahead, Elyas cackled loudly.

Wolf Brother

CHAPTER
28

Footprints in Air

N ynaeve stared in wonder at what lay ahead down the river, the White Bridge gleaming in the sun with a milky glow. *Another legend,* she thought, glancing at the Warder and the Aes Sedai, riding just ahead of her. *Another legend, and they don't even seem to notice.* She resolved not to stare where they could see. *They'll laugh if they see me gaping like a country bumpkin.* The three rode on silently toward the fabled White Bridge.

Since that morning after Shadar Logoth, when she had found Moiraine and Lan on the bank of the Arinelle, there had been little in the way of real conversation between her and the Aes Sedai. There had been talk, of course, but nothing of substance as Nynaeve saw it. Moiraine's attempts to talk her into going to Tar Valon, for instance. Tar Valon. She would go there, if need be, and take their training, but not for the reasons the Aes Sedai thought. If Moiraine had brought harm to Egwene and the boys. . . .

Sometimes, against her will, Nynaeve had found herself thinking of what a Wisdom could do with the One Power, of what she could do. Whenever she realized what was in her head, though, a flash of anger burned it out. The Power was a filthy thing. She would have nothing to do with it. Unless she had to.

The cursed woman only wanted to talk about taking her to

Tar Valon for training. Moiraine would not tell her anything! It was not as if she wanted to know so much.

"How do you mean to find them?" she remembered demanding.

"As I have told you," Moiraine replied without bothering to look back at her, "I will know when I am close to the two who have lost their coins." It was not the first time Nynaeve had asked, but the Aes Sedai's voice was like a still pond that refused to ripple no matter how many stones Nynaeve threw; it made the Wisdom's blood boil every time she was exposed to it. Moiraine went on as if she could not feel Nynaeve's eyes on her back; Nynaeve knew she must be able to, she was staring so hard. "The longer it takes, the closer I must come, but I will know. As for the one who still has his token, so long as he has it in his possession I can follow him across half the world, if need be."

"And then? What do you plan when you've found them, Aes Sedai?" She did not for a minute believe the Aes Sedai would be so intent on finding them if she did not have plans.

"Tar Valon, Wisdom."

"Tar Valon, Tar Valon. That's all you ever say, and I am becoming—"

"Part of the training you will receive in Tar Valon, Wisdom, will teach you to control your temper. You can do nothing with the One Power when emotion rules your mind." Nynaeve opened her mouth, but the Aes Sedai went right on. "Lan, I must speak with you a moment."

The two put their heads together, and Nynaeve was left with a sullen glower that she hated every time she realized it was on her face. It came too often as the Aes Sedai deftly turned her questions off onto another subject, slid easily by her conversational traps, or ignored her shouts until they ended in silence. The scowl made her feel like a girl who had been caught acting the fool by someone in the Women's Circle. That was a feeling Nynaeve was not used to, and the calm smile on Moiraine's face only made it worse.

If only there was some way to get rid of the woman. Lan would be better by himself—a Warder should be able to handle what was needed, she told herself hastily, feeling a sudden flush; no other reason—but one meant the other.

And yet, Lan made her even more furious than Moiraine. She could not understand how he managed to get under her skin so easily. He rarely said anything—sometimes not a dozen words in a day—and he never took part in any of the . . . discussions with Moiraine. He was often apart from the two women, scouting the land, but even when he was there he kept a little to one side, watching them as if watching a duel. Nynaeve wished he would stop. If it was a duel, she had not managed to score once, and Moiraine did not even seem to realize she was in a fight. Nynaeve could have done without his cool blue eyes, without even a silent audience.

That had been the way of their journey, for the most part. Quiet, except when her temper got the best of her, and sometimes when she shouted the sound of her voice seemed to crash in the silence like breaking glass. The land itself was quiet, as if the world were pausing to catch its breath. The wind moaned in the trees, but all else was still. The wind seemed distant, too, even when it was cutting through the cloak on her back.

At first the stillness was restful after everything that had happened. It seemed as if she had not known a moment of quiet since before Winternight. By the end of the first day alone with the Aes Sedai and the Warder, though, she was looking over her shoulder and fidgeting in her saddle as if she had an itch in the middle of her back where she could not reach. The silence seemed like crystal doomed to shatter, and waiting for the first crack put her teeth on edge.

It weighed on Moiraine and Lan, too, as outwardly unperturbable as they were. She soon realized that, beneath their calm surfaces, hour by hour they wound tighter and tighter, like clocksprings being forced to the breaking point. Moiraine seemed to listen to things that were not there, and what she heard put a crease in her forehead. Lan watched the forest and the river as if the leafless trees and wide, slow water carried the signs of traps and ambushes waiting ahead.

Part of her was glad that she was not the only one who apprehended that poised-on-the-brink feel to the world, but if it affected them, it was real, and another part of her wanted nothing so much as for it to be just her imagination. Something of it

tickled the corners of her mind, as when she listened to the
wind, but now she knew that that had to do with the One
Power, and she could not bring herself to embrace those ripples
at the edge of thought.

"It is nothing," Lan said quietly when she asked. He did not
look at her while he spoke; his eyes never ceased their scanning. Then, contradicting what he had just said, he added,
"You should go back to your Two Rivers when we reach
Whitebridge, and the Caemlyn Road. It's too dangerous here.
Nothing will try to stop you going back, though." It was the
longest speech he made all that day.

"She is part of the Pattern, Lan," Moiraine said chidingly.
Her gaze was elsewhere, too. "It is the Dark One, Nynaeve.
The storm has left us . . . for a time, at least." She raised one
hand as though feeling the air, then scrubbed it on her dress
unconsciously, as if she had touched filth. "He is still watching,
however"—she sighed—"and his gaze is stronger. Not on us,
but on the world. How much longer before he is strong enough
to. . . ."

Nynaeve hunched her shoulders; suddenly she could almost
feel someone staring at her back. It was one explanation she
would just as soon the Aes Sedai had not given her.

Lan scouted their path down the river, but where before he
had chosen the way, now Moiraine did so, as surely as if she
followed some unseen track, footprints in air, the scent of
memory. Lan only checked the route she intended, to see that
it was safe. Nynaeve had the feeling that even if he said it was
not, Moiraine would insist on it anyway. And he would go, she
was sure. Straight down the river to. . . .

With a start, Nynaeve pulled out of her thoughts. They were
at the foot of the White Bridge. The pale arch shone in the
sunlight, a milky spiderweb too delicate to stand, sweeping
across the Arinelle. The weight of a man would bring it crash-
ing down, much less that of a horse. Surely it would collapse
under its own weight any minute.

Lan and Moiraine rode unconcernedly ahead, up the gleaming white approach and onto the bridge, hooves ringing, not
like steel on glass, but like steel on steel. The surface of the
bridge certainly looked as slick as glass, wet glass, but it gave
the horses a firm, sure footing.

Nynaeve made herself follow, but from the first step she half waited for the entire structure to shatter under them. *If lace were made of glass,* she thought, *it would look like this.*

It was not until they were almost all the way across that she noticed the tarry smell of char thickening the air. In a moment she saw.

Around the square at the foot of the White Bridge piles of blackened timbers, still leaking smoky threads, replaced half a dozen buildings. Men in poorly fitting red uniforms and tarnished armor patrolled the streets, but they marched quickly, as if afraid of finding anything, and they looked over their shoulders as they went. Townspeople—the few who were out—almost ran, shoulders hunched, as though something were chasing them.

Lan looked grim, even for him, and people walked wide of the three of them, even the soldiers. The Warder sniffed the air and grimaced, growling under his breath. It was no wonder to Nynaeve, with the stink of burn so strong.

"The Wheel weaves as the Wheel wills," Moiraine mumbled. "No eye can see the Pattern until it is woven."

In the next moment she was down off Aldieb and speaking to townsfolk. She did not ask questions; she gave sympathy, and to Nynaeve's surprise it appeared genuine. People who shied away from Lan, ready to hurry from any stranger, stopped to speak with Moiraine. They appeared startled themselves at what they were doing, but they opened up, after a fashion, under Moiraine's clear gaze and soothing voice. The Aes Sedai's eyes seemed to share the people's hurt, to empathize with their confusion, and tongues loosened.

They still lied, though. Most of them. Some denied there had been any trouble at all. Nothing at all. Moiraine mentioned the burned buildings all around the square. Everything was fine, they insisted, staring past what they did not want to see.

One fat fellow spoke with a hollow heartiness, but his cheek twitched at every noise behind him. With a grin that kept slipping, he claimed an overturned lamp had started a fire that spread with the wind before anything could be done. One glance showed Nynaeve that no burned structure stood alongside another.

There were almost as many different stories as there were

people. Several women lowered their voices conspiratorially. The truth of the matter was there was a man somewhere in the town meddling with the One Power. It was time to have the Aes Sedai in; past time, was the way they saw it, no matter what the men said about Tar Valon. Let the Red Ajah settle matters.

One man claimed it had been an attack by bandits, and another said a riot by Darkfriends. "Those ones going to see the false Dragon, you know," he confided darkly. "They're all over the place. Darkfriends, every one."

Still others spoke of some kind of trouble—they were vague about exactly what kind—that had come downriver on a boat.

"We showed them," a narrow-faced man muttered, scrubbing his hand together nervously. "Let them keep that kind of thing in the Borderlands, where it belongs. We went down to the docks and—" He cut off so abruptly his teeth clicked. Without another word he scurried off, peering back over his shoulder at them as if he thought they might chase him down.

The boat had gotten away—that much was clear, eventually, from others—cutting its moorings and fleeing downriver only the day before while a mob poured onto the docks. Nynaeve wondered if Egwene and the boys had been on board. One woman said that a gleeman had been on the boat. If that had been Thom Merrilin. . . .

She tried her opinion on Moiraine, that some of the Emond's Fielders might have fled on the boat. The Aes Sedai listened patiently, nodding, until she was done.

"Perhaps," Moiraine said then, but she sounded doubtful.

An inn still stood in the square, the common room divided in two by a shoulder-high wall. Moiraine paused as she stepped into the inn, feeling the air with her hand. She smiled at whatever it was she felt, but she would say nothing of it, then.

Their meal was consumed in silence, silence not only at their table, but throughout the common room. The handful of people eating there concentrated on their own plates and their own thoughts. The innkeeper, dusting tables with a corner of his apron, muttered to himself continually, but always too low to be heard. Nynaeve thought it would not be pleasant sleeping there; even the air was heavy with fear.

About the time they pushed their plates away, wiped clean

with the last scraps of bread, one of the red-uniformed soldiers appeared in the doorway. He seemed resplendent to Nynaeve, in his peaked helmet and burnished breastplate, until he took a pose just inside the door, with a hand resting on the hilt of his sword and a stern look on his face, and used a finger to ease his too-tight collar. It made her think of Cenn Buie trying to act the way a Village Councilor should.

Lan spared him one glance and snorted. "Militia. Useless."

The soldier looked over the room, letting his eyes come to rest on them. He hesitated, then took a deep breath before stomping over to demand, all in a rush, who they were, what their business was in Whitebridge, and how long they intended to stay.

"We are leaving as soon as I finish my ale," Lan said. He took another slow swallow before looking up at the soldier. "The Light illumine good Queen Morgase."

The red-uniformed man opened his mouth, then took a good look at Lan's eyes and stepped back. He caught himself immediately, with a glance at Moiraine and her. She thought for a moment that he was going to do something foolish to keep from looking the coward in front of two women. In her experience, men were often idiots that way. But too much had happened in Whitebridge; too much uncertainty had escaped from the cellars of men's minds. The militiaman looked back at Lan and reconsidered once more. The Warder's hard-planed face was expressionless, but there were those cold blue eyes. So cold.

The militiaman settled on a brisk nod. "See that you do. Too many strangers around these days for the good of the Queen's peace." Turning on his heel he stomped out again, practicing his stern look on the way. None of the locals in the inn seemed to notice.

"Where are we going?" Nynaeve demanded of the Warder. The mood in the room was such that she kept her voice low, but she made sure it was firm, too. "After the boat?"

Lan looked at Moiraine, who shook her head slightly and said, "First I must find the one I can be sure of finding, and at present he is somewhere to the north of us. I do not think the other two went with the boat in any case." A small, satisfied smile touched her lips. "They were in this room, perhaps a day

ago, no more than two. Afraid, but they left alive. The trace
would not have lasted without that strong emotion."

"Which two?" Nynaeve leaned over the table intently. "Do
you know?" The Aes Sedai shook her head, the slightest of
motions, and Nynaeve settled back. "If they're only a day or
two ahead, why don't we go after them first?"

"I know they were here," Moiraine said in that insufferably
calm voice, "but beyond that I cannot say if they went east or
north or south. I trust they are smart enough to have gone east,
toward Caemlyn, but I do not know, and lacking their tokens, I
will not know where they are until I am perhaps within half a
mile. In two days they could have gone twenty miles, or forty,
in any direction, if fear urged them, and they were certainly
afraid when they left here."

"But—"

"Wisdom, however fearful they were, in whatever direction
they ran, eventually they will remember Caemlyn, and it is
there I will find them. But I will help the one I can find now,
first."

Nynaeve opened her mouth again, but Lan cut her off in a
soft voice. "They had reason to be afraid." He looked around,
then lowered his voice. "There was a Halfman here." He grimaced, the way he had in the square. "I can still smell him
everywhere."

Moiraine sighed. "I will keep hope until I know it is gone. I
refuse to believe the Dark One can win so easily. I will find all
three of them alive and well. I must believe it."

"I want to find the boys, too," Nynaeve said, "but what
about Egwene? You never even mention her, and you ignore
me when I ask. I thought you were going to take her off to"—
she glanced at the other tables, and lowered her voice—"to Tar
Valon."

The Aes Sedai studied the tabletop for a moment before raising her eyes to Nynaeve's, and when she did, Nynaeve started
back from a flash of anger that almost seemed to make
Moiraine's eyes glow. Then her back stiffened, her own anger
rising, but before she could say a word, the Aes Sedai spoke
coldly.

"I hope to find Egwene alive and well, too. I do not easily

give up young women with that much ability once I have found them. But it will be as the Wheel weaves."

Nynaeve felt a cold ball in the pit of her stomach. *Am I one of those young women you won't give up? We'll see about that, Aes Sedai. The Light burn you, we'll see about that!*

The meal was finished in silence, and it was a silent three who rode through the gates and down the Caemlyn Road. Moiraine's eyes searched the horizon to the northeast. Behind them, the smoke-stained town of Whitebridge cowered.

CHAPTER 29

Eyes Without Pity

Elyas pushed for speed across the brown grass flatland as if trying to make up for the time spent with the Traveling People, setting a pace southward that had even Bela grateful to stop when twilight deepened. Despite his desire for haste, though, he took precautions he had not taken before. At night they had a fire only if there was dead wood already on the ground. He would not let them break so much as a twig off of a standing tree. The fires he made were small, and always hidden in a pit carefully dug where he had cut away a plug of sod. As soon as their meal was prepared, he buried the coals and replaced the plug. Before they set out. again in the gray false dawn, he went over the campsite inch by inch to make sure there was no sign that anyone had ever been there. He even righted overturned rocks and straightened bent-down weeds. He did it quickly, never taking more than a few minutes, but they did not leave until he was satisfied.

Perrin did not think the precautions were much good against dreams, but when he began to think of what they might be good against, he wished it were only the dreams. The first time, Egwene asked anxiously if the Trollocs were back, but Elyas only shook his head and urged them on. Perrin said nothing. He knew there were no Trollocs close; the wolves scented only grass and trees and small animals. It was not fear of Trollocs that drove Elyas, but that something else of which even Elyas was not sure. The wolves knew nothing of what it was, but they sensed Elyas's urgent wariness, and they began to scout as if danger ran at their heels or waited in ambush over the next rise.

The land became long, rolling crests, too low to be called hills, rising across their path. A carpet of tough grass, still winter sere and dotted with rank weeds, spread before them, rippled by an east wind that had nothing to cut it for a hundred miles. The groves of trees grew more scattered. The sun rose reluctantly, without warmth.

Among the squat ridges Elyas followed the contours of the land as much as possible, and he avoided topping the rises whenever possible. He seldom talked, and when he did. . . .

"You know how long this is taking, going around every bloody little hill like this? Blood and ashes! I'll be till summer getting you off my hands. No, we can't just go in a straight line! How many times do I have to tell you? You have any idea, even the faintest, how a man stands out on a ridgeline in country like this? Burn me, but we're going back and forth as much as forward. Wiggling like a snake. I could move faster with my feet tied. Well, you going to stare at me, or you going to walk?"

Perrin exchanged glances with Egwene. She stuck her tongue out at Elyas's back. Neither of them said anything. The one time Egwene had protested that Elyas was the one who wanted to go around the hills and he should not blame them, it got her a lecture on how sound carried, delivered in a growl that could have been heard a mile off. He gave the lecture over his shoulder, and he never even slowed to give it.

Whether he was talking or not, Elyas's eyes searched all around them, sometimes staring as if there were something to see except the same coarse grass that was under their feet. If he did see anything, Perrin could not, and neither could the wolves. Elyas's forehead grew extra furrows, but he would not explain, not why they had to hurry, not what he was afraid was hunting them.

Sometimes a longer ridge than usual lay across their path, stretching miles and miles to east and west. Even Elyas had to agree that going around those would take them too far out of their way. He did not let them simply cross over, though. Leaving them at the base of the slope, he would creep up to the crest on his belly, peering over as cautiously as though the wolves had not scouted there ten minutes before. Waiting at the bottom of the ridge, minutes passed like hours, and the not knowing pressed on them. Egwene chewed her lip and unconsciously clicked the beads Aram had given her through her fingers. Perrin waited doggedly. His stomach twisted up in a sick knot, but he managed to keep his face calm, managed to keep the turmoil hidden inside.

The wolves will warn if there's danger. It would be wonderful if they went away, if they just vanished, but right now . . . right now, they'll give warning. What is he looking for? What?

After a long search with only his eyes above the rise, Elyas always motioned them to come ahead. Every time the way ahead was clear—until the next time they found a ridge they could not go around. At the third such ridge, Perrin's stomach lurched. Sour fumes rose in his throat, and he knew if he had to wait even five minutes he would vomit. "I. . . ." He swallowed. "I'm coming, too."

"Keep low," was all Elyas said.

As soon as he spoke Egwene jumped down from Bela.

The fur-clad man pushed his round hat forward and peered at her from under the edge. "You expecting to make that mare crawl?" he said dryly.

Her mouth worked, but no sound came out. Finally she shrugged, and Elyas turned away without another word and began climbing the easy slope. Perrin hurried after him.

Well short of the crest Elyas made a downward motion and a moment later flattened himself on the ground, wriggling forward the last few yards. Perrin flopped on his belly.

At the top, Elyas took off his hat before raising his head ever so slowly. Peering through a clump of thorny weeds, Perrin saw only the same rolling plain that lay behind them. The downslope was bare, though a clump of trees a hundred paces across grew in the hollow, perhaps half a mile south from the ridge. The wolves had already been through it, smelling no trace of Trollocs or Myrddraal.

East and west the land was the same as far as Perrin could see, rolling grassland and wide-scattered thickets. Nothing moved. The wolves were more than a mile ahead, out of sight; at that distance he could barely feel them. They had seen nothing when they covered this ground. *What is he looking for? There's nothing there.*

"We're wasting time," he said, starting to stand, and a flock of ravens burst out of the trees below, fifty, a hundred black birds, spiraling into the sky. He froze in a crouch as they milled over the trees. *The Dark One's Eyes. Did they see me?* Sweat trickled down his face.

As if one thought had suddenly sparked in a hundred tiny minds, every raven broke sharply in the same direction. South. The flock disappeared over the next rise, already descending. To the east another thicket disgorged more ravens. The black mass wheeled twice and headed south.

Shaking, he lowered himself to the ground slowly. He tried to speak, but his mouth was too dry. After a minute he managed to work up some spit. "Was that what you were afraid of? Why didn't you say something? Why didn't the wolves see them?"

"Wolves don't look up in trees much," Elyas growled. "And no, I wasn't looking for this. I told you, I didn't know what. . . ." Far to the west a black cloud rose over yet another grove and winged southward. They were too far off to make out individual birds. "It isn't a big hunt, thank the Light. They don't know. Even after. . . ." He turned to stare back the way they had come.

Perrin swallowed. Even after the dream, Elyas had meant. "Not big?" he said. "Back home you won't see that many ravens in a whole year."

Elyas shook his head. "In the Borderlands I've seen sweeps with a thousand ravens to the flock. Not too often—there's a bounty on ravens there—but it has happened." He was still looking north. "Hush, now."

Perrin felt it, then; the effort of reaching out to the distant wolves. Elyas wanted Dapple and her companions to quit scouting ahead, to hurry back and check their backtrail. His already gaunt face tightened and thinned under the strain. The wolves were so far away Perrin could not even feel them. *Hurry. Watch the sky. Hurry.*

Faintly Perrin caught the reply from far to the south. *We come.* An image flashed in his mind—wolves running, muzzles pointing into the wind of their haste, running as if wildfire raced behind, running—flashed and was gone in an instant.

Elyas slumped and drew a deep breath. Frowning, he peered over the ridge, then back to the north, and muttered under his breath.

"You think there are more ravens behind us?" Perrin asked.

"Could be," Elyas said vaguely. "They do it that way, sometimes. I know a place, if we can reach it by dark. We have to keep moving until full dark anyway, even if we don't get there, but we can't go as fast as I would like. Can't afford to get too close to the ravens ahead of us. But if they're behind us, too. . . ."

"Why dark?" Perrin said. "What place? Somewhere safe from the ravens?"

"Safe from ravens," Elyas said, "but too many people know. . . . Ravens roost for the night. We don't have to worry about them finding us in the dark. The Light send ravens are all we have to worry about then." With one more look over the crest, he rose and waved to Egwene to bring Bela up. "But dark is a long way off. We have to get moving." He started down the far slope in a shambling run, each stride barely catching him on the edge of falling. "Move, burn you!"

Perrin moved, half running, half sliding, after him.

Egwene topped the rise behind them, kicking Bela to a trot. A grin of relief bloomed on her face when she saw them. "What's going on?" she called, urging the shaggy mare to catch up. "When you disappeared like that, I thought. . . . What happened?"

Perrin saved his breath for running until she reached them. He explained about the ravens and Elyas's safe place, but it was a disjointed story. After a strangled, "Ravens!" she kept interrupting with questions for which, as often as not, he had no answers. Between them, he did not finish until they reached the next ridge.

Ordinarily—if anything about the journey could be called ordinary—they would have gone around this one rather than over, but Elyas insisted on scouting anyway.

"You want to just saunter right into the middle of them, boy?" was his sour comment.

Egwene stared at the crest of the ridge, licking her lips, as if she wanted to go with Elyas this time and wanted to stay where she was, too. Elyas was the only one who showed no hesitation. Perrin wondered if the ravens ever doubled back. It would be a fine thing to reach the crest at the same time as a flock of ravens.

At the top he inched his head up until he could just see, and heaved a sigh of relief when all he saw was a copse of trees a little to the west. There were no ravens to be seen. Abruptly a fox burst out of the trees, running hard. Ravens poured from the branches after it. The beat of their wings almost drowned out a desperate whining from the fox. A black whirlwind dove and swirled around it. The fox's jaws snapped at them, but they darted in, and darted away untouched, black beaks glistening wetly. The fox turned back toward the trees, seeking the safety of its den. It ran awkwardly now, head low, fur dark and bloody, and the ravens flapped around it, more and more of them at once, the fluttering mass thickening until it hid the fox completely. As suddenly as they had descended the ravens rose, wheeled, and vanished over the next rise to the south. A misshapen lump of torn fur marked what had been the fox.

Perrin swallowed hard. *Light! They could do that to us. A hundred ravens. They could—*

"Move," Elyas growled, jumping up. He waved to Egwene to come on, and without waiting set off at a trot toward the trees. "Move, burn you!" he called over his shoulder. "Move!"

Egwene galloped Bela over the rise and caught them before they reached the bottom of the slope. There was no time for explanations, but her eyes picked out the fox right away. Her face went as white as snow.

Elyas reached the trees and turned there, at the edge of the copse, waving vigorously for them to hurry. Perrin tried to run faster and stumbled. Arms windmilling, he barely caught himself short of going flat on his face. *Blood and ashes! I'm running as fast as I can!*

A lone raven winged out of the copse. It tilted toward them, screamed, and spun toward the south. Knowing he was already too late, Perrin fumbled his sling from around his waist. He was still trying to get a stone from his pocket to the sling when the raven abruptly folded up in mid-air and plummeted to the

ground. His mouth dropped open, and then he saw the sling
hanging from Egwene's hand. She grinned at him unsteadily.

"Don't stand there counting your toes!" Elyas called.

With a start Perrin hurried into the trees, then jumped out of
the way to avoid being trampled by Egwene and Bela.

Far to the west, almost out of sight, what seemed like a dark
mist rose into the air. Perrin felt the wolves passing in that
direction, heading north. He felt them notice ravens, to the left
and right of them, without slowing. The dark mist swirled
northward as if pursuing the wolves, then abruptly broke off
and flashed to the south.

"Do you think they saw us?" Egwene asked. "We were already in the trees, weren't we? They couldn't see us at that
distance. Could they? Not that far off."

"We saw them at that distance," Elyas said dryly. Perrin
shifted uneasily, and Egwene drew a frightened breath. "If they
had seen us," Elyas growled, "they'd have been down on us
like they were on that fox. Think, if you want to stay alive.
Fear will kill you if you don't control it." His penetrating stare
held on each of them for a moment. Finally he nodded.
"They're gone, now, and we should be, too. Keep those slings
handy. Might be useful again."

As they moved out of the copse, Elyas angled them westward
from the line of march they had been following. Perrin's breath
snagged in his throat; it was as if they were chasing after the
last ravens they had seen. Elyas kept on tirelessly, and there
was nothing for them to do but follow. After all, Elyas knew a
safe place. Somewhere. So he said.

They ran to the next hill, waited till the ravens moved on,
then ran again, waited, ran. The steady progress they had been
keeping had been tiring enough, but all except Elyas quickly
began to flag under this jerky pace. Perrin's chest heaved, and
he gulped air when he had a few minutes to lie on a hilltop,
leaving the search to Elyas. Bela stood head down, nostrils flaring, at every stop. Fear lashed them on, and Perrin did not
know if it was controlled or not. He only wished the wolves
would tell them what was behind them, if anything was, whatever it was.

Ahead were more ravens than Perrin ever hoped to see
again. To the left and right the black birds billowed up, and to

the south. A dozen times they reached the hiding place of a grove or the scant shelter of a slope only moments before ravens swept into the sky. Once, with the sun beginning to slide from its midday height, they stood in the open, frozen as still as statues, half a mile from the nearest cover, while a hundred of the Dark One's feathered spies flashed by a bare mile to the east. Sweat rolled down Perrin's face despite the wind, until the last black shape dwindled to a dot and vanished. He lost count of the stragglers they brought down with their slings.

He saw more than enough evidence lying in the path the ravens had covered to justify his fear. He had stared with a queasy fascination at a rabbit that had been torn to pieces. The eyeless head stood upright, with the other bits—legs, entrails—scattered in a rough circle around it. Birds, too, stabbed to shapeless masses of feathers. And two more foxes.

He remembered something Lan had said. All the Dark One's creatures delight in killing. The Dark One's power is death. And if the ravens found them? Pitiless eyes shining like black beads. Stabbing beaks swirling around them. Needle-sharp beaks drawing blood. A hundred of them. *Or can they call more of their kind? Maybe all of them in the hunt?* A sickening image built up in his mind. A pile of ravens as big as a hill, seething like maggots, fighting over a few bloody shreds.

Suddenly the image was swept away by others, each one clear for an instant, then spinning and fading into another. The wolves had found ravens to the north. Screaming birds dove and whirled and dove again, beaks drawing blood with every swoop. Snarling wolves dodged and leaped, twisting in the air, jaws snapping. Again and again Perrin tasted feathers and the foul taste of fluttering ravens crushed alive, felt the pain of oozing gashes all over his body, knew with a despair that never touched on giving up that all his effort was not enough. Suddenly the ravens broke away, wheeling overhead for one last shriek of rage at the wolves. Wolves did not die as easily as foxes, and they had a mission. A flap of black wings, and they were gone, a few black feathers drifting down on their dead. Wind licked at a puncture on his left foreleg. There was something wrong with one of Hopper's eyes. Ignoring her own hurts, Dapple gathered them and they settled into a painful lope in the direction the ravens had gone. Blood matted their fur. *We come. Danger comes before us.*

Moving in a stumbling trot, Perrin exchanged a glance with Elyas. The man's yellow eyes were expressionless, but he knew. He said nothing, just watched Perrin and waited, all the while maintaining that effortless lope.

Waiting for me. Waiting for me to admit I feel the wolves.

"Ravens," Perrin panted reluctantly. "Behind us."

"He was right," Egwene breathed. "You can talk to them."

Perrin's feet felt like lumps of iron on the ends of wooden posts, but he tried to make them move faster. If he could outrun their eyes, outrun the ravens, outrun the wolves, but above all Egwene's eyes, that knew him now for what he was. *What are you? Tainted, the Light blind me! Cursed!*

His throat burned as it never had from breathing the smoke and heat of Master Luhhan's forge. He staggered and hung on to Egwene's stirrup until she climbed down and all but pushed him into the saddle despite his protests that he could keep going. It was not long, though, before she was clutching the stirrup as she ran, holding up her skirts with her other hand, and only a little while after that until he dismounted, his knees still wobbling. He had to pick her up to make her take his place, but she was too tired to fight him.

Elyas would not slow down. He urged them, and taunted them, and kept them so close behind the searching ravens to the south that Perrin thought all it would take would be for one bird to look back. "Keep moving, burn you! Think you'll do any better than that fox did, if they catch us? The one with its insides piled on its head?" Egwene swayed out of the saddle and vomited noisily. "I knew you'd remember. Just keep going a little more. That's all. Just a little more. Burn you, I thought farm youngsters had endurance. Work all day and dance all night. Sleep all day and sleep all night, looks like to me. Move your bloody feet!"

They began coming down off the hills as soon as the last raven vanished over the next one, then while the last trailers still flapped above the hilltop. *One bird looking back.* To east and west the ravens searched while they hurried across the open spaces between. *One bird is all it will take.*

The ravens behind were coming fast. Dapple and the other wolves worked their way around them and were coming on without stopping to lick their wounds, but they had learned all the lessons they needed about watching the sky. *How close? How long?* The wolves had no notions of time the way men did, no reasons to divide a day into hours. The seasons were time enough for them, and the light and the dark. No need for more. Finally Perrin worked out an image of where the sun would stand in the sky when the ravens overran them from behind. He glanced over his shoulder at the setting sun, and licked his lips with a dry tongue. In an hour the ravens would be on them, maybe less. An hour, and it was a good two hours to sunset, at least two to full dark.

We'll die with the setting sun, he thought, staggering as he ran. Slaughtered like the fox. He fingered his axe, then moved to his sling. That would be more use. Not enough, though. Not against a hundred ravens, a hundred darting targets, a hundred stabbing beaks.

"It's your turn to ride, Perrin," Egwene said tiredly.

"In a bit," he panted. "I'm good for miles, yet." She nodded, and stayed in the saddle. *She is tired. Tell her? Or let her think we still have a chance to escape? An hour of hope, even if it is desperate, or an hour of despair?*

Elyas was watching him again, saying nothing. He must know, but he did not speak. Perrin looked at Egwene again and blinked away hot tears. He touched his axe and wondered if he had the courage. In the last minutes, when the ravens descended on them, when all hope was gone, would he have the courage to spare her the death the fox had died? *Light make me strong!*

The ravens ahead of them suddenly seemed to vanish. Perrin could still make out dark, misty clouds, far to the east and west, but ahead . . . nothing. *Where did they go? Light, if we've overrun them. . . .*

Abruptly a chill ran through him, one cold, clean tingle as if he had jumped into the Winespring Water in midwinter. It rippled through him and seemed to carry away some of his fatigue, a little of the ache in his legs and the burning of his lungs. It left behind . . . something. He could not say what, only he felt different. He stumbled to a halt and looked around, afraid.

Elyas watched him, watched them all, with a gleam behind his eyes. He knew what it was, Perrin was sure of it, but he only watched them.

Egwene reined in Bela and looked around uncertainly, half wondering and half fearful. "It's . . . strange," she whispered. "I feel as if I lost something." Even the mare had her head up expectantly, nostrils flaring as if they detected a faint odor of new-mown hay.

"What . . . what was that?" Perrin asked.

Elyas cackled suddenly. He bent over, shoulders shaking, to rest his hands on his knees. "Safety, that's what. We made it, you bloody fools. No raven will cross that line . . . not one that carries the Dark One's eyes, anyways. A Trolloc would have to be driven across, and there'd need to be something fierce pushing the Myrddraal to make him do the driving. No Aes Sedai, either. The One Power won't work here; they can't touch the True Source. Can't even feel the Source, like it vanished. Makes them itch inside, that does. Gives them the shakes like a seven-day drunk. It's safety."

At first, to Perrin's eyes, the land was unchanged from the rolling hills and ridges they had crossed the whole day. Then he noticed green shoots among the grass; not many, and they were struggling, but more than he had seen anywhere else. There were fewer weeds in the grass, too. He could not imagine what it was, but there was . . . something about this place. And something in what Elyas said tickled his memory.

"What is it?" Egwene asked. "I feel. . . . What is this place? I don't think I like it."

"A *stedding*," Elyas roared. "You never listen to stories? Of course, there hasn't been an Ogier here in three thousand odd years, not since the Breaking of the World, but it's the *stedding* makes the Ogier, not the Ogier make the *stedding*."

"Just a legend," Perrin stammered. In the stories, the *stedding* were always havens, places to hide, whether it was from Aes Sedai or from creatures of the Father of Lies.

Elyas straightened; if not exactly fresh, he gave no sign that he had spent most of a day running. "Come on. We'd better get deeper into this legend. The ravens can't follow, but they can still see us this close to the edge, and there could be enough of them to watch the whole border of it. Let them keep hunting right on by it."

Perrin wanted to stay right there, now that he was stopped; his legs trembled and told him to lie down for a week. Whatever refreshment he had felt had been momentary; all the weariness and aches were back. He forced himself to take one step, then another. It did not get easier, but he kept at it. Egwene flapped the reins to get Bela moving again. Elyas settled into an effortless lope, only slowing to a walk when it became apparent the others could not keep up. A fast walk.

"Why don't—we stay here?" Perrin panted. He was breathing through his mouth, and he forced the words out between deep, wracking breaths. "If it's really—a *stedding*. We'd be safe. No Trollocs. No Aes Sedai. Why don't we—just stay here—until it's all over?" *Maybe the wolves won't come here, either.*

"How long will that be?" Elyas looked over his shoulder with one eyebrow raised. "What would you eat? Grass, like the horse? Besides, there's others know about this place, and nothing keeps men out, not even the worst of them. And there is only one place where there's still water to be found." Frowning uneasily, he turned in a complete circle, scanning the land. When he was done, he shook his head and muttered to himself. Perrin felt him calling to the wolves. *Hurry. Hurry.* "We take our chances on a choice of evils, and the ravens are sure. Come on. It's only another mile or two."

Perrin would have groaned if he had been willing to spare the breath.

Huge boulders began to dot the low hills, irregular lumps of gray, lichen-coated stone half buried in the ground, some as big as a house. Brambles webbed them, and low brush half hid most. Here and there amid the desiccated brown of brambles and brush a lone green shoot announced that this was a special place. Whatever wounded the land beyond its borders hurt it, too, but here the wound did not go quite as deep.

Eventually they straggled over one more rise, and at the base of this hill lay a pool of water. Any of them could have waded across it in two strides, but it was clear and clean enough to show the sandy bottom like a sheet of glass. Even Elyas hurried eagerly down the slope.

Perrin threw himself full length on the ground when he reached the pool and plunged his head in. An instant later he was spluttering from the cold of water that had welled up from the depths of the earth. He shook his head, his long hair spraying a rain of drops. Egwene grinned and splashed back at him. Perrin's eyes grew sober. She frowned and opened her mouth, but he stuck his face back in the water. *No questions. Not now. No explanations. Not ever.* But a small voice taunted him. *But you would have done it, wouldn't you?*

Eventually Elyas called them away from the pool. "Anybody wants to eat, I want some help."

Egwene worked cheerfully, laughing and joking as they prepared their scanty meal. There was nothing left but cheese and dried meat; there had been no chance to hunt. At least there was still tea. Perrin did his share, but silently. He felt Egwene's eyes on him, saw growing worry on her face, but he avoided meeting her eyes as much as he could. Her laughter faded, and the jokes came further apart, each one more strained than the last. Elyas watched, saying nothing. A somber mood descended, and they began their meal in silence. The sun grew red in the west, and their shadows stretched out long and thin.

Not quite an hour till dark. If not for the stedding, *all of you would be dead now. Would you have saved her? Would you have cut her down like so many bushes? Bushes don't bleed, do they? Or scream, and look in your eyes and ask, why?*

Perrin drew in on himself more. He could feel something laughing at him, deep in the back of his mind. Something cruel. Not the Dark One. He almost wished it was. Not the Dark One; himself.

For once Elyas had broken his rule about fires. There were no trees, but he had snapped dead branches from the brush and built his fire against a huge chunk of rock sticking out of the hillside. From the layers of soot staining the stone, Perrin thought the site must have been used by generation after generation of travelers.

What showed above ground of the big rock was rounded somewhat, with a sharp break on one side where moss, old and brown, covered the ragged surface. The grooves and hollows eroded in the rounded part looked odd to Perrin, but he was too absorbed in gloom to wonder about it. Egwene, though, studied it as she ate.

"That," she said finally, "looks like an eye." Perrin blinked; it *did* look like an eye, under all that soot.

"It is," Elyas said. He sat with his back to the fire and the rock, studying the land around them while he chewed a strip of dried meat almost as tough as leather. "Artur Hawkwing's eye. The eye of the High King himself. This is what his power and glory came to, in the end." He said it absently. Even his chewing was absentminded; his eyes and his attention were on the hills.

"Artur Hawkwing!" Egwene exclaimed. "You're joking with me. It isn't an eye at all. Why would somebody carve Artur Hawkwing's eye on a rock out here?"

Elyas glanced over his shoulder at her, muttering, "What do they teach you village whelps?" He snorted and straightened back to his watching, but he went on talking. "Artur Paendrag Tanreall, Artur Hawkwing, the High King, united all the lands from the Great Blight to the Sea of Storms, from the Aryth Ocean to the Aiel Waste, and even some beyond the Waste. He even sent armies the other side of the Aryth Ocean. The stories say he ruled the whole world, but what he really did rule was enough for any man outside of a story. And he brought peace and justice to the land."

"All stood equal before the law," Egwene said, "and no man raised his hand against another."

"So you've heard the stories, at least." Elyas chuckled, a dry sound. "Artur Hawkwing brought peace and justice, but he did it with fire and sword. A child could ride alone with a bag of gold from the Aryth Ocean to the Spine of the World and never have a moment's fear, but the High King's justice was as hard as that rock there for anyone who challenged his power, even if it was just by being who they were, or by people thinking they were a challenge. The common folk had peace, and justice, and full bellies, but he laid a twenty-year siege to Tar Valon and put a price of a thousand gold crowns on the head of every Aes Sedai."

"I thought you didn't like Aes Sedai," Egwene said.

Elyas gave a wry smile. "Doesn't matter what I like, girl.

Artur Hawkwing was a proud fool. An Aes Sedai healer could have saved him when he took sick—or was poisoned, as some say—but every Aes Sedai still alive was penned up behind the Shining Walls, using all their Power to hold off an army that lit up the night with their campfires. He wouldn't have let one near him, anyway. He hated Aes Sedai as much as he hated the Dark One."

Egwene's mouth tightened, but when she spoke, all she said was, "What does all that have to do with whether that's Artur Hawkwing's eye?"

"Just this, girl. With peace except for what was going on across the ocean, with the people cheering him wherever he went—they really loved him, you see; he was a harsh man, but never with the common folk—well, with all of that, he decided it was time to build himself a capital. A new city, not connected in any man's mind with any old cause or faction or rivalry. Here, he'd build it, at the very center of the land bordered by the seas and the Waste and the Blight. Here, where no Aes Sedai would ever come willing or could use the Power if they did. A capital from which, one day, the whole world would receive peace and justice. When they heard the proclamation, the common people subscribed enough money to build a monument to him. Most of them looked on him as only a step below the Creator. A short step. It took five years to carve and build. A statue of Hawkwing, himself, a hundred times bigger than the man. They raised it right here, and the city was to rise around it."

"There was never any city here," Egwene scoffed. "There would have to be something left if there was. Something."

Elyas nodded, still keeping his watch. "Indeed there was not. Artur Hawkwing died the very day the statue was finished, and his sons and the rest of his blood fought over who would sit on Hawkwing's throne. The statue stood alone in the midst of these hills. The sons and the nephews and the cousins died, and the last of the Hawkwing's blood vanished from the earth— except maybe for some of those who went over the Aryth Ocean. There were those who would have erased even the memory of him, if they could. Books were burned just because they mentioned his name. In the end there was nothing left of him but the stories, and most of them wrong. That's what his glory came to.

"The fighting didn't stop, of course, just because the Hawkwing and his kin were dead. There was still a throne to be won, and every lord and lady who could muster fighting men wanted it. It was the beginning of the War of the Hundred Years. Lasted a hundred and twenty-three, really, and most of the history of that time is lost in the smoke of burning towns. Many got a part of the land, but none got the whole, and sometime during those years the statue was pulled down. Maybe they couldn't stand measuring themselves 'against it any longer."

"First you sound as if you despise him," Egwene said, "and now you sound as if you admire him." She shook her head.

Elyas turned to look at her, a flat, unblinking stare. "Get some more tea now, if you want any. I want the fire out before dark."

Perrin could make out the eye clearly now, despite the failing light. It was bigger than a man's head, and the shadows falling across it made it seem like a raven's eye, hard and black and without pity. He wished they were sleeping somewhere else.

CHAPTER
30

Children of Shadow

E gwene sat by the fire, staring up at the fragment of statue, but Perrin went down by the pool to be alone. Day was fading, and the night wind was already rising out of the east, ruffling the surface of the water. He took the axe from the loop on his belt and turned it over in his hands. The ashwood haft was as long as his arm, and smooth and cool to the touch. He hated it. He was ashamed of how proud he had been of the axe back in Emond's Field. Before he knew what he might be willing to do with it.

"You hate her that much?" Elyas said behind him.

Startled, he jumped and half raised the axe before he saw who it was. "Can . . . ? Can you read my mind, too? Like the wolves?"

Elyas cocked his head to one side and eyed him quizzically. "A blind man could read your face, boy. Well, speak up. Do you hate the girl? Despise her? That's it. You were ready to kill her because you despise her, always dragging her feet, holding you back with her womanish ways."

"Egwene never dragged her feet in her life," he protested. "She always does her share. I don't despise her, I love her." He glared at Elyas, daring him to laugh. "Not like that. I mean, she isn't like a sister, but she and Rand. . . . Blood and ashes! If the ravens caught us. . . . If. . . . I don't know."

"Yes, you do. If she had to choose her way of dying, which

do you think she'd pick? One clean blow of your axe, or the way the animals we saw today died? I know which I'd take."
"I don't have any right to choose for her. You won't tell her, will you? About. . . ." His hands tightened on the axe haft; the muscles in his arms corded, heavy muscles for his age, built by long hours swinging the hammer at Master Luhhan's forge. For an instant he thought the thick wooden shaft would snap. "I hate this bloody thing," he growled. "I don't know what I'm doing with it, strutting around like some kind of fool. I couldn't have done it, you know. When it was all pretend and maybe, I could swagger, and play as if I. . . ." He sighed, his voice fading. "It's different, now. I don't ever want to use it again."
"You'll use it."
Perrin raised the axe to throw it in the pool, but Elyas caught his wrist.
"You'll use it, boy, and as long as you hate using it, you will use it more wisely than most men would. Wait. If ever you don't hate it any longer, then will be the time to throw it as far as you can and run the other way."
Perrin hefted the axe in his hands, still tempted to leave it in the pool. *Easy for him to say wait. What if I wait and then* can't *throw it away?*
He opened his mouth to ask Elyas, but no words came out. A sending from the wolves, so urgent that his eyes glazed over. For an instant he forgot what he had been going to say, forgot he had been going to say anything, forgot even how to speak, how to breathe. Elyas's face sagged, too, and his eyes seemed to peer inward and far away. Then it was gone, as quickly as it had come. It had only lasted a heartbeat, but that was enough.
Perrin shook himself and filled his lungs deeply. Elyas did not pause; as soon as the veil lifted from his eyes, he sped toward the fire without any hesitation. Perrin ran wordlessly behind him.
"Douse the fire!" Elyas called hoarsely to Egwene. He gestured urgently, and he seemed to be trying to shout in a whisper. "Get it out!"
She rose to her feet, staring at him uncertainly, then stepped closer to the fire, but slowly, clearly not understanding what was happening.
Elyas pushed roughly past her and snatched up the tea kettle,

cursing when it burned him. Juggling the hot pot, he upended it over the fire just the same. A step behind him, Perrin arrived in time to start kicking dirt over the hissing coals as the last of the tea splashed into the fire, hissing and rising in tendrils of steam. He did not stop until the last vestige of the fire was buried.

Elyas tossed the kettle to Perrin, who immediately let it fall with a choked-off yell. Perrin blew on his hands, frowning at Elyas, but the fur-clad man was too busy giving their campsite a hasty look to pay any attention.

"No chance to hide that somebody's been here," Elyas said. "We'll just have to hurry and hope. Maybe they won't bother. Blood and ashes, but I was sure it was the ravens."

Hurriedly Perrin tossed the saddle on Bela, propping the axe against his thigh while he bent to tighten the girth.

"What is it?" Egwene asked. Her voice shook. "Trollocs? A Fade?"

"Go east or west," Elyas told Perrin. "Find a place to hide, and I'll join you as soon as I can. If they see a wolf. . . ." He darted away, crouching almost as if he intended to go to all fours, and vanished into the lengthening shadows of evening.

Egwene hastily gathered her few belongings, but she still demanded an explanation from Perrin. Her voice was insistent and growing more frightened by the minute as he kept silent. He was frightened, too, but fear made them move faster. He waited until they were headed toward the setting sun. Trotting ahead of Bela and holding the axe across his chest in both hands, he told what he knew over his shoulder in snatches while hunting for a place to go to ground and wait for Elyas.

"There are a lot of men coming, on horses. They came up behind the wolves, but the men didn't see them. They're heading toward the pool. Probably they don't have anything to do with us; it's the only water for miles. But Dapple says. . . ." He glanced over his shoulder. The evening sun painted odd shadows on her face, shadows that hid her expression. *What is she thinking? Is she looking at you as if she doesn't know you anymore? Does she know you?* "Dapple says they smell wrong. It's . . . sort of the way a rabid dog smells wrong." The pool was lost to sight behind them. He could still pick out boulders—fragments of Artur Hawkwing's statue—in the deepening twilight, but not to tell which was the stone where the fire had been. "We'll stay away from them, find a place to wait for Elyas."

"Why should they bother us?" she demanded. "We're supposed to be safe here. It's supposed to be safe. Light, there has to be some place safe."

Perrin began looking harder for somewhere to hide. They could not be very far from the pool, but the twilight was thickening. Soon it would be too dark to travel. Faint light still bathed the crests. From the hollows between, where there was barely enough to see, it seemed bright by contrast. Off to the left a dark shape stood sharp against the sky, a large, flat stone slanting out of a hillside, cloaking the slope beneath in darkness.

"This way," he said.

He trotted toward the hill, glancing over his shoulder for any sign of the men who were coming. There was nothing—yet. More than once he had to stop and wait while the others stumbled after him. Egwene was crouched over Bela's neck, and the mare was picking her way carefully over the uneven ground. Perrin thought they both must be more tired than he had believed. *This had better be a good hiding place. I don't think we can hunt for another.*

At the base of the hill he studied the massive, flat rock outlined against the sky, jutting out the slope almost at the crest. There was an odd familiarity to the way the top of the huge slab seemed to form irregular steps, three up and one down. He climbed the short distance and felt across the stone, walking along it. Despite the weathering of centuries he could still feel four joined columns. He glanced up at the step-like top of the stone, towering over his head like a huge lean-to. Fingers. *We'll shelter in Artur Hawkwing's hand. Maybe some of his justice is left here.*

He motioned for Egwene to join him. She did not move, so he slid back down to the base of the hill and told her what he had found.

Egwene peered up the hill with her head pushed forward. "How can you see anything?" she asked.

Perrin opened his mouth, then shut it. He licked his lips as he looked around, for the first time really aware of what he was seeing. The sun was down. All the way down, now, and clouds

hid the full moon, but it still seemed like the deep purple
fringes of twilight to him. "I felt the rock," he said finally.
"That's what it has to be. They won't be able to pick us out
against the shadow of it even if they come this far." He took
Bela's bridle to lead her to the shelter of the hand. He could
feel Egwene's eyes on his back.

As he was helping her down from the saddle, the night broke
out in shouts back toward the pool. She laid a hand on Perrin's
arm, and he heard her unspoken question.

"The men saw Wind," he said reluctantly. It was difficult to
pick out the meaning of the wolves' thoughts. Something about
fire. "They have torches." He pressed her down at the base of
the fingers and crouched beside her. "They're breaking up into
parties to search. So many of them, and the wolves are all
hurt." He tried to make his voice heartier. "But Dapple and
the others should be able to keep out of their way, even injured, and they don't expect us. People don't see what they
don't expect. They'll give up soon enough and make camp."
Elyas was with the wolves, and would not leave them while
they were hunted. *So many riders. So persistent. Why so persistent?*

He saw Egwene nod, but in the dark she did not realize it.
"We'll be all right, Perrin."

Light, he thought wonderingly, she's *trying to comfort* me.

The shouts went on and on. Small knots of torches moved in
the distance, flickering points of light in the darkness.

"Perrin," Egwene said softly, "will you dance with me at
Sunday? If we're home by then?"

His shoulders shook. He made no sound, and he did not
know if he was laughing or crying. "I will. I promise." Against
his will his hands tightened on the axe, reminding him that he
still held it. His voice dropped to a whisper. "I promise," he
said again, and hoped.

Groups of torch-carrying men now rode through the hills,
bunches of ten or twelve. Perrin could not tell how many
groups there were. Sometimes three or four were in sight at
once, quartering back and forth. They continued to shout to
one another, and sometimes there were screams in the night,
the screams of horses, the screams of men.

He saw it all from more than one vantage. He crouched on

the hillside with Egwene, watching the torches move through the darkness like fireflies, and in his mind he ran in the night with Dapple, and Wind, and Hopper. The wolves had been too hurt by the ravens to run far or fast, so they intended to drive the men out of the darkness, drive them to the shelter of their fires. Men always sought the safety of fires in the end, when wolves roamed the night. Some of the mounted men led strings of horses without riders; they whinnied and reared with wide, rolling eyes when the gray shapes darted among them, screaming and pulling their lead ropes from the hands of the men who held them, scattering in all directions as fast as they could run. Horses with men on their backs screamed, too, when gray shadows flashed out of the dark with hamstringing fangs, and sometimes their riders screamed as well, just before jaws tore out their throats. Elyas was out there, also, more dimly sensed, stalking the night with his long knife, a two-legged wolf with one sharp steel tooth. The shouts became curses more often than not, but the searchers refused to give up.

Abruptly Perrin realized that the men with torches were following a pattern. Each time some of the parties came in view, one of them, at least, was closer to the hillside where he and Egwene were hiding. Elyas had said to hide, but. . . . *What if we run? Maybe we could hide in the dark, if we keep moving. Maybe. It has to be dark enough for that.*

He turned to Egwene, but as he did the decision was taken away from him. Bunched torches, a dozen of them, came around the base of the hill, wavering with the trot of the horses. Lanceheads gleamed in the torchlight. He froze, holding his breath, hands tightening on his axe haft.

The horsemen rode past the hill, but one of the men shouted, and the torches swung back. He thought desperately, seeking for a way to go. But as soon as they moved they would be seen, if they had not already been, and once they were marked they would have no chance, not even with the darkness to help.

The horsemen drew up at the foot of the hill, each man holding a torch in one hand and a long lance in the other, guiding his horse by the pressure of his knees. By the light of the torches Perrin could see the white cloaks of the Children of the Light. They held the torches high and leaned forward in their saddles, peering up at the deep shadows under Artur Hawkwing's fingers.

"There *is* something up there," one of them said. His voice was too loud, as if he was afraid of what lay outside the light of his torch. "I told you somebody could hide in that. Isn't that a horse?"

Egwene laid a hand on Perrin's arm; her eyes were big in the dark. Her silent question plain despite the shadow hiding her features. What to do? Elyas and the wolves still hunted through the night. The horses below shifted their feet nervously. *If we run now, they'll chase us down.*

One of the Whitecloaks stepped his horse forward and shouted up the hill. "If you can understand human speech, come down and surrender. You'll not be harmed if you walk in the Light. If you don't surrender, you will all be killed. You have one minute." The lances lowered, long steel heads bright with torchlight.

"Perrin," Egwene whispered, "we can't outrun them. If we don't give up, they'll kill us. Perrin?"

Elyas and the wolves were still free. Another distant, bubbling scream marked a Whitecloak who had hunted Dapple too closely. *If we run. . . .* Egwene was looking at him, waiting for him to tell her what to do. *If we run. . . .* He shook his head wearily and stood up like a man in a trance, stumbling down the hill toward the Children of the Light. He heard Egwene sigh and follow him, her feet dragging reluctantly. *Why are the Whitecloaks so persistent, as if they hate wolves with a passion? Why do they smell wrong?* He almost thought he could smell the wrongness himself, when the wind gusted from the riders.

"Drop that axe," the leader barked.

Perrin stumbled toward him, wrinkling his nose to get rid of the smell he thought he smelt.

"Drop it, bumpkin!" The leader's lance shifted toward Perrin's chest.

For a moment he stared at the lancehead, enough sharp steel to go completely through him, and abruptly he shouted, "No!" It was not at the horseman he shouted.

Out of the night Hopper came, and Perrin was one with the wolf. Hopper, the cub who had watched the eagles soar, and wanted so badly to fly through the sky as the eagles did. The cub who hopped and jumped and leaped until he could leap higher than any other wolf, and who never lost the cub's yearning to soar through the sky. Out of the night Hopper came and left the ground in a leap, soaring like the eagles. The Whitecloaks had only a moment to begin cursing before Hopper's jaws closed on the throat of the man with his lance leveled at Perrin. The big wolf's momentum carried them both off the other side of the horse. Perrin felt the throat crushing, tasted the blood.

Hopper landed lightly, already apart from the man he had killed. Blood matted his fur, his own blood and that of others. A gash down his face crossed the empty socket where his left eye had been. His good eye met Perrin's two for just an instant. *Run, brother!* He whirled to leap again, to soar one last time, and a lance pinned him to the earth. A second length of steel thrust through his ribs, driving into the ground under him. Kicking, he snapped at the shafts that held him. *To soar.*

Pain filled Perrin, and he screamed, a wordless scream that had something of a wolf's cry in it. Without thinking he leaped forward, still screaming. All thought was gone. The horsemen had bunched too much to be able to use their lances, and the axe was a feather in his hands, one huge wolf's tooth of steel. Something crashed into his head, and as he fell, he did not know if it was Hopper or himself who died.

". . . soar like the eagles."

Mumbling, Perrin opened his eyes woozily. His head hurt, and he could not remember why. Blinking against the light, he looked around. Egwene was kneeling and watching him where he lay. They were in a square tent as big as a medium-sized room in a farmhouse, with a ground cloth for a floor. Oil lamps on tall stands, one in each corner, gave a bright light.

"Thank the Light, Perrin," she breathed. "I was afraid they had killed you."

Instead of answering, he stared at the gray-haired man seated in the lone chair in the tent. A dark-eyed, grandfatherly face looked back at him, a face at odds in his mind with the white-and-gold tabard the man wore, and the burnished armor strapped over his pure-white undercoat. It seemed a kindly face, bluff and dignified, and something about it fit the elegant austerity of the tent's furnishings. A table and a folding bed, a washstand with a plain white basin and pitcher, a single wooden chest inlaid in simple geometric patterns. Where there was wood, it was polished to a soft glow, and the metal gleamed, but not too brightly, and nothing was showy. Everything in the tent had the look of craftsmanship, but only someone who had watched the work of craftsmen—like Master Luhhan, or Master Aydaer, the cabinetmaker—would see it.

Frowning, the man stirred two small piles of objects on the table with a blunt finger. Perrin recognized the contents of his pockets in one of those piles, and his belt knife. The silver coin Moiraine had given him toppled out, and the man pushed it back thoughtfully. Pursing his lips, he left the piles and lifted Perrin's axe from the table, hefting it. His attention came back to the Emond's Fielders.

Perrin tried to get up. Sharp pain stabbing along his arms and legs turned the movement into a flop. For the first time he realized that he was tied, hand and foot. His eyes went to Egwene. She shrugged ruefully, and twisted so that he could see her back. Half a dozen lashings wrapped her wrists and ankles, the cords making ridges in her flesh. A length of rope ran between the bonds around ankles and wrists, short enough to stop her from straightening to more than a crouch if she got to her feet.

Perrin stared. That they were tied was shock enough, but they wore enough ropes to hold horses. *What do they think we are?*

The gray-haired man watched them, curious and thoughtful, like Master al'Vere puzzling out a problem. He held the axe as if he had forgotten it.

The tent flap shifted aside, and a tall man stepped into the tent. His face was long and gaunt, with eyes so deeply set they seemed to look out from caves. There was no excess flesh on him, no fat at all; his skin was pulled tight over the muscle and bone beneath.

Perrin had a glimpse of night outside, and campfires, and two white-cloaked guards at the entrance of the tent, then the flap fell back into place. As soon as the newcomer was into the tent, he stopped, standing as rigid as an iron rod, staring straight ahead of him at the far wall of the tent. His plate-and-mail armor gleamed like silver against his snowy cloak and undercoat.

"My Lord Captain." His voice was as hard as his posture, and grating, but somehow flat, without expression.

The gray-haired man made a casual gesture. "Be at your

ease, Child Byar. You have tallied our costs for this . . . en-
counter?"

The tall man moved his feet apart, but other than that Perrin
did not see anything ease about his stance. "Nine men dead, my
Lord Captain, and twenty-three injured, seven seriously. All can
ride, though. Thirty horses had to be put down. They were
hamstrung!" He emphasized that in his emotionless voice, as if
what had happened to the horses were worse than the deaths and
injuries to men. "Many of the remounts are scattered. We may
find some at daybreak, my Lord Captain, but with wolves to
send them on their way, it will take days to gather them all. The
men who were supposed to be watching them have been assigned
to night guard until we reach Caemlyn."

"We do not have days, Child Byar," the gray-haired man
said mildly. "We ride at dawn. Nothing can change that. We
must be in Caemlyn in time, yes?"

"As you command, my Lord Captain."

The gray-haired man glanced at Perrin and Egwene, then
away again. "And what have we to show for it, aside from
these two younglings?"

Byar drew a deep breath and hesitated. "I have had the wolf
that was with this lot skinned, my Lord Captain. The hide
should make a fine rug for my Lord Captain's tent."

Hopper! Not even realizing what he was doing, Perrin
growled and struggled against his bonds. The ropes dug into his
skin—his wrists became slippery with blood—but they did not
give.

For the first time Byar looked at the prisoners. Egwene started
back from him. His face was as expressionless as his voice, but a
cruel light burned in his sunken eyes, as surely as flames burned
in Ba'alzamon's. Byar hated them as if they were enemies of
long years instead of people never seen before tonight.

· Perrin stared back defiantly. His mouth curled into a tight
smile at the thought of his teeth meeting in the man's throat.

Abruptly his smile faded, and he shook himself. *My teeth?*
I'm a man, not a wolf! Light, there has to be an end to this! But
he still met Byar's glare, hate for hate.

"I do not care about wolf-hide rugs, Child Byar." The re-
buke in the Lord Captain's voice was gentle, but Byar's back
snapped rigid again, his eyes locking to the wall of the tent.

"You were reporting on what we achieved this night, no? If we achieved anything."

"I would estimate the pack that attacked us at fifty beasts or more, my Lord Captain. Of that, we killed at least twenty, perhaps thirty. I did not consider it worth the risk of losing more horses to have the carcasses brought in tonight. In the morning I will have them gathered and burned, those that aren't dragged off in the dark. Besides these two, there were at least a dozen other men. I believe we disposed of four or five, but it is unlikely we will find any bodies, given the Darkfriends' propensity for carrying away their dead to hide their losses. This seems to have been a coordinated ambush, but that raises the question of. . . ."

Perrin's throat tightened as the gaunt man went on. Elyas? Cautiously, reluctantly, he felt for Elyas, for the wolves . . . and found nothing. It was as if he had never been able to feel a wolf's mind. *Either they're dead, or they've abandoned you.* He wanted to laugh, a bitter laugh. At last he had what he had been wishing for, but the price was high.

The gray-haired man did laugh, just then, a rich, wry chuckle that made a red spot bloom on each of Byar's cheeks. "So, Child Byar, it is your considered estimate that we were attacked in a planned ambush by upwards of fifty wolves and better than half a score of Darkfriends? Yes? Perhaps when you've seen a few more actions. . . ."

"But, my Lord Captain Bornhald. . . ."

"I would say six or eight wolves, Child Byar, and perhaps no other humans than these two. You have the true zeal, but no experience outside the cities. It is a different thing, bringing the Light, when streets and houses are far distant. Wolves have a way of seeming more than they are, in the night—and men, also. Six or eight at most, I think." Byar's flush deepened slowly. "I also suspect they were here for the same reason we are: the only easy water for at least a day in any direction. A much simpler explanation than spies or traitors within the Children, and the simplest explanation is usually the truest. You will learn, with experience."

Byar's face went deathly white as the grandfatherly man spoke; by contrast, the two spots in his hollow cheeks deepened from red to purple. He cut his eyes toward the two prisoners for an instant.

He hates us even more, now, Perrin thought, *for hearing this. But why did he hate us in the first place?*

"What do you think of this?" the Lord Captain said, holding up Perrin's axe.

Byar looked a question at his commander and waited for an answering nod before he broke his rigid stance to take the weapon. He hefted the axe and gave a surprised grunt, then whirled it in a tight arc above his head that barely missed the top of the tent. He handled it as surely as if he had been born with an axe in his hands. A look of grudging admiration flickered across his face, but by the time he lowered the axe he was expressionless once more.

"Excellently balanced, my Lord Captain. Plainly made, but by a very good weaponsmith, perhaps even a master." His eyes burned darkly at the prisoners. "Not a villager's weapon, my Lord Captain. Nor a farmer's."

"No." The gray-haired man turned toward Perrin and Egwene with a weary, slightly chiding smile, a kindly grandfather who knew his grandchildren had been up to some mischief. "My name is Geofram Bornhald," he told them. "You are Perrin, I understand. But you, young woman, what is your name?"

Perrin glowered at him, but Egwene shook her head. "Don't be silly, Perrin. I'm Egwene."

"Just Perrin, and just Egwene," Bornhald murmured. "But I suppose if you truly are Darkfriends, you wish to hide your identities as much as possible."

Perrin heaved himself up to his knees; he could rise no further because of the way he was bound. "We aren't Darkfriends," he protested angrily.

The words were not completely out of his mouth before Byar reached him. The man moved like a snake. He saw the handle of his own axe swinging toward him and tried to duck, but the thick haft caught him over the ear. Only the fact that he was moving away from the blow kept his skull from being split. Even so, lights flashed in his eyes. Breath left him as he struck the ground. His head rung, and blood ran down his cheek.

"You have no right," Egwene began, and screamed as the axe handle whipped toward her. She threw herself aside, and the blow whistled through empty air as she tumbled to the ground cloth.

"You will keep a civil tongue," Byar said, "when speaking to an Anointed of the Light,' or you will have no tongue." The worst of it was his voice still had no emotion at all. Cutting out their tongues would give him no pleasure and no regret; it was just something he would do.

"Go easy, Child Byar." Bornhald looked at the captives again. "I expect you·do not know much about the Anointed, or about Lords Captain of the Children of the Light, do you? No, I thought not. Well, for Child Byar's sake, at least, try not to argue or shout, yes? I want no more than that you should walk in the Light, and letting anger get the better of you won't help any of us."

Perrin looked up at the gaunt-faced man standing over them. *For Child Byar's sake?* He noticed that the Lord Captain did not tell Byar to leave them alone. Byar met his eyes and smiled; the smile touched only his mouth, but the skin of his face drew tighter, until it looked like a skull. Perrin shivered.

"I have heard of this thing of men running with wolves," Bornhald said musingly, "though I have not seen it before. Men supposedly talking with wolves, and with other creatures of the Dark One. A filthy business. It makes me fear the Last Battle is indeed coming soon."

"Wolves aren't—" Perrin cut off as Byar's boot drew back. Taking a deep breath, he went on in a milder tone. Byar lowered his foot with a disappointed grimace. "Wolves aren't creatures of the Dark One. They hate the Dark One. At least, they hate Trollocs, and Fades." He was surprised to see the gaunt-faced man nod as if to himself.

Bornhald raised an eyebrow. "Who told you that?"

"A Warder," Egwene said. She scrunched away from Byar's heated eyes. "He said wolves hate Trollocs, and Trollocs are afraid of wolves." Perrin was glad she had not mentioned Elyas.

"A Warder," the gray-haired man sighed. "A creature of the Tar Valon witches. What else would that sort tell you, when he is a Darkfriend himself, and a servant of Darkfriends? Do you not know Trollocs have wolves' muzzles and teeth, and wolves' fur?"

Perrin blinked, trying to clear his head. His brain still felt like jellied pain, but there was something wrong here. He could not get his thoughts straight enough to puzzle it out.

"Not all of them," Egwene muttered. Perrin gave Byar a wary look, but the gaunt man only watched her. "Some of them have horns, like rams or goats, or hawks' beaks, or . . . or . . . all sorts of things."

Bornhald shook his head sadly. "I give you every chance, and you dig yourself deeper with every word." He held up one finger. "You run with wolves, creatures of the Dark One." A second finger. "You admit to being acquainted with a Warder, another creature of the Dark One. I doubt he would have told you what he did if it was only in passing." A third finger. "You, boy, carry a Tar Valon mark in your pocket. Most men outside Tar Valon get rid of those as fast as they can. Unless they serve the Tar Valon witches." A fourth. "You carry a fighting man's weapon while you dress like a farmboy. A skulker, then." The thumb rose. "You know Trollocs, and Myrddraal. This far south, only a few scholars and those who have traveled in the Borderlands believe they are anything but stories. Perhaps you have been to the Borderlands? If so, tell me where? I have traveled a good deal in the Borderlands; I know them well. No? Ah, well, then." He looked at his spread hand, then dropped it hard on the table. The grandfatherly expression said the grandchildren had been up to some very serious mischief indeed. "Why do you not tell me the truth of how you came to be running in the night with wolves?"

Egwene opened her mouth, but Perrin saw the stubborn set of her jaw and knew right away she was going to tell one of the stories they had worked out. That would not do. Not now, not here. His head ached, and he wished he had time to think it out, but there was no time. Who could tell where this Bornhald had traveled, with what lands and cities he was familiar? If he caught them in a lie, there would be no going back to the truth. Bornhald would be convinced they were Darkfriends, then.

"We're from the Two Rivers," he said quickly.

Egwene stared at him openly before she caught herself, but he pressed on with the truth—or a version of it. The two of them had left the Two Rivers to see Caemlyn. On the way they had heard of the ruins of a great city, but when they found Shadar Logoth, there were Trollocs there. The two of them managed to escape across the River Arinelle, but by that time they were completely lost. Then they fell in with a man who offered to guide them to Caemlyn. He had said his name was none of their business, and he hardly seemed friendly, but they needed a guide. The first either of them had seen of wolves had been after the Children of the Light appeared. All they had been trying to do was hide so they would not get eaten by wolves or killed by the men on horses.

". . . If we'd known you were Children of the Light," he finished, "we'd have gone to you for help."

Byar snorted with disbelief. Perrin did not care overmuch; if the Lord Captain was convinced, Byar could not harm them. It was plain that Byar would stop breathing if Lord Captain Bornhald told him to.

"There is no Warder in that," the gray-haired man said after a moment.

Perrin's invention failed him; he knew he should have taken time to think it out. Egwene leaped into the breach. "We met him in Baerlon. The city was crowded with men who had come down from the mines after the winter, and we were put at the same table in an inn. We only talked to him for the length of a meal."

Perrin breathed again. *Thank you, Egwene.*

"Give them back their belongings, Child Byar. Not the weapons, of course." When Byar looked at him in surprise, Bornhald added, "Or are you one of those who have taken to looting the unenlightened, Child Byar? It is a bad business, that, yes? No man can be a thief and walk in the Light." Byar seemed to struggle with disbelief at the suggestion.

"Then you're letting us go?" Egwene sounded surprised. Perrin lifted his head to stare at the Lord Captain.

"Of course not, child," Bornhald said sadly. "You may be telling the truth about being from the Two Rivers, since you know about Baerlon, and the mines. But Shadar Logoth . . . ? That is a name very, very few know, most of them Darkfriends, and anyone who knows enough to know the name, knows enough not to go there. I suggest you think of a better story on the journey to Amador. You will have time, since we must pause in Caemlyn. Preferably the truth, child. There is freedom in truth and the Light."

Byar forgot some of his diffidence toward the gray-haired

man. He spun from the prisoners, and there was an outraged snap to his words. "You can't! It is not allowed!" Bornhald raised one eyebrow quizzically, and Byar pulled himself up short, swallowing. "Forgive me, my Lord Captain. I forgot myself, and I humbly beg pardon and submit myself for penance, but as my Lord Captain himself has pointed out, we must reach Caemlyn in time, and with most of our remounts gone, we will be hard pressed enough without carrying prisoners along."

"And what would you suggest?" Bornhald asked calmly.

"The penalty for Darkfriends is death." The flat voice made it all the more jarring. He might have been suggesting stepping on a bug. "There is no truce with the Shadow. There is no mercy for Darkfriends."

"Zeal is to be applauded, Child Byar, but, as I must often tell my son, Dain, overzealousness can be a grievous fault. Remember that the Tenets also say, 'No man is so lost that he cannot be brought to the Light.' These two are young. They cannot yet be deep in the Shadow. They can yet be led to the Light, if they will only allow the Shadow to be lifted from their eyes. We must give them that chance."

For a moment Perrin almost felt affection for the grandfatherly man who stood between them and Byar. Then Bornhald turned his grandfather's smile on Egwene.

"If you refuse to come to the Light by the time we reach Amador, I will be forced to turn you over to the Questioners, and beside them Byar's zeal is but a candle beside the sun." The gray-haired man sounded like a man who regretted what he must do, but who had no intention of ever doing anything but his duty as he saw it. "Repent, renounce the Dark One, come to the Light, confess your sins and tell what you know of this vileness with wolves, and you will be spared that. You will walk free, in the Light." His gaze centered on Perrin, and he sighed sadly. Ice filled Perrin's spine. "But you, just Perrin from the Two Rivers. You killed two of the Children." He touched the axe that Byar still held. "For you, I fear, a gibbet waits in Amador."

CHAPTER

31

Play for Your Supper

R and narrowed his eyes, watching the dust-tail that rose ahead, three or four bends of the road away. Mat was already headed toward the wild hedgerow alongside the roadway. Its evergreen leaves and densely intermeshed branches would hide them as well as a stone wall, if they could find a way through to the other side. The other side of the road was marked by the sparse brown skeletons of head-high bushes, and beyond was an open field for half a mile to the woods. It might have been part of a farm not too long abandoned, but it offered no quick hiding place. He tried to judge the speed of the dust-tail, and the wind.

A sudden gust swirled road dust up around him, obscuring everything. He blinked and adjusted the plain, dark scarf across his nose and mouth. None too clean now, it made his face itch, but it kept him from inhaling dust with every breath. A farmer had given it to him, a long-faced man with grooves in his cheeks from worry.

"I don't know what you're running from," he had said with an anxious frown, "and I don't want to. You understand? My family." Abruptly the farmer had dug two long scarves out of his coat pocket and pushed the tangle of wool at them. "It's not much, but here. Belong to my boys. They have others. You don't know me, understand? It's hard times."

Rand treasured the scarf. The list of kindnesses he had made in his mind in the days since Whitebridge was a short one, and he did not believe it would get much longer.

Mat, all but his eyes hidden by the scarf wrapped around his head, hunted swiftly along the tall hedgerow, pulling at the leafy branches. Rand touched the heron-marked hilt at his belt, but let his hand fall away. Once already, cutting a hole through a hedge had almost given them away. The dust-tail was moving toward them, and staying together too long. Not the wind. At least it was not raining. Rain settled the dust. No matter how hard it fell, it never turned the hard-packed road to mud, but when it rained there was no dust. Dust was the only warning they had before whoever it was came close enough to hear. Sometimes that was too late.

"Here," Mat called softly. He seemed to step right through the hedge.

Rand hurried to the spot. Someone had cut a hole there, once. It was partly grown over, and from three feet away it looked as solid as the rest, but close up there was only a thin screen of branches. As he pushed through, he heard horses coming. Not the wind.

He crouched behind the barely covered opening, clutching the hilt of his sword as the horsemen rode by. Five . . . six . . . seven of them. Plainly dressed men, but swords and spears said they were not villagers. Some wore leather tunics with metal studs, and two had round steel caps. Merchants' guards, perhaps, between hirings. Perhaps.

One of them casually swung his eyes toward the hedge as he went by the opening, and Rand bared an inch of his sword. Mat snarled silently like a cornered badger, squinting above his scarf. His hand was under his coat; he always clutched the dagger from Shadar Logoth when there was danger. Rand was no longer sure if it was to protect himself or to protect the ruby-hilted dagger. Of late Mat seemed to forget he had a bow, sometimes.

The riders passed at a slow trot, going somewhere with a purpose but not too great a haste. Dust sifted through the hedge.

Rand waited until the clop of the hooves faded before he stuck his head cautiously back through the hole. The dust-tail was well down the road, going the way they had come. Eastward the sky was clear. He climbed out onto the roadway, watching the column of dust move west.

"Not after us," he said, halfway between a statement and a question.

Mat scrambled out after him, looking warily in both directions. "Maybe," he said. "Maybe."

Rand had no idea which way he meant it, but he nodded. Maybe. It had not begun like this, their journey down the Caemlyn Road.

For a long time after leaving Whitebridge, Rand would suddenly find himself staring back down the road behind them. Sometimes he would see someone who made his breath catch, a tall, skinny man hurrying up the road, or a lanky, white-haired fellow up beside the driver on a wagon, but it was always a pack-peddler, or farmers making their way to market, never Thom Merrilin. Hope faded as the days passed.

There was considerable traffic on the road, wagons and carts, people on horses and people afoot. They came singly and in groups, a train of merchants' wagons or a dozen horsemen together. They did not jam the road, and often there was nothing in sight except the all but leafless trees lining the hard-packed roadbed, but there were certainly more people traveling than Rand had ever seen in the Two Rivers.

Most traveled in the same direction that they did, eastward toward Caemlyn. Sometimes they got a ride in a farmer's wagon for a little distance, a mile, or five, but more often they walked. Men on horseback they avoided; when they spotted even one rider in the distance they scrambled off the road and hid until he was past. None ever wore a black cloak, and Rand did not really think a Fade would let them see him coming, but there was no point in taking chances. In the beginning it was just the Halfmen they feared.

The first village after Whitebridge looked so much like Emond's Field that Rand's steps dragged when he saw it. Thatched roofs with high peaks, and goodwives in their aprons gossiping over the fences between their houses, and children playing on a village green. The women's hair hung unbraided around their shoulders, and other small things were different, too, but the whole together was like home. Cows cropped on the green, and geese waddled self-importantly across the road.

The children tumbled, laughing, in the dust where the grass was gone altogether. They did not even look around when Rand and Mat went by. That was another thing that was different. Strangers were no oddity there; two more did not draw so much as a second glance. Village dogs only raised their heads to sniff as he and Mat passed; none stirred themselves.

It was coming on evening as they went through the village, and he felt a pang of homesickness as lights appeared in the windows. *No matter what it looks like,* a small voice whispered in his mind, *it isn't really home. Even if you go into one of those houses Tam won't be there. If he was, could you look him in the face? You know, now, don't you? Except for little things like where you come from and who you are. No fever-dreams.* He hunched his shoulders against taunting laughter inside his head. *You might as well stop,* the voice snickered. *One place is as good as another when you aren't from anywhere, and the Dark One has you marked.*

Mat tugged at his sleeve, but he pulled loose and stared at the houses. He did not want to stop, but he did want to look and remember. *So much like home, but you'll never see that again, will you?*

Mat yanked at him again. His face was taut, the skin around his mouth and eyes white. "Come on," Mat muttered. "Come on." He looked at the village as if he suspected something of hiding there. "Come on. We can't stop yet."

Rand turned in a complete circle, taking in the whole village, and sighed. They were not very far from Whitebridge. If the Myrddraal could get past Whitebridge's wall without being seen, it would have no trouble at all searching this small village. He let himself be drawn on into the countryside beyond, until the thatch-roofed houses were left behind.

Night fell before they found a spot by moonlight, under some bushes still bearing their dead leaves. They filled their bellies with cold water from a shallow rivulet not far away and curled up on the ground, wrapped in their cloaks, without a fire. A fire could be seen; better to be cold.

Uneasy with his memories, Rand woke often, and every time he could hear Mat muttering and tossing in his sleep. He did not dream, that he could remember, but he did not sleep well. *You'll never see home again.*

That was not the only night they spent with just their cloaks to protect them from the wind, and sometimes the rain, cold and soaking. It was not the only meal they made from nothing but cold water. Between them they had enough coins for a few meals at an inn, but a bed for the night would take too much. Things cost more outside the Two Rivers, more this side of the Arinelle than in Baerlon. What money they had left had to be saved for an emergency.

One afternoon Rand mentioned the dagger with the ruby in its hilt, while they were trudging down the road with bellies too empty to rumble, and the sun low and weak, and nothing in view for the coming night but more bushes. Dark clouds built up overhead for rain during the night. He hoped they were lucky; maybe no more than an icy drizzle.

He went on a few steps before he realized that Mat had stopped. He stopped, too, wriggling his toes in his boots. At least his feet felt warm. He eased the straps across his shoulders. His blanketroll and Thom's bundled cloak were not heavy, but even a few pounds weighed heavy after miles on an empty stomach. "What's the matter, Mat?" he said.

"Why are you so anxious to sell it?" Mat demanded angrily. "I found it, after all. You ever think I might like to keep it? For a while, anyway. If you want to sell something, sell that bloody sword!"

Rand rubbed his hand along the heron-marked hilt. "My father gave this sword to me. It was his. I wouldn't ask you to sell something your father gave you. Blood and ashes, Mat, do you like going hungry? Anyway, even if I could find somebody to buy it, how much would a sword bring? What would a farmer want with a sword? That ruby would fetch enough to take us all the way to Caemlyn in a carriage. Maybe all the way to Tar Valon. And we'd eat every meal in an inn, and sleep every night in a bed. Maybe you like the idea of walking halfway across the world and sleeping on the ground?" He glared at Mat, and his friend glared back.

They stood like that in the middle of the road until Mat suddenly gave an uncomfortable shrug, and dropped his eyes to the road. "Who would I sell it to, Rand? A farmer would have to pay in chickens; we couldn't buy a carriage with chickens. And if I even showed it in any village we've been through, they'd probably think we stole it. The Light knows what would happen then."

After a minute Rand nodded reluctantly. "You're right. I know it. I'm sorry; I didn't mean to snap at you. It's only that I'm hungry and my feet hurt."

"Mine, too." They started down the road again, walking even more wearily than before. The wind gusted up, blowing dust in their faces. "Mine, too." Mat coughed.

Farms did provide some meals and a few nights out of the cold. A haystack was nearly as warm as a room with a fire, at least compared to lying under the bushes, and a haystack, even one without a tarp over it, kept all but the heaviest rain off, if you dug yourself in deeply enough. Sometimes Mat tried his hand at stealing eggs, and once he attempted to milk a cow left unattended, staked out on a long rope to crop in a field. Most farms had dogs, though, and farm dogs were watchful. A two-mile run with baying hounds at their heels was too high a price for two or three eggs as Rand saw it, especially when the dogs sometimes took hours to go away and let them down out of the tree where they had taken shelter. The hours were what he regretted.

He did not really like doing it, but Rand preferred to approach a farmhouse openly in broad daylight. Now and again they had the dogs set on them anyway, without a word being said, for the rumors and the times made everyone who lived apart from other people nervous about strangers, but often an hour or so chopping wood or hauling water would earn a meal and a bed, even if the bed was a pile of straw in the barn. But an hour or two doing chores was an hour or two of daylight when they were standing still, an hour or two for the Myrddraal to catch up. Sometimes he wondered how many miles a Fade could cover in an hour. He begrudged every minute of it— though admittedly not so much when he was wolfing down a goodwife's hot soup. And when they had no food, knowing they had spent every possible minute moving toward Caemlyn did not do much to soothe an empty belly. Rand could not make up his mind if it was worse to lose time or go hungry, but Mat went beyond worrying about his belly or pursuit.

"What do we know about them, anyway?" Mat demanded

one afternoon while they were mucking out stalls on a small farm.

"Light, Mat, what do they know about us?" Rand sneezed. They were working stripped to the waist, and sweat and straw covered them both liberally, and motes of straw-dust hung in the air. "What I know is they'll give us some roast lamb and a real bed to sleep in."

Mat dug his hayfork into the straw and manure and gave a sidelong frown at the farmer, coming from the back of the barn with a bucket in one hand and his milking stool in the other. A stooped old man with skin like leather and thin, gray hair, the farmer slowed when he saw Mat looking at him, then looked away quickly and hurried on out of the barn, slopping milk over the rim of the bucket in his haste.

"He's up to something, I tell you," Mat said. "See the way he wouldn't meet my eye? Why are they so friendly to a couple of wanderers they never laid eyes on before? Tell me that."

"His wife says we remind her of their grandsons. Will you stop worrying about them? What we have to worry about is behind us. I hope."

"He's up to something," Mat muttered.

When they finished, they washed up at the trough in front of the barn, their shadows stretching long with the sinking sun. Rand toweled off with his shirt as they walked to the farmhouse. The farmer met them at the door; he leaned on a quarterstaff in a too-casual manner. Behind him his wife clutched her apron and peered past his shoulder, chewing her lip. Rand sighed; he did not think he and Mat reminded them of their grandsons any longer.

"Our sons are coming to visit tonight," the old man said. "All four of them. I forgot. They're all four coming. Big lads. Strong. Be here any time, now. I'm afraid we don't have the bed we promised you."

His wife thrust a small bundle wrapped in a napkin past him. "Here. It's bread, and cheese, and pickles, and lamb. Enough for two meals, maybe. Here." Her wrinkled face asked them to please take it and go.

Rand took the bundle. "Thank you. I understand. Come on, Mat."

Mat followed him, grumbling while he pulled his shirt over his head. Rand thought it best to cover as many miles as they could before stopping to eat. The old farmer had a dog.

It could have been worse, he thought. Three days earlier, while they were still working, they'd had the dogs set on them. The dogs, and the farmer, and his two sons waving cudgels chased them out to the Caemlyn Road and half a mile down it before giving up. They had barely had time to snatch up their belongings and run. The farmer had carried a bow with a broad-head arrow nocked.

"Don't come back, hear!" he had shouted after them. "I don't know what you're up to, but don't let me see your shifty eyes again!"

Mat had started to turn back, fumbling at his quiver, but Rand pulled him on. "Are you crazy?" Mat gave him a sullen look, but at least he kept running.

Rand sometimes wondered if it was worthwhile stopping at farms. The further they went, the more suspicious of strangers Mat became, and the less he was able to hide it. Or bothered to. The meals got skimpier for the same work, and sometimes not even the barn was offered as a place to sleep. But then a solution to all their problems came to Rand, or so it seemed, and it came at Grinwell's farm.

Master Grinwell and his wife had nine children, the eldest a daughter not more than a year younger than Rand and Mat. Master Grinwell was a sturdy man, and with his children he probably had no need of any more help, but he looked them up and down, taking in their travel-stained clothes and dusty boots, and allowed as how he could always find work for more hands. Mistress Grinwell said that if they were going to eat at her table, they would not do it in those filthy things. She was about to do laundry, and some of her husband's old clothes would fit them well enough for working. She smiled when she said it, and for a minute she looked to Rand just like Mistress al'Vere, though her hair was yellow; he had never seen hair that color before. Even Mat seemed to lose some of his tension when her smile touched him. The eldest daughter was another matter.

Dark-haired, big-eyed, and pretty, Else grinned impudently at them whenever her parents were not looking. While they

worked, moving barrels and sacks of grain in the barn, she
hung over a stall door, humming to herself and chewing the end
of one long pigtail, watching them. Rand she watched especially. He tried to ignore her, but after a few minutes he put on
the shirt Master Grinwell had loaned him. It was tight across
the shoulders and too short, but it was better than nothing.
Else laughed out loud when he tugged it on. He began to think
that this time it would not be Mat's fault when they were
chased off.

Perrin would know how to handle this, he thought. *He'd
make some offhand comment, and pretty soon she'd be laughing
at his jokes instead of mooning around where her father can see.*
Only he could not think of any offhand comment, or any jokes,
either. Whenever he looked in her direction, she smiled at him
in a way that would have her father loosing the dogs on them if
he saw. Once she told him she liked tall men. All the boys on
the farms around there were short. Mat gave a nasty snicker.
Wishing he could think of a joke, Rand tried to concentrate on
his hayfork.

The younger children, at least, were a blessing in Rand's
eyes. Mat's wariness always eased a little when there were children around. After supper they all settled in front of the fireplace, with Master Grinwell in his favorite chair thumbing his
pipe full of tabac and Mistress Grinwell fussing with her sewing
box and the shirts she had washed for him and Mat. Mat dug
out Thom's colored balls and began to juggle. He never did
that unless there were children. The children laughed when he
pretended to be dropping the balls, snatching them at the last
minute, and they clapped for fountains and figure-eights and a
six-ball circle that he really did almost drop. But they took it in
good part, Master Grinwell and his wife applauding as hard as
their children. When Mat was done, bowing around the room
with as many flourishes as Thom might have made, Rand took
Thom's flute from its case.

He could never handle the instrument without a pang of sadness. Touching its gold-and-silver scrollwork was like touching
Thom's memory. He never handled the harp except to see that
it was safe and dry—Thom had always said the harp was
beyond a farmboy's clumsy hands—but whenever a farmer allowed them to stay, he always played one tune on the flute

after supper. It was just a little something extra to pay the farmer, and maybe a way of keeping Thom's memory fresh.

With a laughing mood already set by Mat's juggling, he played "Three Girls in the Meadow." Master and Mistress Grinwell clapped along, and the smaller children danced around the floor, even the smallest boy, who could barely walk, stomping his feet in time. He knew he would win no prizes at Bel Tine, but after Thom's teaching he would not be embarrassed to enter.

Else was sitting cross-legged in front of the fire, and as he lowered the flute after the last note, she leaned forward with a long sigh and smiled at him. "You play so beautifully. I never heard anything so beautiful."

Mistress Grinwell suddenly paused in her sewing and raised an eyebrow at her daughter, then gave Rand a long, appraising look.

He had picked up the leather case to put the flute away, but under her stare he dropped the case and almost the flute, too. If she accused him of trifling with her daughter. . . . In desperation he put the flute back to his lips and played another song, then another, and another. Mistress Grinwell kept watching him. He played "The Wind That Shakes the Willow," and "Coming Home From Tarwin's Gap," and "Mistress Aynora's Rooster," and "The Old Black Bear." He played every song he could think of, but she never took her eyes off him. She never said anything, either, but she watched, and weighed.

It was late when Master Grinwell finally stood up, chuckling and rubbing his hands together. "Well, this has been rare fun, but it's way past our bedtime. You traveling lads make your own hours, but morning comes early on a farm. I'll tell you lads, I have paid good money at an inn for no better entertainment than I've had this night. For worse."

"I think they should have a reward, father," Mistress Grinwell said as she picked up her youngest boy, who had long since fallen asleep in front of the fire. "The barn is no fit place to sleep. They can sleep in Else's room tonight, and she will sleep with me."

Else grimaced. She was careful to keep her head down, but Rand saw it. He thought her mother did, too.

Master Grinwell nodded. "Yes, yes, much better than the

barn. If you don't mind sleeping two to a bed, that is." Rand
flushed; Mistress Grinwell was still looking at him. "I do wish I
could hear more of that flute. And your juggling, too. I like
that. You know, there's a little task you could help with tomorrow, and—"

"They'll be wanting an early start, father," Mistress Grinwell
cut in. "Arien is the next village the way they're going, and if
they intend to try their luck at the inn there, they'll have to
walk all day to get there before dark."

"Yes, mistress," Rand said, "we will. And thank you."

She gave him a tight-lipped smile as if she knew very well
that his thanks were for more than her advice, or even supper
and a warm bed.

The whole next day Mat twitted him about Else as they made
their way down the road. He kept trying to change the subject,
and what the Grinwells had suggested about performing at inns
was the easiest thing to mind. In the morning, with Else pout-
ing as he left, and Mistress Grinwell watching with a sharp-eyed
look of good-riddance and soonest-mended, it was just something to keep Mat from talking. By the time they did reach the
next village, it was something else again.

With dusk descending, they entered the only inn in Arien,
and Rand spoke to the innkeeper. He played "Ferry O'er the
River"—which the plump innkeeper called "Darling Sara"—
and part of "The Road to Dun Aren," and Mat did a little
juggling, and the upshot was that they slept in a bed that night
and ate roasted potatoes and hot beef. It was the smallest room
in the inn, to be sure, up under the eaves in the back, and the
meal came in the middle of a long night of playing and juggling,
but it was still a bed beneath a roof. Even better, to Rand,
every daylight hour had been spent traveling. And the inn's
patrons did not seem to care if Mat stared at them suspiciously.
Some of them even looked askance at one another. The times
made suspicion of strangers a commonplace, and there were
always strangers at an inn.

Rand slept better than he had since leaving Whitebridge, despite sharing a bed with Mat and his nocturnal muttering. In
the morning the innkeeper tried to talk them into staying another day or two, but when he could not, he called over a
bleary-eyed farmer who had drunk too much to drive his cart

home the night before. An hour later they were five miles further east, sprawling on their backs on the straw in the back of Eazil Forney's cart.

That became the way of their traveling. With a little luck, and maybe a ride or two, they could almost always reach the next village by dark. If there was more than one inn in a village, the innkeepers would bid for them once they heard Rand's flute and saw Mat juggle. Together they still did not come close to a gleeman, but they were more than most villages saw in a year. Two or three inns in a town meant a better room, with two beds, and more generous portions of a better cut of meat, and sometimes even a few coppers in their pockets when they left besides. In the mornings there was almost always someone to offer a ride, another farmer who had stayed too late and drunk too much, or a merchant who had liked their entertainment enough not to mind if they hopped up on the back of one of his wagons. Rand began to think their problems were over till they reached Caemlyn. But then they came to Four Kings.

A Questioner

CHAPTER
32

Four Kings in Shadow

The village was bigger than most, but still a scruffy town to bear a name like Four Kings. As usual, the Caemlyn Road ran straight through the center of the town, but another heavily traveled highway came in from the south, too. Most villages were markets and gathering places for the farmers of the area, but there were few farmers to be seen here. Four Kings survived as a stopover for merchants' wagon trains on their way to Caemlyn and to the mining towns in the Mountains of Mist beyond Baerlon, as well as the villages between. The southern road carried Lugard's trade with the mines in the west; Lugarder merchants going to Caemlyn had a more direct route. The surrounding country held few farms, barely enough to feed themselves and the town, and everything in the village centered on the merchants and their wagons, the men who drove them and the laborers who loaded the goods.

Plots of bare earth, ground to dust, lay scattered through Four Kings, filled with wagons parked wheel to wheel and abandoned except for a few bored guards. Stables and horse-lots lined the streets, all of which were wide enough to allow wagons to pass and deeply rutted from too many wheels. There was no village green, and the children played in the ruts, dodging wagons and the curses of wagon drivers. Village women, their heads covered with scarves, kept their eyes down and walked quickly, sometimes followed by wagoneers' comments that made Rand blush; even Mat gave a start at some of them.

No woman stood gossiping over the fence with a neighbor. Drab wooden houses stood cheek by jowl, with only narrow alleys between and whitewash—where anyone had bothered to whitewash the weathered boards—faded as if it had not been freshened in years. Heavy shutters on the houses had not been open in so long that the hinges were solid lumps of rust. Noise hung over everything, clanging from blacksmiths, shouts from the wagon drivers, raucous laughter from the town's inns.

Rand swung down from the back of a merchant's canvas-topped wagon as they came abreast of a garishly painted inn, all greens and yellows that caught the eye from afar among the leaden houses. The line of wagons kept moving. None of the drivers even seemed to notice that he and Mat had gone; dusk was falling, and they all had their eyes on unhitching the horses and reaching the inns. Rand stumbled in a rut, then leaped quickly to avoid a heavy-laden wagon clattering the other way. The driver shouted a curse at him as the wagon rolled by. A village woman stepped around him and hurried on without ever meeting his eye.

"I don't know about this place," he said. He thought he could hear music mixed in the din, but he could not tell from where it was coming. From the inn, maybe, but it was hard to be sure. "I don't like it. Maybe we'd better go on this time."

Mat gave him a scornful look, then rolled his eyes at the sky. Dark clouds thickened overhead. "And sleep under a hedge tonight? In that? I'm used to a bed again." He cocked his head to listen, then grunted. "Maybe one of these places doesn't have musicians. Anyway, I'll bet they don't have a juggler." He slung his bow across his shoulders and started for the bright yellow door, studying everything through narrowed eyes. Rand followed doubtfully.

There were musicians inside, their zither and drum almost drowned in coarse laughter and drunken shouting. Rand did not bother to find the landlord. The next two inns had musicians as well, and the same deafening cacophony. Roughly dressed men filled the tables and stumbled across the floor, waving mugs and trying to fondle serving maids who dodged with fixed, long-suffering smiles. The buildings shook with the racket, and the smell was sour, a stench of old wine and unwashed bodies. Of the merchants, in their silk and velvet and

lace, there was no sign; private dining rooms abovestairs protected their ears and noses. He and Mat only put their heads in
the doors before leaving. He was beginning to think they would
have no choice but to move on.

The fourth inn, The Dancing Cartman, stood silent.

It was as gaudy as the other inns, yellow trimmed in bright
red and bilious, eye-wrenching green, though here the paint
was cracked and peeling. Rand and Mat stepped inside.

Only half a dozen men sat at the tables that filled the common room, hunched over their mugs, each one glumly alone
with his thoughts. Business was definitely not good, but it had
been better once. Exactly as many serving maids as there were
patrons busied themselves around the room. There was plenty
for them to do—dirt crusted the floor and cobwebs filled the
corners of the ceiling—but most were not doing anything really
useful, only moving so they would not be seen standing still.

A bony man with long, stringy hair to his shoulders turned to
scowl at them as they came through the door. The first slow
peal of thunder rumbled across Four Kings. "What do you
want?" He was rubbing his hands on a greasy apron that hung
to his ankles. Rand wondered if more grime was coming off on
the apron or on the man's hands. He was the first skinny innkeeper Rand had seen. "Well? Speak up, buy a drink, or get
out! Do I look like a raree show?"

Flushing, Rand launched into the spiel he had perfected at
inns before this. "I play the flute, and my friend juggles, and
you'll not see two better in a year. For a good room and a good
meal, we'll fill this common room of yours." He remembered
the filled common rooms he had already seen that evening, especially the man who had vomited right in front of him at the
last one. He had had to step lively to keep his boots untouched.
He faltered, but caught himself and went on. "We'll fill your
inn with men who will repay the little we cost twenty times over
with the food and drink they buy. Why should—"

"I've got a man plays the dulcimer," the innkeeper said
sourly.

"You have a drunk, Saml Hake," one of the serving maids
said. She was passing him with a tray and two mugs, and she
paused to give Rand and Mat a plump smile. "Most times, he

can't see well enough to find the common room," she confided in a loud whisper. "Haven't even seen him in two days."

Without taking his eyes off Rand and Mat, Hake casually backhanded her across the face. She gave a surprised grunt and fell heavily to the unwashed floor; one of the mugs broke, and the spilled wine washed rivulets in the dirt. "You're docked for the wine and breakage. Get 'em fresh drinks. And hurry. Men don't pay to wait while you laze around." His tone was as offhand as the blow. None of the patrons looked up from their wine, and the other serving maids kept their eyes averted.

The plump woman rubbed her cheek and stared pure murder at Hake, but she gathered the empty mug and the broken pieces on her tray and went off without a word.

Hake sucked his teeth thoughtfully, eyeing Rand and Mat. His gaze clung to the heron-mark sword before he pulled it away. "Tell you what," he said finally. "You can have a couple of pallets in an empty storeroom in the back. Rooms are too expensive to give away. You eat when everybody's gone. There ought to be something left."

Rand wished there was an inn in Four Kings they had not yet tried. Since leaving Whitebridge he had met coolness, indifference, and outright hostility, but nothing that gave him the sense of unease that this man and this village did. He told himself it was just the dirt and squalor and noise, but the misgivings did not go away. Mat was watching Hake as if he suspected some trap, but he gave no sign of wanting to give up The Dancing Cartman for a bed under a hedge. Thunder rattled the windows. Rand sighed.

"The pallets will do if they're clean, and if there are enough clean blankets. But we eat two hours after full dark, no later, and the best you have. Here. We'll show you what we can do." He reached for the flute case, but Hake shook his head.

"Don't matter. This lot'll be satisfied with any kind of screeching so long as it sounds something like music." His eyes touched Rand's sword again; his thin smile touched nothing but his lips. "Eat when you want, but if you don't bring the crowd in, out you go in the street." He nodded over his shoulder at two hard-faced men sitting against the wall. They were not drinking, and their arms were thick enough for legs. When

Hake nodded at them, their eyes shifted to Rand and Mat, flat and expressionless.

Rand put one hand on his sword hilt, hoping the twisting in his stomach did not show on his face. "As long as we get what's agreed on," he said in a level tone.

Hake blinked, and for a moment he seemed uneasy himself. Abruptly he nodded. "What I said, isn't it? Well, get started. You won't bring anybody in just standing there." He stalked off, scowling and shouting at the serving maids as if there were fifty customers they were neglecting.

There was a small, raised platform at the far end of the room, near the door to the back. Rand lifted a bench up on it, and settled his cloak, blanketroll, and Thom's bundled cloak behind the bench with the sword lying atop them.

He wondered if he had been wise to keep wearing the sword openly. Swords were common enough, but the heron-mark attracted attention and speculation. Not from everybody, but any notice at all made him uncomfortable. He could be leaving a clear trail for the Myrddraal—if Fades needed that kind of trail. They did not seem to. In any case, he was reluctant to stop wearing it. Tam had given it to him. His father. As long as he wore the sword, there was still some connection between Tam and him, a thread that gave him the right to still call Tam father. *Too late now,* he thought. He was not sure what he meant, but he was sure it was true. *Too late.*

At the first note of "Cock o' the North" the half-dozen patrons in the common room lifted their heads out of their wine. Even the two bouncers sat forward a little. They all applauded when he finished, including the two toughs, and once more when Mat sent a shower of colored balls spinning through his hands. Outside, the sky muttered again. The rain was holding off, but the pressure of it was palpable; the longer it waited, the harder it would fall.

Word spread, and by the time it was dark outside the inn was packed full with men laughing and talking so loud that Rand could barely hear what he was playing. Only the thunder overpowered the noise in the common room. Lightning flashed in the windows, and in the momentary lulls he could faintly hear rain drumming on the roof. Men who came in now dripped trails across the floor.

Whenever he paused, voices shouted the names of tunes through the din. A good many names he did not recognize, though when he got someone to hum a bit of it, he often found he did know the song. It had been that way other places, before. "Jolly Jaim" was "Rhea's Fling" here, and had been "Colors of the Sun" at an earlier stop. Some names stayed the same; others changed with ten miles' distance, and he had learned new songs, too. "The Drunken Peddler" was a new one, though sometimes it was called "Tinker in the Kitchen." "Two Kings Came Hunting" was "Two Horses Running" and several other names besides. He played the ones he knew, and men pounded the tables for more.

Others called for Mat to juggle again. Sometimes fights broke out between those wanting music and those who fancied juggling. Once a knife flashed, and a woman screamed, and a man reeled back from a table with blood streaming down his face, but Jak and Strom, the two bouncers, closed in swiftly and with complete impartiality threw everyone involved into the street with lumps on their heads. That was their tactic with any trouble. The talk and the laughing went on as if nothing had occurred. Nobody even looked around except those the bouncers jostled on their way to the door.

The patrons were free with their hands, too, when one of the serving maids let herself grow unwary. More than once Jak or Strom had to rescue one of the women, though they were none too quick about it. The way Hake carried on, screaming and shaking the woman involved, he always considered it her fault, and the teary eyes and stammered apologies said she was willing to accept his opinion. The women jumped whenever Hake frowned, even if he was looking somewhere else. Rand wondered why any of them put up with it.

Hake smiled when he looked at Rand and Mat. After a while Rand realized Hake was not smiling at them; the smiles came when his eyes slid behind them, to where the heron-mark sword lay. Once, when Rand set the gold-and-silver-chased flute down beside his stool, the flute got a smile, too.

The next time he changed places with Mat at the front of the dais, he leaned over to speak in Mat's ear. Even that close he had to speak loudly, but with all the noise he doubted if anyone else could hear. "Hake's going to try to rob us."

Mat nodded as if it was nothing he had not expected. "We'll have to bar our door tonight."

"Bar our door? Jak and Strom could break down a door with their fists. Let's get out of here."

"Wait till after we eat, at least. I'm hungry. They can't do anything here," Mat added. The packed common room shouted impatiently for them to get on with it. Hake was glaring at them. "Anyway, you want to sleep outside tonight?" An especially strong crack of lightning drowned out everything else, and for an instant the light through the windows was stronger than the lamps.

"I just want to get out without my head being broken," Rand said, but Mat was already slouching back to take his rest on the stool. Rand sighed and launched into "The Road to Dun Aren." A lot of them seemed to like that one; he had already played it four times, and they still shouted for it.

The trouble was that Mat was right, as far as he went. He was hungry, too. And he could not see how Hake could give them any trouble while the common room was full, and getting fuller. For every man who left or was thrown out by Jak and Strom, two came in from the street. They shouted for the juggling or for a particular tune, but mostly they were interested in drinking and fondling the serving maids. One man was different, though.

He stood out in every way among the crowd in The Dancing Cartman. Merchants apparently had no use for the run-down inn; there were not even any private dining rooms for them, as far as he could make out. The patrons were all rough-dressed, with the tough skin of men who labored in the sun and wind. This man was sleekly fleshy, with a soft look to his hands, and a velvet coat, and a dark green velvet cloak lined with blue silk was slung around his shoulders. All of his clothes had an expensive cut to them. His shoes—soft velvet slippers, not boots—were not made for the rutted streets of Four Kings, or for any streets at all, for that matter.

He came in well after dark, shaking the rain off his cloak as he looked around, a twist of distaste on his mouth. He scanned the room once, already turning to go, then suddenly gave a start at nothing Rand could see and sat down at a table Jak and Strom had just emptied. A serving maid stopped at his table, then brought him a mug of wine which he pushed to one side and never touched again. She seemed in a hurry to leave his table both times, though he did not try to touch her or even look at her. Whatever it was about him that made her uneasy, others who came close to him noticed it, too. For all of his soft look, whenever some callus-handed wagon driver decided to share his table, one glance was all it took to send the man looking elsewhere. He sat as if there were no one else in the room but him—and Rand and Mat. Them he watched over steepled hands that glittered with a ring on each finger. He watched them with a smile of satisfied recognition.

Rand murmured to Mat as they were changing places again, and Mat nodded. "I saw him," he muttered. "Who *is* he? I keep thinking I know him."

The same thought had occurred to Rand, tickling the back of his memory, but he could not bring it forward. Yet he was sure that face was one he had never seen before.

When they had been performing for two hours, as near as Rand could estimate, he slipped the flute into its case and he and Mat gathered up their belongings. As they were stepping down from the low platform, Hake came bustling up, anger twisting his narrow face.

"It's time to eat," Rand said to forestall him, "and we don't want our things stolen. You want to tell the cook?" Hake hesitated, still angry, trying unsuccessfully to keep his eyes off what Rand held in his arms. Casually Rand shifted his bundles so he could rest one hand on the sword. "Or you can *try* throwing us out." He made the emphasis deliberately, then added, "There's a lot of night left for us to play, yet. We have to keep our strength up if we're going to perform well enough to keep this crowd spending money. How long do you think this room will stay full if we fall over from hunger?"

Hake's eyes twitched over the room full of men putting money in his pocket, then he turned and stuck his head through the door to the rear of the inn. "Feed 'em!" he shouted. Rounding on Rand and Mat, he snarled, "Don't be all night about it. I expect you up there till the last man's gone."

Some of the patrons were shouting for the musician and the

juggler, and Hake turned to soothe them. The man in the velvet cloak was one of the anxious ones. Rand motioned Mat to follow him.

A stout door separated the kitchen from the front of the inn, and, except when it opened to let a serving maid through, the rain pounding the roof was louder in the kitchen than the shouts from the common room. It was a big room, hot and steamy from stoves and ovens, with a huge table covered with half-prepared food and dishes ready to be served. Some of the serving maids sat clustered on a bench near the rear door, rubbing their feet and chattering away all at once with the fat cook, who talked back at the same time and waved a big spoon to emphasize her points. They all glanced up as Rand and Mat came in, but it did not slow their conversation or stop their foot rubbing.

"We ought to get out of here while we have the chance," Rand said softly, but Mat shook his head, his eyes fixed on the two plates the cook was filling with beef and potatoes and peas. She hardly looked at the two of them, keeping up her talk with the other women while she pushed things aside on the table with her elbows and set the plates down, adding forks.

"After we eat is time enough." Mat slid onto a bench and began using his fork as if it were a shovel.

Rand sighed, but he was right behind Mat. He had had only a butt-end of bread to eat since the night before. His belly felt as empty as a beggar's purse, and the cooking smells that filled the kitchen did not help. He quickly had his mouth full, though Mat was getting his plate refilled by the cook before he had finished half of his.

He did not mean to eavesdrop on the women's talk, but some of the words reached out and grabbed him.

"Sounds crazy to me."

"Crazy or not, it's what I hear. He went to half the inns in town before he came here. Just walked in, looked around, and walked out without saying one word, even at the Royal Inn. Like it wasn't raining at all."

"Maybe he thought here was the most comfortable." That brought gales of laughter.

"What I hear is he didn't even get to Four Kings till after nightfall, and his horses blowing like they'd been pushed hard."

"Where'd he come from, to get caught out after dark? Nobody but a fool or a madman travels anywhere and plans it that badly."

"Well, maybe he's a fool, but he's a rich one. I hear he even has another carriage for his servants and baggage. There's money there, mark my words. Did you see that cloak of his? I wouldn't mind having that my ownself."

"He's a little plump for my taste, but I always say a man can't be too fat if enough gold comes with it." They all doubled over giggling, and the cook threw back her head and roared with laughter.

Rand dropped his fork on his plate. A thought he did not like bubbled in his head. "I'll be back in a minute," he said. Mat barely nodded, stuffing a piece of potato into his mouth.

Rand picked up his sword belt along with his cloak as he stood, and buckled it around his waist on the way to the back door. No one paid him any mind.

The rain was bucketing down. He swung his cloak around his shoulders and pulled the hood over his head, holding the cloak closed as he trotted across the stableyard. A curtain of water hid everything except when lightning flashed, but he found what he was hunting. The horses had been taken into the stable, but the two black-lacquered carriages glistened wetly outside. Thunder grumbled, and a bolt of lightning streaked above the inn. In the brief burst of light he made out a name in gold script on the coach doors. Howal Gode.

Unmindful of the rain beating at him, he stood staring at the name he could no longer see. He remembered where he had last seen black-lacquered coaches with their owners' names on the door, and sleek, overfed men in silk-lined velvet cloaks and velvet slippers. Whitebridge. A Whitebridge merchant could have a perfectly legitimate reason to be on his way to Caemlyn. *A reason that sends him to half the inns in town before he chooses the one where you are? A reason that makes him look at you as if he's found what he's searching for?*

Rand shivered, and suddenly he was aware of rain trickling down his back. His cloak was tightly woven, but it had never been meant to stand up to this kind of downpour. He hurried back to the inn, splashing through deepening puddles. Jak blocked the door as he started through.

"Well, well, well. Out here alone in the dark. Dark's dangerous, boy."

Rain slicked Rand's hair down across his forehead. The stableyard was empty except for them. He wondered if Hake had decided he wanted the sword and the flute badly enough to forgo keeping the crowd in the common room.

Brushing water out of his eyes with one hand, he put the other on his sword. Even wet, the nobby leather made a sure grip for his fingers. "Has Hake decided all those men will stay just for his ale, instead of going where there's entertainment, too? If he has, we'll call the meal even for what we've done so far and be on our way."

Dry in the doorway, the big man looked out at the rain and snorted. "In this?" His eyes slid down to Rand's hand on the sword. "You know, me and Strom got a bet. He figures you stole that from your old grandmother. Me, I figure your grandmother'd kick you round the pigpen and hang you out to dry." He grinned. His teeth were crooked and yellow, and the grin made him look even meaner. "Night's long yet, boy."

Rand brushed past him, and Jak let him by with an ugly chuckle.

Inside, he tossed off his cloak and dropped on the bench at the table he had left only minutes before. Mat was done with his second plate and working on a third, eating more slowly now, but intently, as if he planned to finish every bite if it killed him. Jak took up a place by the door to the stableyard, leaning against the wall and watching them. Even the cook seemed to feel no urge to talk with him there.

"He's from Whitebridge," Rand said softly. There was no need to say who "he" was. Mat's head swiveled toward him, a piece of beef on the end of the fork suspended halfway to his mouth. Conscious of Jak watching, Rand stirred the food on his plate. He could not have gotten a mouthful down if he had been starving, but he tried to pretend an interest in the peas as he told Mat about the carriages, and what the women had said, in case Mat had not been listening.

Obviously he had not been. Mat blinked in surprise and whistled between his teeth, then frowned at the meat on his fork and grunted as he tossed the fork onto his plate. Rand wished he would make at least an effort to be circumspect.

"After us," Mat said when he finished. The creases in Mat's forehead deepened. "A Darkfriend?"

"Maybe. I don't know." Rand glanced at Jak and the big man stretched elaborately, shrugging shoulders as big as any blacksmith's. "Do you think we can get past him?"

"Not without him making enough noise to bring Hake and the other one. I knew we should never have stopped here."

Rand gaped, but before he could say anything Hake pushed through the door from the common room. Strom bulked large over his shoulder. Jak stepped in front of the back door. "You going to eat all night?" Hake barked. "I didn't feed you so you could lie around out here."

Rand looked at his friend. Later, Mat mouthed, and they gathered their things under the watchful eyes of Hake, Strom, and Jak.

In the common room, cries for juggling and the names of tunes burst through the clamor as soon as Rand and Mat appeared. The man in the velvet cloak—Howal Gode—still appeared to ignore everyone around him, but he was nonetheless seated on the edge of his chair. At the sight of them he leaned back, the satisfied smile returning to his lips.

Rand took the first turn at the front of the dais, playing "Drawing Water From the Well" with only half his mind on it. No one seemed to notice the few wrong notes. He tried to think of how they were going to get away, and tried to avoid looking at Gode, too. If he was after them, there was no point in letting him know they knew it. As for getting away. . . .

He had never realized before what a good trap an inn made. Hake, Jak, and Strom did not even have to keep a close eye on them; the crowd would let them know if he or Mat left the dais. As long as the common room was full of people, Hake could not send Jak and Strom after them, but as long as the common room was full of people they could not get away without Hake knowing. And Gode was watching their every move, too. It was so funny he would have laughed if he had not been on the point of throwing up. They would just have to be wary and wait their chance.

When he changed places with Mat, Rand groaned to himself. Mat glared at Hake, at Strom, at Jak, without a care to whether they noticed or wondered why. When he was not actu-

ally handling the balls, his hand rested under his coat. Rand
hissed at him, but he paid no attention. If Hake saw that ruby,
he might not wait until they were alone. If the men in the common room saw it, half of them might join in with Hake.

Worst of all, Mat stared at the Whitebridge merchant—the
Darkfriend?—twice as hard as at anyone else, and Gode noticed. There was no way he could avoid noticing. But it did not
disturb his aplomb in the least. His smile deepened, if anything,
and he nodded to Mat as if to an old acquaintance, then looked
at Rand and raised a questioning eyebrow. Rand did not want
to know what the question was. He tried to avoid looking at the
man, but he knew it was too late for that. *Too late. Too late
again.*

Only one thing seemed to shake the velvet-cloaked man's
equilibrium. Rand's sword. He had left it on. Two or three men
staggered up to ask if he thought his playing was so bad that he
needed protection, but none of them had noticed the heron on
the hilt. Gode noticed. His pale hands clenched, and he
frowned at the sword for a long time before his smile came
back. When it did, it was not as sure as before.

One good thing, at least, Rand thought. *If he believes I can
live up to the heron-mark, maybe he'll leave us alone. Then all
we have to worry about is Hake and his bullies.* It was hardly a
comforting thought, and, sword or no sword, Gode kept watching. And smiling.

To Rand the night seemed to last a year. All those eyes looking at him: Hake and Jak and Strom like vultures watching a
sheep caught in a bog, Gode waiting like something even
worse. He began to think that everybody in the room was
watching with some hidden motive. Sour wine fumes and
the stench of dirty, sweating bodies made his head swim, and
the din of voices beat at him till his eyes blurred and even the
sound of his own flute scratched at his ears. The crash of the
thunder seemed to be inside his skull. Weariness hung on him
like an iron weight.

Eventually the need to be up with the dawn began to pull
men reluctantly out into the dark. A farmer had only himself to
answer to, but merchants were notoriously unfeeling about
hangovers when they were paying drivers' wages. In the small

hours the common room slowly emptied as even those who had
rooms abovestairs staggered off to find their beds.

Gode was the last patron. When Rand reached for the
leather flute case, yawning, Gode stood up and slung his cloak
over his arm. The serving maids were cleaning up, muttering
among themselves about the mess of spilled wine and broken
crockery. Hake was locking the front door with a big key.
Gode cornered Hake for a moment, and Hake called one of the
women to show him to a room. The velvet-cloaked man gave
Mat and Rand a knowing smile before he disappeared upstairs.

Hake was looking at Rand and Mat. Jak and Strom stood at
his shoulders.

Rand hastily finished hanging his things from his shoulders,
holding them all awkwardly behind him with his left hand so he
could reach his sword. He made no move toward it, but he
wanted to know it was ready. He suppressed a yawn; how tired
he was was something they should not know.

Mat shouldered his bow and his few other belongings awkwardly, but he put his hand under his coat as he watched Hake
and his toughs approach.

Hake was carrying an oil lamp, and to Rand's surprise he
gave a little bow and gestured to a side door with it. "Your
pallets are this way." Only a slight twist of his lips spoiled his
act.

Mat thrust his chin out at Jak and Strom. "You need those
two to show us our beds?"

"I'm a man of property," Hake said, smoothing the front of
his soiled apron, "and men of property can't be too careful." A
crash of thunder rattled the windows, and he glanced signifi-
cantly at the ceiling, then gave them a toothy grin. "You want
to see your beds or not?"

Rand wondered what would happen if he said they wanted to
leave. *If you really did know more about using a sword than the
few exercises Lan showed you. . . .* "Lead the way," he said,
trying to make his voice hard. "I don't like having anybody
behind me."

Strom snickered, but Hake nodded placidly and turned toward the side door, and the two big men swaggered after him.
Taking a deep breath, Rand gave a wishful glance at the door
to the kitchen. If Hake had already locked the back door, run-

ning now would only begin what he was hoping to avoid. He followed the innkeeper glumly.

At the side door he hesitated, and Mat crowded into his back. The reason for Hake's lamp was apparent. The door let into a hall as black as pitch. Only the lamp Hake carried, silhouetting Jak and Strom, gave him the courage to keep on. If they turned, he would know it. *And do what?* The floor creaked under his boots.

The hall ended in a rough, unpainted door. He had not seen if there were any other doors along the way. Hake and his bullies went through, and he followed quickly, before they could have a chance to set a trap, but Hake merely lifted the lamp high and gestured at the room.

"Here it is."

An old storeroom, he had called it, and by the look of it not used in some time. Weathered barrels and broken crates filled half the floor. Steady drips fell from more than one place on the ceiling, and a broken pane in the filthy window let the rain blow in freely. Unidentifiable odds and ends littered the shelves, and thick dust covered almost everything. The presence of the promised pallets was a surprise.

The sword makes him nervous. He won't try anything until we're sound asleep. Rand had no intention of sleeping under Hake's roof. As soon as the innkeeper left, he intended to be out the window. "It'll do," he said. He kept his eyes on Hake, wary for a signal to the two grinning men at the innkeeper's side. It was an effort not to wet his lips. "Leave the lamp."

Hake grunted, but pushed the lamp onto a shelf. He hesitated, looking at them, and Rand was sure he was about to give the word for Jak and Strom to jump them, but his eyes went to Rand's sword with a calculating frown, and he jerked his head at the two big men. Surprise flashed across their broad faces, but they followed him out of the room without a backward glance.

Rand waited for the *creak-creak-creak* of their footsteps to fade away, then counted to fifty before sticking his head into the hall. The blackness was broken only by a rectangle of light that seemed as distant as the moon: the door to the common room. As he pulled his head in, something big moved in the darkness near the far door. Jak or Strom, standing guard.

A quick examination of the door told him all he needed to know, little of it good. The boards were thick and stout, but there was no lock, and no bar on the inside. It did open into the room, though.

"I thought they were going for us," Mat said. "What are they waiting for?" He had the dagger out, gripped in a white-knuckled fist. Lamplight flickered on the blade. His bow and quiver lay forgotten on the floor.

"For us to go to sleep." Rand started rummaging through the barrels and crates. "Help me find something to block the door."

"Why? You don't really intend to sleep here, do you? Let's get out the window and gone. I'd rather be wet than dead."

"One of them is at the end of the hall. We make any noise, and they'll be down on us before we can blink. I think Hake would rather face us awake than risk letting us get away."

Muttering, Mat joined his search, but there was nothing useful in any of the litter on the floor. The barrels were empty, the crates splintered, and the whole lot of them piled in front of the door would not stop anyone from opening it. Then something familiar on a shelf caught Rand's eye. Two splitting wedges, covered with rust and dust. He took them down with a grin.

Hastily he shoved them under the door and, when the next roll of thunder rattled the inn, drove them in with two quick kicks of his heel. The thunder faded, and he held his breath, listening. All he heard was the rain pounding on the roof. No floorboards creaking under running feet.

"The window," he said.

It had not been opened in years, from the dirt crusted around it. They strained together, pushing up with all their might. Rand's knees wobbled before the sash budged; it groaned with each reluctant inch. When the opening was wide enough for them to slip through, he crouched, then stopped.

"Blood and ashes!" Mat growled. "No wonder Hake wasn't worried about us slipping out."

Iron bars in an iron frame glistened wetly in the light from the lamp. Rand pushed at them; they were as solid as a boulder.

"I saw something," Mat said. He pawed hurriedly through

the litter on the shelves and came back with a rusty crowbar. He rammed the end of it under the iron frame on one side, and Rand winced.

"Remember the noise, Mat."

Mat grimaced and muttered under his breath, but he waited. Rand put his hands on the crowbar and tried to find good footing in the growing puddle of water under the window. Thunder rolled and they heaved. With a tortured squeal of nails that made the hairs lift on Rand's neck, the frame shifted—a quarter of an inch, if that. Timing themselves to peals of thunder and lightning cracks, they heaved on the crowbar again and again. Nothing. A quarter of an inch. Nothing. A hairsbreadth. Nothing. Nothing.

Suddenly Rand's feet slipped in the water, and they crashed to the floor. The crowbar clattered against the bars like a gong. He lay in a puddle holding his breath and listening. Silence but for the rain.

Mat nursed bruised knuckles and glared at him. "We'll never get out at this rate." The iron frame was pushed out from the window not quite far enough to get two fingers under it. Dozens of thick nails crossed the narrow opening.

"We just have to keep trying," Rand said, getting up. But as he set the crowbar under the edge of the frame, the door creaked as someone tried to open it. The splitting wedges held it shut. He exchanged a worried look with Mat. Mat pulled the dagger out again. The door gave another screak.

Rand took a deep breath and tried to make his voice steady. "Go away, Hake. We're trying to sleep."

"I fear you mistake me." The voice was so sleek and full of itself that it named its owner. Howal Gode. "Master Hake and his . . . minions will not trouble us. They sleep soundly, and in the morning they will only be able to wonder where you vanished to. Let me in, my young friends. We must talk."

"We don't have anything to talk to you about," Mat said. "Go away and let us sleep."

Gode's chuckle was nasty. "Of course we have things to talk about. You know that as well as I. I saw it in your eyes. I know what you are, perhaps better than you do. I can feel it coming from you in waves. Already you halfway belong to my master. Stop running and accept it. Things will be so much easier for you. If the Tar Valon hags find you, you'll wish you could cut your own throat before they are done, but you won't be able to. Only my master can protect you from them."

Rand swallowed hard. "We don't know what you're talking about. Leave us alone." The floorboards in the hall squeaked. Gode was not alone. How many men could he have brought in two carriages?

"Stop being foolish, my young friends. You know. You know very well. The Great Lord of the Dark has marked you for his own. It is written that when he awakes, the new Dreadlords will be there to praise him. You must be two of them, else I would not have been sent to find you. Think of it. Life everlasting, and power beyond dreams." His voice was thick with hunger for that power himself.

Rand glanced back at the window just as lightning split the sky, and he almost groaned. The brief flash of light showed men outside, men ignoring the rain that drenched them as they stood watching the window.

"I tire of this," Gode announced. "You will submit to my master—to your master—or you will be made to submit. That would not be pleasant for you. The Great Lord of the Dark rules death, and he can give life in death or death in life as he chooses. Open this door. One way or another, your running is at an end. Open it, I say!"

He must have said something else, too, for suddenly a heavy body thudded against the door. It shivered, and the wedges slid a fraction of an inch with a grate of rust rubbing off on wood. Again and again the door trembled as bodies hurled themselves at it. Sometimes the wedges held; sometimes they slid another tiny bit, and bit by tiny bit the door crept inexorably inward.

"Submit," Gode demanded from the hall, "or spend eternity wishing that you had!"

"If we don't have any choice—" Mat licked his lips under Rand's stare. His eyes darted like the eyes of a badger in a trap; his face was pale, and he panted as he spoke. "We could say yes, and then get away later. Blood and ashes, Rand, there's no way out!"

The words seemed to drift to Rand through wool stuffed in his ears. *No way out.* Thunder muttered overhead, and was drowned in a slash of lightning. *Have to find a way out.* Gode called to them, demanding, appealing; the door slid another inch toward being open. *A way out!*

Light filled the room, flooding vision; the air roared and burned. Rand felt himself picked up and dashed against the wall. He slid down in a heap, ears ringing and every hair on his body trying to stand on end. Dazed, he staggered to his feet. His knees wobbled, and he put a hand against the wall to steady himself. He looked around in amazement.

The lamp, lying on its side on the edge of one of the few shelves still clinging to the walls, still burned and gave light. All the barrels and crates, some blackened and smoldering, lay toppled where they had been hurled. The window, bars and all, and most of the wall, too, had vanished, leaving a splintered hole. The roof sagged, and tendrils of smoke fought the rain around the jagged edges of the opening. The door hung off its hinges, jammed in the doorframe at an angle slanting into the hall.

With a feeling of woozy unreality he stood the lamp up. It seemed the most important thing in the world was making sure it did not break.

A pile of crates suddenly heaved apart, and Mat stood up in the middle of it. He weaved on his feet, blinking and fumbling at himself as if wondering if everything was still attached. He peered toward Rand. "Rand? Is that you? You're alive. I thought we were both—" He broke off, biting his lip and shaking. It took Rand a moment to realize he was laughing, and on the edge of hysteria.

"What happened, Mat? Mat? Mat! What happened?"

One last shiver wracked Mat, and then he was still. "Lightning, Rand. I was looking right at the window when it hit the bars. Lightning. I can't see worth—" He broke off, squinting at the aslant door, and his voice went sharp. "Where's Gode?"

Nothing moved in the dark corridor beyond the door. Of Gode and his companions there was neither sign nor sound, though anything could have lain in the blackness. Rand found himself hoping they were dead, but he would not have put his head into the hall to find out for sure if he had been offered a crown. Nothing moved out in the night beyond where the wall had been, either, but others were up and about. Confused shouts came from abovestairs in the inn, and the pounding of running feet.

"Let's go while we can," Rand said.

Hastily helping separate their belongings from the rubble, he grabbed Mat's arm and half pulled, half guided his friend through the gaping hole into the night. Mat clutched his arm, stumbling beside him with his head pushed forward in an effort to see.

As the first rain hit Rand's face, lightning forked above the inn, and he came to a convulsive stop. Gode's men were still there, lying with their feet toward the opening. Pelted by the rain, their open eyes stared at the sky.

"What is it?" Mat asked. "Blood and ashes! I can hardly see my own bloody hand!"

"Nothing," Rand said. *Luck. The Light's own. . . . Is it?* Shivering, he carefully guided Mat around the bodies. "Just the lightning."

There was no light save the lightning, and he stumbled in the ruts as they ran staggering away from the inn. With Mat almost hanging on him, every stumble almost pulled them both down, but tottering, panting, they ran.

Once he looked back. Once, before the rain thickened to a deafening curtain that blotted The Dancing Cartman from sight. Lightning silhouetted the figure of a man at the back of the inn, a man shaking his fist at them, or at the sky. Gode or Hake, he did not know, but either one was as bad as the other. The rain came in a deluge, isolating them in a wall of water. He hurried through the night, listening through the roar of the storm for the sound of pursuit.

CHAPTER
33

The Dark Waits

Under a leaden sky the high-wheeled cart bumped east along the Caemlyn Road. Rand pulled himself out of the straw in back to look over the side. It was easier than it had been an hour earlier. His arms felt as if they might stretch instead of drawing him up, and for a minute his head wanted to keep on going and float away, but it was easier. He hooked his elbows over the low slats and watched the land roll past. The sun, still hidden by dull clouds, yet stood high overhead, but the cart was clattering into another village of vine-covered, red brick houses. Towns had been getting closer together since Four Kings.

Some of the people waved or called a greeting to Hyam Kinch, the farmer whose cart it was. Master Kinch, leathery-faced and taciturn, shouted back a few words each time, around the pipe in his teeth. The clenched teeth made what he said all but unintelligible, but it sounded jovial and seemed to satisfy; they went back to what they were doing without another glance at the cart. No one appeared to pay any mind to the farmer's two passengers.

The village inn moved through Rand's field of vision. It was whitewashed, with a gray slate roof. People bustled in and out, nodding casually and waving to one another. Some of them stopped to speak. They knew one another. Villagers, mostly, by their clothes—boots and trousers and coats not much different from what he wore himself, though with an inordinate fondness for colorful stripes. The women wore deep bonnets that hid their faces and white aprons with stripes. Maybe they were all townsmen and local farmfolk. *Does that make any difference?*

He dropped back on the straw, watching the village dwindle between his feet. Fenced fields and trimmed hedges lined the road, and small farmhouses with smoke rising from red brick chimneys. The only woods near the road were coppices, well tended for firewood, tame as a farmyard. But the branches stood leafless against the sky, as stark as in the wild woods to the west.

A line of wagons heading the other way rumbled down the center of the road, crowding the cart over onto the verge. Master Kinch shifted his pipe to the corner of his mouth and spat between his teeth. With one eye on his off-side wheel, to make sure it did not tangle in the hedge, he kept the cart moving. His mouth tightened as he glanced at the merchants' train.

None of the wagon drivers cracking their long whips in the air above eight-horse teams, none of the hard-faced guards slouching in their saddles alongside the wagons, looked at the cart. Rand watched them go, his chest tight. His hand was under his cloak, gripping his sword hilt, until the last wagon lurched by.

As that final wagon rattled away toward the village they had just left, Mat turned on the seat beside the farmer and leaned back until he found Rand's eyes. The scarf that did duty for dust, when need be, shaded his own eyes, folded over thickly and tied low around his forehead. Even so he squinted in the gray daylight. "You see anything back there?" he asked quietly. "What about the wagons?"

Rand shook his head, and Mat nodded. He had seen nothing either.

Master Kinch glanced at them out of the corner of his eye, then shifted his pipe again, and flapped the reins. That was all, but he had noticed. The horse picked up the pace a step.

"Your eyes still hurt?" Rand asked.

Mat touched the scarf around his head. "No. Not much. Not unless I look almost right at the sun, anyway. What about you? Are you feeling any better?"

"Some." He really was feeling better, he realized. It was a

wonder to get over being sick so fast. More than that, it was a gift of the Light. *It has to be the Light. It has to be.*

Suddenly a body of horsemen was passing the cart, heading west like the merchants' wagons. Long white collars hung down over their mail and plate, and their cloaks and undercoats were red, like the gatetenders' uniforms in Whitebridge, but better made and better fitting. Each man's conical helmet shone like silver. They sat their horses with straight backs. Thin red streamers fluttered beneath the heads of their lances, every lance held at the same angle.

Some of them glanced into the cart as they passed in two columns. A cage of steel bars masked each face. Rand was glad his cloak covered his sword. A few nodded to Master Kinch, not as if they knew him, but in a neutral greeting. Master Kinch nodded back in much the same way, but despite his unchanging expression there was a hint of approval in his nod.

Their horses were at a walk, but with the speed of the cart added, they went by quickly. With a part of his mind Rand counted them. Ten . . . twenty . . . thirty . . . thirty-two. He raised his head to watch the columns move on down the Caemlyn Road.

"Who were they?" Mat asked, half wondering, half suspicious.

"Queen's Guards," Master Kinch said around his pipe. He kept his eyes on the road ahead. "Won't go much further than Breen's Spring, 'less they're called for. Not like the old days." He sucked on his pipe, then added, "I suppose, these days, there's parts of the Realm don't see the Guards in a year or more. Not like the old days."

"What are they doing?" Rand asked.

The farmer gave him a look. "Keeping the Queen's peace and upholding the Queen's law." He nodded to himself as if he liked the sound of that, and added, "Searching out malefactors and seeing them before a magistrate. Mmmph!" He let out a long streamer of smoke. "You two must be from pretty far off not to recognize the Queen's Guard. Where you from?"

"Far off," Mat said at the same instant that Rand said, "The Two Rivers." He wished he could take it back as soon as he said it. He still was not thinking clearly. Trying to hide, and mentioning a name a Fade would hear like a bell.

Master Kinch glanced at Mat out of the corner of his eye, and puffed his pipe in silence for a while. "That's far off, all right," he said finally. "Almost to the border of the Realm. But things must be worse than I thought if there's places in the Realm where people don't even *recognize* the Queen's Guards. Not like the old days at all."

Rand wondered what Master al'Vere would say if someone told him the Two Rivers was part of some Queen's Realm. The Queen of Andor, he supposed. Perhaps the Mayor did know— he knew a lot of things that surprised Rand—and maybe others did, too, but he had never heard anyone mention it. The Two Rivers was the Two Rivers. Each village handled its own problems, and if some difficulty involved more than one village the Mayors, and maybe the Village Councils, solved it between them.

Master Kinch pulled on the reins, drawing the cart to a halt. "Far as I go." A narrow cart path led off to the north; several farmhouses were visible in that direction across open fields, plowed but still bare of crops. "Two days will see you in Caemlyn. Least, it would if your friend had his legs under him."

Mat hopped down and retrieved his bow and other things, then helped Rand climb off the tail of the cart. Rand's bundles weighed on him, and his legs wobbled, but he shrugged off his friend's hand and tried a few steps on his own. He still felt unsteady, but his legs held him up. They even seemed to grow stronger as he used them.

The farmer did not start his horse up again right away. He studied them for a minute, sucking on his pipe. "You can rest up a day or two at my place, if you want. Won't miss anything in that time, I suppose. Whatever sickness you're getting over, young fellow . . . well, the old woman and me, we already had about every sickness you can think of before you were born, and nursed our younglings through 'em, too. I expect you're past the catching stage, anyway."

Mat's eyes narrowed, and Rand caught himself frowning. *Not everyone is part of it. It can't be everybody.*

"Thank you," he said, "but I'm all right. Really. How far to the next village?"

"Carysford? You can reach it before dark, walking." Master

Kinch took his pipe from between his teeth and pursed his lips thoughtfully before going on. "First off, I reckoned you for runaway 'prentices, but now I expect it's something more serious you're running from. Don't know what. Don't care. I'm a good enough judge to say you're not Darkfriends, and not likely to rob or hurt anybody. Not like some on the road these days. I got in trouble a time or two myself when I was your age. You need a place to keep out of sight a few days, my farm is five miles that way"—he jerked his head toward the cart track—"and don't nobody ever come out there. Whatever's chasing you, won't likely find you there." He cleared his throat as if embarrassed by speaking so many words together.

"How would you know what Darkfriends look like?" Mat demanded. He backed away from the cart, and his hand went under his coat. "What do you know about Darkfriends?"

Master Kinch's face tightened. "Suit yourselves," he said, and clucked to his horse. The cart rolled off down the narrow path, and he never looked back.

Mat looked at Rand, and his scowl faded. "Sorry, Rand. You need a place to rest. Maybe if we go after him. . . ." He shrugged. "I just can't get over the feeling that everybody's after us. Light, I wish I knew why they were. I wish it was over. I wish. . . ." He trailed off miserably.

"There are still some good people," Rand said. Mat started toward the cart path, jaw clenched as if it were the last thing he wanted to do, but Rand stopped him. "We can't afford to stop just to rest, Mat. Besides, I don't think there is anywhere to hide."

Mat nodded, his relief evident. He tried to take some of Rand's burdens, the saddlebags and Thom's cloak wrapped around the cased harp, but Rand held onto them. His legs really did feel stronger. *Whatever's chasing us?* he thought as they started off down the road. *Not chasing. Waiting.*

The rain had continued through the night they staggered away from The Dancing Cartman, hammering at them as hard as the thunder out of a black sky split by lightning. Their clothes became sodden in minutes; in an hour Rand's skin felt sodden, too, but they had left Four Kings behind them. Mat was all but blind in the dark, squinting painfully at the sharp

flashes that made trees stand out starkly for an instant. Rand
led him by the hand, but Mat still felt out each step uncertainly.
Worry creased Rand's forehead. If Mat did not regain his sight,
they would be slowed to a crawl. They would never get away.

Mat seemed to sense his thought. Despite the hood of his
cloak, the rain had plastered Mat's hair across his face.
"Rand," he said, "you won't leave me, will you? If I can't keep
up?" His voice quavered.

"I won't leave you." Rand tightened his grip on his friend's
hand. "I won't leave you no matter what." *Light help us!*
Thunder crashed overhead, and Mat stumbled, almost falling,
almost pulling him down, too. "We have to stop, Mat. If we
keep going, you'll break a leg."

"Gode." Lightning split the dark right above them as Mat
spoke, and the thunder crack pounded every other sound into
the ground, but in the flash Rand could make out the name on
Mat's lips.

"He's dead." *He has to be. Light, let him be dead.*

He led Mat to some bushes the lightning flash had showed
him. They had leaves enough to give a little shelter from the
driving rain. Not as much as a good tree might, but he did not
want to risk another lightning strike. They might not be so
lucky, next time.

Huddled together beneath the bushes, they tried to arrange
their cloaks to make a little tent over the branches. It was far
too late to think of staying dry, but just stopping the incessant
pelting of the raindrops would be something. They crouched
against each other to share what little body warmth was left to
them. Dripping wet as they were, and more drips coming
through the cloaks, they shivered themselves into sleep.

Rand knew right away it was a dream. He was back in Four
Kings, but the town was empty except for him. The wagons
were there, but no people, no horses, no dogs. Nothing alive.
He knew someone was waiting for him, though.

As he walked down the rutted street, the buildings seemed to
blur as they slid behind him. When he turned his head, they
were all there, solid, but the indistinctness remained at the corners of his vision. It was as if only what he saw really existed,
and then just while he was seeing. He was sure if he turned

quickly enough he would see. . . . He was not sure what, but it made him uneasy, thinking about it.

The Dancing Cartman appeared in front of him. Somehow its garish paint seemed gray and lifeless. He went in. Gode was there, at a table.

He only recognized the man from his clothes, his silk and dark velvets. Gode's skin was red, burned and cracked and oozing. His face was almost a skull, his lips shriveled to bare teeth and gums. As Gode turned his head, some of his hair cracked off, powdering to soot when it hit his shoulder. His lidless eyes stared at Rand.

"So you are dead," Rand said. He was surprised that he was not afraid. Perhaps it was knowing that it was a dream this time.

"Yes," said Ba'alzamon's voice, "but he did find you for me. That deserves some reward, don't you think?"

Rand turned, and discovered he could be afraid, even knowing it was a dream. Ba'alzamon's clothes were the color of dried blood, and rage and hate and triumph battled on his face.

"You see, youngling, you cannot hide from me forever. One way or another I find you. What protects you also makes you vulnerable. One time you hide, the next you light a signal fire. Come to me, youngling." He held out his hand to Rand. "If my hounds must pull you down, they may not be gentle. They are jealous of what you will be, once you have knelt at my feet. It is your destiny. You belong to me." Gode's burned tongue made an angry, eager garble of sound.

Rand tried to wet his lips, but he had no spit in his mouth. "No," he managed, and then the words came more easily. "I belong to myself. Not you. Not ever. Myself. If your Darkfriends kill me, you'll never have me."

The fires in Ba'alzamon's face heated the room till the air swam. "Alive or dead, youngling, you are mine. The grave belongs to me. Easier dead, but better alive. Better for you, youngling. The living have more power in most things." Gode made a gabbling sound again. "Yes, my good hound. Here is your reward."

Rand looked at Gode just in time to see the man's body crumble to dust. For an instant the burned face held a look of sublime joy that turned to horror in the final moment, as if he had seen something waiting he did not expect. Gode's empty velvet garments settled on the chair and the floor among the ash.

When he turned back, Ba'alzamon's outstretched hand had become a fist. "You are mine, youngling, alive or dead. The Eye of the World will never serve you. I mark you as mine." His fist opened, and a ball of flame shot out. It struck Rand in the face, exploding, searing.

Rand lurched awake in the dark, water dripping through the cloaks onto his face. His hand trembled as he touched his cheeks. The skin felt tender, as if sunburned.

Suddenly he realized Mat was twisting and moaning in his sleep. He shook him, and Mat came awake with a whimper.

"My eyes! Oh, Light, my eyes! He took my eyes!"

Rand held him close, cradling him against his chest as if he were a baby. "You're all right, Mat. You're all right. He can't hurt us. We won't let him." He could feel Mat shaking, sobbing into his coat. "He can't hurt us," he whispered, and wished he believed it. *What protects you makes you vulnerable. I am going mad.*

Just before first light the downpour dwindled, the last drizzle fading as dawn came. The clouds remained, threatening until well into the morning. The wind came up, then, driving the clouds off to the south, baring a warmthless sun and slicing through their dripping wet clothes. They had not slept again, but groggily they donned their cloaks and set off eastward, Rand leading Mat by the hand. After a while Mat even felt well enough to complain about what the rain had done to his bowstring. Rand would not let him stop to exchange it for a dry string from his pocket, though; not yet.

They came on another village shortly after midday. Rand shivered harder at the sight of snug brick houses and smoke rising from chimneys, but he kept clear, leading Mat through the woods and fields to the south. A lone farmer working with a spading fork in a muddy field was the only person he saw, and he took care that the man did not see them, crouching through the trees. The farmer's attention was all on his work, but Rand kept one eye on him till he was lost to sight. If any of Gode's men were alive, perhaps they would believe he and Mat had taken the southern road out of Four Kings when they could not find anyone who had seen them in this village. They came back to the road out of sight of the town, and walked their clothes, if not dry, at least to just damp.

An hour beyond the town a farmer gave them a ride in his half-empty haywain. Rand had been taken by surprise while lost in worry about Mat. Mat shielded his eyes from the sun with his hand, weak as the afternoon light was, squinting through slitted lids even so, and he muttered continually about how bright the sun was. When Rand heard the rumble of the haywain, it was too late already. The sodden road deadened sound, and the wagon with its two-horse hitch was only fifty yards behind them, the driver already peering at them.

To Rand's surprise he drew up and offered them a lift. Rand hesitated, but it was too late to avoid being seen, and refusing a ride might fix them in the man's mind. He helped Mat up to the seat beside the farmer, then climbed up behind him.

Alpert Mull was a stolid man, with a square face and square hands, both worn and grooved from hard work and worry, and he wanted someone to talk to. His cows had gone dry, his chickens had stopped laying, and there was no pasture worth the name. For the first time in memory he had had to buy hay, and half a wagon was all "old Bain" would let him have. He wondered whether there was any chance of getting hay on his own land this year, or any kind of crop.

"The Queen should do something, the Light illumine her," he muttered, knuckling his forehead respectfully but absent-mindedly.

He hardly looked at Rand or Mat, but when he let them down by the narrow, rail-lined track that led off to his farm, he hesitated, then said, almost as if to himself, "I don't know what you're running from, and I don't want to. I have a wife and children. You understand? My family. It's hard times for helping strangers."

Mat tried to stick his hand under his coat, but Rand had his wrist and he held on. He stood in the road, looking at the man without speaking.

"If I was a good man," Mull said, "I'd offer a couple of lads soaked to the skin a place to dry out and get warm in front of my fire. But it's hard times, and strangers. . . . I don't know what you're running from, and I don't want to. You understand? My family." Suddenly he pulled two long, woolen scarves, dark and thick, out of his coat pocket. "It's not much, but here. Belong to my boys. They have others. You don't know me, understand? It's hard times."

"We never even saw you," Rand agreed as he took the scarves. "You *are* a good man. The best we've met in days." The farmer looked surprised, then grateful. Gathering his reins, he turned his horses down the narrow lane. Before he completed the turn Rand was leading Mat on down the Caemlyn Road.

The wind stiffened as dusk closed in. Mat began to ask querulously when they were going to stop, but Rand kept moving, pulling Mat behind him, searching for more shelter than a spot under a hedge. With their clothes still clammy and the wind getting colder by the minute, he was not sure they could survive another night in the open. Night fell without him spotting anything useful. The wind grew icy, beating his cloak. Then, through the darkness ahead, he saw lights. A village.

His hand slid into his pocket, feeling the coins there. More than enough for a meal and a room for the two of them. A room out of the cold night. If they stayed in the open, in the wind and cold in damp clothes, anyone who found them would likely as not find only two corpses. They just had to keep from attracting any more notice than they could help. No playing the flute, and with his eyes, Mat certainly could not juggle. He grasped Mat's hand again and set out toward the beckoning lights.

"When are we going to stop?" Mat asked again. The way he peered ahead, with his head stuck forward, Rand was not sure if Mat could see him, much less the village lights.

"When we're somewhere warm," he replied.

Pools of light from house windows lit the streets of the town, and people walked them unconcerned with what might be out in the dark. The only inn was a sprawling building, all on one floor, with the look of having had rooms added in bunches over the years without any particular plan. The front door opened to let someone out, and a wave of laughter rolled out after him.

Rand froze in the street, the drunken laughter at The Dancing Cartman echoing in his head. He watched the man go down the street with a none-too-steady stride, then took a deep breath and pushed the door open. He took care that his cloak covered his sword. Laughter swept over him.

Lamps hanging from the high ceiling made the room bright, and right away he could see and feel the difference from Saml Hake's inn. There was no drunkenness here, for one thing. The room was filled with people who looked to be farmers and townsmen, if not entirely sober, not too far from it. The laughter was real, if a bit forced around the edges. People laughing to forget their troubles, but with true mirth in it, too. The common room itself was neat and clean, and warm from a fire roaring in a big fireplace at the far end. The serving maids' smiles were as warm as the fire, and when they laughed Rand could tell it was because they wanted to.

The innkeeper was as clean as his inn, with a gleaming white apron around his bulk. Rand was glad to see he was a stout man; he doubted if he would ever again trust a skinny innkeeper. His name was Rulan Allwine—a good omen, Rand thought, with so much of the sound of Emond's Field to it— and he eyed them up and down, then politely mentioned paying in advance.

"Not suggesting you're the sort, understand, but there's some on the road these days aren't too particular about paying up come morning. Seems to be a lot of young folks headed for Caemlyn."

Rand was not offended, not as damp and bedraggled as he was. When Master Allwine mentioned the price, though, his eyes widened, and Mat made a sound as if he had choked on something.

The innkeeper's jowls swung as he shook his head regretfully, but he seemed to be used to it. "Times are hard," he said in a resigned voice. "There isn't much, and what there is costs five times what it used to. It'll be more next month, I'll lay oath on it."

Rand dug his money out and looked at Mat. Mat's mouth tightened stubbornly. "You want to sleep under a hedge?" Rand asked. Mat sighed and reluctantly emptied his pocket. When the reckoning was paid, Rand grimaced at the little that remained to divide with Mat.

But ten minutes later they were eating stew at a table in a corner near the fireplace, pushing it onto their spoons with chunks of bread. The portions were not as large as Rand could have wished, but they were hot, and filling. Warmth from the hearth seeped into him slowly. He pretended to keep his eyes on his plate, but he watched the door intently. Those who came in or went out all looked like farmers, but it was not enough to quiet his fear.

Mat ate slowly, savoring each bite, though he muttered about the light from the lamps. After a time he dug out the scarf Alpert Mull had given him and wound it around his forehead, pulling it down until his eyes were almost hidden. That got them some looks Rand wished they could have avoided. He cleaned his plate hurriedly, urging Mat to do the same, then asked Master Allwine for their room.

The innkeeper seemed surprised that they were retiring so early, but he made no comment. He got a candle and showed them through a jumble of corridors to a small room, with two narrow beds, back in a far corner of the inn. When he left, Rand dropped his bundles beside his bed, tossed his cloak over a chair, and fell on the coverlet fully dressed. All of his clothes were still damp and uncomfortable, but if they had to run, he wanted to be ready. He left the sword belt on, too, and slept with his hand on the hilt.

A rooster crowing jerked him awake in the morning. He lay there, watching dawn lighten the window, and wondered if he dared sleep a little longer. Sleep during daylight, when they could be moving. A yawn made his jaws crack.

"Hey," Mat exclaimed, "I can see!" He sat up on his bed, squinting around the room. "Some, anyway. Your face is still a little blurry, but I can tell who you are. I knew I'd be all right. By tonight I'll see better than you do. Again."

Rand sprang out of bed, scratching as he scooped up his cloak. His clothes were wrinkled from drying on him while he slept, and they itched. "We're wasting daylight," he said. Mat scrambled up as fast as he had; he was scratching, too.

Rand did feel good. They were a day away from Four Kings, and none of Gode's men had showed up. A day closer to Caemlyn, where Moiraine would be waiting for them. She would. No more worrying about Darkfriends once they were back with the Aes Sedai and the Warder. It was strange to be looking forward so much to being with an Aes Sedai. *Light, when I see Moiraine again, I'll kiss her!* He laughed at the thought. He felt good enough to invest some of their dwindling stock of coins in breakfast—a big loaf of bread and a pitcher of milk, cold from the springhouse.

They were eating in the back of the common room when a young man came in, a village youth by the look of him, with a cocky spring to his walk and twirling a cloth cap, with a feather in it, on one finger. The only other person in the room was an old man sweeping out; he never looked up from his broom. The young man's eyes swept jauntily around the room, but when they lit on Rand and Mat, the cap fell off his finger. He stared at them for a full minute before snatching the cap from the floor, then stared some more, running his fingers through his thick head of dark curls. Finally he came over to their table, his feet dragging.

He was older than Rand, but he stood looking down at them diffidently. "Mind if I sit down?" he asked, and immediately swallowed hard as if he might have said the wrong thing.

Rand thought he might be hoping to share their breakfast, though he looked able to buy his own. His blue-striped shirt was embroidered around the collar, and his dark blue cloak all around the hem. His leather boots had never been near any work that scuffed them, that Rand could see. He nodded to a chair.

Mat stared at the fellow as he drew the chair to the table. Rand could not tell if he was glaring or just trying to see clearly. In any case, Mat's frown had an effect. The young man froze halfway to sitting, and did not lower himself all the way until Rand nodded again.

"What's your name?" Rand asked.

"My name? My name. Ah . . . call me Paitr." His eyes shifted nervously. "Ah . . . this is not my idea, you understand. I have to do it. I didn't want to, but they made me. You have to understand that. I don't—"

Rand was beginning to tense when Mat growled, "Darkfriend."

Paitr gave a jerk and half lifted out of his chair, staring wildly around the room as if there were fifty people to overhear. The old man's head was still bent over the broom, his attention on the floor. Paitr sat back down and looked from Rand to Mat and back uncertainly. Sweat beaded on his upper lip. It was accusation enough to make anyone sweat, but he said not a word against it.

Rand shook his head slowly. After Gode, he knew that Darkfriends did not necessarily have the Dragon's Fang on their foreheads, but except for his clothes this Paitr could have fit right in Emond's Field. Nothing about him hinted at murder and worse. Nobody would have remarked him twice. At least Gode had been . . . different.

"Leave us alone," Rand said. "And tell your friends to leave us alone. We want nothing from them, and they'll get nothing from us."

"If you don't," Mat added fiercely, "I'll name you for what you are. See what your village friends think of that."

Rand hoped he did not really mean it. That could cause as much trouble for the two of them as it did for Paitr.

Paitr seemed to take the threat seriously. His face grew pale. "I . . . I heard what happened at Four Kings. Some of it, anyway. Word travels. We have ways of hearing things. But there's nobody here to trap you. I'm alone, and . . . and I just want to talk."

"About what?" Mat asked at the same time that Rand said, "We're not interested." They looked at each other, and Mat shrugged. "We're not interested," he said.

Rand gulped the last of the milk and stuffed the heel of his half of the bread into his pocket. With their money almost gone, it might be their next meal.

How to leave the inn? If Paitr discovered that Mat was almost blind, he would tell others . . . other Darkfriends. Once Rand had seen a wolf separate a crippled sheep from the flock; there were other wolves around, and he could neither leave the flock nor get a clear shot with his bow. As soon as the sheep was alone, bleating with terror, hobbling frantically on three legs, the one wolf chasing it became ten as if by magic. The memory of it turned his stomach. They could not stay there, either. Even if Paitr was telling the truth about being alone, how long would he stay that way?

"Time to go, Mat," he said, and held his breath. As Mat started to stand, he pulled Paitr's eyes to himself by leaning forward and saying, "Leave us alone, Darkfriend. I won't tell you again. Leave—us—alone."

Paitr swallowed hard and pressed back in his chair; there was
no blood left in his face at all. It made Rand think of a Myrddraal.

By the time he looked back at Mat, Mat was on his feet, his
awkwardness unseen. Rand hastily hung his own saddlebags
and other bundles around him, trying to keep his cloak over the
sword as he did. Maybe Paitr already knew about it; maybe
Gode had told Ba'alzamon, and Ba'alzamon had told Paitr; but
he did not think so. He thought Paitr had only the vaguest idea
of what had happened in Four Kings. That was why he was so
frightened.

The comparatively bright outline of the door helped Mat
make a beeline for it, if not quickly, then not slow enough to
seem unnatural, either. Rand followed closely, praying for him
not to stumble. He was thankful Mat had a clear, straight path,
with no tables or chairs in the way.

Behind him Paitr suddenly leaped to his feet. "Wait," he said
desperately. "You have to wait."

"Leave us alone," Rand said without looking back. They
were almost to the door, and Mat had not put a foot wrong yet.

"Just listen to me," Paitr said, and put his hand on Rand's
shoulder to stop him.

Images spun in his head. The Trolloc, Narg, leaping at him in
his own home. The Myrddraal threatening at the Stag and Lion
in Baerlon. Halfmen everywhere, Fades chasing them to
Shadar Logoth, coming for them in Whitebridge. Darkfriends
everywhere. He whirled, his hand balling up. "I said, leave us
alone!" His fist took Paitr flush on the nose.

The Darkfriend fell on his bottom and sat there on the floor
staring at Rand. Blood trickled from his nose. "You won't get
away," he spat angrily. "No matter how strong you are, the
Great Lord of the Dark is stronger. The Shadow will swallow
you!"

There was a gasp from further into the common room, and
the clatter of a broom handle hitting the floor. The old man
with the broom had finally heard. He stood staring wide-eyed
at Paitr. The blood drained from his wrinkled face and his
mouth worked, but no sound came out. Paitr stared back for an
instant, then gave a wild curse and sprang to his feet, darting
out of the inn and down the street as if starving wolves were at

his heels. The old man shifted his attention to Rand and Mat, looking not a whit less frightened.

Rand hustled Mat out of the inn and out of the village as fast as he could, listening all the while for a hue and cry that never came but was no less loud in his ears for that.

"Blood and ashes," Mat growled, "they're always there, always right on our heels. We'll never get away."

"No they're not," Rand said. "If Ba'alzamon knew we were here, do you think he'd have left it to that fellow? There'd have been another Gode, and twenty or thirty bullyboys. They're still hunting, but they won't know until Paitr tells them, and maybe he really is alone. He might have to go all the way to Four Kings, for all we know."

"But he said—"

"I don't care." He was unsure which "he" Mat meant, but it changed nothing. "We're not going to lie down and let them take us."

They got six rides, short ones, during the day. A farmer told them that a crazy old man at the inn in Market Sheran was claiming there were Darkfriends in the village. The farmer could hardly talk for laughing; he kept wiping tears off his cheeks. Darkfriends in Market Sheran! It was the best story he had heard since Ackley Farren got drunk and spent the night on the inn roof.

Another man, a round-faced wagonwright with tools hanging from the sides of his cart and two wagon wheels in the back, told a different story. Twenty Darkfriends had held a gathering in Market Sheran. Men with twisted bodies, and the women worse, all dirty and in rags. They could make your knees grow weak and your stomach heave just by looking at you, and when they laughed, the filthy cackles rang in your ears for hours and your head felt as if it were splitting open. He had seen them himself, just at a distance, far enough off to be safe. If the Queen would not do something, then somebody ought to ask the Children of the Light for help. Somebody should do something.

It was a relief when the wagonwright let them down.

With the sun low behind them they walked into a small village, much like Market Sheran. The Caemlyn Road split the town neatly in two, but on both sides of the wide road stood rows of small brick houses with thatched roofs. Webs of vine covered the bricks, though only a few leaves hung on them. The village had one inn, a small place no bigger than the Winespring Inn, with a sign on a bracket out front, creaking back and forth in the wind. The Queen's Man.

Strange, to think of the Winespring Inn as small. Rand could remember when he thought it was about as big as a building could be. Anything bigger would be a palace. But he had seen a few things, now, and suddenly he realized that nothing would look the same to him when he got back home. *If you ever do.*

He hesitated in front of the inn, but even if prices at The Queen's Man were not as high as in Market Sheran, they could not afford a meal or a room, either one.

Mat saw where he was looking and patted the pocket where he kept Thom's colored balls. "I can see well enough, as long as I don't try to get too fancy." His eyes had been getting better, though he still wore the scarf around his forehead, and had squinted whenever he looked at the sky during the day. When Rand said nothing, Mat went on. "There can't be Darkfriends at every inn between here and Caemlyn. Besides, I don't want to sleep under a bush if I can sleep in a bed." He made no move toward the inn, though, just stood waiting for Rand.

After a moment Rand nodded. He felt as tired as he had at any time since leaving home. Just thinking of a night in the open made his bones ache. *It's all catching up. All the running, all the looking over your shoulder.*

"They can't be everywhere," he agreed.

With the first step he took into the common room, he wondered if he had made a mistake. It was a clean place, but crowded. Every table was filled, and some men leaned against the walls because there was nowhere for them to sit. From the way the serving maids scurried between the tables with harried looks—and the landlord, too—it was a larger crowd than they were used to. Too many for this small village. It was easy to pick out the people who did not belong there. They were dressed no differently from the rest, but they kept their eyes on their food and drink. The locals watched the strangers as much as anything else.

A drone of conversation hung in the air, enough that the innkeeper took them into the kitchen when Rand made him understand that they needed to talk to him. The noise was almost as bad there, with the cook and his helpers banging pots and darting about.

The innkeeper mopped his face with a large handkerchief. "I suppose you're on your way to Caemlyn to see the false Dragon like every other fool in the Realm. Well, it's six to a room and two or three to a bed, and if that doesn't suit, I've nothing for you."

Rand gave his spiel with a feeling of queasiness. With so many people on the road, every other one could be a Darkfriend, and there was no way to pick them out from the rest. Mat demonstrated his juggling—he kept it to three balls, and was careful even then—and Rand took out Thom's flute. After only a dozen notes of "The Old Black Bear," the innkeeper nodded impatiently.

"You'll do. I need something to take those idiots' minds off this Logain. There's been three fights already over whether or not he's really the Dragon. Stow your things in the corner, and I'll go clear a space for you. If there's any room to. Fools. The world's full of fools who don't know enough to stay where they belong. That's what's causing all the trouble. People who won't stay where they belong." Mopping his face again, he hurried out of the kitchen, muttering under his breath.

The cook and his helpers ignored Rand and Mat. Mat kept adjusting the scarf around his head, pushing it up, then blinking at the light and tugging it back down again. Rand wondered if he could see well enough to do anything more complicated than juggle three balls. As for himself. . . .

The queasiness in his stomach grew thicker. He dropped on a low stool, holding his head in his hands. The kitchen felt cold. He shivered. Steam filled the air; stoves and ovens crackled with heat. His shivers became stronger, his teeth chattering. He wrapped his arms around himself, but it did no good. His bones felt as if they were freezing.

Dimly he was aware of Mat asking him something, shaking his shoulder, and of someone cursing and running out of the room. Then the innkeeper was there, with the cook frowning at his side, and Mat was arguing loudly with them both. He could not make out any of what they said; the words were a buzz in his ears, and he could not seem to think at all.

Suddenly Mat took his arm, pulling him to his feet. All of

their things—saddlebags, blanketrolls, Thom's bundled cloak and instrument cases—hung from Mat's shoulders with his bow. The innkeeper was watching them, wiping his face anxiously. Weaving, more than half supported by Mat, Rand let his friend steer him toward the back door.

"S-s-sorry, M-m-mat," he managed. He could not stop his teeth from chattering. "M-m-must have . . . b-been t-the . . . rain. O-one m-more . . . night out . . . w-won't h-hurt . . . I guess." Twilight darkened the sky, spotted by a handful of stars.

"Not a bit of it," Mat said. He was trying to sound cheerful, but Rand could hear the hidden worry. "He was scared the other folk would find out there was somebody sick in his inn. I told him if he kicked us out, I'd take you into the common room. That'd empty half his rooms in ten minutes. For all his talk about fools, he doesn't want that."

"Then w-where?"

"Here," Mat said, pulling open the stable door with a loud creak of hinges.

It was darker inside than out, and the air smelled of hay and grain and horses, with a strong undersmell of manure. When Mat lowered him to the straw-covered floor, he folded over with his chest on his knees, still hugging himself and shaking from head to toe. All of his strength seemed to go for the shaking. He heard Mat stumble and curse and stumble again, then a clatter of metal. Suddenly light blossomed. Mat held up a battered old lantern.

If the inn was full, so was its stable. Every stall had a horse, some raising their heads and blinking at the light. Mat eyed the ladder to the hayloft, then looked at Rand, crouched on the floor, and shook his head.

"Never get you up there," Mat muttered. Hanging the lantern on a nail, he scrambled up the ladder and began tossing down armloads of hay. Hurriedly climbing back down, he made a bed at the back of the stable and got Rand onto it. Mat covered him with both their cloaks, but Rand pushed them off almost immediately.

"Hot," he murmured. Vaguely he knew that he had been cold only a moment before, but now he felt as if he were in an oven. He tugged at his collar, tossing his head. "Hot." He felt Mat's hand on his forehead.

"I'll be right back," Mat said, and disappeared.

He twisted fitfully on the hay, how long he was not sure, until Mat returned with a heaped plate in one hand, a pitcher in the other, and two white cups dangling from fingers by their handles.

"There's no Wisdom here," he said, dropping to his knees beside Rand. He filled one of the cups and held it to Rand's mouth. Rand gulped the water down as if he had had nothing to drink in days; that was how he felt. "They don't even know what a Wisdom is. What they do have is somebody called Mother Brune, but she's off somewhere birthing a baby, and nobody knows when she'll be back. I did get some bread, and cheese, and sausage. Good Master Inlow will give us anything as long as we stay out of sight of his guests. Here, try some."

Rand turned his head away from the food. The sight of it, the thought of it, made his stomach heave. After a minute Mat sighed and settled down to eat himself. Rand kept his eyes averted, and tried not to listen.

The chills came once more, and then the fever, to be replaced by the chills, and the fever again. Mat covered him when he shook, and fed him water when he complained of thirst. The night deepened, and the stable shifted in the flickering lantern light. Shadows took shape and moved on their own. Then he saw Ba'alzamon striding down the stable, eyes burning, a Myrddraal at either side with faces hidden in the depths of their black cowls.

Fingers scrabbling for his sword hilt, he tried to get to his feet, yelling, "Mat! Mat, they're here! Light, they're here!"

Mat jerked awake where he sat cross-legged against the wall. "What? Darkfriends? Where?"

Wavering on his knees, Rand pointed frantically down the stable . . . and gaped. Shadows stirred, and a horse stamped in its sleep. Nothing more. He fell back on the straw.

"There's nobody but us," Mat said. "Here, let me take that." He reached for Rand's sword belt, but Rand tightened his grip on the hilt.

"No. No. I have to keep it. He's my father. You understand? He's m-my f-father!" The shivering swept over him once more, but he clung to the sword as if to a lifeline. "M-my f-father!" Mat gave up trying to take it and pulled the cloaks back over him.

There were other visitations in the night, while Mat dozed. Rand was never sure if they were really there or not. Sometimes he looked at Mat, with his head on his chest, wondering if he would see them, too, if he woke.

Egwene stepped out of the shadows, her hair in a long, dark braid as it had been in Emond's Field, her face pained and mournful. "Why did you leave us?" she asked. "We're dead because you left us."

Rand shook his head weakly on the hay. "No, Egwene. I didn't want to leave you. Please."

"We're all dead," she said sadly, "and death is the kingdom of the Dark One. The Dark One has us, because you abandoned us."

"No. I had no choice, Egwene. Please. Egwene, don't go. Come back, Egwene!"

But she turned into the shadows, and was shadow.

Moiraine's expression was serene, but her face was bloodless and pale. Her cloak might as well have been a shroud, and her voice was a lash. "That is right, Rand al'Thor. You have no choice. You must go to Tar Valon, or the Dark One will take you for his own. Eternity chained in the Shadow. Only Aes Sedai can save you, now. Only Aes Sedai."

Thom grinned at him sardonically. The gleeman's clothes hung in charred rags that made him see the flashes of light as Thom wrestled with the Fade to give them time to run. The flesh under the rags was blackened and burned. "Trust Aes Sedai, boy, and you'll wish you were dead. Remember, the price of Aes Sedai help is always smaller than you can believe, always greater than you can imagine. And what Ajah will find you first, eh? Red? Maybe Black. Best to run, boy. Run."

Lan's stare was as hard as granite, and blood covered his face. "Strange to see a heron-mark blade in the hands of a sheepherder. Are you worthy of it? You had better be. You're alone, now. Nothing to hold to behind you, and nothing before, and anyone can be a Darkfriend." He smiled a wolf's smile, and blood poured out of his mouth. "Anyone."

Perrin came, accusing, pleading for help. Mistress al'Vere, weeping for her daughter, and Bayle Domon, cursing him for bringing Fades down on his vessel, and Master Fitch, wringing his hands over the ashes of his inn, and Min, screaming in a

Trolloc's clutches, people he knew, people he had only met. But the worst was Tam. Tam stood over him, frowning and shaking his head, and said not a word.

"You have to tell me," Rand begged him. "Who am I? Tell me, please. Who am I? *Who am I?*" he shouted.

"Easy, Rand."

For a moment he thought it was Tam answering, but then he saw that Tam was gone. Mat bent over him, holding a cup of water to his lips.

"Just rest easy. You're Rand al'Thor, that's who you are, with the ugliest face and the thickest head in the Two Rivers. Hey, you're sweating! The fever's broken."

"Rand al'Thor?" Rand whispered. Mat nodded, and there was something so comforting in it that Rand drifted off to sleep without even touching the water.

It was a sleep untroubled by dreams—at least by any he remembered—but light enough that his eyes drifted open whenever Mat checked on him. Once he wondered if Mat was getting any sleep at all, but he fell back asleep himself before the thought got very far.

The squeal of the door hinges roused him fully, but for a moment he only lay there in the hay wishing he was still asleep. Asleep he would not be aware of his body. His muscles ached like wrung-out rags, and had about as much strength. Weakly he tried to raise his head; he made it on the second try.

Mat sat in his accustomed place against the wall, within arm's reach of Rand. His chin rested on his chest, which rose and fell in the easy rhythm of deep sleep. The scarf had slipped down over his eyes.

Rand looked toward the door.

A woman stood there holding it open with one hand. For a moment she was only a dark shape in a dress, outlined by the faint light of early morning, then she stepped inside, letting the door swing shut behind her. In the lantern light he could see her more clearly. She was about the same age as Nynaeve, he thought, but she was no village woman. The pale green silk of her dress shimmered as she moved. Her cloak was a rich, soft gray, and a frothy net of lace caught up her hair. She fingered a heavy gold necklace as she looked thoughtfully at Mat and him.

"Mat," Rand said, then louder, "Mat!"

Mat snorted and almost fell over as he came awake. Scrubbing sleep from his eyes, he stared at the woman.

"I came to look at my horse," she said, gesturing vaguely at the stalls. She never took her eyes away from the two of them, though. "Are you ill?"

"He's all right," Mat said stiffly. "He just caught a chill in the rain, that's all."

"Perhaps I should look at him," she said. "I have some knowledge. . . ."

Rand wondered if she were Aes Sedai. Even more than her clothes, her self-assured manner, the way she held her head as if on the point of giving a command, did not belong here. *And if she is Aes Sedai, of what Ajah?*

"I'm fine, now," he told her. "Really, there's no need."

But she came down the length of the stable, holding her skirt up and placing her gray slippers gingerly. With a grimace for the straw, she knelt beside him and felt his forehead.

"No fever," she said, studying him with a frown. She was pretty, in a sharp-featured fashion, but there was no warmth in her face. It was not cold, either; it just seemed to lack any feeling whatsoever. "You *were* sick, though. Yes. Yes. And still weak as a day-old kitten. I think. . . ." She reached under her cloak, and suddenly things were happening too fast for Rand to do more than give a strangled shout.

Her hand flashed from under her cloak; something glittered as she lunged across Rand toward Mat. Mat toppled sideways in a flurry of motion, and there was a solid *tchunk* of metal driven into wood. It all took just an instant, and then everything was still.

Mat lay half on his back, one hand gripping her wrist just above the dagger she had driven into the wall where his chest had been, his other hand holding the blade from Shadar Logoth to her throat.

Moving nothing but her eyes, she tried to look down at the dagger Mat held. Eyes widening, she drew a ragged breath and tried to pull back from it, but he kept the edge against her skin. After that, she was as still as a stone.

Licking his lips, Rand stared at the tableau above him. Even if he had not been so weak, he did not believe he could have moved. Then his eyes fell on her dagger, and his mouth went dry. The wood around the blade was blackening; thin tendrils of smoke rose from the char.

"Mat! Mat, her dagger!"

Mat flicked a glance at the dagger, then back to the woman, but she had not moved. She was licking *her* lips nervously. Roughly Mat pried her hand off the hilt and gave her a push; she toppled back, sprawling away from them and catching herself with her hands behind her, still watching the blade in his hand. "Don't move," he said. "I'll use this if you move. Believe me, I will." She nodded slowly; her eyes never left Mat's dagger. "Watch her, Rand."

Rand was not sure what he was supposed to do if she tried anything—shout, maybe; he certainly could not run after her if she tried to flee—but she sat there without twitching while Mat yanked her dagger free of the wall. The black spot stopped growing, though a faint wisp of smoke still trailed up from it.

Mat looked around for somewhere to put the dagger, then thrust it toward Rand. He took it gingerly, as if it were a live adder. It looked ordinary, if ornate, with a pale ivory hilt and a narrow, gleaming blade no longer than the palm of his hand. Just a dagger. Only he had seen what it could do. The hilt was not even warm, but his hand began to sweat. He hoped he did not drop it in the hay.

The woman did not move from her sprawl as she watched Mat slowly turn toward her. She watched him as if wondering what he would do next, but Rand saw the sudden tightening of Mat's eyes, the tightening of his hand on the dagger. "Mat, no!"

"She tried to kill me, Rand. She'd have killed you, too. She's a Darkfriend." Mat spat the word.

"But we're not," Rand said. The woman gasped as if she had just realized what Mat had intended. "We are not, Mat."

For a moment Mat remained frozen, the blade in his fist catching the lantern light. Then he nodded. "Move over there," he told the woman, gesturing with the dagger toward the door to the tack room.

She got to her feet slowly, pausing to brush the straw from her dress. Even when she started in the direction Mat indicated, she moved as if there were no reason to hurry. But Rand noticed that she kept a wary eye on the ruby-hilted dagger in

Mat's hand. "You really should stop struggling," she said. "It would be for the best, in the end. You will see."

"The best?" Mat said wryly, rubbing his chest where her blade would have gone if he had not moved. "Get over there."

She gave a casual shrug as she obeyed. "A mistake. There has been considerable . . . confusion since what happened with that egotistical fool Gode. Not to mention whoever the idiot was who started the panic in Market Sheran. No one is sure what happened there, or how. That makes it more dangerous for you, don't you see? You will have honored places if you come to the Great Lord of your own free will, but as long as you run, there will be pursuit, and who can tell what will happen then?"

Rand felt a chill. *My hounds are jealous, and may not be gentle.*

"So you're having trouble with a couple of farmboys." Mat's laugh was grim. "Maybe you Darkfriends aren't as dangerous as I've always heard." He flung open the door of the tack room and stepped back.

She paused just through the doorway, looking at him over her shoulder. Her gaze was ice, and her voice colder still. "You will find out how dangerous we are. When the Myrddraal gets here—"

Whatever else she had to say was cut off as Mat slammed the door and pulled the bar down into its brackets. When he turned, his eyes were worried. "Fade," he said in a tight voice, tucking the dagger back under his coat. "Coming here, she says. How are your legs?"

"I can't dance," Rand muttered, "but if you'll help me get on my feet, I can walk." He looked at the blade in his hand and shuddered. "Blood and ashes, I'll run."

Hurriedly hanging himself about with their possessions, Mat pulled Rand to his feet. Rand's legs wobbled, and he had to lean on his friend to stay upright, but he tried not to slow Mat down. He held the woman's dagger well away from himself. Outside the door was a bucket of water. He tossed the dagger into it as they passed. The blade entered the water with a hiss; steam rose from the surface. Grimacing, he tried to take faster steps.

With light come, there were plenty of people in the streets, even so early. They were about their own business, though, and no one had any attention to spare for two young men walking out of the village, not with so many strangers about. Just the same, Rand stiffened every muscle, trying to stand straight. With each step he wondered if any of the folk hurrying by were Darkfriends. *Are any of them waiting for the woman with the dagger? For the Fade?*

A mile outside the village his strength gave out. One minute he was panting along, hanging on Mat; the next they were both on the ground. Mat tugged him over to the side of the road.

"We have to keep going," Mat said. He scrubbed his hand through his hair, then tugged the scarf down above his eyes. "Sooner or later, somebody will let her out, and they'll be after us again."

"I know," Rand panted. "I know. Give me a hand."

Mat pulled him up again, but he wavered there, knowing it was no good. The first time he tried to take a step, he would be flat on his face again.

Holding him upright, Mat waited impatiently for a horse-cart, approaching from the village, to pass them. Mat gave a grunt of surprise when the cart slowed to a stop before them. A leathery-faced man looked down from the driver's seat.

"Something wrong with him?" the man asked around his pipe.

"He's just tired," Mat said.

Rand could see that was not going to do, not leaning on Mat the way he was. He let go of Mat and took a step away from him. His legs quivered, but he willed himself to stay erect. "I haven't slept in two days," he said. "Ate something that made me sick. I'm better, now, but I haven't slept."

The man blew a streamer of smoke from the corner of his mouth. "Going to Caemlyn, are you? Was your age, I expect I might be off to see this false Dragon myself."

"Yes." Mat nodded. "That's right. We're going to see the false Dragon."

"Well, climb on up, then. Your friend in the back. If he's sick again, best it's on the straw, not up here. Name's Hyam Kinch."

CHAPTER
34

The Last Village

I t was after dark when they reached Carysford, longer than Rand had thought it would take from what Master Kinch said when he let them down. He wondered if his whole sense of time was getting skewed. Only three nights since Howal Gode and Four Kings, two since Paitr had surprised them in Market Sheran. Just a bare day since the nameless Darkfriend woman tried to kill them in the stable of The Queen's Man, but even that seemed a year ago, or a lifetime.

Whatever was happening to time, Carysford appeared normal enough, on the surface, at least. Neat, vine-covered brick houses and narrow lanes, except for the Caemlyn Road itself, quiet and outwardly peaceful. *But what's underneath?* he wondered. Market Sheran had been peaceful to look at, and so had the village where the woman. . . . He had never learned the name of that one, and he did not want to think about it.

Light spilled from the windows of the houses into streets all but empty of people. That suited Rand. Slinking from corner to corner, he avoided the few people abroad. Mat stuck to his shoulder, freezing when the crunch of gravel announced the approach of a villager, dodging from shadow to shadow when the dim shape had gone past.

The River Cary was a bare thirty paces wide there, and the black water moved sluggishly, but the ford had long since been bridged over. Centuries of rain and wind had worn the stone abutments until they seemed almost like natural formations.

Years of freight wagons and merchant trains had ground at the thick wooden planks, too. Loose boards rattled under their boots, sounding as loud as drums. Until long after they were through the village and into the countryside beyond, Rand waited for a voice to demand to know who they were. Or worse, knowing who they were.

The countryside had been filling up the further they went, becoming more and more settled. There were always the lights of farmhouses in sight. Hedges and rail fences lined the road and the fields beyond. Always the fields were there, and never a stretch of woods close to the road. It seemed as if they were always on the outskirts of a village, even when they were hours from the nearest town. Neat and peaceful. And with never an indication that Darkfriends or worse might be lurking.

Abruptly Mat sat down in the road. He had pushed the scarf up on top of his head, now that the only light came from the moon. "Two paces to the span," he muttered. "A thousand spans to the mile, four miles to the league. . . . I'm not walking another ten paces unless there's a place to sleep at the end of it. Something to eat wouldn't be amiss, either. You haven't been hiding anything in your pockets, have you? An apple, maybe? I won't hold it against you if you have. You could at least look."

Rand peered down the road both ways. They were the only things moving in the night. He glanced at Mat, who had pulled off one boot and was rubbing his foot. Or they had been. His own feet hurt, too. A tremor ran up his legs as if to tell him he had not yet regained as much strength as he thought.

Dark mounds stood in a field just ahead of them. Haystacks, diminished by winter feeding, but still haystacks.

He nudged Mat with his toe. "We'll sleep there."

"Haystacks again." Mat sighed, but he tugged on his boot and got up.

The wind was rising, the night chill growing deeper. They climbed over the smooth poles of the fence and quickly were burrowing into the hay. The tarp that kept the rain off the hay cut the wind, too.

Rand twisted around in the hollow he had made until he found a comfortable position. Hay still managed to poke at him through his clothes, but he had learned to put up with that. He tried counting the haystacks he had slept in since Whitebridge.

Heroes in the stories never had to sleep in haystacks, or under hedges. But it was not easy to pretend, anymore, that he was a hero in a story, even for a little while. With a sigh, he pulled his collar up in the hopes of keeping hay from getting down his back.

"Rand?" Mat said softly. "Rand, do you think we'll make it?"

"Tar Valon? It's a long way yet, but—"

"Caemlyn. Do you think we'll make it to Caemlyn?"

Rand raised his head, but it was dark in their burrow; the only thing that told him where Mat was was his voice. "Master Kinch said two days. Day after tomorrow, the next day, we'll get there."

"If there aren't a hundred Darkfriends waiting for us down the road, or a Fade or two." There was silence for a moment, then Mat said, "I think we're the last ones left, Rand." He sounded frightened. "Whatever it's all about, it's just us two, now. Just us."

Rand shook his head. He knew Mat could not see in the darkness, but it was more for himself than Mat, anyway. "Go to sleep, Mat," he said tiredly. But he lay awake a long time himself, before sleep came. *Just us.*

A cock's crow woke him, and he scrambled out into the false dawn, brushing hay off his clothes. Despite his precautions some had worked its way down his back; the straws clung between his shoulder blades, itching. He took off his coat and pulled his shirt out of his breeches to get to it. It was while he had one hand down the back of his neck and the other twisted up behind him that he became aware of the people.

The sun was not yet truly up, but already a steady trickle moved down the road in ones and twos, trudging toward Caemlyn, some with packs or bundles on their backs, others with nothing but a walking staff, if that. Most were young men, but here and there was a girl, or someone older. One and all they had the travel-stained look of having walked a long way. Some had their eyes on their feet and a weary slump to their shoulders, early as it was; others had their gaze fixed on something out of sight ahead, something toward the dawn.

Mat rolled out of the haystack, scratching vigorously. He only paused long enough to wrap the scarf around his head; it shaded his eyes a little less this morning. "You think we might get something to eat today?"

Rand's stomach rumbled in sympathy. "We can think about that when we're on the road," he said. Hastily arranging his clothes, he dug his share of their bundles out of the haystack.

By the time they reached the fence, Mat had noticed the people, too. He frowned, stopping in the field while Rand climbed over. A young man, not much older than they, glanced at them as he passed. His clothes were dusty, and so was the blanketroll strapped across his back.

"Where are you bound?" Mat called.

"Why, Caemlyn, for to see the Dragon," the fellow shouted back without stopping. He raised an eyebrow at the blankets and saddlebags hanging from their shoulders, and added, "Just like you." With a laugh he went on, his eyes already seeking eagerly ahead.

Mat asked the same question several times during the day, and the only people who did not give much the same answer were local folk. If those answered at all, it was by spitting and turning away in disgust. They turned away, but they kept a watchful eye, too. They looked at all the travelers the same way, out of the corners of their eyes. Their faces said strangers might get up to anything if not watched.

People who lived in the area were not only wary of the strangers, they seemed more than a little put out. Just enough people were on the road, scattered out just enough, that when farmers' carts and wagons appeared with the sun peeking over the horizon, even their usually slow pace was halved. None of them was in any mood to give a ride. A sour grimace, and maybe a curse for the work they were missing, were more likely.

The merchants' wagons rolled by with little hindrance beyond shaken fists, whether they were going toward Caemlyn or away from it. When the first merchants' train appeared, early on in the morning, coming at a stiff trot with the sun barely above the horizon behind the wagons, Rand stepped out of the road. They gave no sign of slowing for anything, and he saw other folk scrambling out of the way. He moved all the way over onto the verge, but kept walking.

A flicker of motion as the first wagon rumbled close was all the warning he had. He went sprawling on the ground as the wagon driver's whip cracked in the air where his head had been. From where he lay he met the driver's eyes as the wagon rolled by. Hard eyes above a mouth in a tight grimace. Not a care that he might have drawn blood, or taken an eye.

"Light blind you!" Mat shouted after the wagon. "You can't—" A mounted guard caught him on the shoulder with the butt of his spear, knocking him down atop Rand.

"Out of the way, you dirty Darkfriend!" the guard growled without slowing.

After that, they kept their distance from the wagons. There were certainly enough of them. The rattle and clatter of one hardly faded before another could be heard coming. Guards and drivers, they all stared at the travelers heading for Caemlyn as if seeing dirt walk.

Once Rand misjudged a driver's whip, just by the length of the tip. Clapping his hand to the shallow gash over his eyebrow, he swallowed hard to keep from vomiting at how close it had come to his eye. The driver smirked at him. With his other hand he grabbed Mat, to stop him nocking an arrow.

"Let it go," he said. He jerked his head at the guards riding alongside the wagons. Some of them were laughing; others gave Mat's bow a hard eye. "If we're lucky, they'd just beat us with their spears. If we're lucky."

Mat grunted sourly, but he let Rand pull him on down the road.

Twice squadrons of the Queen's Guards came trotting down the road, streamers on their lances fluttering in the wind. Some of the farmers hailed them, wanting something done about the strangers, and the Guards always paused patiently to listen. Near midday Rand stopped to listen to one such conversation.

Behind the bars of his helmet, the Guard captain's mouth was a tight line. "If one of them steals something, or trespasses on your land," he growled at the lanky farmer frowning beside his stirrup, "I'll haul him before a magistrate, but they break no Queen's Law by walking on the Queen's Highway."

"But they're all over the place," the farmer protested. "Who knows who they are, or what they are. All this talk about the Dragon. . . ."

"Light, man! You only have a handful here. Caemlyn's walls

are bulging with them, and more coming every day." The captain's scowl deepened as he caught sight of Rand and Mat, standing in the road nearby. He gestured down the road with a steel-backed gauntlet. "Get on with you, or I'll have you in for blocking traffic."

His voice was no rougher with them than with the farmer, but they moved on. The captain's eyes followed them for a time; Rand could feel them on his back. He suspected the Guards had little patience left with the wanderers, and no sympathy for a hungry thief. He decided to stop Mat if he suggested stealing eggs again.

Still, there was a good side to all the wagons and people on the road, especially all the young men heading for Caemlyn. For any Darkfriends hunting them, it would be like trying to pick out two particular pigeons in a flock. If the Myrddraal on Winternight had not known exactly who it was after, maybe its fellow would do no better here.

His stomach rumbled frequently, reminding him that they had next to no money left, certainly not enough for a meal at the prices charged this close to Caemlyn. He realized once he had a hand on the flute case, and firmly pushed it around to his back. Gode had known all about the flute, and the juggling. There was no telling how much Ba'alzamon had learned from him before the end—if what Rand had seen had *been* the end—or how much had been passed to other Darkfriends.

He looked regretfully at a farm they were passing. A man patrolled the fences with a pair of dogs, growling and tugging at their leashes. The man looked as if he wanted nothing more than an excuse to let them loose. Not every farm had the dogs out, but no one was offering jobs to travelers.

Before the sun went down, he and Mat walked through two more villages. The village folk stood in knots, talking among themselves and watching the steady stream pass by. Their faces were no friendlier than the faces of the farmers, or the wagon drivers, or the Queen's Guards. All these strangers going to see the false Dragon. Fools who did not know enough to stay where they belonged. Maybe followers of the false Dragon. Maybe even Darkfriends. If there was any difference between the two.

With evening coming, the stream began to thin at the second

town. The few who had money disappeared into the inn, though there seemed to be some argument about letting them inside; others began hunting for handy hedges or fields with no dogs. By dusk he and Mat had the Caemlyn Road to themselves. Mat began talking about finding another haystack, but Rand insisted on keeping on.

"As long as we can see the road," he said. "The further we go before stopping, the further ahead we are." *If they are chasing you. Why should they chase now, when they've been waiting for you to come to them so far?*

It was argument enough for Mat. With frequent glances over his shoulder, he quickened his step. Rand had to hurry to keep up.

The night thickened, relieved only a bit by scant moonlight. Mat's burst of energy faded, and his complaints started up again. Aching knots formed in Rand's calves. He told himself he had walked further in a hard day working on the farm with Tam, but repeat it as often as he would, he could not make himself believe it. Gritting his teeth, he ignored the aches and pains and would not stop.

With Mat complaining and him concentrating on the next step, they were almost on the village before he saw the lights. He tottered to a stop, suddenly aware of a burning that ran from his feet right up his legs. He thought he had a blister on his right foot.

At the sight of the village lights, Mat sagged to his knees with a groan. "Can we stop now?" he panted. "Or do you want to find an inn and hang out a sign for the Darkfriends? Or a Fade."

"The other side of the town," Rand answered, staring at the lights. From this distance, in the dark, it could have been Emond's Field. *What's waiting there?* "Another mile, that's all."

"All! I'm not walking another span!"

Rand's legs felt like fire, but he made himself take a step, and then another. It did not get any easier, but he kept on, one step at a time. Before he had gone ten paces he heard Mat staggering after him, muttering under his breath. He thought it was just as well he could not make out what Mat was saying.

It was late enough for the streets of the village to be empty, though most houses had a light in at least one window. The inn in the middle of town was brightly lit, surrounded by a golden pool that pushed back the darkness. Music and laughter, dimmed by thick walls, drifted from the building. The sign over the door creaked in the wind. At the near end of the inn, a cart and horse stood in the Caemlyn Road with a man checking the harness. Two men stood at the far end of the building, on the very edge of the light.

Rand stopped in the shadows beside a house that stood dark. He was too tired to hunt through the lanes for a way around. A minute resting could not hurt. Just a minute. Just until the men went away. Mat slumped against the wall with a grateful sigh, leaning back as if he meant to go to sleep right there.

Something about the two men at the rim of the shadows made Rand uneasy. He could not put a finger on anything, at first, but he realized the man at the cart felt the same way about them. He reached the end of the strap he was checking, adjusted the bit in the horse's mouth, then went back and started over from the beginning again. He kept his head down the whole while, his eyes on what he was doing and away from the other men. It could have been that he simply was not aware of them, though they were less than fifty feet off, except for the stiff way he moved and the way he sometimes turned awkwardly in what he was doing so he would not be looking toward them.

One of the men in the shadows was only a black shape, but the other stood more into the light, with his back to Rand. Even so it was plain he was not overjoyed at the conversation he was having. He wrung his hands and kept his eyes on the ground, jerking his head in a nod now and then at something the other had said. Rand could not hear anything, but he got the impression that the man in the shadows was doing all the talking; the nervous man just listened, and nodded, and wrung his hands anxiously.

Eventually the one who was wrapped in darkness turned away, and the nervous fellow started back into the light. Despite the chill he was mopping his face with the long apron he wore, as if he were drenched in sweat.

Skin prickling, Rand watched the shape moving off in the night. He did not know why, but his uneasiness seemed to fol-

low that one, a vague tingling in the back of his neck and the
hair stirring on his arms as if he had suddenly realized something was sneaking up on him. With a quick shake of his head,
he rubbed his arms briskly. *Getting as foolish as Mat, aren't
you?*

At that moment the form slipped by the edge of the light
from a window—just on the brink of it—and Rand's skin
crawled. The inn's sign went *scree-scree-scree* in the wind, but
the dark cloak never stirred.

"Fade," he whispered, and Mat jerked to his feet as if he had
shouted.

"What—?"

He clamped a hand over Mat's mouth. "Softly." The dark
shape was lost in the darkness. *Where?* "It's gone, now. I think.
I hope." He took his hand away; the only sound Mat made was
a long, indrawn breath.

The nervous man was almost to the inn door. He stopped
and smoothed down his apron, visibly composing himself before he went inside.

"Strange friends you've got, Raimun Holdwin," the man by
the cart said suddenly. It was an old man's voice, but strong.
The speaker straightened, shaking his head. "Strange friends in
the dark for an innkeeper."

The nervous man jumped when the other spoke, looking
around as if he had not seen the cart and the other man until
right then. He drew a deep breath and gathered himself, then
asked sharply, "And what do you mean by that, Almen Bunt?"

"Just what I said, Holdwin. Strange friends. He's not from
around here, is he? Lot of odd folk coming through the last few
weeks. Awful lot of odd folk."

"You're a fine one to talk." Holdwin cocked an eye at the
man by the cart. "I know a lot of men, even men from
Caemlyn. Not like you, cooped up alone·out on that farm of
yours." He paused, then went on as if he thought he had to
explain further. "He's from Four Kings. Looking for a couple
of thieves. Young men. They stole a heron-mark sword from
him."

Rand's breath had caught at the mention of Four Kings; at
the mention of the sword he glanced at Mat. His friend had his
back pressed hard against the wall and was staring into the

darkness with eyès so wide they seemed to be all whites. Rand
wanted to stare into the night, too—the Halfman could be anywhere—but his eyes went back to the two men in front of the
inn.

"A heron-mark sword!" Bunt exclaimed. "No wonder he
wants it back."

Holdwin nodded. "Yes, and them, too. My friend's a rich
man, a . . . a merchant, and they've been stirring up trouble
with the men who work for him. Telling wild stories and getting
people upset. They're Darkfriends, and followers of Logain,
too."

"Darkfriends *and* followers of the false Dragon? And telling
wild stories, too? Getting up to a lot for young fellows. You did
say they were young?" There was a sudden note of amusement
in Bunt's voice, but the innkeeper did not seem to notice.

"Yes. Not yet twenty. There's a reward—a hundred crowns
in gold—for the two of them." Holdwin hesitated, then added,
"They've sly tongues, these two. The Light knows what kind of
tales they'll tell, trying to turn people against one another. And
dangerous, too, even if they don't look it. Vicious. Best you
stay clear if you think you see them. Two young men, one with
a sword, and both looking over their shoulders. If they're the
right ones, my . . . my friend will pick them up once they're
located."

"You sound almost as if you know them to look at."

"I'll know them when I see them," Holdwin said confidently.
"Just don't try to take them yourself. No need for anyone to
get hurt. Come tell me if you see them. My . . . friend will deal
with them. A hundred crowns for the two, but he wants the
pair."

"A hundred crowns for the two," Bunt mused. "How much
for this sword he wants so bad?"

Abruptly Holdwin appeared to realize the other man was
making fun of him. "I don't know why I'm telling you," he
snapped. "You're still fixed on that fool plan of yours, I see."

"Not such a fool plan," Bunt replied placidly. "There might
not be another false Dragon to see before I die—Light send it
so!—and I'm too old to eat some merchant's dust all the way to
Caemlyn. I'll have the road to myself, and I'll be in Caemlyn
bright and early tomorrow."

"To yourself?" The innkeeper's voice had a nasty quiver. "You can never tell what might be out in the night, Almen Bunt. All alone on the road, in the dark. Even if somebody hears you scream, there's no one will unbar a door to help. Not these days, Bunt. Not your nearest neighbor."

None of that seemed to ruffle the old farmer at all; he answered as calmly as before. "If the Queen's Guards can't keep the road safe this close to Caemlyn, then we're none of us safe even in our own beds. If you ask me, one thing the Guards could do to make sure the roads are safe would be clap that friend of yours in irons. Sneaking around in the dark, afraid to let anybody get a look at him. Can't tell me he's not up to no good."

"Afraid!" Holdwin exclaimed. "You old fool, if you knew—" His teeth clicked shut abruptly, and he gave himself a shake. "I don't know why I'm wasting time on you. Get off with you! Stop cluttering up the front of my place of business." The door of the inn boomed shut behind him.

Muttering to himself, Bunt took hold of the edge of the cart seat and set his foot on the wheelhub.

Rand hesitated only a moment. Mat caught his arm as he started forward.

"Are you crazy, Rand? He'll recognize us for sure!"

"You'd rather stay here? With a Fade around? How far do you think we'll get on foot before it finds us?" He tried not to think of how far they would get in a cart if it found them. He shook free of Mat and trotted up the road. He carefully held his cloak shut so the sword was hidden; the wind and the cold were excuse enough for that.

"I couldn't help overhearing you're going to Caemlyn," he said.

Bunt gave a start, jerking a quarterstaff out of the cart. His leathery face was a mass of wrinkles and half his teeth were gone, but his gnarled hands held the staff steady. After a minute he lowered one end of the staff to the ground and leaned on it. "So you two are going to Caemlyn. To see the Dragon, eh?"

Rand had not realized that Mat had followed him. Mat was keeping well back, though, out of the light, watching the inn and the old farmer with as much suspicion as he was the night.

"The false Dragon," Rand said with emphasis.

Bunt nodded. "Of course. Of course." He threw a sideways look at the inn, then abruptly shoved his staff back under the cart seat. "Well, if you want a ride, get in. I've wasted enough time." He was already climbing to the seat.

Rand clambered over the back as the farmer flicked the reins. Mat ran to catch up as the cart started off. Rand caught his arms and pulled him aboard.

The village faded quickly into the night at the pace Bunt set. Rand lay back on the bare boards, fighting the lulling creak of the wheels. Mat stifled his yawns with a fist, warily staring into the countryside. Darkness weighed heavily on the fields and farms, dotted with the lights of farmhouses. The lights seemed distant, seemed to struggle vainly against the night. An owl called, a mourner's cry, and the wind moaned like lost souls in the Shadow.

It could be out there anywhere, Rand thought.

Bunt seemed to feel the oppression of the night, too, for he suddenly spoke up. "You two ever been to Caemlyn before?" He gave a little chuckle. "Don't suppose you have. Well, wait till you see it. The greatest city in the world. Oh, I've heard all about Illian and Ebou Dar and Tear and all—there's always some fool thinks a thing is bigger and better just because it's off somewheres over the horizon—but for my money, Caemlyn is the grandest there is. Couldn't be grander. No, it couldn't. Unless maybe Queen Morgase, the Light illumine her, got rid of that witch from Tar Valon."

Rand was lying back with his head pillowed on his blanketroll atop the bundle of Thom's cloak, watching the night drift by, letting the farmer's words wash by him. A human voice kept the darkness at bay and muted the mournful wind. He twisted around to look up at the dark mass of Bunt's back. "You mean an Aes Sedai?"

"What else would I mean? Sitting there in the Palace like a spider. I'm a good Queen's man—never say I'm not—but it just isn't right. I'm not one of those saying Elaida's got too much influence over the Queen. Not me. And as for the fools who claim Elaida's really the queen in all but name. . . ." He spat into the night. "That for them. Morgase is no puppet to dance for any Tar Valon witch."

Another Aes Sedai. If . . . when Moiraine got to Caemlyn,

she might well go to a sister Aes Sedai. If the worst happened, this Elaida might help them reach Tar Valon. He looked at Mat, and just as if he had spoken aloud Mat shook his head. He could not see Mat's face, but he knew it was fixed in denial.

Bunt went right on talking, flicking the reins whenever his horse slowed but otherwise letting his hands rest on his knees. "I'm a good Queen's man, like I said, but even fools say something worthwhile now and again. Even a blind pig finds an acorn sometimes. There's got to be some changes. This weather, the crops failing, cows drying up, calves and lambs born dead, or with two heads. Bloody ravens don't even wait for things to die. People are scared. They want somebody to blame. Dragon's Fang turning up on people's doors. Things creeping about in the night. Barns getting burned. Fellows around like that friend of Holdwin, scaring people. The Queen's got to do something before it's too late. You see that, don't you?" Rand made a noncommittal sound. It sounded as if they had been even luckier than he had thought to find this old man and his cart. They might not have gotten further than that last village if they had waited for daylight. Things creeping about in the night. He lifted up to look over the side of the cart at the darkness. Shadows and shapes seemed to writhe in the black. He dropped back before his imagination convinced him there was something there.

Bunt took it for agreement. "Right. I'm a good Queen's man, and I'll stand against any who try to harm her, but I'm right. You take the Lady Elayne and the Lord Gawyn, now. There's a change wouldn't harm anything, and might do some good. Sure, I know we've always done it that way in Andor. Send the Daughter-Heir off to Tar Valon to study with the Aes Sedai, and the eldest son off to study with the Warders. I believe in tradition, I do, but look what it got us last time. Luc dead in the Blight before he was ever anointed First Prince of the Sword, and Tigraine vanished—run off or dead—when it came time for her to take the throne. Still troubling us, that.

"There's some saying she's still alive, you know, that Morgase isn't the rightful Queen. Bloody fools. I remember what happened. Remember like it was yesterday. No Daughter-Heir to take the throne when the old Queen died, and every House in Andor scheming and fighting for the right. And Taringail

Damodred. You wouldn't have thought he'd lost his wife, him hot to figure which House would win so he could marry again and become Prince Consort after all. Well, he managed it, though why Morgase chose . . . ah, no man knows the mind of a woman, and a queen is twice a woman, wed to a man, wed to the land. He got what he wanted, anyway, if not the way he wanted it.

"Brought Cairhien into the plotting before he was done, and you know how that ended. The Tree chopped down, and black-veiled Aiel coming over the Dragonwall. Well, he got himself decently killed after he'd fathered Elayne and Gawyn, so there's an end to it, I suppose. But why send them to Tar Valon? It's time men didn't think of the throne of Andor and Aes Sedai in the same thought anymore. If they've got to go some place else to learn what they need, well, Illian's got libraries as good as Tar Valon, and they'll teach the Lady Elayne as much about ruling and scheming as ever the witches could. Nobody knows more about scheming than an Illianer. And if the Guards can't teach the Lord Gawyn enough about soldiering, well, they've soldiers in Illian, too. And in Shienar, and Tear, for that matter. I'm a good Queen's man, but I say let's stop all this truck with Tar Valon. Three thousand years is long enough. Too long. Queen Morgase can lead us and put things right without help from the White Tower. I tell you, there's a woman makes a man proud to kneel for her blessing. Why, once. . . ."

Rand fought the sleep his body cried out for, but the rhythmic creak and sway of the cart lulled him and he floated off on the drone of Bunt's voice. He dreamed of Tam. At first they were at the big oak table in the farmhouse, drinking tea while Tam told him about Prince Consorts, and Daughter-Heirs, and the Dragonwall, and black-veiled Aielmen. The heron-mark sword lay on the table between them, but neither of them looked at it. Suddenly he was in the Westwood, pulling the makeshift litter through the moon-bright night. When he looked over his shoulder, it was Thom on the litter, not his father, sitting cross-legged and juggling in the moonlight.

"The Queen is wed to the land," Thom said as brightly colored balls danced in a circle, "but the Dragon . . . the Dragon is one with the land, and the land is one with the Dragon."

Further back Rand saw a Fade coming, black cloak un-
disturbed by the wind, horse ghosting silently through the trees.
Two severed heads hung at the Myrddraal's saddlebow, dripping blood that ran in darker streams down its mount's coal-
black shoulder. Lan and Moiraine, faces distorted in grimaces
of pain. The Fade pulled on a fistful of tethers as it rode. Each
tether ran back to the bound wrists of one of those who ran
behind the soundless hooves, their faces blank with despair.
Mat and Perrin. And Egwene.

"Not her!" Rand shouted. "The Light blast you, it's me you
want, not her!"

The Halfman gestured, and flames consumed Egwene, flesh
crisping to ash, bone blacking and crumbling.

"The Dragon is one with the land," Thom said, still juggling
unconcernedly, "and the land is one with the Dragon."

Rand screamed . . . and opened his eyes.

The cart creaked along the Caemlyn Road, filled with night
and the sweetness of long-vanished hay and the faint smell of
horse. A shape blacker than the night rested on his chest, and
eyes blacker than death looked into his.

"You are mine," the raven said, and the sharp beak stabbed
into his eye. He screamed as it plucked his eyeball out of his
head.

With a throat-ripping shriek, he sat up, clapping both hands
to his face.

Early morning daylight bathed the cart. Dazed, he stared at
his hands. No blood. No pain. The rest of the dream was already fading, but that. . . . Gingerly he felt his face and shuddered.

"At least. . . ." Mat yawned, cracking his jaws. "At least
you got some sleep." There was little sympathy in his bleary
eyes. He was huddled under his cloak, with his blanketroll doubled up beneath his head. "He talked all bloody night."

"You all the way awake?" Bunt said from the driver's seat.
"Gave me a start, you did, yelling like that. Well, we're there."
He swept a hand out in front of them in a grand gesture.
"Caemlyn, the grandest city in the world."

CHAPTER
35

Caemlyn

Rand twisted up to kneel behind the driver's seat. He could not help laughing with relief. "We made it, Mat! I told you we'd. . . ."

Words died in his mouth as his eyes fell on Caemlyn. After Baerlon, even more after the ruins of Shadar Logoth, he had thought he knew what a great city would look like, but this . . . this was more than he would have believed.

Outside the great wall, buildings clustered as if every town he had passed through had been gathered and set down there, side-by-side and all pushed together. Inns thrust their upper stories above the tile roofs of houses, and squat warehouses, broad and windowless, shouldered against them all. Red brick and gray stone and plastered white, jumbled and mixed together, they spread as far as the eye could see. Baerlon could have vanished into it without being noticed, and Whitebridge swallowed up twenty times over with hardly a ripple.

And the wall itself. The sheer, fifty-foot height of pale gray stone, streaked with silver and white, swept out in a great circle, curving to north and south till he wondered how far it must run. All along its length towers rose, round and standing high above the wall's own height, red-and-white banners whipping in the wind atop each one. From inside the wall other towers peeked out, slender towers even taller than those at the walls, and domes gleaming white and gold in the sun. A thousand stories had painted cities in his mind, the great cities of kings

and queens, of thrones and powers and legends, and Caemlyn
fit into those mind-deep pictures as water fits into a jug.

The cart creaked down the wide road toward the city, toward
tower-flanked gates. The wagons of a merchants' train rolled
out of those gates, under a vaulting archway in the stone that
could have let a giant through, or ten giants abreast. Unwalled
markets lined the road on both sides, roof tiles glistening red
and purple, with stalls and pens in the spaces between. Calves
bawled, cattle lowed, geese honked, chickens clucked, goats
bleated, sheep baaed, and people bargained at the top of their
lungs. A wall of noise funneled them toward the gates of
Caemlyn.

"What did I tell you?" Bunt had to raise his voice to near a
shout in order to be heard. "The grandest city in the world.
Built by Ogier, you know. Least, the Inner City and the Palace
were. It's that old, Caemlyn is. Caemlyn, where good Queen
Morgase, the Light illumine her, makes the law and holds the
peace for Andor. The greatest city on earth."

Rand was ready to agree. His mouth hung open, and he
wanted to put his hands over his ears to shut out the din. People crowded the road, as thick as folk in Emond's Field
crowded the Green at Bel Tine. He remembered thinking there
were too many people in Baerlon to be believed, and almost
laughed. He looked at Mat and grinned. Mat did have his
hands over his ears, and his shoulders were hunched up as if he
wanted to cover them with those, too.

"How are we going to hide in this?" he demanded loudly
when he saw Rand looking. "How can we tell who to trust with
so many? So bloody many. Light, the noise!"

Rand looked at Bunt before answering. The farmer was
caught up in staring at the city; with the noise, he might not
have heard anyway. Still, Rand put his mouth close to Mat's
ear. "How can they find us among so many? Can't you see it,
you wool-headed idiot? We're safe, if you ever learn to watch
your bloody tongue!" He flung out a hand to take in everything, the markets, the city walls still ahead. "Look at it, Mat!
Anything could happen here. Anything! We might even find
Moiraine waiting for us, and Egwene, and all the rest."

"If they're alive. If you ask me, they're as dead as the
gleeman."

The grin faded from Rand's face, and he turned to watch the gates come nearer. Anything could happen in a city like Caemlyn. He held that thought stubbornly.

The horse could not move any faster, flap the reins as Bunt would; the closer to the gates they came, the thicker the crowd grew, jostling together shoulder to shoulder, pressing against the carts and wagons heading in. Rand was glad to see a good many were dusty young men afoot with little in the way of belongings. Whatever their ages, a lot of the crowd pushing toward the gates had a travel-worn look, rickety carts and tired horses, clothes wrinkled from many nights of sleeping rough, dragging steps and weary eyes. But weary or not, those eyes were fixed on the gates as if getting inside the walls would strip away all their fatigue.

Half a dozen of the Queen's Guards stood at the gates, their clean red-and-white tabards and burnished plate-and-mail a sharp contrast to most of the people streaming under the stone arch. Backs rigid and heads straight, they eyed the incomers with disdainful wariness. It was plain they would just as soon have turned away most of those coming in. Aside from keeping a way clear for traffic leaving the city, though, and having a hard word with those who tried to push too fast, they did not hinder anyone.

"Keep your places. Don't push. Don't push, the Light blind you! There's room for everybody, the Light help us. Keep your places."

Bunt's cart rolled past the gates with the slow tide of the throng, into Caemlyn.

The city rose on low hills, like steps climbing to a' center. Another wall encircled that center, shining pure white and running over the hills. Inside that were even more towers and domes, white and gold and purple, their elevation atop the hills making them seem to look down on the rest of Caemlyn. Rand thought that must be the Inner City of which Bunt had spoken.

The Caemlyn Road itself changed as soon as it was inside the city, becoming a wide boulevard, split down the middle by broad strips of grass and trees. The grass was brown and the tree branches bare, but people hurried by as if they saw nothing unusual, laughing, talking, arguing, doing all the things that people do. Just as if they had no idea that there had been no

spring yet this year and might be none. They did not see, Rand
realized, could not or would not. Their eyes slid away from
leafless branches, and they walked across the dead and dying
grass without once looking down. What they did not see, they
could ignore; what they did not see was not really there.

Gaping at the city and the people, Rand was taken by surprise when the cart turned down a side street, narrower than
the boulevard, but still twice as wide as any street in Emond's
Field. Bunt drew the horse to a halt and turned to look back at
them hesitantly. The traffic was a bit lighter here; the crowd
split around the cart without breaking stride.

"What you're hiding under your cloak, is it really what Holdwin says?"

Rand was in the act of tossing his saddlebags over his shoulder. He did not even twitch. "What do you mean?" His voice
was steady, too. His stomach was a sour knot, but his voice was
steady.

Mat stifled a yawn with one hand, but he shoved the other
under his coat—clutching the dagger from Shadar Logoth,
Rand knew—and his eyes had a hard, hunted look under the
scarf around his head. Bunt avoided looking at Mat, as if he
knew there was a weapon in that hidden hand.

"Don't mean nothing, I suppose. Look, now, if you heard I
was coming to Caemlyn, you were there long enough to hear
the rest. Was I after a reward, I'd have made some excuse to go
in the Goose and Crown, speak to Holdwin. Only I don't much
like Holdwin, and I don't like that friend of his, not at all.
Seems like he wants you two more than he wants . . . anything
else."

"I don't know what he wants," Rand said. "We've never
seen him before." It might even be the truth; he could not tell
one Fade from another.

"Uh-huh. Well, like I say, I don't know nothing, and I guess
I don't want to. There's enough trouble around for everybody
without I go looking for more."

Mat was slow in gathering his things, and Rand was already
in the street before he started climbing down. Rand waited impatiently. Mat turned stiffly from the cart, hugging bow and
quiver and blanketroll to his chest, muttering under his breath.
Heavy shadows darkened the undersides of his eyes.

Rand's stomach rumbled, and he grimaced. Hunger combined with a sour twisting in his gut made him afraid he was going to vomit. Mat was staring at him now, expectantly. *Which way to go? What to do now?*

Bunt leaned over and beckoned him closer. He went, hoping for advice about Caemlyn.

"I'd hide that. . . ." The old farmer paused and looked around warily. People pushed by on both sides of the cart, but except for a few passing curses about blocking the way, no one paid them any attention. "Stop wearing it," he said, "hide it, sell it. Give it away. That's my advice. Thing like that's going to draw attention, and I guess you don't want any of that."

Abruptly he straightened, clucking to his horse, and drove slowly on down the crowded street without another word or a backward glance. A wagon loaded with barrels rumbled toward them. Rand jumped out of the way, staggered, and when he looked again Bunt and his cart were lost to sight.

"What do we do now?" Mat demanded. He licked his lips, staring wide-eyed at all the people pushing by and the buildings towering as much as six stories above the street. "We're in Caemlyn, but what do we do?" He had uncovered his ears, but his hands twitched as if he wanted to put them back. A hum lay on the city, the low, steady drone of hundreds of shops working, thousands of people talking. To Rand it was like being inside a giant beehive, constantly buzzing. "Even if they are here, Rand, how could we find them in all of this?"

"Moiraine will find us," Rand said slowly. The immensity of the city was a weight on his shoulders; he wanted to get away, to hide from all the people and noise. The void eluded him despite Tam's teachings; his eyes drew the city into it. He concentrated instead on what was right around him, ignoring everything that lay beyond. Just looking at that one street, it almost seemed like Baerlon. Baerlon, the last place they had all thought they were safe. *Nobody's safe anymore. Maybe they are all dead. What do you do then?*

"They're alive! Egwene's alive!" he said fiercely. Several passersby looked at him oddly.

"Maybe," Mat said. "Maybe. What if Moiraine doesn't find us? What if nobody does but the . . . the. . . ." He shuddered, unable to say it.

"We'll think about that when it happens," he told Mat
firmly. "If it happens." The worst meant seeking out Elaida,
the Aes Sedai in the Palace. He would go on to Tar Valon,
first. He did not know if Mat remembered what Thom had said
about the Red Ajah—and the Black—but he surely did. His
stomach twisted again. "Thom said to find an inn called The
Queen's Blessing. We'll go there first."

"How? We can't afford one meal between the two of us."

"At least it's a place to start. Thom thought we could find
help there."

"I can't. . . . Rand, they're everywhere." Mat dropped his
eyes to the paving stones and seemed to shrink in on himself,
trying to pull away from the people that were all around them.
"Wherever we go, they're right behind us, or they're waiting
for us. They'll be at The Queen's Blessing, too. I can't. . . .
I. . . . Nothing's going to stop a Fade."

Rand grabbed Mat's collar in a fist that he was trying hard to
keep from trembling. He needed Mat. Maybe the others were
alive—*Light, please!*—but right then and there, it was just Mat
and him. The thought of going on alone. . . . He swallowed
hard, tasting bile.

He looked around quickly. No one seemed to have heard
Mat mention the Fade; the crowd pressed past lost in its own
worries. He put his face close to Mat's. "We've made it this far,
haven't we?" he asked in a hoarse whisper. "They haven't
caught us yet. We can make it all the way, if we just don't quit.
I won't just quit and wait for them like a sheep for slaughter. I
won't! Well? Are you going to stand here till you starve to
death? Or until they come pick you up in a sack?"

He let go of Mat and turned away. His fingernails dug into
his palms, but his hands still trembled. Suddenly Mat was walking alongside him, his eyes still down, and Rand let out a long
breath.

"I'm sorry, Rand," Mat mumbled.

"Forget it," Rand said.

Mat barely looked up enough to keep from walking into people while the words poured out in a lifeless voice. "I can't stop
thinking I'll never see home again. I want to go home. Laugh if
you want; I don't care. What I wouldn't give to have my
mother blessing me out for something right now. It's like

weights on my brain; hot weights. Strangers all around, and no
way to tell who to trust, if I can trust anybody. Light, the Two
Rivers is so far away it might as well be on the other side of the
world. We're alone, and we'll never get home. We're going to
die, Rand."

"Not yet, we won't," Rand retorted. "Everybody dies. The
Wheel turns. I'm not going to curl up and wait for it to happen,
though."

"You sound like Master al'Vere," Mat grumbled, but his
voice had a little spirit in it.

"Good," Rand said. "Good." *Light, let the others be all
right. Please don't let us be alone.*

He began asking directions to The Queen's Blessing. The re-
sponses varied widely, a curse for all those who did not stay
where they belonged or a shrug and a blank look being the
most common. Some stalked on by with no more than a glance,
if that.

A broad-faced man, nearly as big as Perrin, cocked his head
and said, "The Queen's Blessing, eh? You country boys
Queen's men?" He wore a white cockade on his wide-brimmed
hat, and a white armband on his long coat. "Well, you've come
too late."

He went off roaring with laughter, leaving Rand and Mat to
stare at one another in puzzlement. Rand shrugged; there were
plenty of odd folk in Caemlyn, people like he had never seen
before.

Some of them stood out in the crowd, skins too dark or too
pale, coats of strange cut or bright colors, hats with pointed
peaks or long feathers. There were women with veils across
their faces, women in stiff dresses as wide as the wearer was
tall, women in dresses that left more skin bare than any tav-
ernmaid he had seen. Occasionally a carriage, all vivid paint
and gilt, squeezed through the thronged streets behind a four-
or six-horse team with plumes on their harness. Sedan chairs
were everywhere, the polemen pushing along with never a care
for who they shoved aside.

Rand saw one fight start that way, a brawling heap of men
swinging their fists while a pale-skinned man in a red-striped
coat climbed out of the sedan chair lying on its side. Two
roughly dressed men, who seemed to have been just passing by

up till then, jumped on him before he was clear. The crowd
that had stopped to watch began to turn ugly, muttering and
shaking fists. Rand pulled at Mat's sleeve and hurried on. Mat
needed no second urging. The roar of a small riot followed
them down the street.

Several times men approached the two of them instead of the
other way around. Their dusty clothes marked them as newcomers, and seemed to act like a magnet on some types. Fur-
tive fellows who offered relics of Logain for sale with darting
eyes and feet set to run. Rand calculated he was offered
enough scraps of the false Dragon's cloak and fragments of his
sword to make two swords and half a dozen cloaks. Mat's face
brightened with interest, the first time at least, but Rand gave
them all a curt no, and they took it with a bob of the head and
a quick, "Light illumine the Queen, good master," and vanished. Most of the shops had plates and cups painted with fanciful scenes purporting to show the false Dragon being
displayed before the Queen in chains. And there were Whitecloaks in the streets. Each walked in an open space that moved
with him, just as in Baerlon.

Staying unnoticed was something Rand thought about a great
deal. He kept his cloak over his sword, but that would not be
good enough for very long. Sooner or later someone would
wonder what he was hiding. He would not—could not—take
Bunt's advice to stop wearing it, not his link to Tam. To his
father.

Many others among the throng wore swords, but none with
the heron-mark to pull the eye. All the Caemlyn men, though,
and some of the strangers, had their swords wound in strips of
cloth, sheath and hilt, red bound with white cord, or white
bound with red. A hundred heron-marks could be hidden under those wrappings and no one would see. Besides, following
local fashion would make them seem to fit in more.

A good many shops were fronted with tables displaying the
cloth and cord, and Rand stopped at one. The red cloth was
cheaper than the white, though he could see no difference apart
from the color, so he bought that and the white cord to go with
it, despite Mat's complaints about how little money they had
left. The tight-lipped shopkeeper eyed them up and down with

a twist to his mouth while he took Rand's coppers, and cursed them when Rand asked for a place inside to wrap his sword.

"We didn't come to see Logain," Rand said patiently. "We just came to see Caemlyn." He remembered Bunt, and added, "The grandest city in the world." The shopkeeper's grimace remained in place. "The Light illumine good Queen Morgase," Rand said hopefully.

"You make any trouble," the man said sourly, "and there's a hundred men in sound of my voice will take care of you even if the Guards won't." He paused to spit, just missing Rand's foot. "Get on about your filthy business."

Rand nodded as if the man had bid him a cheerful farewell, and pulled Mat away. Mat kept looking back over his shoulder toward the shop, growling to himself; until Rand tugged him into an empty alleyway. With their backs to the street no passerby could see what they were doing. Rand pulled off the sword belt and set to wrapping the sheath and hilt.

"I'll bet he charged you double for that bloody cloth," Mat said. "Triple."

It was not as easy as it looked, fastening the strips of cloth and the cord so the whole thing would not fall off.

"They'll all be trying to cheat us, Rand. They think we've come to see the false Dragon, like everybody else. We'll be lucky if somebody doesn't hit us on the head while we sleep. This is no place to be. There are too many people. Let's leave for Tar Valon now. Or south, to Illian. I wouldn't mind seeing them gather for the Hunt of the Horn. If we can't go home, let's just go."

"I'm staying," Rand said. "If they're not here already, they'll come here sooner or later, looking for us."

He was not sure if he had the wrappings done the way everyone else did, but the herons on scabbard and hilt were hidden and he thought it was secure. As he went back out on the street, he was sure that he had one less thing to worry about causing trouble. Mat trailed along beside him as reluctantly as if he were being pulled on a leash.

Bit by bit Rand did get the directions he wanted. At first they were vague, on the order of "somewhere in that direction" and "over that way." The nearer they came, though, the clearer the instructions, until at last they stood before a broad stone building with a sign over the door creaking in the wind. A man kneeling before a woman with red-gold hair and a crown, one of her hands resting on his bowed head. The Queen's Blessing.

"Are you sure about this?" Mat asked.

"Of course," Rand said. He took a deep breath and pushed open the door.

The common room was large and paneled with dark wood, and fires on two hearths warmed it. A serving maid was sweeping the floor, though it was clean, and another was polishing candlesticks in the corner. Each smiled at the two newcomers before going back to her work.

Only a few tables had people at them, but a dozen men was a crowd for so early in the day, and if none looked exactly happy to see him and Mat, at least they looked clean and sober. The smells of roasting beef and baking bread drifted from the kitchen, making Rand's mouth water.

The innkeeper was fat, he was pleased to see, a pink-faced man in a starched white apron, with graying hair combed back over a bald spot that it did not quite cover. His sharp eye took them in from head to toe, dusty clothes and bundles and worn boots, but he had a ready, pleasant smile, too. Basel Gill was his name.

"Master Gill," Rand said, "a friend of ours told us to come here. Thom Merrilin. He—" The innkeeper's smile slipped. Rand looked at Mat, but he was too busy sniffing the aromas coming from the kitchen to notice anything else. "Is something wrong? You do know him?"

"I know him," Gill said curtly. He seemed more interested in the flute case at Rand's side now, than in anything else. "Come with me." He jerked his head toward the back. Rand gave Mat a jerk to get him started, then followed, wondering what was going on.

In the kitchen, Master Gill paused to speak to the cook, a round woman with her hair in a bun at the back of her head who almost matched the innkeeper pound for pound. She kept stirring her pots while Master Gill talked. The smells were so good—two days' hunger made a fine sauce for anything, but this smelled as good as Mistress al'Vere's kitchen—that Rand's stomach growled. Mat was leaning toward the pots, nose first.

Rand nudged him; Mat hastily wiped his chin where he had begun drooling.

Then the innkeeper was hurrying them out the back door. In the stableyard he looked around to make sure no one was close, then rounded on them. On Rand. "What's in the case, lad?"

"Thom's flute," Rand said slowly. He opened the case, as if showing the gold-and-silver-chased flute would help. Mat's hand crept under his coat.

Master Gill did not take his eyes off Rand. "Aye, I recognize it. I saw him play it often enough, and there's not likely two like that outside a royal court." The pleasant smiles were gone, and his sharp eyes were suddenly as sharp as a knife. "How did you come by it? Thom would part with his arm as soon as that flute."

"He gave it to me." Rand took Thom's bundled cloak from his back and set it on the ground, unfolding enough to show the colored patches, as well as the end of the harp case. "Thom's dead, Master Gill. If he was your friend, I'm sorry. He was mine, too."

"Dead, you say. How?"

"A . . . a man tried to kill us. Thom pushed this at me and told us to run." The patches fluttered in the wind like butterflies. Rand's throat caught; he folded the cloak carefully back up again. "We'd have been killed if it hadn't been for him. We were on our way to Caemlyn together. He told us to come here, to your inn."

"I'll believe he's dead," the innkeeper said slowly, "when I see his corpse." He nudged the bundled cloak with his toe and cleared his throat roughly. "Nay, nay, I believe you saw whatever it was you saw; I just don't believe he's dead. He's a harder man to kill than you might believe, is old Thom Merrilin."

Rand put a hand on Mat's shoulder. "It's all right, Mat. He's a friend."

Master Gill glanced at Mat, and sighed. "I suppose I am at that."

Mat straightened up slowly, folding his arms over his chest. He was still watching the innkeeper warily, though, and a muscle in his cheek twitched.

"Coming to Caemlyn, you say?" The innkeeper shook his
head. "This is the last place on earth I'd expect Thom to come,
excepting maybe it was Tar Valon." He waited for a stableman
to pass, leading a horse, and even then he lowered his voice.
"You've trouble with the Aes Sedai, I take it."

"Yes," Mat grumbled at the same time that Rand said,
"What makes you think that?"

Master Gill chuckled dryly. "I know the man, that's what.
He'd jump into that kind of trouble, especially to help a couple
of lads about the age of you. . . ." The reminiscence in his eyes
flickered out, and he stood up straight with a chary look. "Now
. . . ah . . . I'm not making any accusations, mind, but . . . ah
. . . I take it neither of you can . . . ah . . . what I'm getting at
is . . . ah . . . what exactly is the nature of your trouble with
Tar Valon, if you don't mind my asking?"

Rand's skin prickled as he realized what the man was suggesting. The One Power. "No, no, nothing like that. I swear.
There was even an Aes Sedai helping us. Moiraine was. . . ."
He bit his tongue, but the innkeeper's expression never
changed.

"Glad to hear it. Not that I've all that much love for Aes
Sedai, but better them than . . . that other thing." He shook
his head slowly. "Too much talk of that kind of thing, with
Logain being brought here. No offense meant, you understand,
but . . . well, I had to know, didn't I?"

"No offense," Rand said. Mat's murmur could have been
anything, but the innkeeper appeared to take it for the same as
Rand had said.

"You two look the right sort, and I do believe you were—
are—friends of Thom, but it's hard times and stony days. I
don't suppose you can pay? No, I didn't think so. There's not
enough of anything, and what there is costs the earth, so I'll
give you beds—not the best, but warm and dry—and something to eat, and I cannot promise more, however much I'd
like."

"Thank you," Rand said with a quizzical glance at Mat. "It's
more than I expected." What was the right sort, and why
should he promise more?

"Well, Thom's a good friend. An old friend. Hot-headed and
liable to say the worst possible thing to the one person he

shouldn't, but a good friend all the same. If he doesn't show up
. . . well, we'll figure something out then. Best you don't talk
any more talk about Aes Sedai helping you. I'm a good
Queen's man, but there are too many in Caemlyn right now
who'd take it wrong, and I don't mean just the Whitecloaks."

Mat snorted. "For all I care, the ravens can take every Aes
Sedai straight to Shayol Ghul!"

"Watch your tongue," Master Gill snapped. "I said I don't
love them; I didn't say I'm a fool thinks they're behind everything that's wrong. The Queen supports Elaida, and the Guards
stand for the Queen. The Light send things don't go so bad that
changes. Anyway, lately some Guards have forgotten themselves enough to be a little rough with folks they overhear
speaking against Aes Sedai. Not on duty, thank the Light, but
it's happened, just the same. I don't need off-duty Guards
breaking up my common room to teach you a lesson, and I
don't need Whitecloaks egging somebody on to paint the
Dragon's Fang on my door, so if you want any help out of me,
you just keep thoughts about Aes Sedai to yourself, good or
bad." He paused thoughtfully, then added, "Maybe it's best
you don't mention Thom's name, either, where anyone but me
can hear. Some of the Guards have long memories, and so does
the Queen. No need taking chances."

"Thom had trouble with the Queen?" Rand said incredulously, and the innkeeper laughed.

"So he didn't tell you everything. Don't know why he
should. On the other hand, I don't know why you shouldn't
know, either. Not like it's a secret, exactly. Do you think every
gleeman thinks as much of himself as Thom does? Well, come
to think of it, I guess they do, but it always seemed to me
Thom had an extra helping of thinking a lot of himself. He
wasn't always a gleeman, you know, wandering from village to
village and sleeping under a hedge as often as not. There was a
time Thom Merrilin was Court-bard right here in Caemlyn, and
known in every royal court from Tear to Maradon."

"Thom?" Mat said.

Rand nodded slowly. He could picture Thom at a Queen's
court, with his stately manner and grand gestures.

"That he was," Master Gill said. "It was not long after Taringail Damodred died that the . . . trouble about his nephew

cropped up. There were some said Thom was, shall we say, closer to the Queen than was proper. But Morgase was a young widow, and Thom was in his prime, then, and the Queen can do as she wishes is the way I look at it. Only she's always had a temper, has our good Morgase, and he took off without a word when he learned what kind of trouble his nephew was in. The Queen didn't much like that. Didn't like him meddling in Aes Sedai matters, either. Can't say I think it was right, either, nephew or no. Anyway, when he came back, he said some words, all right. Words you don't say to a Queen. Words you don't say to any woman with Morgase's spirit. Elaida was set against him because of his trying to mix in the business with his nephew, and between the Queen's temper and Elaida's animosity, Thom left Caemlyn half a step ahead of a trip to prison, if not the headsman's axe. As far as I know, the writ still stands."

"If it was a long time ago," Rand said, "maybe nobody remembers."

Master Gill shook his head. "Gareth Bryne is Captain-General of the Queen's Guards. He personally commanded the Guardsmen Morgase sent to bring Thom back in chains, and I misdoubt he'll ever forget returning empty-handed to find Thom had already been back to the Palace and left again. And the Queen never forgets *anything*. You ever know a woman who did? My, but Morgase was in a taking. I'll swear the whole city walked soft and whispered for a month. Plenty of other Guardsmen old enough to remember, too. No, best you keep Thom as close a secret as you keep that Aes Sedai of yours. Come, I'll get you something to eat. You look as if your bellies are gnawing at your backbones."

CHAPTER
36

Web of the Pattern

Master Gill took them to a corner table in the common room and had one of the serving maids bring them food. Rand shook his head when he saw the plates, with a few thin slices of gravy-covered beef, a spoonful of mustard greens, and two potatoes on each. It was a rueful, resigned headshake, though, not angry. Not enough of anything, the innkeeper had said. Picking up his knife and fork, Rand wondered what would happen when there was nothing left. It made his half-covered plate seem like a feast. It made him shiver.

Master Gill had chosen a table well away from anyone else, and he sat with his back to the corner, where he could watch the room. Nobody could get close enough to overhear what they said without him seeing. When the maid left, he said softly, "Now, why don't you tell me about this trouble of yours? If I'm going to help, I'd best know what I'm getting into."

Rand looked at Mat, but Mat was frowning at his plate as if he were mad at the potato he was cutting. Rand took a deep breath. "I don't really understand it myself," he began.

He kept the story simple, and he kept Trollocs and Fades out of it. When somebody offered help, it would not do to tell them it was all about fables. But he did not think it was fair to understate the danger, either, not fair to pull someone in when they had no idea what they were getting into. Some men were after him and Mat, and a couple of friends of theirs, too. They appeared where they were least expected, these men, and they were deadly dangerous and set on killing him and his friends, or worse. Moiraine said some of them were Darkfriends. Thom did not trust Moiraine completely, but he stayed on with them, he said, because of his nephew. They had been separated during an attack while trying to reach Whitebridge, and then, in Whitebridge, Thom died saving them from another attack. And there had been other tries. He knew there were holes in it, but it was the best he could do on short notice without telling more than was safe.

"We just kept on till we reached Caemlyn," he explained. "That was the plan, originally. Caemlyn, and then Tar Valon." He shifted uncomfortably on the edge of his chair. After keeping everything secret for so long, it felt odd to be telling somebody even as much as he was. "If we stay on that route, the others will be able to find us, sooner or later."

"If they're alive," Mat muttered at his plate.

Rand did not even glance at Mat. Something compelled him to add, "It could bring you trouble, helping us."

Master Gill waved it off with a plump hand. "Can't say as I want trouble, but it wouldn't be the first I've seen. No bloody Darkfriend will make me turn my back on Thom's friends. This friend of yours from up north, now—if she comes to Caemlyn, I'll hear. There are people keep their eyes on comings and goings like that around here, and word spreads."

Rand hesitated, then asked, "What about Elaida?"

The innkeeper hesitated, too, and finally shook his head. "I don't think so. Maybe if you didn't have a connection to Thom. She'd winkle it out, and then where would you be? No telling. Maybe in a cell. Maybe worse. They say she has a way of feeling things, what's happened, what's going to happen. They say she can cut right through to what a man wants to hide. I don't know, but I wouldn't risk it. If it wasn't for Thom, you could go to the Guards. They'd take care of any Darkfriends quick enough. But even if you could keep Thom quiet from the Guards, word would reach Elaida as soon as you mentioned Darkfriends, and then you're back where we started."

"No Guards," Rand agreed. Mat nodded vigorously while stuffing a fork into his mouth and got gravy on his chin.

"Trouble is, you're caught up in the fringes of politics, lad, even if it's none of your doing, and politics is a foggy mire full of snakes."

"What about—" Rand began, but the innkeeper grimaced suddenly, his chair creaking under his bulk as he sat up straight.

The cook was standing in the doorway to the kitchen, wiping her hands with her apron. When she saw the innkeeper looking she motioned for him to come, then vanished back into the kitchen.

"Might as well be married to her." Master Gill sighed. "Finds things that need fixing before I know there's anything wrong. If it's not the drains stopped up, or the downspouts clogged, it's rats. I keep a clean place, you understand, but with so many people in the city, rats are everywhere. Crowd people together and you get rats, and Caemlyn has a plague of them all of a sudden. You wouldn't believe what a good cat, a prime ratter, fetches these days. Your room is in the attic. I'll tell the girls which; any of them can show you to it. And don't worry about Darkfriends. I can't say much good about the Whitecloaks, but between them and the Guards, that sort won't dare show their filthy faces in Caemlyn." His chair squeaked again as he pushed it back and stood. "I hope it isn't the drains again."

Rand went back to his food, but he saw that Mat had stopped eating. "I thought you were hungry," he said. Mat kept staring at his plate, pushing one piece of potato in a circle with his fork. "You have to eat, Mat. We need to keep up our strength if we're going to reach Tar Valon."

Mat let out a low, bitter laugh. "Tar Valon! All this time it's been Caemlyn. Moiraine would be waiting for us in Caemlyn. We'd find Perrin and Egwene in Caemlyn. Everything would be all right if we only got to Caemlyn. Well, here we are, and nothing's right. No Moiraine, no Perrin, no anybody. Now it's everything will be all right if we only get to Tar Valon."

"We're alive," Rand said, more sharply than he had intended. He took a deep breath and tried to moderate his tone. "We are alive. That much is all right. And I intend to stay alive. I intend to find out why we're so important. I won't give up."

"All these people, and any of them could be Darkfriends.

Master Gill promised to help us awfully quick. What kind of man just shrugs off Aes Sedai and Darkfriends? It isn't natural. Any decent person would tell us to get out, or . . . or . . . or something."

"Eat," Rand said gently, and watched until Mat began chewing a piece of beef.

He left his own hands resting beside his plate for a minute, pressing them against the table to keep them from shaking. He was scared. Not about Master Gill, of course, but there was enough without that. Those tall city walls would not stop a Fade. Maybe he should tell the innkeeper about that. But even if Gill believed, would he be as willing to help if he thought a Fade might show up at The Queen's Blessing? And the rats. Maybe rats did thrive where there were a lot of people, but he remembered the dream that was not a dream in Baerlon, and a small spine snapping. *Sometimes the Dark One uses carrion eaters as his eyes,* Lan had said. *Ravens, crows, rats. . . .*

He ate, but when he was done he could not remember tasting a single bite.

A serving maid, the one who had been polishing candlesticks when they came in, showed them up to the attic room. A dormer window pierced the slanting outer wall, with a bed on either side of it and pegs beside the door for hanging their belongings. The dark-eyed girl had a tendency to twist her skirt and giggle whenever she looked at Rand. She was pretty, but he knew if he said anything to her he would just make a fool of himself. She made him wish he had Perrin's way with girls; he was glad when she left.

He expected some comment from Mat, but as soon as she was gone, Mat threw himself on one of the beds, still in his cloak and boots, and turned his face to the wall.

Rand hung his things up, watching Mat's back. He thought Mat had his hand under his coat, clutching that dagger again.

"You just going to lie up here hiding?" he said finally.

"I'm tired," Mat mumbled.

"We have questions to ask Master Gill, yet. He might even be able to tell us how to find Egwene, and Perrin. They could be in Caemlyn already if they managed to hang onto their horses."

"They're dead," Mat said to the wall.

Rand hesitated, then gave up. He closed the door softly behind him, hoping Mat really would sleep.

Downstairs, however, Master Gill was nowhere to be found, though the sharp look in the cook's eye said she was looking for him, too. For a while Rand sat in the common room, but he found himself eyeing every patron who came in, every stranger who could be anyone—or anything—especially in the moment when he was first silhouetted as a cloaked black shape in the doorway. A Fade in the room would be like a fox in a chicken coop.

A Guardsman entered from the street. The red-uniformed man stopped just inside the door, running a cool eye over those in the room who were obviously from outside the city. Rand studied the tabletop when the Guardsman's eyes fell on him; when he looked up again, the man was gone.

The dark-eyed maid was passing with her arms full of towels. "They do that sometimes," she said in a confiding tone as she went by. "Just to see there's no trouble. They look after good Queen's folk, they do. Nothing for you to worry about." She giggled.

Rand shook his head. Nothing for him to worry about. It was not as if the Guardsman would have come over and demanded to know if he knew Thom Merrilin. He was getting as bad as Mat. He scraped back his chair.

Another maid was checking the oil in the lamps along the wall.

"Is there another room where I could sit?" he asked her. He did not want to go back upstairs and shut himself up with Mat's sullen withdrawal. "Maybe a private dining room that's not being used?"

"There's the library." She pointed to a door. "Through there, to your right, at the end of the hall. Might be empty, this hour."

"Thank you. If you see Master Gill, would you tell him Rand al'Thor needs to talk to him if he can spare a minute?"

"I'll tell him," she said, then grinned. "Cook wants to talk to him, too."

The innkeeper was probably hiding, he thought as he turned away from her.

When he stepped into the room to which she had directed

him, he stopped and stared. The shelves must have held three
or four hundred books, more than he had ever seen in one
place before. Clothbound, leatherbound with gilded spines.
Only a few had wooden covers. His eyes gobbled up the titles,
picking out old favorites. *The Travels of Jain Farstrider. The
Essays of Willim of Maneches.* His breath caught at the sight of
a leatherbound copy of *Voyages Among the Sea Folk.* Tam had
always wanted to read that.

Picturing Tam, turning the book over in his hands with a
smile, getting the feel of it before settling down before the fireplace with his pipe to read, his own hand tightened on his
sword hilt with a sense of loss and emptiness that dampened all
his pleasure in the books.

A throat cleared behind him, and he suddenly realized he
was not alone. Ready to apologize for his rudeness, he turned.
He was used to being taller than almost everyone he met, but
this time his eyes traveled up and up and up, and his mouth fell
open. Then he came to the head almost reaching the ten-foot
ceiling. A nose as broad as the face, so wide it was more a
snout than a nose. Eyebrows that hung down like tails, framing
pale eyes as big as teacups. Ears that poked up to tufted points
through a shaggy, black mane. *Trolloc!* He let out a yell and
tried to back up and draw his sword. His feet got tangled, and
he sat down hard, instead.

"I wish you humans wouldn't do that," rumbled a voice as
deep as a drum. The tufted ears twitched violently, and the
voice became sad. "So few of you remember us. It's our own
fault, I suppose. Not many of us have gone out among men
since the Shadow fell on the Ways. That's . . . oh, six generations, now. Right after the War of the Hundred Years, it was."
The shaggy head shook and let out a sigh that would have done
credit to a bull. "Too long, too long, and so few to travel and
see, it might as well have been none."

Rand sat there for a minute with his mouth hanging open,
staring up at the apparition in wide-toed, knee-high boots and a
dark blue coat that buttoned from the neck to the waist, then
flared out to his boot tops like a kilt over baggy trousers. In one
hand was a book, seeming tiny by comparison, with a finger
broad enough for three marking the place.

"I thought you were—" he began, then caught himself.

"What are—?" That was not any better. Getting to his feet, he gingerly offered his hand. "My name is Rand al'Thor."

A hand as big as a ham engulfed his; it was accompanied by a formal bow. "Loial, son of Arent son of Halan. Your name sings in my ears, Rand al'Thor."

That sounded like a ritual greeting to Rand. He returned the bow. "Your name sings in my ears, Loial, son of Arent . . . ah . . . son of Halan."

It was all a little unreal. He still did not know *what* Loial was. The grip of Loial's huge fingers was surprisingly gentle, but he was still relieved to get his hand back in one piece.

"You humans are very excitable," Loial said in that bass rumble. "I had heard all the stories, and read the books, of course, but I didn't realize. My first day in Caemlyn, I could not believe the uproar. Children cried, and women screamed, and a mob chased me all the way across the city, waving clubs and knives and torches, and shouting, 'Trolloc!' I'm afraid I was almost beginning to get a little upset. There's no telling what would have happened if a party of the Queen's Guards hadn't come along."

"A lucky thing," Rand said faintly.

"Yes, but even the Guardsmen seemed almost as afraid of me as the others. Four days in Caemlyn now, and I haven't been able to put my nose outside this inn. Good Master Gill even asked me not to use the common room." His ears twitched. "Not that he hasn't been very hospitable, you understand. But there was a bit of trouble that first night. All the humans seemed to want to leave at once. Such screaming and shouting, everyone trying to get through the door at the same time. Some of them could have been hurt."

Rand stared in fascination at those twitching ears.

"I'll tell you, it was not for this I left the *stedding*."

"You're an Ogier!" Rand exclaimed. "Wait! Six generations? You said the War of the Hundred Years! How old are you?" He knew it was rude as soon as he said it, but Loial became defensive rather than offended.

"Ninety years," the Ogier said stiffly. "In only ten more I'll be able to address the Stump. I think the Elders should have let me speak, since they were deciding whether I could leave or not. But then they always worry about anyone of any age going

Outside. You humans are so hasty, so erratic." He blinked and gave a short bow. "Please forgive me. I shouldn't have said that. But you do fight all the time, even when there's no need to."

"That's all right," Rand said. He was still trying to take in Loial's age. Older than old Cenn Buie, and still not old enough to. . . . He sat down in one of the high-backed chairs. Loial took another, made to hold two; he filled it. Sitting, he was as tall as most men standing. "At least they did let you go."

Loial looked at the floor, wrinkling his nose and rubbing at it with one thick finger. "Well, as to that, now. You see, the Stump had not been meeting very long, not even a year, but I could tell from what I heard that by the time they reached a decision I would be old enough to go without their permission. I am afraid they'll say I put a long handle on my axe, but I just . . . left. The Elders always said I was too hot-headed, and I fear I've proven them right. I wonder if they have realized I'm gone, yet? But I had to go."

Rand bit his lip to keep from laughing. If Loial was a hot-headed Ogier, he could imagine what most Ogier were like. Had not been meeting very long, not even a year? Master al'Vere would just shake his head in wonder; a Village Council meeting that lasted half a day would have everybody jumping up and down, even Haral Luhhan. A wave of homesickness swept over him, making it hard to breathe for memories of Tam, and Egwene, and the Winespring Inn, and Bel Tine on the Green in happier days. He forced them away.

"If you don't mind my asking," he said, clearing his throat, "why did you want to go . . . ah, Outside, so much? I wish I'd never left my home, myself."

"Why, to see," Loial said as if it were the most obvious thing in the world. "I read the books, all the travelers' accounts, and it began to burn in me that I had to see, not just read." His pale eyes brightened, and his ears stiffened. "I studied every scrap I could find about traveling, about the Ways, and customs in human lands, and the cities we built for you humans after the Breaking of the World. And the more I read, the more I knew that I had to go Outside, go to those places we had been, and see the groves for myself."

Rand blinked. "Groves?"

Web of the Pattern 203

"Yes, the groves. The trees. Only a few of the Great Trees, of course, towering to the sky to keep memories of the *stedding* fresh." His chair groaned as he shifted forward, gesturing with his hands, one of which still held the book. His eyes were brighter than ever, and his ears almost quivered. "Mostly they used the trees of the land and the place. You cannot make the land go against itself. Not for long; the land will rebel. You must shape the vision to the land, not the land to the vision. In every grove was planted every tree that would grow and thrive in that place, each balanced against the next, each placed to complement the others, for the best growing, of course, but also so that the balance would sing in the eye and the heart. Ah, the books spoke of groves to make Elders weep and laugh at the same time, groves to remain green in memory forever."

"What about the cities?" Rand asked. Loial gave him a puzzled look. "The cities. The cities the Ogier built. Here, for instance. Caemlyn. Ogier built Caemlyn, didn't you? The stories say so."

"Working with stone. . . ." His shoulders gave a massive shrug. "That was just something learned in the years after the Breaking, during the Exile, when we were still trying to find the *stedding* again. It is a fine thing, I suppose, but not the true thing. Try as you will—and I have read that the Ogier who built those cities truly did try—you cannot make stone live. A few still do work with stone, but only because you humans damage the buildings so often with your wars. There were a handful of Ogier in . . . ah . . . Cairhien, it's called now . . . when I passed through. They were from another *stedding*, luckily, so they didn't know about me, but they were still suspicious that I was Outside alone so young. I suppose it's just as well there was no reason for me to linger there. In any case, you see, working with stone is just something that was thrust on us by the weaving of the Pattern; the groves came from the heart."

Rand shook his head. Half the stories he had grown up with had just been stood on their heads. "I didn't know Ogier believed in the Pattern, Loial."

"Of course, we believe. The Wheel of Time weaves the Pattern of the Ages, and lives are the threads it weaves. No one can tell how the thread of his own life will be woven into the

Pattern, or how the thread of a people will be woven. It gave us
the Breaking of the World, and the Exile, and Stone, and the
Longing, and eventually it gave us back the *stedding* before we
all died. Sometimes I think the reason you humans are the way
you are is because your threads are so short. They must jump
around in the weaving. Oh, there, I've done it again. The Elders say you humans don't like to be reminded of how short a
time you live. I hope I didn't hurt your feelings."

Rand laughed and shook his head. "Not at all. I suppose it'd
be fun to live as long as you do, but I never really thought
about it. I guess if I live as long as old Cenn Buie, that'll be
long enough for anybody."

"He is a very old man?"

Rand just nodded. He was not about to explain that old
Cenn Buie was not quite as old as Loial.

"Well," Loial said, "perhaps you humans do have short lives,
but you do so much with them, always jumping around, always
so hasty. And you have the whole world to do it in. We Ogier
are bound to our *stedding*."

"You're Outside."

"For a time, Rand. But I must go back, eventually. This
world is yours, yours and your kind's. The *stedding* are mine.
There's too much hurly-burly Outside. And so much is changed
from what I read about."

"Well, things do change over the years. Some, anyway."

"Some? Half the cities I read about aren't even there any
longer, and most of the rest are known by different names. You
take Cairhien. The city's proper name is Al'cair'rahienallen,
Hill of the Golden Dawn. They don't even remember, for all of
the sunrise on their banners. And the grove there. I doubt if it
has been tended since the Trolloc Wars. It's just another forest,
now, where they cut firewood. The Great Trees are all gone,
and no one remembers them. And here? Caemlyn is still
Caemlyn, but they let the city grow right over the grove. We're
not a quarter of a mile from the center of it right where we
sit—from where the center of it should be. Not a tree of it left.
I've been to Tear and Illian, too. Different names, and no
memories. There's only pasture for their horses where the
grove was at Tear, and at Illian the grove is the King's park,
where he hunts his deer, and none allowed inside without his

permission. It has all changed, Rand. I fear very much that I will find the same everywhere I go. All the groves gone, all the memories gone, all the dreams dead."

"You can't give up, Loial. You can't ever give up. If you give up, you might as well be dead." Rand sank back in his chair as far as he could go, his face turning red. He expected the Ogier to laugh at him, but Loial nodded gravely instead.

"Yes, that's the way of your kind, isn't it?" The Ogier's voice changed, as if he were quoting something. "Till shade is gone, till water is gone, into the Shadow with teeth bared, screaming defiance with the last breath, to spit in Sightblinder's eye on the Last Day." Loial cocked his shaggy head expectantly, but Rand had no idea what it was he expected.

A minute went by with Loial waiting, then another, and his long eyebrows began to draw down in puzzlement. But he still waited, the silence growing uncomfortable for Rand.

"The Great Trees," Rand said finally, just for something to break that silence. "Are they like *Avendesora*?"

Loial sat up sharply; his chair squealed and cracked so loudly Rand thought it was going to come apart. "You know better than that. You, of all people."

"Me? How would I know?"

"Are you playing a joke on me? Sometimes you Aielmen think the oddest things are funny."

"What? I'm not an Aielman! I'm from the Two Rivers. I never even saw an Aielman!"

Loial shook his head, and the tufts on his ears drooped outward. "You see? Everything is changed, and half of what I know is useless. I hope I did not offend you. I'm sure your Two Rivers is a very fine place, wherever it is."

"Somebody told me," Rand said, "that it was once called Manetheren. I'd never heard it, but maybe you. . . ."

The Ogier's ears had perked up happily. "Ah! Yes. Manetheren." The tufts went down again. "There was a very fine grove there. Your pain sings in my heart, Rand al'Thor. We could not come in time."

Loial bowed where he sat, and Rand bowed back. He suspected Loial would be hurt if he did not, would think he was rude at the least. He wondered if Loial thought he had the same sort of memories the Ogier seemed to. The corners of

Loial's mouth and eyes were certainly turned down as if he were sharing the pain of Rand's loss, just as if the destruction of Manetheren were not something that happened two thousand years ago, near enough, something that Rand only knew about because of Moiraine's story.

After a time Loial sighed. "The Wheel turns," he said, "and no one knows its turning. But you have come almost as far from your home as I have. A very considerable distance, as things are now. When the Ways were freely open, of course— but that is long past. Tell me, what brings you so far? Is there something you want to see, too?"

Rand opened his mouth to say that they had come to see the false Dragon—and he could not say it. Perhaps it was because Loial acted as if he were no older than Rand, ninety years old or no ninety years old. Maybe for an Ogier ninety years was not any older than he was. It had been a long time since he had been able to really talk to anyone about what was happening. Always the fear that they might be Darkfriends, or think he was. Mat was so drawn in on himself, feeding his fears on his own suspicions, that he was no good for talking. Rand found himself telling Loial about Winternight. Not a vague story about Darkfriends; the truth about Trollocs breaking in the door, and a Fade on the Quarry Road.

Part of him was horrified at what he was doing, but it was almost as if he were two people, one trying to hold his tongue while the other only felt the relief at being able to tell it all finally. The result was that he stumbled and stuttered and jumped around in the story. Shadar Logoth and losing his friends in the night, not knowing if they were alive or dead. The Fade in Whitebridge, and Thom dying so they could escape. The Fade in Baerlon. Darkfriends later, Howal Gode, and the boy who was afraid of them, and the woman who tried to kill Mat. The Halfman outside the Goose and Crown.

When he started babbling about dreams, even the part of him that wanted to talk felt the hackles rising on the back of his neck. He bit his tongue clamping his teeth shut. Breathing heavily through his nose, he watched the Ogier warily, hoping he thought he had meant nightmares. The Light knew it all sounded like a nightmare, or enough to give anyone nightmares. Maybe Loial would just think he was going mad. Maybe. . . .

"*Ta'veren*," Loial said.

Rand blinked. "What?"

"*Ta'veren.*" Loial rubbed behind a pointed ear with one blunt finger and gave a little shrug. "Elder Haman always said I never listened, but sometimes I did. Sometimes, I listened. You know how the Pattern is woven, of course?"

"I never really thought about it," he said slowly. "It just is."

"Um, yes, well. Not exactly. You see, the Wheel of Time weaves the Pattern of the Ages, and the threads it uses are lives. It is not fixed, the Pattern, not always. If a man tries to change the direction of his life and the Pattern has room for it, the Wheel just weaves on and takes it in. There is always room for small changes, but sometimes the Pattern simply won't accept a big change, no matter how hard you try. You understand?"

Rand nodded. "I could live on the farm or in Emond's Field, and that would be a small change. If I wanted to be a king, though. . . ." He laughed, and Loial gave a grin that almost split his face in two. His teeth were white, and as broad as chisels.

"Yes, that's it. But sometimes the change chooses you, or the Wheel chooses it for you. And sometimes the Wheel bends a life-thread, or several threads, in such a way that all the surrounding threads are forced to swirl around it, and those force other threads, and those still others, and on and on. That first bending to make the Web, that is *ta'veren*, and there is nothing you can do to change it, not until the Pattern itself changes. The Web—*ta'maral'ailen*, it's called—can last for weeks, or for years. It can take in a town, or even the whole Pattern. Artur Hawkwing was *ta'veren*. So was Lews Therin Kinslayer, for that matter, I suppose." He let out a booming chuckle. "Elder Haman would be proud of me. He always droned on, and the books about traveling were much more interesting, but I did listen sometimes."

"That's all very well," Rand said, "but I don't see what it has to do with me. I'm a shepherd, not another Artur Hawkwing. And neither is Mat, or Perrin. It's just . . . ridiculous."

"I didn't say you were, but I could almost feel the Pattern

swirl just listening to you tell your tale, and I have no Talent there. You are *ta'veren,* all right. You, and maybe your friends, too." The Ogier paused, rubbing the bridge of his broad nose thoughtfully. Finally he nodded to himself as if he had reached a decision. "I wish to travel with you, Rand."

For a minute Rand stared, wondering if he had heard correctly. "With me?" he exclaimed when he could speak. "Didn't you hear what I said about . . . ?" He eyed the door suddenly. It was shut tight, and thick enough that anyone trying to listen on the other side would hear only a murmur, even with his ear pressed against the wooden panels. Just the same he went on in a lower voice. "About who's chasing me? Anyway, I thought you wanted to go see your trees."

"There is a very fine grove at Tar Valon, and I have been told the Aes Sedai keep it well tended. Besides, it is not just the groves I want to see. Perhaps you are not another Artur Hawkwing, but for a time, at least, part of the world will shape itself around you, perhaps is even now shaping itself around you. Even Elder Haman would want to see that."

Rand hesitated. It would be good to have someone else along. The way Mat was behaving, being with him was almost like being alone. The Ogier was a comforting presence. Maybe he was young as Ogier reckoned age, but he seemed as unflappable as a rock, just like Tam. And Loial had been all of those places, and knew about others. He looked at the Ogier, sitting there with his broad face a picture of patience. Sitting there, and taller sitting than most men standing. *How do you hide somebody almost ten feet tall?* He sighed and shook his head.

"I don't think that is a good idea, Loial. Even if Moiraine finds us here, we'll be in danger all the way to Tar Valon. If she does not. . . ." *If she doesn't, then she's dead and so is everyone else. Oh, Egwene.* He gave himself a shake. Egwene was not dead, and Moiraine would find them.

Loial looked at him sympathetically and touched his shoulder. "I am sure your friends are well, Rand."

Rand nodded his thanks. His throat was too tight to speak.

"Will you at least talk with me sometimes?" Loial sighed, a bass rumble. "And perhaps play a game of stones? I have not had anyone to talk to in days, except good Master Gill, and he is busy most of the time. The cook seems to run him unmercifully. Perhaps she really owns the inn?"

"Of course, I will." His voice was hoarse. He cleared his throat and tried to grin. "And if we meet in Tar Valon, you can show me the grove there." *They have to be all right. Light send they're all right.*

Loiar of the Ogier

CHAPTER
37

The Long Chase

Nynaeve gripped the reins of the three horses and peered into the night as if she could somehow pierce the darkness and find the Aes Sedai and the Warder. Skeletal trees surrounded her, stark and black in the dim moonlight. The trees and the night made an effective screen for whatever Moiraine and Lan were doing, not that either of them had paused to let her know what that was. A low "Keep the horses quiet," from Lan, and they were gone, leaving her standing like a stableboy. She glanced at the horses and sighed with exasperation.

Mandarb blended into the night almost as well as his master's cloak. The only reason the battle-trained stallion was letting her get this close was because Lan had handed her the reins himself. He seemed calm enough now, but she remembered all too well the lips drawing back silently when she reached for his bridle without waiting for Lan's approval. The silence had made the bared teeth seem that much more dangerous. With a last wary look at the stallion, she turned to peer in the direction the other two had gone, idly stroking her own horse. She gave a startled jump when Aldieb pushed a pale muzzle under her hand, but after a minute she gave the white mare a pat, too.

"No need to take it out on you, I suppose," she whispered, "just because your mistress is a cold-faced—" She strained at the darkness again. *What were they doing?*

After leaving Whitebridge they had ridden through villages

that seemed unreal in their normality, ordinary market villages that seemed to Nynaeve unconnected to a world that had Fades and Trollocs and Aes Sedai. They had followed the Caemlyn Road, until at last Moiraine sat forward in Aldieb's saddle, peering eastward as if she could see the whole length of the great highway, all the many miles to Caemlyn, and see, too, what waited there.

Eventually the Aes Sedai let out a long breath and settled back. "The Wheel weaves as the Wheel wills," she murmured, "but I cannot believe it weaves an end to hope. I must first take care of that of which I can be certain. It will be as the Wheel weaves." And she turned her mare north, off the road into the forest. One of the boys was in that direction with the coin Moiraine had given him. Lan followed.

Nynaeve gave a long last look at the Caemlyn Road. Few people shared the roadway with them there, a couple of high-wheeled carts and one empty wagon in the distance, a handful of folk afoot with their belongings on their backs or piled on pushcarts. Some of those were willing to admit they were on their way to Caemlyn to see the false Dragon, but most denied it vehemently, especially those who had come through White-bridge. At Whitebridge she had begun to believe Moiraine. Somewhat. More, at any rate. And there was no comfort in that.

The Warder and the Aes Sedai were almost out of sight through the trees before she started after them. She hurried to catch up. Lan looked back at her frequently, and waved for her to come on, but he kept at Moiraine's shoulder, and the Aes Sedai had her eyes fixed ahead.

One evening after they left the road, the invisible trail failed. Moiraine, the unflappable Moiraine, suddenly stood up beside the small fire where the tea kettle was boiling, her eyes widen-ing. "It is gone," she whispered at the night.

"He is . . . ?" Nynaeve could not finish the question. *Light, I don't even know which one it is!*

"He did not die," the Aes Sedai said slowly, "but he no longer has the token." She sat down, her voice level and her hands steady as she took the kettle off the flames and tossed in a handful of tea. "In the morning we will keep on as we've been going. When I get close enough, I can find him without the coin."

As the fire burned down to coals, Lan rolled himself in his cloak and went to sleep. Nynaeve could not sleep. She watched the Aes Sedai. Moiraine had her eyes closed, but she sat upright, and Nynaeve knew she was awake.

Long after the last glow had faded from the coals, Moiraine opened her eyes and looked at her. She could feel the Aes Sedai's smile even in the dark. "He has regained the coin, Wisdom. All will be well." She lay down on her blankets with a sigh and almost at once was breathing deep in slumber.

Nynaeve had a hard time joining her, tired as she was. Her mind conjured up the worst no matter how she tried to stop it. *All will be well.* After Whitebridge, she could no longer make herself believe that so easily.

Abruptly Nynaeve was jerked from memory back to the night; there really was a hand on her arm. Stifling the cry that rose in her throat, she fumbled for the knife at her belt, her hand closing on the hilt before she realized that the hand was Lan's.

The Warder's hood was thrown back, but his chameleon-like cloak blended so well with the night that the dim blur of his face seemed to hang suspended in the night. The hand on her arm appeared to come out of thin air.

She drew a shuddering breath. She expected him to comment on how easily he had come on her unaware, but instead he turned to dig into his saddlebags. "You are needed," he said, and knelt to fasten hobbles on the horses.

As soon as the horses were secured, he straightened, grasped her hand, and headed off into the night again. His dark hair fit into the night almost as well as his cloak, and he made even less noise than she did. Grudgingly she had to admit that she could never have followed him through the darkness without his grip as a guide. She was not certain she could pull loose if he did not want to release her, anyway; he had very strong hands.

As they came up on a small rise, barely enough to be called a hill, he sank to one knee, pulling her down beside him. It took her a moment to see that Moiraine was there, too. Unmoving, the Aes Sedai could have passed for a shadow in her dark cloak. Lan gestured down the hillside to a large clearing in the trees.

Nynaeve frowned in the dim moonlight, then suddenly smiled in understanding. Those pale blurs were tents in regular rows, a darkened encampment.

"Whitecloaks," Lan whispered, "two hundred of them, maybe more. There's good water down there. And the lad we're after."

"In the camp?" She felt, more than saw, Lan nod.

"In the middle of it. Moiraine can point right to him. I went close enough to see he's under guard."

"A prisoner?" Nynaeve said. "Why?"

"I don't know. The Children should not be interested in a village boy, not unless there was something to make them suspicious. The Light knows it doesn't take much to make Whitecloaks suspicious, but it still worries me."

"How are you going to free him?" It was not until he glanced at her that she realized how much assurance there had been in her that he could march into the middle of two hundred men and come back with the boy. *Well, he is a Warder. Some of the stories must be true.*

She wondered if he was laughing at her, but his voice was flat and businesslike. "I can bring him out, but he'll likely be in no shape for stealth. If we're seen, we may find two hundred Whitecloaks on our heels, and us riding double. Unless they are too busy to chase us. Are you willing to take a chance?"

"To help an Emond's Fielder? Of course! What kind of chance?"

He pointed into the darkness again, beyond the tents. This time she could make out nothing but shadows. "Their horselines. If the picket-ropes are cut, not all the way through, but enough so they'll break when Moiraine creates a diversion, the Whitecloaks will be too busy chasing their own horses to come after us. There are two guards on that side of the camp, beyond the picket-lines, but if you are half as good as I think you are, they'll never see you."

She swallowed hard. Stalking rabbits was one thing; guards, though, with spears and swords. . . . *So he thinks I'm good, does he?* "I'll do it."

Lan nodded again, as if he had expected no less. "One other

thing. There are wolves about, tonight. I saw two, and if I saw that many, there are probably more." He paused, and though his voice did not change she had the feeling he was puzzled. "It was almost as if they wanted me to see them. Anyway, they shouldn't bother you. Wolves usually stay away from people."

"I wouldn't have known that," she said sweetly. "I only grew up around shepherds." He grunted, and she smiled into the darkness.

"We'll do it now, then," he said.

Her smile faded as she peered down at the camp full of armed men. Two hundred men with spears and swords and. . . . Before she could reconsider, she eased her knife in its sheath and started to slip away. Moiraine caught her arm in a grip almost as strong as Lan's.

"Take care," the Aes Sedai said softly. "Once you cut the ropes, return as quickly as you can. You are a part of the Pattern, too, and I would not risk you, any more than any of the others, if the whole world was not at risk in these days."

Nynaeve rubbed her arm surreptitiously when Moiraine released it. She was not about to let the Aes Sedai know the grip had hurt. But Moiraine turned back to watching the camp below as soon as she let go. And the Warder was gone, Nynaeve realized with a start. She had not heard him leave. *Light blind the bloody man!* Quickly she tied her skirts up to give her legs freedom, and hurried into the night.

After that first rush, with fallen branches cracking under her feet, she slowed down, glad there was no one there to see her blush. The idea was to be quiet, and she was not in any kind of competition with the Warder. *Oh, no?*

She shook off the thought and concentrated on making her way through the dark woods. It was not hard in and of itself; the faint light of the waning moon was more than enough for anyone who had been taught by her father, and the ground had a slow, easy roll. But the trees, bare and stark against the night sky, constantly reminded her that this was no childhood game, and the keening wind sounded all too much like Trolloc horns. Now that she was alone in the darkness, she remembered that the wolves that usually ran away from people had been behaving differently in the Two Rivers this winter.

Relief flooded through her like warmth when she finally

caught the smell of horses. Almost holding her breath, she got down on her stomach and crawled upwind, toward the smell.

She was nearly on the guards before she saw them, marching toward her out of the night, white cloaks flapping in the wind and almost shining in the moonlight. They might as well have carried torches; torchlight could not have made them much more visible. She froze, trying to make herself a part of the ground. Nearly in front of her, not ten paces away, they marched to a halt with a stomp of feet, facing each other, spears shouldered. Just beyond them she could make out shadows that had to be the horses. The stable smell, horse and manure, was strong.

"All is well with the night," one white-cloaked shape announced. "The Light illumine us, and protect us from the Shadow."

"All is well with the night," the other replied. "The Light illumine us, and protect us from the Shadow."

With that they turned and marched off into the darkness again.

Nynaeve waited, counting to herself while they made their circuit twice. Each time they took exactly the same count, and each time they rigidly repeated the same formula, not a word more or less. Neither so much as glanced to one side; they stared straight ahead as they marched up, then marched away. She wondered if they would have noticed her even if she had been standing up.

Before the night swallowed the pale swirls of their cloaks a third time, she was already on her feet, running in a crouch toward the horses. As she came close, she slowed so as not to startle the animals. The Whitecloak guards might not see what was not shoved under their noses, but they would certainly investigate if the horses suddenly began whickering.

The horses along the picket-lines—there was more than one row—were barely realized masses in the darkness, heads down. Occasionally one snorted or stamped a foot in its sleep. In the dim moonlight she was nearly on the endpost of the picket-line before she saw it. She reached for the picket-line, and froze when the nearest horse raised its head and looked at her. Its single lead-rein was tied in a big loop around the thumb-thick line that ended at the post. *One whinny.* Her heart tried to

pound its way out of her chest, sounding loud enough to bring
the guards.

Never taking her eyes off the horse, she sliced at the picket-
rope, feeling in front of her blade to see how far she had cut.
The horse tossed its head, and her breath went cold. *Just one
whinny.*

Only a few thin strands of hemp remained whole under her
fingers. Slowly she headed toward the next line, watching the
horse until she could no longer see if it was looking at her or
not, then drew a ragged breath. If they were all like that, she
did not think she would last.

At the next picket-rope, though, and the next, and the next,
the horses remained asleep, even when she cut her thumb and
bit off a yelp. Sucking the cut, she looked warily back the way
she had come. Upwind as she was, she could no longer hear the
guards make their exchange, but they might have heard her if
they were in the right place. If they were coming to see what
the noise had been, the wind would keep her from hearing
them until they were right on top of her. *Time to go. With four
horses out of five running loose, they won't be chasing anyone.*

But she did not move. She could imagine Lan's eyes when he
heard what she had done. There would be no accusation in
them; her reasoning was sound, and he would not expect any
more of her. She was a Wisdom, not a bloody great invincible
Warder who could make himself all but invisible. Jaw set, she
moved to the last picket-line. The first horse on it was Bela.

There was no mistaking that squat, shaggy shape; for there to
be another horse like that, here and now, was too big a coinci-
dence. Suddenly she was so glad that she had not left off this
last line that she was shaking. Her arms and legs trembled so
that she was afraid to touch the picket-rope, but her mind was
as clear as the Winespring Water. Whichever of the boys was in
the camp, Egwene was there, too. And if they left riding double, some of the Children would catch them no matter how well
the horses were scattered, and some of them would die. She
was as certain as if she were listening to the wind. That stuck a
spike of fear into her belly, fear of *how* she was certain. This
had nothing to do with weather or crops or sickness. *Why did
Moiraine tell me I can use the Power? Why couldn't she leave me
alone?*

Strangely, the fear stilled her trembling. With hands as steady as if she were grinding herbs in her own house she slit the picket-rope as she had the others. Thrusting the dagger back into its sheath, she untied Bela's lead-rein. The shaggy mare woke with a start, tossing her head, but Nynaeve stroked her nose and spoke comforting words softly in her ear. Bela gave a low snort and seemed content.

Other horses along that line were awake, too, and looking at her. Remembering Mandarb, she reached hesitantly to the next lead-rein, but that horse gave no objection to a strange hand. Indeed, it seemed to want some of the muzzle-stroking that Bela had received. She gripped Bela's rein tightly and wrapped the other around her other wrist, all the while watching the camp nervously. The pale tents were only thirty yards off, and she could see men moving among them. If they noticed the horses stirring and came to see what caused it. . . .

Desperately she wished for Moiraine not to wait on her return. Whatever the Aes Sedai was going to do, let her do it now. *Light, make her do it now, before.* . . .

Abruptly lightning shattered the night overhead, for a moment obliterating darkness. Thunder smote her ears, so hard she thought her knees would buckle, as a jagged trident stabbed the ground just beyond the horses, splashing dirt and rocks like a fountain. The crash of riven earth fought the thunderstroke. The horses went mad, screaming and rearing; the picket-ropes snapped like thread where she had cut them. Another lightning bolt sliced down before the image of the first faded.

Nynaeve was too busy to exult. At the first clash Bela jerked one way while the other horse reared away in the opposite direction. She thought her arms were being pulled out of their sockets. For an endless minute she hung suspended between the horses, her feet off the ground, her scream flattened by the second crash. Again the lightning struck, and again, and again, in one continuous, raging roar from the heavens. Balked in the way they wanted to go, the horses surged back, letting her drop. She wanted to crouch on the ground and soothe her tortured shoulders, but there was no time. Bela and the other horse buffeted her, eyes rolling wildly till only whites showed, threatening to knock her down and trample her. Somehow she made her arms lift, clutched her hands in Bela's mane, pulled herself onto the heaving mare's back. The other rein was still around her wrist, pulled tight into the flesh.

Her jaw dropped as a long, gray shadow snarled past, seeming to ignore her and the horses with her, but teeth snapping at the crazed animals now darting in every direction. A second shadow of death followed close behind. Nynaeve wanted to scream again, but nothing came out. *Wolves! Light help us! What is Moiraine doing?*

The heels she dug into Bela's sides were not needed. The mare ran, and the other was more than happy to follow. Anywhere, so long as they could run, so long as they could escape the fire from the sky that killed the night.

Wolves! What is Moiraine doing?

CHAPTER
38

Rescue

Perrin shifted as best he could with his wrists bound behind him and finally gave up with a sigh. Every rock he avoided brought him two more. Awkwardly he tried to work his cloak back over him. The night was cold, and the ground seemed to draw all the heat out of him, as it had every night since the Whitecloaks took them. The Children did not think prisoners needed blankets, or shelter. Especially not dangerous Darkfriends.

Egwene lay huddled against his back for warmth, sleeping the deep sleep of exhaustion. She never even murmured at his shifting. The sun was long hours below the horizon, and he ached from head to foot after a day walking behind a horse with a halter around his neck, but sleep would not come for him.

The column did not move that fast. With most of their remounts lost to the wolves in the *stedding*, the Whitecloaks could not push on as hard as they wanted; the delay was another thing they held against the Emond's Fielders. The sinuous double line did move steadily, though—Lord Bornhald meant to reach Caemlyn in time for whatever it was—and always in the back of Perrin's mind was the fear that if he fell the Whitecloak holding his leash would not stop, no matter Lord Captain Bornhald's orders to keep them alive for the Questioners in Amador. He knew he could not save himself if that happened; the only times they freed his hands were when he was fed and for visits to the latrine pit. The halter made every step momentous, every rock underfoot potentially fatal. He walked with muscles tense, scanning the ground with anxious eyes. Whenever he glanced at Egwene, she was doing the same. When she met his eyes, her face was tight and frightened. Neither of them dared take their eyes off the ground long enough for more than a glance.

Usually he collapsed like a wrung-out rag as soon as the Whitecloaks let him stop, but tonight his mind was racing. His skin crawled with dread that had been building for days. If he closed his eyes, he would see only the things Byar promised for them once they reached Amador.

He was sure Egwene still did not believe what Byar told them in that flat voice. If she did, she would not be able to sleep no matter how tired she was. In the beginning he had not believed Byar either. He still did not want to; people just did not do things like that to other people. But Byar did not really threaten; as if he were talking about getting a drink of water he talked about hot irons and pincers, about knives slicing away skin and needles piercing. He did not appear to be trying to frighten them. There was never even a touch of gloating in his eyes. He just did not care if they were frightened or not, if they were tortured or not, if they were alive or not. That was what brought cold sweat to Perrin's face once it got through to him. That was what finally convinced him Byar was telling the simple truth.

The two guards' cloaks gleamed grayly in the faint moonlight. He could not make out their faces, but he knew they were watching. As if they could try something, tied hand and foot the way they were. From when there had still been light enough to see, he remembered the disgust in their eyes and the pinched looks on their faces, as though they had been set to guard filth-soaked monsters, stinking and repellent to look at. All the Whitecloaks looked at them that way. It never changed. *Light, how do I make them believe we aren't Darkfriends when they're already convinced we are?* His stomach twisted sickeningly. In the end, he would probably confess to anything just to make the Questioners stop.

Someone was coming, a Whitecloak carrying a lantern. The man stopped to speak with the guards, who answered respectfully. Perrin could not hear what was said, but he recognized the tall, gaunt shape.

He squinted as the lantern was held close to his face. Byar had Perrin's axe in his other hand; he had appropriated the weapon as his own. At least, Perrin never saw him without it.

"Wake up," Byar said emotionlessly, as if he thought Perrin slept with his head raised. He accompanied the words with a heavy kick in the ribs.

Perrin gave a grunt through gritted teeth. His sides were a mass of bruises already from Byar's boots.

"I said, wake up." The foot went back again, and Perrin spoke quickly.

"I'm awake." You had to acknowledge what Byar said, or he found ways to get your attention.

Byar set the lantern on the ground and bent to check his bonds. The man jerked roughly at his wrist, twisting his arms in their sockets. Finding those knots still as tight as he had left them, Byar pulled at his ankle rope, scraping him across the rocky ground. The man looked too skeletal to have any strength, but Perrin might as well have been a child. It was a nightly routine.

As Byar straightened, Perrin saw that Egwene was still asleep. "Wake up!" he shouted. "Egwene! Wake up!"

"Wha . . . ? What?" Egwene's voice was frightened and still thick with sleep. She lifted her head, blinking in the lantern light.

Byar gave no sign of disappointment at not being able to kick her awake; he never did. He just jerked at her ropes the same way he had Perrin's, ignoring her groans. Causing pain was another of those things that seemed not to affect him one way or another; Perrin was the only one he really went out of his way to hurt. Even if Perrin could not remember it, Byar remembered that he had killed two of the Children.

"Why should Darkfriends sleep," Byar said dispassionately, "when decent men must stay awake to guard them?"

"For the hundredth time," Egwene said wearily, "we aren't Darkfriends."

Perrin tensed. Sometimes such a denial brought a lecture delivered in a grating near monotone, on confession and repentance, leading into a description of the Questioners' methods of obtaining them. Sometimes it brought the lecture and a kick. To his surprise, this time Byar ignored it.

Instead the man squatted in front of him, all angles and sunken hollows, with the axe across his knees. The golden sun on his cloak's left breast, and the two golden stars beneath it, glittered in the lantern light. Taking off his helmet, he set it beside the lantern. For a change there was something besides disdain or hatred on his face, something intent and unreadable. He rested his arms on the axehandle and studied Perrin silently. Perrin tried not to shift under that hollow-eyed stare.

"You are slowing us down, Darkfriend, you and your wolves. The Council of the Anointed has heard reports of such things, and they want to know more, so you must be taken to Amador and given to the Questioners, but you are slowing us down. I had hoped we could move fast enough, even without the remounts, but I was wrong." He fell silent, frowning at them.

Perrin waited; Byar would tell him when he was ready.

"The Lord Captain is caught in the cleft of a dilemma," Byar said finally. "Because of the wolves he must take you to the Council, but he must reach Caemlyn, too. We have no spare horses to carry you, but if we continue to let you walk, we will not reach Caemlyn by the appointed time. The Lord Captain sees his duties with a single-minded vision, and he intends to see you before the Council."

Egwene made a sound. Byar was staring at Perrin, and he stared back, almost afraid to blink. "I don't understand," he said slowly.

"There is nothing to understand," Byar replied. "Nothing but idle speculation. If you escaped, we would not have time to track you down. We don't have an hour to spare if we are to reach Caemlyn in time. If you frayed your ropes on a sharp rock, say, and vanished into the night, the Lord Captain's problem would be solved." Never taking his gaze from Perrin, he reached under his cloak and tossed something on the ground.

Automatically Perrin's eyes followed it. When he realized what it was, he gasped. A rock. A split rock with a sharp edge.

"Just idle speculation," Byar said. "Your guards tonight also speculate."

Perrin's mouth was suddenly dry. *Think it through! Light help me, think it through and don't make any mistakes!*

Could it be true? Could the Whitecloaks' need to get to Caemlyn quickly be important enough for this? Letting suspected Darkfriends escape? There was no use trying that way; he did not know enough. Byar was the only Whitecloak who would talk to them, aside from Lord Captain Bornhald, and neither was exactly free with information. Another way. If Byar wanted them to escape, why not simply cut their bonds? If Byar wanted them to escape? Byar, who was convinced to his marrow that they were Darkfriends. Byar, who hated Darkfriends worse than he did the Dark One himself. Byar, who looked for any excuse to cause him pain because he had killed two Whitecloaks. *Byar* wanted them to escape?

If he had thought his mind was racing before, now it sped like an avalanche. Despite the cold, sweat ran down his face in rivulets. He glanced at the guards. They were only shadows of pale gray, but it seemed to him that they were poised, waiting. If he and Egwene were killed trying to escape, and their ropes had been cut on a rock that could have been lying there by chance. . . . The Lord Captain's dilemma would be solved, all right. And Byar would have them dead, the way he wanted them.

The gaunt man picked up his helmet from beside the lantern and started to stand.

"Wait," Perrin said hoarsely. His thoughts tumbled over and over as he searched in vain for some way out. "Wait, I want to talk. I—"

Help comes!

The thought blossomed in his mind, a clear burst of light in the midst of chaos, so startling that for a moment he forgot everything else, even where he was. Dapple was alive. *Elyas,* he thought at the wolf, demanding without words to know if the man was alive. An image came back. Elyas, lying on a bed of evergreen branches beside a small fire in a cave, tending a wound in his side. It all took only an instant. He gaped at Byar, and his face broke into a foolish grin. Elyas was alive. Dapple was alive. Help was coming.

Byar paused, risen only to a crouch, looking at him. "Some thought has come to you, Perrin of the Two Rivers, and I would know what it is."

For a moment Perrin thought he meant the thought from

Dapple. Panic fled across his face, followed by relief. Byar could not possibly know.

Byar watched his changes of expression, and for the first time the Whitecloak's eyes went to the rock he had tossed on the ground.

He was reconsidering, Perrin realized. If he changed his mind about the rock, would he dare risk leaving them alive to talk? Ropes could be frayed after the people wearing them were dead, even if it made for risk of discovery. He looked into Byar's eyes—the shadowed hollows of the man's eye sockets made them appear to stare at him from dark caves—and he saw death decided.

Byar opened his mouth, and as Perrin waited for sentence to be pronounced, things began to happen too fast for thought.

Suddenly one of the guards vanished. One minute there were two dim shapes, the next the night swallowed one of them. The second guard turned, the beginning of a cry on his lips, but before the first syllable was uttered there was a solid *tchunk* and he toppled over like a felled tree.

Byar spun, swift as a striking viper, the axe whirling in his hands so fast that it hummed. Perrin's eyes bulged as the night seemed to flow into the lantern light. His mouth opened to yell, but his throat locked tight with fear. For an instant he even forgot that Byar wanted to kill them. The Whitecloak was another human being, and the night had come alive to take them all.

Then the darkness invading the light became Lan, cloak swirling through shades of gray and black as he moved. The axe in Byar's hands lashed out like lightning . . . and Lan seemed to lean casually aside, letting the blade pass so close he must have felt the wind of it. Byar's eyes widened as the force of his blow carried him off balance, as the Warder struck with hands and feet in rapid succession, so quick that Perrin was not sure what he had just seen. What he was sure of was Byar collapsing like a puppet. Before the falling Whitecloak had finished settling to the ground, the Warder was on his knees extinguishing the lantern.

In the sudden return to darkness, Perrin stared blindly. Lan seemed to have vanished again.

"Is it really . . . ?" Egwene gave a stifled sob. "We thought you were dead. We thought you were all dead."

"Not yet." The Warder's deep whisper was tinged with amusement.

Hands touched Perrin, found his bonds. A knife sliced through the ropes with barely a tug, and he was free. Aching muscles protested as he sat up. Rubbing his wrists, he peered at the graying mound that marked Byar. "Did you . . . ? Is he . . . ?"

"No," Lan's voice answered quietly from the darkness. "I do not kill unless I mean to. But he won't bother anyone for a while. Stop asking questions and get a pair of their cloaks. We do not have much time."

Perrin crawled to where Byar lay. It took an effort to touch the man, and when he felt the Whitecloak's chest rising and falling he almost jerked his hands away. His skin crawled as he made himself unfasten the white cloak and pull it off. Despite what Lan said, he could imagine the skull-faced man suddenly rearing up. Hastily he fumbled around till he found his axe, then crawled to another guard. It seemed strange, at first, that he felt no reluctance to touch this unconscious man, but the reason came to him. All the Whitecloaks hated him, but that was a human emotion. Byar felt nothing beyond that he should die; there was no hate in it, no emotion at all.

Gathering the two cloaks in his arms, he turned—and panic grabbed him. In the darkness he suddenly had no sense of direction, of how to find his way back to Lan and the others. His feet rooted to the ground, afraid to move. Even Byar was hidden by the night without his white cloak. There was nothing by which to orient himself. Any way he went might be out into the camp.

"Here."

He stumbled toward Lan's whisper until hands stopped him. Egwene was a dim shadow, and Lan's face was a blur; the rest of the Warder seemed not to be there at all. He could feel their eyes on him, and he wondered if he should explain.

"Put on the cloaks," Lan said softly. "Quickly. Bundle your own. And make no sound. You aren't safe yet."

Hurriedly Perrin passed one of the cloaks to Egwene, relieved at being saved from having to tell of his fear. He made his own cloak into a bundle to carry, and swung the white cloak around his shoulders in its place. He felt a prickle as it settled around his shoulders, a stab of worry between his shoulder blades. Was it Byar's cloak he had ended up with? He almost thought he could smell the gaunt man on it.

Lan directed them to hold hands, and Perrin gripped his axe in one hand and Egwene's hand with the other, wishing the Warder would get on with their escape so he could stop his imagination from running wild. But they just stood there, surrounded by the tents of the Children, two shapes in white cloaks and one that was sensed but not seen.

"Soon," Lan whispered. "Very soon."

Lightning broke the night above the camp, so close that Perrin felt the hair on his arms, his head, lifting as the bolt charged the air. Just beyond the tents the earth erupted from the blow, the explosion on the ground merging with that in the sky. Before the light faded Lan was leading them forward.

At their first step another strike sliced open the blackness. Lightning came like hail, so that the night flickered as if the darkness were coming in momentary flashes. Thunder drummed wildly, one roar rumbling into the next, one continuous, rippling peal. Fear-stricken horses screamed, their whinnies drowned except for moments when the thunder faded. Men tumbled out of their tents, some in their white cloaks, some only half clothed, some dashing to and fro, some standing as if stunned.

Through the middle of it Lan pulled them at a trot, Perrin bringing up the rear. Whitecloaks looked at them, wild-eyed, as they passed. A few shouted at them, the shouts lost in the pounding from the heavens, but with their white cloaks gathered around them no one tried to stop them. Through the tents, out of the camp and into the night, and no one raised a hand against them.

The ground turned uneven under Perrin's feet, and brush slapped at him as he let himself be drawn along. The lightning flickered fitfully and was gone. Echoes of thunder rolled across the sky before they, too, faded away. Perrin looked over his shoulder. A handful of fires burned back there, among the tents. Some of the lightning must have struck home, or perhaps men had knocked over lamps in their panic. Men still shouted, voices tiny in the night, trying to restore order, to find out what had happened. The land began to slope upwards, and tents and fires and shouting were left behind.

Suddenly he almost trod on Egwene's heels as Lan stopped. Ahead in the moonlight stood three horses.

A shadow stirred, and Moiraine's voice came, weighted with irritation. "Nynaeve has not returned. I fear that young woman has done something foolish." Lan spun on his heel as if to return the way they had come, but a single whip-crack word from Moiraine halted him. "No!" He stood looking at her sideways, only his face and hands truly visible, and they but dimly shadowed blurs. She went on in a gentler tone; gentler but no less firm. "Some things are more important than others. You know that." The Warder did not move, and her voice hardened again. "Remember your oaths, al'Lan Mandragoran, Lord of the Seven Towers! What of the oath of a Diademed Battle Lord of the Malkieri?"

Perrin blinked. Lan was all of that? Egwene was murmuring, but he could not take his eyes off the tableau in front of him, Lan standing like a wolf from Dapple's pack, a wolf at bay before the diminutive Aes Sedai and vainly seeking escape from doom.

The frozen scene was broken by a crash of breaking branches in the woods. In two long strides Lan was between Moiraine and the sound, the pale moonlight rippling along his sword. To the crackle and snap of underbrush a pair of horses burst from the trees, one with a rider.

"Bela!" Egwene exclaimed at the same time that Nynaeve said from the shaggy mare's back, "I almost didn't find you again. Egwene! Thank the Light you're alive!"

She slid down off Bela, but as she started toward the Emond's Fielders Lan caught her arm and she stopped short, staring up at him.

"We must go, Lan," Moiraine said, once more sounding unruffled, and the Warder released his grip.

Nynaeve rubbed her arm as she hurried to hug Egwene, but Perrin thought he heard her give a low laugh, too. It puzzled him because he did not think it had anything to do with her happiness at seeing them again.

"Where are Rand and Mat?" he asked.

"Elsewhere," Moiraine replied, and Nynaeve muttered something in a sharp tone that made Egwene gasp. Perrin blinked; he had caught the edge of a wagoneer's oath, and a coarse one. "The Light send they are well," the Aes Sedai went on as if she had not noticed.

"We will none of us be well," Lan said, "if the Whitecloaks find us. Change your cloaks, and get mounted."

Perrin scrambled up onto the horse Nynaeve had brought behind Bela. The lack of a saddle did not hamper him; he did not ride often at home, but when he did it was more likely bareback than not. He still carried the white cloak, now rolled up and tied to his belt. The Warder said they must leave no more traces for the Children to find than they could help. He still thought he could smell Byar on it.

As they started out, the Warder leading on his tall black stallion, Perrin felt Dapple's touch on his mind once more. *One day again.* More a feeling than words, it sighed with the promise of a meeting foreordained, with anticipation of what was to come, with resignation to what was to come, all streaked in layers. He tried to ask when and why, fumbling in haste and sudden fear. The trace of the wolves grew fainter, fading. His frantic questions brought only the same heavy-laden answer. *One day again.* It hung haunting in his mind long after awareness of the wolves winked out.

Lan pressed southward slowly but steadily. The night-draped wilderness, all rolling ground and underbrush hidden until it was underfoot, shadowed trees thick against the sky, allowed no great speed in any case. Twice the Warder left them, riding back toward the slivered moon, he and Mandarb becoming one with the night behind. Both times he returned to report no sign of pursuit.

Egwene stayed close beside Nynaeve. Soft-spoken scraps of excited talk floated back to Perrin. Those two were as buoyed up as if they had found home again. He hung back at the tail of their little column. Sometimes the Wisdom turned in her saddle to look back at him, and each time he gave her a wave, as if to say that he was all right, and stayed where he was. He had a lot to think about, though he could not get any of it straight in his head. *What was to come. What was to come?*

Perrin thought it could not be much short of dawn when

Moiraine finally called a halt. Lan found a gully where he could build a fire hidden within a hollow in one of the banks.

Finally they were allowed to rid themselves of the white cloaks, burying them in a hole dug near the fire. As he was about to toss in the cloak he had used, the embroidered golden sun on the breast caught his eye, and the two golden stars beneath. He dropped the cloak as if it stung and walked away, scrubbing his hands on his coat, to sit alone.

"Now," Egwene said, once Lan was shoveling dirt into the hole, "will somebody tell me where Rand and Mat are?"

"I believe they are in Caemlyn," Moiraine said carefully, "or on their way there." Nynaeve gave a loud, disparaging grunt, but the Aes Sedai went on as if she had not been interrupted. "If they are not, I will yet find them. That I promise."

They made a quiet meal on bread and cheese and hot tea. Even Egwene's enthusiasm succumbed to weariness. The Wisdom produced an ointment from her bag for the weals the ropes had left on Egwene's wrists, and a different one for her other bruises. When she came to where Perrin sat on the edge of the firelight, he did not look up.

She stood looking at him silently for a time, then squatted with her bag beside her, saying briskly, "Take your coat and shirt off, Perrin. They tell me one of the Whitecloaks took a dislike to you."

He complied slowly, still half lost in Dapple's message, until Nynaeve gasped. Startled, he stared at her, then at his own bare chest. It was a mass of color, the newer, purple blotches overlaying older ones faded into shades of brown and yellow. Only thick slabs of muscle earned by hours at Master Luhhan's forge had saved him from broken ribs. With his mind filled by the wolves, he had managed to forget the pain, but he was reminded of it now, and it came back gladly. Involuntarily he took a deep breath, and clamped his lips on a groan.

"How could he have disliked you so much?" Nynaeve asked wonderingly.

I killed two men. Aloud, he said, "I don't know."

She rummaged in her bag, and he flinched when she began spreading a greasy ointment over his bruises. "Ground ivy, five-finger, and sunburst root," she said.

It was hot and cold at the same time, making him shiver

while he broke into a sweat, but he did not protest. He had had experience of Nynaeve's ointments and poultices before. As her fingers gently rubbed the mixture in, the heat and cold vanished, taking the pain with them. The purple splotches faded to brown, and the brown and yellow paled, some disappearing altogether. Experimentally, he took a deep breath; there was barely a twinge.

"You look surprised," Nynaeve said. She looked a little surprised herself, and strangely frightened. "Next time, you can go to *her*."

"Not surprised," he said soothingly, "just glad." Sometimes Nynaeve's ointments worked fast and sometimes slow, but they always worked. "What . . . what happened to Rand and Mat?"

Nynaeve began stuffing her vials and pots back into her bag, jamming each one in as if she were thrusting it through a barrier. "*She* says they're all right. *She* says we'll find them. In Caemlyn, *she* says. *She* says it's too important for us not to, whatever *that* means. *She* says a great many things."

Perrin grinned in spite of himself. Whatever else had changed, the Wisdom was still herself, and she and the Aes Sedai were still far from fast friends.

Abruptly Nynaeve stiffened, staring at his face. Dropping her bag, she pressed the backs of her hands to his cheeks and forehead. He tried to pull back, but she caught his head in both hands and thumbed back his eyelids, peering into his eyes and muttering to herself. Despite her small size she held his face easily; it was never easy to get away from Nynaeve when she did not want you to.

"I don't understand," she said finally, releasing him and settling back to sit on her heels. "If it was yelloweye fever, you wouldn't be able to stand. But you don't have any fever, and the whites of your eyes aren't yellowed, just the irises."

"Yellow?" Moiraine said, and Perrin and Nynaeve both jumped where they sat. The Aes Sedai's approach had been utterly silent. Egwene was asleep by the fire, wrapped in her cloaks, Perrin saw. His own eyelids wanted to slide closed.

"It isn't anything," he said, but Moiraine put a hand under his chin and turned his face up so she could peer into his eyes the way Nynaeve had. He jerked away, prickling. The two women were handling him as if he were a child. "I said it isn't anything."

"There was no foretelling this." Moiraine spoke as if to herself. Her eyes seemed to look at something beyond him. "Something ordained to be woven, or a change in the Pattern? If a change, by what hand? The Wheel weaves as the Wheel wills. It must be that."

"Do you know what it is?" Nynaeve asked reluctantly, then hesitated. "Can you do something for him? Your Healing?" The request for aid, the admission that she could do nothing, came out of her as if dragged.

Perrin glared at both the women. "If you're going to talk about me, talk to me. I'm sitting right here." Neither looked at him.

"Healing?" Moiraine smiled. "Healing can do nothing about this. It is not an illness, and it will not. . . ." She hesitated briefly. She did glance at Perrin, then, a quick look that regretted many things. The look did not include him, though, and he muttered sourly as she turned back to Nynaeve. "I was going to say it will not harm him, but who can say what the end will be? At least I can say it will not harm him directly."

Nynaeve stood, dusting off her knees, and confronted the Aes Sedai eye to eye. "That's not good enough. If there's something wrong with—"

"What is, is. What is woven already is past changing." Moiraine turned away abruptly. "We must sleep while we can and leave at first light. If the Dark One's hand grows too strong. . . . We must reach Caemlyn quickly."

Angrily, Nynaeve snatched up her bag and stalked off before Perrin could speak. He started to growl an oath, but a thought hit him like a blow and he sat there gaping silently. Moiraine knew. The Aes Sedai knew about the wolves. And she thought it could be the Dark One's doing. A shiver ran through him. Hastily he shrugged back into his shirt, tucking it in awkwardly, and pulled his coat and cloak back on. The clothing did not help very much; he felt chilled right down to his bones, his marrow like frozen jelly.

Lan dropped to the ground cross-legged, tossing back his cloak. Perrin was glad of that. It was unpleasant, looking at the Warder and having his eyes slide past.

For a long moment they simply stared at one another. The hard planes of the Warder's face were unreadable, but in his eyes Perrin thought he saw . . . something. Sympathy? Curiosity? Both?

"You know?" he said, and Lan nodded.

"I know some, not all. Did it just come to you, or did you meet a guide, an intermediary?"

"There was a man," Perrin said slowly. *He knows, but does he think the same as Moiraine?* "He said his name was Elyas. Elyas Machera." Lan drew a deep breath, and Perrin looked at him sharply. "You know him?"

"I knew him. He taught me much, about the Blight, and about this." Lan touched his sword hilt. "He was a Warder, before . . . before what happened. The Red Ajah. . . ." He glanced to where Moiraine was, lying before the fire.

It was the first time Perrin could remember any uncertainty in the Warder. At Shadar Logoth Lan had been sure and strong, and when he was facing Fades and Trollocs. He was not afraid now—Perrin was convinced of that—but he was wary, as if he might say too much. As if what he said could be dangerous.

"I've heard of the Red Ajah," he told Lan.

"And most of what you've heard is wrong, no doubt. You must understand, there are . . . factions within Tar Valon. Some would fight the Dark One one way, some another. The goal is the same, but the differences . . . the differences can mean lives changed, or ended. The lives of men or nations. He is well, Elyas?"

"I think so. The Whitecloaks said they killed him, but Dapple—" Perrin glanced at the Warder uncomfortably. "I don't know." Lan seemed to accept that he did not, reluctantly, and it emboldened him to go on. "This communicating with the wolves. Moiraine seems to think it's something the . . . something the Dark One did. It isn't, is it?" He would not believe Elyas was a Darkfriend.

But Lan hesitated, and sweat started on Perrin's face, chill beads made colder by the night. They were sliding down his cheeks by the time the Warder spoke.

"Not in itself, no. Some believe it is, but they are wrong; it was old and lost long before the Dark One was found. But what of the chance involved, blacksmith? Sometimes the Pattern has a randomness to it—to our eyes, at least—but what chance that you should meet a man who could guide you in this thing, and you one who could follow the guiding? The Pattern is forming a Great Web, what some call the Lace of Ages, and you lads are central to it. I don't think there is much chance left in your lives, now. Have you been chosen out, then? And if so, by the Light, or by the Shadow?"

"The Dark One can't touch us unless we name him." Immediately Perrin thought of the dreams of Ba'alzamon, the dreams that were more than dreams. He scrubbed the sweat off his face. "He can't."

"Rock-hard stubborn," the Warder mused. "Maybe stubborn enough to save yourself, in the end. Remember the times we live in, blacksmith. Remember what Moiraine Sedai told you. In these times many things are dissolving, and breaking apart. Old barriers weaken, old walls crumble. The barriers between what is and what was, between what is and what will be." His voice turned grim. "The walls of the Dark One's prison. This may be the end of an Age. We may see a new Age born before we die. Or perhaps it is the end of Ages, the end of time itself. The end of the world." Suddenly he grinned, but his grin was as dark as a scowl; his eyes sparkled merrily, laughing at the foot of the gallows. "But that's not for us to worry about, eh, blacksmith? We'll fight the Shadow as long as we have breath, and if it overruns us, we'll go under biting and clawing. You Two Rivers folk are too stubborn to surrender. Don't you worry whether the Dark One has stirred in your life. You are back among friends, now. Remember, the Wheel weaves as the Wheel wills, and even the Dark One cannot change that, not with Moiraine to watch over you. But we had better find your friends soon."

"What do you mean?"

"They have no Aes Sedai touching the True Source to protect them. Blacksmith, perhaps the walls have weakened enough for the Dark One himself to touch events. Not with a free hand, or we'd be done already, but maybe tiny shiftings in the threads. A chance turning of one corner instead of another, a chance meeting, a chance word, or what seems like chance, and they could be so far under the Shadow not even Moiraine could bring them back."

"We have to find them," Perrin said, and the Warder gave a grunt of a laugh.

"What have I been saying? Get some sleep, blacksmith." Lan's cloak swung back around him as he stood. In the faint light from fire and moon he seemed almost part of the shadows beyond. "We have a hard few days to Caemlyn. Just you pray we find them there."

"But Moiraine . . . she can find them anywhere, can't she? She says she can."

"But can she find them in time? If the Dark One is strong enough to take a hand himself, time is running out. You pray we find them in Caemlyn, blacksmith, or we may all be lost."

CHAPTER

39

Weaving of the Web

Rand looked down on the crowds from the high window of his room in The Queen's Blessing. They ran shouting along the street, all streaming in the same direction, waving pennants and banners, the white lion standing guard on a thousand fields of red. Caemlyners and outlanders, they ran together, and for a change no one appeared to want to bash anyone else's head. Today, maybe, there was only one faction.

He turned from the window grinning. Next to the day when Egwene and Perrin walked in, alive and laughing over what they had seen, this was the day he had been waiting for most.

"Are you coming?" he asked again.

Mat glowered from where he lay curled up in a ball on his bed. "Take that Trolloc you're so friendly with."

"Blood and ashes, Mat, he's not a Trolloc. You're just being stubborn stupid. How many times do you want to have this argument? Light, it's not as if you'd never heard of Ogier before."

"I never heard they looked like Trollocs." Mat pushed his face into his pillow and curled himself tighter.

"Stubborn stupid," Rand muttered. "How long are you going to hide up here? I'm not going to keep bringing you your meals up all those stairs forever. You could do with a bath, too." Mat shrugged around on the bed as if he were trying to burrow deeper into it. Rand sighed, then went to the door. "Last chance to go together, Mat. I'm leaving now." He closed the door slowly, hoping that Mat would change his mind, but his friend did not stir. The door clicked shut.

In the hallway, he leaned against the doorframe. Master Gill said there was an old woman two streets over, Mother Grubb, who sold herbs and poultices, besides birthing babies, tending the sick, and telling fortunes. She sounded a little like a Wisdom. Nynaeve was who Mat needed, or maybe Moiraine, but Mother Grubb was who he had. Bringing her to The Queen's Blessing might bring the wrong kind of attention as well, though, if she would even come. For her as well as for Mat and him.

Herbalists and hedge-doctors were lying low in Caemlyn right now; there was talk against anyone who did any kind of healing, or fortunetelling. Every night the Dragon's Fang was scrawled on doors with a free hand, sometimes even in the daylight, and people might forget who had cured their fevers and poulticed their toothaches when the cry of Darkfriend went up. That was the temper in the city.

It was not as if Mat were really sick. He ate everything Rand carried up from the kitchen—he would take nothing from anyone else's hand, though—and never complained about aches or fever. He just refused to leave the room. But Rand had been sure today would bring him out.

He settled his cloak on his shoulders and hitched his sword belt around so the sword, and the red cloth wrapped around it, was covered more.

At the foot of the stairs he met Master Gill just starting up. "There's someone been asking after you in the city," the innkeeper said around his pipe. Rand felt a surge of hope. "Asking after you and those friends of yours, by name. You younglings, anyway. Seems to want you three lads most."

Anxiety replaced hope. "Who?" Rand asked. He still could not help glancing up and down the hall. Except for they two, it was empty, from the exit into the alley to the common room door.

"Don't know his name. Just heard about him. I hear most things in Caemlyn, eventually. Beggar." The innkeeper grunted. "Half mad, I hear. Even so, he could take the Queen's Bounty at the Palace, even with things as hard as they are. On High Days, the Queen gives it out with her own hands, and there's never anyone turned away for any reason. No one needs to beg in Caemlyn. Even a man under warrant can't be arrested while he's taking the Queen's Bounty."

"A Darkfriend?" Rand said reluctantly. *If the Darkfriends know our names.* . . .

"You've got Darkfriends on the brain, young fellow. They're around, certainly, but just because the Whitecloaks have everybody stirred up is no reason for you to think the city's full of them. Do you know what rumor those idiots have started now? 'Strange shapes.' Can you believe it? Strange shapes creeping around outside the city in the night." The innkeeper chuckled till his belly shook.

Rand did not feel like laughing. Hyam Kinch had talked about strange shapes, and there had surely enough been a Fade back there. "What kind of shapes?"

"What kind? I don't know what kind. Strange shapes. Trollocs, probably. The Shadowman. Lews Therin Kinslayer himself, come back fifty feet high. What kind of shapes do you *think* people will imagine now the idea's in their heads? It's none of our worry." Master Gill eyed him for a moment. "Going out, are you? Well, I can't say I care for it, myself, even today, but there's hardly anybody left here but me. Not your friend?"

"Mat's not feeling very well. Maybe later."

"Well, be that as it may. You watch yourself, now. Even today good Queen's men will be outnumbered out there, Light burn the day I ever thought to see it so. Best you leave by the alleyway. There's two of those blood-be-damned traitors sitting across the street watching my front door. They know where I stand, by the Light!"

Rand stuck his head out and looked both ways before slipping into the alley. A bulky man Master Gill had hired stood at the head of the alley, leaning on a spear and watching the people run past with an apparent lack of interest. It was only apparent, Rand knew. The fellow—his name was Lamgwin—saw everything through those heavy-lidded eyes, and for all his bullish bulk he could move like a cat. He also thought Queen Morgase was the Light made flesh, or near enough. There were a dozen like him scattered around The Queen's Blessing.

Lamgwin's ear twitched when Rand reached the mouth of

the alley, but he never took his disinterest off the street. Rand knew the man had heard him coming.

"Watch your back today, man." Lamgwin's voice sounded like gravel in a pan. "When the trouble starts, you'll be a handy one to have here, not somewhere with a knife in your back."

Rand glanced at the blocky man, but his surprise was muted. He always tried to keep the sword out of sight, but this was not the first time one of Master Gill's men had assumed he would know his way in a fight. Lamgwin did not look back at him. The man's job was guarding the inn, and he did it.

Pushing his sword back a little further under his cloak, Rand joined the flow of people. He saw the two men the innkeeper had mentioned, standing on upturned barrels across the street from the inn so they could see over the crowd. He did not think they noticed him coming out of the alley. They made no secret of their allegiance. Not only were their swords wrapped in white tied with red, they wore white armbands and white cockades on their hats.

He had not been in Caemlyn long before learning that red wrappings on a sword, or a red armband or cockade, meant support for Queen Morgase. White said the Queen and her involvement with Aes Sedai and Tar Valon were to blame for everything that had gone wrong. For the weather, and the failed crops. Maybe even for the false Dragon.

He did not want to get involved in Caemlyn politics. Only, it was too late, now. It was not just that he had already chosen—by accident, but there it was. Matters in the city had gone beyond letting anyone stay neutral. Even outlanders wore cockades and armbands, or wrapped their swords, and more wore the white than the red. Maybe some of them did not think that way, but they were far from home and that was the way sentiment was running in Caemlyn. Men who supported the Queen went about in groups for their own protection, when they went out at all.

Today, though, it was different. On the surface, at least. Today, Caemlyn celebrated a victory of the Light over the Shadow. Today the false Dragon was being brought into the city, to be displayed before the Queen before he was taken north to Tar Valon.

No one talked about that part of it. No one but the Aes

Sedai could deal with a man who could actually wield the One
Power, of course, but no one wanted to talk about it. The Light
had defeated the Shadow, and soldiers from Andor had been in
the forefront of the battle. For today, that was all that was
important. For today, everything else could be forgotten.
Or could it, Rand wondered. The crowd ran, singing and
waving banners, laughing, but men displaying the red kept together in knots of ten or twenty, and there were no women or
children with them. He thought there were at least ten men
showing white for every one proclaiming allegiance to the
Queen. Not for the first time, he wished white cloth had been
the cheaper. *But would Master Gill have helped if you'd been
showing the white?*
The crowd was so thick that jostling was inevitable. Even
Whitecloaks did not enjoy their little open spaces in the throng
today. As Rand let the crowd carry him toward the Inner City,
he realized that not all animosities were being reined in. He
saw one of the Children of the Light, one of three, bumped so
hard he almost fell. The Whitecloak barely caught himself and
started an angry oath at the man who had bumped him when
another man staggered him with a deliberate, aimed shoulder.
Before matters could go any further the Whitecloak's companions pulled him over to the side of the street to where they
could shelter in a doorway. The three seemed caught between
their normal glaring stare and disbelief. The crowd streamed on
by as if none had noticed, and perhaps none had.
No one would have dared do such a thing two days earlier.
More, Rand realized, the men who had done the bumping wore
white cockades on their hats. It was widely believed the Whitecloaks supported those who opposed the Queen and her Aes
Sedai advisor, but that made no difference. Men were doing
things of which they had never before thought. Jostling a
Whitecloak, today. Tomorrow, perhaps pulling down a Queen?
Suddenly he wished there were a few more men close to him
showing red; jostled by white cockades and armbands, he
abruptly felt very alone.
The Whitecloaks noticed him looking at them and stared
back as if meeting a challenge. He let a singing swirl in the
crowd sweep him out of their sight, and joined in their song.

"Forward the Lion,
forward the Lion,
the White Lion takes the field.
Roar defiance at the Shadow.
Forward the Lion,
forward, Andor triumphant."

The route that would bring the false Dragon into Caemlyn was well known. Those streets themselves were kept clear by solid lines of the Queen's Guards and red-cloaked pikemen, but people packed the edges of them shoulder to shoulder, even the windows and the rooftops. Rand worked his way into the Inner City, trying to get closer to the Palace. He had some thought of actually seeing Logain displayed before the Queen. To see the false Dragon and a Queen, both . . . that was something he had never dreamed of back home.

The Inner City was built on hills, and much of what the Ogier had made still remained. Where streets in the New City mostly ran every which way in a crazy-quilt, here they followed the curves of the hills as if they were a natural part of the earth. Sweeping rises and dips presented new and surprising vistas at every turn. Parks seen from different angles, even from above, where their walks and monuments made patterns pleasing to the eye though barely touched with green. Towers suddenly revealed, tile-covered walls glittering in the sunlight with a hundred changing colors. Sudden rises where the gaze was thrown out across the entire city to the rolling plains and forests beyond. All in all, it would have been something to see if not for the crowd that hurried him along before he had a chance to really take it in. And all those curving streets made it impossible to see very far ahead.

Abruptly he was swept around a bend, and there was the Palace. The streets, even following the natural contours of the land, had been laid out to spiral in on this—this gleeman's tale of pale spires and golden domes and intricate stonework traceries, with the banner of Andor waving from every prominence, a centerpiece for which all the other vistas had been designed. It seemed more sculpted by an artist than simply built like ordinary buildings.

That glimpse showed him he would get no nearer. No one was being allowed close to the Palace. Queen's Guards made scarlet ranks ten deep flanking the Palace gates. Along the tops of the white walls, on high balconies and towers, more Guards stood rigidly straight, bows precisely slanted across breastplated chests. They, too, looked like something out of a gleeman's tale, a guard of honor, but Rand did not believe that was why they were there. The clamoring crowd lining the streets was almost solid with white-wrapped swords, white armbands, and white cockades. Only here and there was the white wall broken by a knot of red. The red-uniformed guards seemed a thin barrier against all that white.

Giving up on making his way closer to the Palace, he sought a place where he could use his height to advantage. He did not have to be in the front row to see everything. The crowd shifted constantly, people shoving to get nearer the front, people hurrying off to what they thought was a better vantage point. In one of those shifts he found himself only three people from the open street, and all in front of him were shorter than he, including the pikemen. Almost everyone was. People crowded against him from both sides, sweating from the press of so many bodies. Those behind him muttered about not being able to see, and tried to wriggle past. He stood his ground, making an impervious wall with those to either side. He was content. When the false Dragon passed by, he would be close enough to see the man's face clearly.

Across the street and down toward the gates to the New City, a ripple passed through the tight-packed crowd; around the curve, an eddy of people was drawing back to let something go by. It was not like the clear space that followed Whitecloaks on any day but today. These people jerked themselves back with startled glances that became grimaces of distaste. Pressing themselves out of the way, they turned their faces from whatever it was, but watched out of the corners of their eyes until it was past.

Other eyes around him noted the disturbance, too. Keyed for the coming of the Dragon but with nothing to do now but wait, the crowd found anything at all worthy of comment. He heard speculation ranging from an Aes Sedai to Logain himself, and a

few coarser suggestions that brought rough laughter from the
men and disdainful sniffs from the women.

The ripple meandered through the crowd, drawing closer to
the edge of the street as it came. No one seemed to hesitate in
letting it go where it wanted, even if that meant losing a good
spot for viewing as the crowd flowed back in on itself behind
the passing. Finally, directly across from Rand, the crowd
bulged into the street, pushing aside red-cloaked pikemen who
struggled to shove them back, and broke open. The stooped
shape that shuffled hesitantly out into the open looked more
like a pile of filthy rags than a man. Rand heard murmurs of
disgust around him.

The ragged man paused on the far edge of the street. His
cowl, torn and stiff with dirt, swung back and forth as if searching for something, or listening. Abruptly he gave a wordless cry
and flung out a dirty claw of a hand, pointing straight at Rand.
Immediately he began to scuttle across the street like a bug.

The beggar. Whatever ill chance had led the man to find him
like this, Rand was suddenly sure that, Darkfriend or not, he
did not want to meet him face-to-face. He could feel the beggar's eyes, like greasy water on his skin. Especially he did not
want the man close to him here, surrounded by people balanced on the brink of violence. The same voices that had
laughed before now cursed him as he pushed his way back,
away from the street.

He hurried, knowing the densely packed mass through which
he had to shove and wriggle would give way before the filthy
man. Struggling to force a path through the crowd, he staggered and almost fell when he abruptly broke free. Flailing his
arms to keep his balance he turned the stagger into a run. People pointed at him; he was the only one not pressing the other
way, and running at that. Shouts followed him. His cloak
flapped behind him, exposing his red-clad sword. When he realized that, he ran faster. A lone supporter of the Queen, running, could well spark a white-cockaded mob to pursuit, even
today. He ran, letting his long legs eat paving stones. Not until
the shouts were left far behind did he allow himself to collapse
against a wall, panting.

He did not know where he was, except that he was still

within the Inner City. He could not remember how many twists and turns he had taken along those curving streets. Poised to run again, he looked back the way he had come. Only one person moved on the street, a woman walking placidly along with her shopping basket. Almost everyone in the city was gathered for a glimpse of the false Dragon. *He can't have followed me. I must have left him behind.*

The beggar would not give up; he was sure of it, though he could not say why. That ragged shape would be working its way through the crowds at that very minute, searching, and if Rand returned to see Logain he ran the risk of a meeting. For a moment he considered going back to The Queen's Blessing, but he was sure he would never get another chance to see a Queen, and he hoped he would never have another to see a false Dragon. There seemed to be something cowardly in letting a bent beggar, even a Darkfriend, chase him into hiding.

He looked around, considering. The way the Inner City was laid out, buildings were kept low, if there were buildings at all, so that someone standing at a particular spot would have nothing to interrupt the planned view. There had to be places from where he could see the procession pass with the false Dragon. Even if he could not see the Queen, he could see Logain. Suddenly determined, he set off.

In the next hour he found several such places, every last one already packed cheek-to-cheek with people avoiding the crush along the procession route. They were a solid front of white cockades and armbands. No red at all. Thinking what the sight of his sword might do in a crowd like that, he slipped away carefully, and quickly.

Shouting floated up from the New City, cries and the blaring of trumpets, the martial beat of drums. Logain and his escort were already in Caemlyn, already on their way to the Palace.

Dispirited, he wandered the all but empty streets, still half-heartedly hoping to find some way to see Logain. His eyes fell on the slope, bare of buildings, rising above the street where he was walking. In a normal spring the slope would be an expanse of flowers and grass, but now it was brown all the way to the high wall along its crest, a wall over which the tops of trees were visible.

This part of the street had not been designed for any grand

view, but just ahead, over the rooftops, he could see some of
the Palace spires, topped by White Lion banners fluttering in
the wind. He was not sure exactly where the curve of the street
ran after it rounded the hill beyond his sight, but he suddenly
had a thought about that hilltop wall.

The drums and trumpets were drawing nearer, the shouting
growing louder. Anxiously he scrambled up the slope. It was
not meant to be climbed, but he dug his boots into the dead sod
and pulled himself up using leafless shrubs as handholds. Panting as much with desire as effort, he scrambled the last yards to
the wall. It reared above him, easily twice his height and more.
The air thundered with the drumbeat, rang with trumpet blasts.

The face of the wall had been left much in the natural state
of the stone, the huge blocks fitted together so well that the
joins were nearly invisible, the roughness making it seem almost a natural cliff. Rand grinned. The cliffs just beyond the
Sand Hills were higher, and even Perrin had climbed those. His
hands sought rocky knobs, his booted feet found ridges. The
drums raced him as he climbed. He refused to let them win. He
would reach the top before they reached the Palace. In his
haste, the stone tore his hands and scraped his knees through
his breeches, but he flung his arms over the top and heaved
himself up with a sense of victory.

Hastily he twisted himself around to a seat on the flat, narrow top of the wall. The leafy branches of a towering tree stuck
out over his head, but he had no thought for that. He looked
across tiled rooftops, but from the wall his line of sight was
clear. He leaned out, just a little, and could see the Palace
gate, and the Queen's Guards drawn up there, and the expectant crowd. Expectant. Their shouts drowned out by the
thunder of drums and trumpets, but waiting still. He grinned. *I
won.*

Even as he settled in place, the first part of the procession
rounded the final curve before the Palace. Twenty ranks of
trumpeters came first, splitting the air with peal after triumphant peal, a fanfare of victory. Behind them, as many drum-
mers thundered. Then came the banners of Caemlyn, white
lions on red, borne by mounted men, followed by the soldiers
of Caemlyn, rank on rank on rank of horsemen, armor gleaming, lances proudly held, crimson pennants fluttering. Treble

rows of pikemen and archers flanked them, and came on and on after the horsemen began passing between the waiting Guards and through the Palace gates.

The last of the foot soldiers rounded the curve, and behind them was a massive wagon. Sixteen horses pulled it in hitches of four. In the center of its flat bed was a large cage of iron bars, and on each corner of the wagonbed sat two women, watching the cage as intently as if the procession and the crowd did not exist. Aes Sedai, he was certain. Between the wagon and the footmen, and to either side, rode a dozen Warders, their cloaks swirling and tangling the eye. If the Aes Sedai ignored the crowd, the Warders scanned it as if there were no other guards but they.

With all of that, it was the man in the cage who caught and held Rand's eyes. He was not close enough to see Logain's face, as he had wanted to, but suddenly he thought he was as close as he cared for. The false Dragon was a tall man, with long, dark hair curling around his broad shoulders. He held himself upright against the sway of the wagon with one hand on the bars over his head. His clothes seemed ordinary, a cloak and coat and breeches that would not have caused comment in any farming village. But the way he wore them. The way he held himself. Logain was a king in every inch of him. The cage might as well not have been there. He held himself erect, head high, and looked over the crowd as if they had come to do him honor. And wherever his gaze swept, there the people fell silent, staring back in awe. When Logain's eyes left them, they screamed with redoubled fury as if to make up for their silence, but it made no difference in the way the man stood, or in the silence that passed along with him. As the wagon rolled through the Palace gates, he turned to look back at the assembled masses. They howled at him, beyond words, a wave of sheer animal hate and fear, and Logain threw back his head and laughed as the Palace swallowed him.

Other contingents followed behind the wagons, with banners representing more who had fought and defeated the false Dragon. The Golden Bees of Illian, the three White Crescents of Tear, the Rising Sun of Cairhien, others, many others, of nations and of cities, and of great men with their own trumpets, their own drums to thunder their grandeur. It was anticlimactic after Logain.

Rand leaned out a bit further to try to catch one last sight of the caged man. *He* was *defeated, wasn't he? Light, he wouldn't be in a bloody cage if he wasn't defeated.*

Overbalanced, he slipped and grabbed at the top of the wall, pulled himself back to a somewhat safer seat. With Logain gone, he became aware of the burning in his hands, where the stone had scraped his palms and fingers. Yet he could not shake free of the images. The cage and the Aes Sedai. Logain, undefeated. No matter the cage, that had not been a defeated man. He shivered and rubbed his stinging hands on his thighs.

"Why were the Aes Sedai watching him?" he wondered aloud.

"They're keeping him from touching the True Source, silly."

He jerked to look up, toward the girl's voice, and suddenly his precarious seat was gone. He had only time to realize that he was toppling backward, falling, when something struck his head and a laughing Logain chased him into spinning darkness.

Logain Ablar

CHAPTER
40

The Web Tightens

I t seemed to Rand that he was sitting at table with Logain and Moiraine. The Aes Sedai and the false Dragon sat watching him silently, as if neither knew the other was there. Abruptly he realized the walls of the room were becoming indistinct, fading off into gray. A sense of urgency built in him. Everything was going, blurring away. When he looked back to the table, Moiraine and Logain had vanished, and Ba'alzamon sat there instead. Rand's whole body vibrated with urgency; it hummed inside his head, louder and louder. The hum became the pounding of blood in his ears.

With a jerk he sat up, and immediately groaned and clutched his head, swaying. His whole skull hurt; his left hand found sticky dampness in his hair. He was sitting on the ground, on green grass. That troubled him, vaguely, but his head spun and everything he looked at lurched, and all he could think of was lying down until it stopped.

The wall! The girl's voice!

Steadying himself with one hand flat on the grass, he looked around slowly. He had to do it slowly; when he tried to turn his head quickly everything started whirling again. He was in a garden, or a park; a slate-paved walk meandered by through flowering bushes not six feet away, with a white stone bench beside it and a leafy arbor over the bench for shade. He *had* fallen inside the wall. *And the girl?*

He found the tree, close behind his back, and found her

too—climbing down out of it. She reached the ground and
turned to face him, and he blinked and groaned again. A deep
blue velvet cloak lined with pale fur rested on her shoulders, its
hood hanging down behind to her waist with a cluster of silver
bells at the peak. They jingled when she moved. A silver fil-
igree circlet held her long, red-gold curls, and delicate silver
rings hung at her ears, while a necklace of heavy silver links
and dark green stones he thought were emeralds lay around her
throat. Her pale blue dress was smudged with bark stains from
her tree climbing, but it was still silk, and embroidered with
painstakingly intricate designs, the skirt slashed with inserts the
color of rich cream. A wide belt of woven silver encircled her
waist, and velvet slippers peeked from under the hem of her
dress.

He had only ever seen two women dressed in this fashion,
Moiraine and the Darkfriend who had tried to kill Mat and
him. He could not begin to imagine who would choose to climb
trees in clothes like that, but he was sure she had to be someone important. The way she was looking at him redoubled the
impression. She did not seem in the least troubled at having a
stranger tumble into her garden. There was a self-possession
about her that made him think of Nynaeve, or Moiraine.

He was so enmeshed in worrying whether or not he had gotten himself into trouble, whether or not she was someone who
could and would call the Queen's Guards even on a day when
they had other things to occupy them, that it took him a few
moments to see past the elaborate clothes and lofty attitude to
the girl herself. She was perhaps two or three years younger
than he, tall for a girl, and beautiful, her face a perfect oval
framed by that mass of sunburst curls, her lips full and red, her
eyes bluer than he could believe. She was completely different
from Egwene in height and face and body, but every bit as
beautiful. He felt a twinge of guilt, but told himself that denying what his eyes saw would not bring Egwene safely to
Caemlyn one whit faster.

A scrabbling sound came from up in the tree and bits of bark
fell, followed by a boy dropping lightly to the ground behind
her. He was a head taller than she and a little older, but his
face and hair marked him as her close kin. His coat and cloak
were red and white and gold, embroidered and brocaded, and

for a male even more ornate than hers. That increased Rand's anxiety. Only on a feastday would any ordinary man dress in anything like that, and never with that much grandeur. This was no public park. Perhaps the Guards were too busy to bother with trespassers.

The boy studied Rand over the girl's shoulder, fingering the dagger at his waist. It seemed more a nervous habit than any thought that he might use it. Not completely, though. The boy had the same self-possession as the girl, and they both looked at him as if he were a puzzle to be solved. He had the odd feeling that the girl, at least, was cataloguing everything about him from the condition of his boots to the state of his cloak.

"We will never hear the end of this, Elayne, if mother finds out," the boy said suddenly. "She told us to stay in our rooms, but you just had to get a look at Logain, didn't you? Now look what it has got us."

"Be quiet, Gawyn." She was clearly the younger of the two, but she spoke as though she took it for granted that he would obey. The boy's face struggled as if he had more to say, but to Rand's surprise he held his peace. "Are you all right?" she said suddenly.

It took-Rand a minute to realize she was speaking to him. When he did, he tried to struggle to his feet. "I'm fine. I just—" He tottered, and his legs gave way. He sat back down hard. His head swam. "I'll just climb back over the wall," he muttered. He attempted to stand again, but she put a hand on his shoulder, pressing him down. He was so dizzy the slight pressure was enough to hold him in place.

"You *are* hurt." Gracefully she knelt beside him. Her fingers gently parted the blood-matted hair on the left side of his head. "You must have struck a branch coming down. You will be lucky if you didn't break anything more than your scalp. I don't think I ever saw anyone as skillful at climbing as you, but you don't do so well falling."

"You'll get blood on your hands," he said, drawing back.

Firmly she pulled his head back to where she could get at it. "Hold still." She did not speak sharply, but again there was that note in her voice as if she expected to be obeyed. "It does not look *too* bad, thank the Light." From pockets on the inside of her cloak she began taking out an array of tiny vials and twisted packets of paper, finishing with a handful of wadded bandage.

He stared at the collection in amazement. It was the sort of thing he would have expected a Wisdom to carry, not someone dressed as she was. She had gotten blood on her fingers, he saw, but it did not seem to bother her.

"Give me your water flask, Gawyn," she said. "I need to wash this."

The boy she called Gawyn unfastened a leather bottle from his belt and handed it to her, then squatted easily at Rand's feet with his arms folded on his knees. Elayne went about what she was doing in a very workmanlike manner. He did not flinch at the sting of cold water when she washed the cut in his scalp, but she held the top of his head with one hand as if she expected him to try to pull away again and would have none of it. The ointment she smoothed on after, from one of her small vials, soothed almost as much as one of Nynaeve's preparations would have.

Gawyn smiled at him as she worked, a calming smile, as if he, too, expected Rand to jerk away and maybe even run. "She's always finding stray cats and birds with broken wings. You are the first human being she has had to work on." He hesitated, then added, "Do not be offended. I am not calling you a stray." It was not an apology, just a statement of fact.

"No offense taken," Rand said stiffly. But the pair were acting as if he were a skittish horse.

"She does know what she is doing," Gawyn said. "She has had the best teachers. So do not fear, you are in good hands."

Elayne pressed some of the bandaging against his temple and pulled a silk scarf from her belt, blue and cream and gold. For any girl in Emond's Field it would have been a treasured feast-day cloth. Elayne deftly began winding it around his head to hold the wad of bandage in place.

"You can't use that," he protested.

She went on winding. "I told you to hold still," she said calmly.

Rand looked at Gawyn. "Does she always expect everybody to do what she tells them?"

A flash of surprise crossed the young man's face, and his

mouth tightened with amusement. "Most of the time she does. And most of the time they do."

"Hold this," Elayne said. "Put your hand there while I tie—" She exclaimed at the sight of his hands. "You did not do that falling. Climbing where you should not have been climbing is more like it." Quickly finishing her knot, she turned his hands palms upward in front of him, muttering to herself about how little water was left. The washing made the lacerations burn, but her touch was surprisingly delicate. "Hold still, this time."

The vial of ointment was produced again. She spread it thinly along the scrapes, all of her attention apparently on rubbing it in without hurting him. A coolness spread through his hands, as if she were rubbing the torn places away.

"Most of the time they do exactly what she says," Gawyn went on with an affectionate grin at the top of her head. "Most people. Not Mother, of course. Or Elaida. And not Lini. Lini was her nurse. You can't give orders to someone who switched you for stealing figs when you were little. And even not so little." Elayne raised her head long enough to give him a dangerous look. He cleared his throat and carefully blanked his expression before hurrying on. "And Gareth, of course. No one gives orders to Gareth."

"Not even Mother," Elayne said, bending her head back over Rand's hands. "She makes suggestions, and he always does what she suggests, but I've never heard her give him a command." She shook her head.

"I don't know why that always surprises you," Gawyn answered her. "Even you don't try telling Gareth what to do. He's served three Queens and been Captain-General, and First Prince Regent, for two. I daresay there are some think he's more a symbol of the Throne of Andor than the Queen is."

"Mother should go ahead and marry him," she said absently. Her attention was on Rand's hands. "She wants to; she can't hide it from me. And it would solve so many problems."

Gawyn shook his head. "One of them must bend first. Mother cannot, and Gareth will not."

"If she commanded him. . . ."

"He would obey. I think. But she won't. You know she won't."

Abruptly they turned to stare at Rand. He had the feeling

they had forgotten he was there. "Who . . . ?" He had to stop
to wet his lips. "Who is your mother?"

Elayne's eyes widened in surprise, but Gawyn spoke in an
ordinary tone that made his words all the more jarring. "Morgase, by the Grace of the Light, Queen of Andor, Defender of
the Realm, Protector of the People, High Seat of the House
Trakand."

"The Queen," Rand muttered, shock spreading through him
in waves of numbness. For a minute he thought his head was
going to begin spinning again. *Don't attract any attention. Just
fall into the Queen's garden and let the Daughter-Heir tend your
cuts like a hedge-doctor.* He wanted to laugh, and knew it for
the fringes of panic.

Drawing a deep breath, he scrambled hastily to his feet. He
held himself tightly in rein against the urge to run, but the need
to get away filled him, to get away before anyone else discovered him there.

Elayne and Gawyn watched him calmly, and when he leaped
up they rose gracefully, not hurried in the least. He put up a
hand to pull the scarf from his head, and Elayne seized his
elbow. "Stop that. You will start the bleeding again." Her
voice was still calm, still sure that he would do as he was told.

"I have to go," Rand said. "I'll just climb back over the wall
and—"

"You really didn't know." For the first time she seemed as
startled as he was. "Do you mean you climbed up on that wall
to see Logain without even knowing where you were? You
could have gotten a much better view down in the streets."

"I . . . I don't like crowds," he mumbled. He sketched a bow
to each of them. "If you'll pardon me, ah . . . my Lady." In the
stories, royal courts were full of people all calling one another
Lord and Lady and Royal Highness and Majesty, but if he had
ever heard the correct form of address for the Daughter-Heir,
he could not think clearly enough to remember. He could not
think clearly about anything beyond the need to be far away.
"If you will pardon me, I'll just leave now. Ah . . . thank you
for the. . . ." He touched the scarf around his head. "Thank
you."

"Without even telling us your name?" Gawyn said. "A poor
payment for Elayne's care. I've been wondering about you.

You sound like an Andorman, though not a Caemlyner, certainly, but you look like. . . . Well, you know our names. Courtesy would suggest you give us yours." ·

Looking longingly at the wall, Rand gave his right name before he thought what he was doing, and even added, "From Emond's Field, in the Two Rivers."

"From the west," Gawyn murmured. "Very far to the west." Rand looked around at him sharply. There had been a note of surprise in the young man's voice, and Rand caught some of it still on his face when he turned. Gawyn replaced it with a pleasant smile so quickly, though, that he almost doubted what he had seen.

"Tabac and wool," Gawyn said. "I have to know the principal products of every part of the Realm. Of every land, for that matter. Part of my training. Principal products and crafts, and what the people are like. Their customs, their strengths and weaknesses. It's said Two Rivers people are stubborn. They can be led, if they think you are worthy, but the harder you try to push them, the harder they dig in. Elayne ought to choose her husband from there. It'll take a man with a will like stone to keep from being trampled by her."

Rand stared at him. Elayne was staring, too. Gawyn looked as much under control as ever, but he was babbling. *Why?*

"What's this?"

All three of them jumped at the sudden voice, and spun to face it.

The young man who stood there was the handsomest man Rand had ever seen, almost too handsome for masculinity. He was tall and slender, but his movements spoke of whipcord strength and a sure confidence. Dark of hair and eye, he wore his clothes, only a little less elaborate in red and white than Gawyn's, as if they were of no importance. One hand rested on his sword hilt, and his eyes were steady on Rand.

"Stand away from him, Elayne," the man said. "You, too, Gawyn."

Elayne stepped in front of Rand, between him and the newcomer, head high and as confident as ever. "He is a loyal subject of our mother, and a good Queen's man. And he is under my protection, Galad."

Rand tried to remember what he had heard from Master

Kinch, and since from Master Gill. Galadedrid Damodred was Elayne's half-brother, Elayne's and Gawyn's, if he remembered correctly; the three shared the same father. Master Kinch might not have liked Taringail Damodred too well—neither did anyone else that he had heard—but the son was well thought of by wearers of the red and the white alike, if talk in the city was any guide.

"I am aware of your fondness for strays, Elayne," the slender man said reasonably, "but the fellow is armed, and he hardly looks reputable. In these days, we cannot be too careful. If he's a loyal Queen's man, what is he doing here where he does not belong? It is easy enough to change the wrappings on a sword, Elayne."

"He is here as my guest, Galad, and I vouch for him. Or have you appointed yourself my nurse, to decide whom I may talk to, and when?"

Her voice was rich with scorn, but Galad seemed unmoved. "You know I make no claims for control over your actions, Elayne, but this . . . guest of yours is not proper, and you know that as well as I. Gawyn, help me convince her. Our mother would—"

"Enough!" Elayne snapped. "You are right that you have no say over my actions, nor have you any right to judge them. You may leave me. Now!"

Galad gave Gawyn a rueful look; at one and the same time it seemed to ask for help while saying that Elayne was too headstrong to be helped. Elayne's face darkened, but just as she opened her mouth again, he bowed, in all formality yet with the grace of a cat, took a step back, then turned and strode down the paved path, his long legs carrying him quickly out of sight beyond the arbor.

"I hate him," Elayne breathed. "He is vile and full of envy."

"There you go too far, Elayne," Gawyn said. "Galad does not know the meaning of envy. Twice he has saved my life, with none to know if he held his hand. If he had not, he would be your First Prince of the Sword in my place."

"Never, Gawyn. I would choose anyone before Galad. Anyone. The lowest stableboy." Suddenly she smiled and gave her brother a mock-stern look. "You say I am fond of giving orders. Well, I command you to let nothing happen to you. I command you to be my First Prince of the Sword when I take the throne—the Light send that day is far off!—and to lead the armies of Andor with the sort of honor Galad cannot dream of."

"As you command, my Lady." Gawyn laughed, his bow a parody of Galad's.

Elayne gave Rand a thoughtful frown. "Now we must get you out of here quickly."

"Galad always does the right thing," Gawyn explained, "even when he should not. In this case, finding a stranger in the gardens, the right thing is to notify the Palace guards. Which I suspect he is on his way to do right this minute."

"Then it's time I was back over the wall," Rand said. *A fine day for going unnoticed! I might as well carry a sign!* He turned to the wall, but Elayne caught his arm.

"Not after the trouble I went to with your hands. You'll only make fresh scrapes and then let some back-alley crone put the Light knows what on them. There is a small gate on the other side of the garden. It's overgrown, and no one but me even remembers it's there."

Suddenly Rand heard boots pounding toward them over the slate paving stones.

"Too late," Gawyn muttered. "He must have started running as soon as he was out of eyeshot."

Elayne growled an oath, and Rand's eyebrows shot up. He had heard that one from the stablemen at The Queen's Blessing and had been shocked then. The next moment she was in cool self-possession once more.

Gawyn and Elayne appeared content to remain where they were, but he could not make himself stay for the Queen's Guards with such equanimity. He started once more for the wall, knowing he would be no more than halfway up before the guards arrived, but unable to stand still.

Before he had taken three steps red-uniformed men burst into sight, breastplates catching the sun as they dashed up the path. Others came like breaking waves of scarlet and polished steel, seemingly from every direction. Some held drawn swords; others only waited to set their boots before raising bows and nocking feathered shafts. Behind the barred face-guards every eye was grim, and every broadhead arrow was pointed unwaveringly at him.

Elayne and Gawyn leaped as one, putting themselves between him and the arrows, their arms spread to cover him. He stood very still and kept his hands in plain sight, away from his sword.

While the thud of boots and the creak of bowstrings still hung in the air, one of the soldiers, with the golden knot of an officer on his shoulder, shouted, "My Lady, my Lord, down, quickly!"

Despite her outstretched arms Elayne drew herself up regally. "You dare to bring bare steel into my presence, Tallanvor? Gareth Bryne will have you mucking stables with the meanest trooper for this, if you are lucky!"

The soldiers exchanged puzzled glances, and some of the bowmen uneasily half lowered their bows. Only then did Elayne let her arms down, as if she had only held them up because she wished to. Gawyn hesitated, then followed her example. Rand could count the bows that had not been lowered. The muscles of his stomach tensed as though they could stop a broadhead shaft at twenty paces.

The man with the officer's knot seemed the most perplexed of all. "My Lady, forgive me, but Lord Galadedrid reported a dirty peasant skulking in the gardens, armed and endangering my Lady Elayne and my Lord Gawyn." His eyes went to Rand, and his voice firmed. "If my Lady and my Lord will please to step aside, I will take the villain into custody. There is too much riff-raff in the city these days."

"I doubt very much if Galad reported anything of the kind," Elayne said. "Galad does not lie."

"Sometimes I wish he would," Gawyn said softly, for Rand's ear. "Just once. It might make living with him easier."

"This man is my guest," Elayne continued, "and here under my protection. You may withdraw, Tallanvor."

"I regret that will not be possible, My Lady. As My Lady knows, the Queen, your lady mother, has given orders regarding anyone on Palace grounds without Her Majesty's permission, and word has been sent to Her Majesty of this intruder." There was more than a hint of satisfaction in Tallanvor's voice.

Rand suspected the officer had had to accept other commands from Elayne that he did not think proper; this time the man was not about to, not when he had a perfect excuse.

Elayne stared back at Tallanvor; for once she seemed at a loss.

Rand looked a question at Gawyn, and Gawyn understood. "Prison," he murmured. Rand's face went white, and the young man added quickly, "Only for a few days, and you will not be harmed. You'll be questioned by Gareth Bryne, the Captain-General, personally, but you will be set free once it's clear you meant no harm." He paused, hidden thoughts in his eyes. "I hope you were telling the truth, Rand al'Thor from the Two Rivers."

"You will conduct all three of us to my mother," Elayne announced suddenly. A grin bloomed on Gawyn's face.

Behind the steel bars across his face, Tallanvor appeared taken aback. "My Lady, I—"

"Or else conduct all three of us to a cell," Elayne said. "We will remain together. Or will you give orders for hands to be laid upon my person?" Her smile was victorious, and the way Tallanvor looked around as if he expected to find help in the trees said he, too, thought she had won.

Won what? How?

"Mother is viewing Logain," Gawyn said softly, as if he had read Rand's thoughts, "and even if she was not busy, Tallanvor would not dare troop into her presence with Elayne and me, as if *we* were under guard. Mother has a bit of a temper, sometimes."

Rand remembered what Master Gill had said about Queen Morgase. *A bit of a temper?*

Another red-uniformed soldier came running down the path, skidding to a halt to salute with an arm across his chest. He spoke softly to Tallanvor, and his words brought satisfaction back to Tallanvor's face.

"The Queen, your lady mother," Tallanvor announced, "commands me to bring the intruder to her immediately. It is also the Queen's command that my Lady Elayne and my Lord Gawyn attend her. Also immediately."

Gawyn winced, and Elayne swallowed hard. Her face composed, she still began industriously brushing at the stains on her dress. Aside from dislodging a few pieces of bark, her effort did little good.

"If my Lady pleases?" Tallanvor said smugly. "My Lord?" The soldiers formed around them in a hollow box that started along the slate path with Tallanvor leading. Gawyn and Elayne walked on either side of Rand, both appearing lost in unpleasant thoughts. The soldiers had sheathed their swords and returned arrows to quivers, but they were no less on guard than when they had had weapons in hand. They watched Rand as if they expected him at any moment to snatch his sword and try to cut his way to freedom.

Try anything? I won't try anything. *Unnoticed! Hah!*

Watching the soldiers watching him, he suddenly became aware of the garden. One thing had happened after another, each new shock coming before the last had a chance to fade, and his surroundings had been a blur, except for the wall and his devout wish to be back on the other side of it. Now he *saw* the green grass that had only tickled the back of his mind before. *Green!* A hundred shades of green. Trees and bushes green and thriving, thick with leaves and fruit. Lush vines covering arbors over the path. Flowers everywhere. So many flowers, spraying the garden with color. Some he knew—bright golden sunburst and tiny pink tallowend, crimson starblaze and purple Emond's Glory, roses in every color from purest white to deep, deep red—but others were strange, so fanciful in shape and hue he wondered if they could be real.

"It's green," he whispered. "Green." The soldiers muttered to themselves; Tallanvor gave them a sharp look over his shoulder and they fell silent.

"Elaida's work," Gawyn said absently.

"It is not right," Elayne said. "She asked if I wanted to pick out the one farm she could do the same for, while all around it the crops still failed, but it still isn't right for us to have flowers when there are people who do not have enough to eat." She drew a deep breath, and refilled her self-possession. "Remember yourself," she told Rand briskly. "Speak up clearly when you are spoken to, and keep silent otherwise. And follow my lead. All will be well."

Rand wished he could share her confidence. It would have helped if Gawyn had seemed to have it as well. As Tallanvor led them into the Palace, he looked back at the garden, at all the green streaked with blossoms, colors wrought for a Queen by an Aes Sedai's hand. He was in deep water, and there was no bank in sight.

Palace servants filled the halls, in red liveries with collars and cuffs of white, the White Lion on the left breast of their tunics, scurrying about intent on tasks that were not readily apparent. When the soldiers trooped by with Elayne and Gawyn, and Rand, in their midst, they stopped dead in their tracks to stare openmouthed.

Through the middle of all the consternation a gray-striped tomcat wandered unconcernedly down the hall, weaving between the goggling servants. Suddenly the cat struck Rand as odd. He had been in Baerlon long enough to know that even the meanest shop had cats lurking in every corner. Since entering the Palace, the tom was the only cat he had seen.

"You don't have rats?" he said in disbelief. *Every* place had rats.

"Elaida doesn't like rats," Gawyn muttered vaguely. He was frowning worriedly down the hall, apparently already seeing the coming meeting with the Queen. "We never have rats."

"Both of you be quiet." Elayne's voice was sharp, but as absent as her brother's. "I am trying to think."

Rand watched the cat over his shoulder until the guards took him round a corner, hiding the tom from sight. A lot of cats would have made him feel better; it would have been nice if there was one thing normal about the Palace, even if it was rats.

The path Tallanvor took turned so many times that Rand lost his sense of direction. Finally the young officer stopped before tall double doors of dark wood with a rich glow, not so grand as some they had passed, but still carved all over with rows of lions, finely wrought in detail. A liveried servant stood to either side.

"At least it isn't the Grand Hall." Gawyn laughed unsteadily. "I never heard that Mother commanded anyone's head cut off from here." He sounded as if he thought she might set a precedent.

Tallanvor reached for Rand's sword, but Elayne moved to cut him off. "He is my guest, and by custom and law, guests of the royal family may go armed even in Mother's presence. Or will you deny my word that he is my guest?"

Tallanvor hesitated, locking eyes with her, then nodded. "Very well, my Lady." She smiled at Rand as Tallanvor stepped back, but it lasted only a moment. "First rank to accompany me," Tallanvor commanded. "Announce the Lady Elayne and the Lord Gawyn to Her Majesty," he told the door-keepers. "Also Guardsman-Lieutenant Tallanvor, at Her Majesty's command, with the intruder under guard."

Elayne scowled at Tallanvor, but the doors were already swinging open. A sonorous voice sounded, announcing those who came.

Grandly Elayne swept through the doors, spoiling her regal entrance only a little by motioning for Rand to keep close behind her. Gawyn squared his shoulders and strode in flanking her, one measured pace to her rear. Rand followed, uncertainly keeping level with Gawyn on her other side. Tallanvor stayed close to Rand, and ten soldiers came with him. The doors closed silently behind them.

Suddenly Elayne dropped into a deep curtsy, simultaneously bowing from the waist, and stayed there, holding her skirt wide. Rand gave a start, then hastily emulated Gawyn and the other men, shifting awkwardly until he had it right. Down on his right knee, head bowed, bending forward to press the knuckles of his right hand against the marble tiles, his left hand resting on the end of his sword hilt. Gawyn, without a sword, put his hand on his dagger the same way.

Rand was just congratulating himself on getting it right when he noticed Tallanvor, his head still bent, glaring sideways at him from behind his face-guard. *Was I supposed to do something else?* He was suddenly angry that Tallanvor expected him to know what to do when no one had told him. And angry over being afraid of the guards. He had done nothing to be fearful for. He knew his fear was not Tallanvor's fault, but he was angry at him anyway.

Everyone held their positions, frozen as if waiting for the spring thaw. He did not know what they were waiting for, but he took the opportunity to study the place to which he had been brought. He kept his head down, just turning it enough to see. Tallanvor's scowl deepened, but he ignored it.

The square chamber was about the size of the common room at The Queen's Blessing, its walls presenting hunting scenes carved in relief in stone of the purest white. The tapestries between the carvings were gentle images of bright flowers and brilliantly plumaged hummingbirds, except for the two at the far end of the room, where the White Lion of Andor stood taller than a man on scarlet fields. Those two hangings flanked a dais, and on the dais a carved and gilded throne where sat the Queen.

A bluff, blocky man stood bareheaded by the Queen's right hand in the red of the Queen's Guards, with four golden knots on the shoulder of his cloak and wide golden bands breaking the white of his cuffs. His temples were heavy with gray, but he looked as strong and immovable as a rock. That had to be the Captain-General, Gareth Bryne. Behind the throne and to the other side a woman in deep green silk sat on a low stool, knitting something out of dark, almost black, wool. At first the knitting made Rand think she was old, but at second glance he could not put an age to her at all. Young, old, he did not know. Her attention seemed to be entirely on her needles and yarn, just as if there were not a Queen within arm's reach of her. She was a handsome woman, outwardly placid, yet there was something terrible in her concentration. There was no sound in the room except for the click of her needles.

He tried to look at everything, yet his eyes kept going back to the woman with the gleaming wreath of finely wrought roses on her brow, the Rose Crown of Andor. A long red stole, the Lion of Andor marching along its length, hung over her silken dress of red and white pleats, and when she touched the Captain-General's arm with her left hand, a ring in the shape of the Great Serpent, eating its own tail, glittered. Yet it was not the grandeur of clothes or jewelry or even crown that drew Rand's eyes again and again: it was the woman who wore them.

Morgase had her daughter's beauty, matured and ripened. Her face and figure, her presence, filled the room like a light that dimmed the other two with her. If she had been a widow in Emond's Field, she would have had a line of suitors outside her door even if she was the worst cook and most slovenly housekeeper in the Two Rivers. He saw her studying him and ducked his head, afraid she might be able to tell his thoughts from his face. *Light, thinking about the Queen like she was a village woman! You fool!*

"You may rise," Morgase said in a rich, warm voice that held Elayne's assurance of obedience a hundred times over.

Rand stood with the rest.

"Mother—" Elayne began, but Morgase cut her off.

"You have been climbing trees, it seems, daughter." Elayne plucked a stray fragment of bark from her dress and, finding there was no place to put it, held it clenched in her hand. "In fact," Morgase went on calmly, "it would seem that despite my orders to the contrary you have contrived to take your look at this Logain. Gawyn, I have thought better of you. You must learn not only to obey your sister, but at the same time to be counterweight for her against disaster." The Queen's eyes swung to the blocky man beside her, then quickly away again. Bryne remained impassive, as if he had not noticed, but Rand thought those eyes noticed everything. "That, Gawyn, is as much the duty of the First Prince as is leading the armies of Andor. Perhaps if your training is intensified, you will find less time for letting your sister lead you into trouble. I will ask the Captain-General to see that you do not lack for things to do on the journey north."

Gawyn shifted his feet as if about to protest, then bowed his head instead. "As you command, mother."

Elayne grimaced. "Mother, Gawyn cannot keep me out of trouble if he is not with me. It was for that reason alone he left his rooms. Mother, surely there could be no harm in just looking at Logain. Almost everyone in the city was closer to him than we."

"Everyone in the city is not the Daughter-Heir." Sharpness underlay the Queen's voice. "I have seen this fellow Logain from close, and he is dangerous, child. Caged, with Aes Sedai to guard him every minute, he is still as dangerous as a wolf. I wish he had never been brought near Caemlyn."

"He will be dealt with in Tar Valon." The woman on the stool did not take her eyes from her knitting as she spoke. "What is important is that the people see that the Light has once again vanquished the Dark. And that they see you are part of that victory, Morgase."

. Morgase waved a dismissive hand. "I would still rather he had never come near Caemlyn. Elayne, I know your mind."

"Mother," Elayne protested, "I do mean to obey you. Truly I do."

"You do?" Morgase asked in mock surprise, then chuckled. "Yes, you do try to be a dutiful daughter. But you constantly test how far you may go. Well, I did the same with my mother. That spirit will stand you in good stead when you ascend to the throne, but you are not Queen yet, child. You have disobeyed me and had your look at Logain. Be satisfied with that. On the journey north you will not be allowed within one hundred paces of him, neither you nor Gawyn. If I did not know just how hard your lessons will be in Tar Valon, I would send Lini along to see that you obey. She, at least, seems able to make you do as you must."

Elayne bowed her head sullenly.

The woman behind the throne seemed occupied with counting her stitches. "In one week," she said suddenly, "you will be wanting to come home to your mother. In a month you will be wanting to run away with the Traveling People. But my sisters will keep you away from the unbeliever. That sort of thing is not for you, not yet." Abruptly she turned on the stool to look intently at Elayne, all her placidity gone as if it had never been. "You have it in you to be the greatest Queen that Andor has ever seen, that any land has seen in more than a thousand years. It is for that we will shape you, if you have the strength for it."

Rand stared at her. She had to be Elaida, the Aes Sedai. Suddenly he was glad he had not come to her for help, no matter what her Ajah. A sternness far beyond Moiraine's radiated from her. He had sometimes thought of Moiraine as steel covered with velvet; with Elaida the velvet was only an illusion.

"Enough, Elaida," Morgase said, frowning uneasily. "She has heard that more than enough. The Wheel weaves as the Wheel wills." For a moment she was silent, looking at her daughter. "Now there is the problem of this young man"—she gestured to Rand without taking her eyes off Elayne's face— "and how and why he came here, and why you claimed guest-right for him to your brother."

"May I speak, mother?" When Morgase nodded her assent,

Elayne told of events simply, from the time she first saw Rand climbing up the slope to the wall. He expected her to finish by proclaiming the innocence of what he had done, but instead she said, "Mother, often you tell me I must know our people, from the highest to the lowest, but whenever I meet any of them it is with a dozen attendants. How can I come to know anything real or true under such circumstances? In speaking with this young man I have already learned more about the people of the Two Rivers, what kind of people they are, than I ever could from books. It says something that he has come so far and has put on the red, when so many incomers wear the white from fear. Mother, I beg you not to misuse a loyal subject, and one who has taught me much about the people you rule."

"A loyal subject from the Two Rivers." Morgase sighed. "My child, you should pay more heed to those books. The Two Rivers has not seen a tax collector in six generations, nor the Queen's Guards in seven. I daresay they seldom even think to remember they are part of the Realm." Rand shrugged uncomfortably, recalling his surprise when he was told the Two Rivers was part of the Realm of Andor. The Queen saw him, and smiled ruefully at her daughter. "You see, child?"

Elaida had put down her knitting, Rand realized, and was studying him. She rose from her stool and slowly came down from the dais to stand before him. "From the Two Rivers?" she said. She reached a hand toward his head; he pulled away from her touch, and she let her hand drop. "With that red in his hair, and gray eyes? Two Rivers people are dark of hair and eye, and they seldom have such height." Her hand darted out to push back his coat sleeve, exposing lighter skin the sun had not reached so often. "Or such skin."

It was an effort not to clench his fists. "I was born in Emond's Field," he said stiffly. "My mother was an outlander; that's where my eyes come from. My father is Tam al'Thor, a shepherd and farmer, as I am."

Elaida nodded slowly, never taking her eyes from his face. He met her gaze with a levelness that belied the sour feeling in his stomach. He saw her note the steadiness of his look. Still meeting him eye to eye, she moved her hand slowly toward him again. He resolved not to flinch this time.

It was his sword she touched, not him, her hand closing

around the hilt at the very top. Her fingers tightened and her eyes opened wide with surprise. "A shepherd from the Two Rivers," she said softly, a whisper meant to be heard by all, "with a heron-mark sword."

Those last few words acted on the chamber as if she had announced the Dark One. Leather and metal creaked behind Rand, boots scuffling on the marble tiles. From the corner of his eye he could see Tallanvor and another of the guardsmen backing away from him to gain room, hands on their swords, prepared to draw and, from their faces, prepared to die. In two quick strides Gareth Bryne was at the front of the dais, between Rand and the Queen. Even Gawyn put himself in front of Elayne, a worried look on his face and a hand on his dagger. Elayne herself looked at him as if she were seeing him for the first time. Morgase did not change expression, but her hands tightened on the gilded arms of her throne.

Only Elaida showed less reaction than the Queen. The Aes Sedai gave no sign that she had said anything out of the ordinary. She took her hand from the sword, causing the soldiers to tense even more. Her eyes stayed on his, unruffled and calculating.

"Surely," Morgase said, her voice level, "he is too young to have earned a heron-mark blade. He cannot be any older than Gawyn."

"It belongs with him," Gareth Bryne said.

The Queen looked at him in surprise. "How can that be?"

"I do not know, Morgase," Bryne said slowly. "He *is* too young, yet still it belongs with him, and he with it. Look at his eyes. Look how he stands, how the sword fits him, and he it. He is too young, but the sword is his."

When the Captain-General fell silent, Elaida said, "How did you come by this blade, Rand al'Thor from the Two Rivers?" She said it as if she doubted his name as much as she did where he was from.

"My father gave it to me," Rand said. "It was his. He thought I'd need a sword, out in the world."

"Yet *another* shepherd from the Two Rivers with a heron-mark blade." Elaida's smile made his mouth go dry. "When did you arrive in Caemlyn?"

He had had enough of telling this woman the truth. She

made him as afraid as any Darkfriend had. It was time to start
hiding again. "Today," he said. "This morning."

"Just in time," she murmured. "Where are you staying?
Don't say you have not found a room somewhere. You look a
little tattered, but you have had a chance to freshen. Where?"

"The Crown and Lion." He remembered passing The Crown
and Lion while looking for The Queen's Blessing. It was on the
other side of the New City from Master Gill's inn. "I have a
bed there. In the attic." He had the feeling that she knew he
was lying, but she only nodded.

"What chance this?" she said. "Today the unbeliever is
brought into Caemlyn. In two days he will be taken north to
Tar Valon, and with him goes the Daughter-Heir for her training. And at just this juncture a young man appears in the Palace gardens, claiming to be a loyal subject from the Two
Rivers . . ."

"I *am* from the Two Rivers." They were all looking at him,
but all ignored him. All but Tallanvor and the guards; those
eyes never blinked.

". . . with a story calculated to entice Elayne and bearing a
heron-mark blade. He does not wear an armband or a cockade
to proclaim his allegiance, but wrappings that carefully conceal
the heron from inquisitive eyes. What chance this, Morgase?"

The Queen motioned the Captain-General to stand aside,
and when he did she studied Rand with a troubled look. It was
to Elaida that she spoke, though. "What are you naming him?
Darkfriend? One of Logain's followers?"

"The Dark One stirs in Shayol Ghul," the Aes Sedai replied.
"The Shadow lies across the Pattern, and the future is balanced
on the point of a pin. This one is dangerous."

Suddenly Elayne moved, throwing herself onto her knees before the throne. "Mother, I beg you not to harm him. H ;
would have left immediately had I not stopped him. He wanted
to go. It was I who made him stay. I cannot believe he is a
Darkfriend."

Morgase made a soothing gesture toward her daughter, but
her eyes remained on Rand. "Is this a Foretelling, Elaida? Are
you reading the Pattern? You say it comes on you when you
least expect it and goes as suddenly as it comes. If this is a
Foretelling, Elaida, I command you to speak the truth clearly,

without your usual habit of wrapping it in so much mystery that no one can tell if you have said yes or no. Speak. What do you see?"

"This I Foretell," Elaida replied, "and swear under the Light that I can say no clearer. From this day Andor marches toward pain and division. The Shadow has yet to darken to its blackest, and I cannot see if the Light will come after. Where the world has wept one tear, it will weep thousands. This I Foretell."

A pall of silence clung to the room, broken only by Morgase expelling her breath as if it were her last.

Elaida continued to stare into Rand's eyes. She spoke again, barely moving her lips, so softly that he could barely hear her less than an arm's length away. "This, too, I Foretell. Pain and division come to the whole world, and this man stands at the heart of it. I obey the Queen," she whispered, "and speak it clearly."

Rand felt as if his feet had become rooted in the marble floor. The cold and stiffness of the stone crept up his legs and sent a shiver up his spine. No one else could have heard. But she was still looking at him, and he had heard.

"I'm a shepherd," he said for the entire room. "From the Two Rivers. A shepherd."

"The Wheel weaves as the Wheel wills," Elaida said aloud, and he could not tell if there was a touch of mockery in her tone or not.

"Lord Gareth," Morgase said, "I need the advice of my Captain-General."

The blocky man shook his head. "Elaida Sedai says the lad is dangerous, My Queen, and if she could tell more I would say summon the headsman. But all she says is what any of us can see with our own eyes. There's not a farmer in the countryside won't say things will get worse, without any Foretelling. Myself, I believe the boy is here through mere happenstance, though an ill one for him. To be safe, My Queen, I say clap him in a cell till the Lady Elayne and the Lord Gawyn are well on their way, then let him go. Unless, Aes Sedai, you have more to Foretell concerning him?"

"I have said all that I have read in the Pattern, Captain-General," Elaida said. She flashed a hard smile at Rand, a smile that barely bent her lips, mocking his inability to say that she was not telling the truth. "A few weeks imprisoned will not harm him, and it may give me a chance to learn more." Hunger filled her eyes, deepening his chill. "Perhaps another Foretelling will come."

For a time Morgase considered, chin on her fist and elbow on the arm of her throne. Rand would have shifted under her frowning gaze if he could have moved at all, but Elaida's eyes froze him solid. Finally the Queen spoke.

"Suspicion is smothering Caemlyn, perhaps all of Andor. Fear and black suspicion. Women denounce their neighbors for Darkfriends. Men scrawl the Dragon's Fang on the doors of people they have known for years. I will not become part of it."

"Morgase—" Elaida began, but the Queen cut her off.

"I will not become part of it. When I took the throne I swore to uphold justice for the high and the low, and I will uphold it even if I am the last in Andor to remember justice. Rand al'Thor, do you swear under the Light that your father, a shepherd in the Two Rivers, gave you this heron-mark blade?"

Rand worked his mouth to get enough moisture to speak. "I do." Abruptly remembering to whom he was speaking he hastily added, "My Queen." Lord Gareth raised a heavy eyebrow, but Morgase did not seem to mind.

"And you climbed the garden wall simply to gain a look at the false Dragon?"

"Yes, my Queen."

"Do you mean harm to the throne of Andor, or to my daughter, or my son?" Her tone said the last two would gain him even shorter shrift than the first.

"I mean no harm to anyone, my Queen. To you and yours least of all."

"I will give you justice then, Rand al'Thor," she said. "First, because I have the advantage of Elaida and Gareth in having heard Two Rivers speech when I was young. You have not the look, but if a dim memory can serve me you have the Two Rivers on your tongue. Second, no one with your hair and eyes would claim that he is a Two Rivers shepherd unless it was true. And that your father gave you a heron-mark blade is too preposterous to be a lie. And third, the voice that whispers to me that the best lie is often one too ridiculous to be taken for a

lie . . . that voice is not proof. I will uphold the laws I have
made. I give you your freedom, Rand al'Thor, but I suggest
you take a care where you trespass in the future. If you are
found on the Palace grounds again, it will not go so easily with
you."

"Thank you, my Queen," he said hoarsely. He could feel
Elaida's displeasure like a heat on his face.

"Tallanvor," Morgase said, "escort this . . . escort my
daughter's guest from the Palace, and show him every courtesy.
The rest of you go as well. No, Elaida, you stay. And if you
will too, please, Lord Gareth. I must decide what to do about
these Whitecloaks in the city."

Tallanvor and the guardsmen sheathed their swords reluctantly, ready to draw again in an instant. Still Rand was glad to
let the soldiers form a hollow box around him and to follow
Tallanvor. Elaida was only half attending what the Queen was
saying; he could feel her eyes on his back. *What would have
happened if Morgase had not kept the Aes Sedai with her?* The
thought made him wish the soldiers would walk faster.

To his surprise, Elayne and Gawyn exchanged a few words
outside the door, then fell in beside him. Tallanvor was surprised, too. The young officer looked from them back to the
doors, closing now.

"My mother," Elayne said, "ordered him to be escorted
from the Palace, Tallanvor. With every courtesy. What are you
waiting for?"

Tallanvor scowled at the doors, behind which the Queen was
conferring with her advisors. "Nothing, my Lady," he said
sourly, and needlessly ordered the escort forward.

The wonders of the Palace slid by Rand unseen. He was be-
fuddled, snatches of thought spinning by too fast to grasp. *You
have not the look. This man stands at the heart of it.*

The escort stopped. He blinked, startled to find himself in
the great court at the front of the Palace, standing at the tall,
gilded gates, gleaming in the sun. Those gates would not be
opened for a single man, certainly not for a trespasser, even if
the Daughter-Heir did claim guest-right for him. Wordlessly
Tallanvor unbarred a sally-port, a small door set within one
gate.

"It is the custom," Elayne said, "to escort guests as far as the gates, but not to watch them go. It is the pleasure of a guest's company that should be remembered, not the sadness of parting."

"Thank you, my Lady," Rand said. He touched the scarf bandaging his head. "For everything. Custom in the Two Rivers is for a guest to bring a small gift. I'm afraid I have nothing. Although," he added dryly, "apparently I did teach you something of the Two Rivers folk."

"If I had told Mother I think you are handsome, she certainly would have had you locked in a cell." Elayne favored him with a dazzling smile. "Fare you well, Rand al'Thor."

Gaping, he watched her go, a younger version of Morgase's beauty and majesty.

"Do not try to bandy words with her." Gawyn laughed. "She will win every time."

Rand nodded absently. *Handsome? Light, the Daughter-Heir to the throne of Andor!* He gave himself a shake to clear his head.

Gawyn seemed to be waiting for something. Rand looked at him for a moment.

"My Lord, when I told you I was from the Two Rivers you were surprised. And everybody else, your mother, Lord Gareth, Elaida Sedai"—a shiver ran down his back—"none of them. . . ." He could not finish it; he was not even sure why he started. *I am Tam al'Thor's son, even if I was not born in the Two Rivers.*

Gawyn nodded as if it was for this he had been waiting. Still he hesitated. Rand opened his mouth to take back the unspoken question, and Gawyn said, "Wrap a *shoufa* around your head, Rand, and you would be the image of an Aielman. Odd, since Mother seems to think you *sound* like a Two Rivers man, at least. I wish we could have come to know one another, Rand al'Thor. Fare you well."

An Aielman.

Rand stood watching Gawyn's retreating back until an impatient cough from Tallanvor reminded him where he was. He ducked through the sally-port, barely clearing his heels before Tallanvor slammed it behind him. The bars inside were jammed into place loudly.

The oval plaza in front of the Palace was empty, now. All the soldiers gone, all the crowds, trumpets, and drums vanished in silence. Nothing left but a scattering of litter blowing across the pavement and a few people hurrying about their business now that the excitement was done. He could not make out if they showed the red or the white.

Aielman.

With a start he realized he was standing right in front of the Palace gates, right where Elaida could find him easily once she finished with the Queen. Pulling his cloak close, he broke into a trot, across the plaza and into the streets of the Inner City. He looked back frequently to see if anyone was following him, but the sweeping curves kept him from seeing very far. He could remember Elaida's eyes all too well, though, and imagined them watching. By the time he reached the gates to the New City, he was running.

CHAPTER
41

Old Friends and New Threats

Back at The Queen's Blessing, Rand threw himself against the front doorframe, panting. He had run all the way, not caring if anyone saw that he wore the red, or even if they took his running as an excuse to chase him. He did not think even a Fade could have caught him.

Lamgwin was sitting on a bench by the door, a brindle cat in his arms, when he came running up. The man stood to look for trouble the way Rand had come, still calmly scratching behind the cat's ears. Seeing nothing, he sat back down again, careful not to disturb the animal. "Fools tried to steal some of the cats a while back," he said. He examined his knuckles before going back to his scratching. "Good money in cats these days."

The two men showing the white were still across the way, Rand saw, one with a black eye and a swollen jaw. That one wore a sour scowl and rubbed his sword hilt with a sullen eagerness as he watched the inn.

"Where's Master Gill?" Rand asked.

"Library," Lamgwin replied. The cat began purring, and he grinned. "Nothing bothers a cat for long, not even somebody trying to stick him in a sack."

Rand hurried inside, through the common room, now with its usual complement of men wearing the red and talking over their ale. About the false Dragon, and whether the White-cloaks would make trouble when he was taken north. No one cared what happened to Logain, but they all knew the Daughter-Heir and Lord Gawyn would be traveling in the party, and no man there would countenance any risk to them.

He found Master Gill in the library, playing stones with Loial. A plump tabby sat on the table, feet tucked under her, watching their hands move over the cross-hatched board.

The Ogier placed another stone with a touch oddly delicate for his thick fingers. Shaking his head, Master Gill took the excuse of Rand's appearance to turn from the table. Loial almost always won at stones. "I was beginning to worry where you were, lad. Thought you might have had trouble with some of those white-flashing traitors, or run into that beggar or something."

For a minute Rand stood there with his mouth open. He had forgotten all about that bundle-of-rags of a man. "I saw him," he said finally, "but that's nothing. I saw the Queen, too, and Elaida; that's where the trouble is."

Master Gill snorted a laugh. "The Queen, eh? You don't say. We had Gareth Bryne out in the common room an hour or so ago, arm-wrestling the Lord Captain-Commander of the Children, but the Queen, now . . . that's something."

"Blood and ashes," Rand growled, "everybody thinks I'm lying today." He tossed his cloak across the back of a chair and threw himself onto another. He was too wound up to sit back. He perched on the front edge, mopping his face with a handkerchief. "I saw the beggar, and he saw me, and I thought. . . . That's not important. I climbed up on a wall around a garden, where I could see the plaza in front of the Palace, where they took Logain in. And I fell off, on the inside."

"I almost believe you aren't making fun," the innkeeper said slowly.

"*Ta'veren,*" Loial murmured.

"Oh, it happened," Rand said. "Light help me, it did."

Master Gill's skepticism melted slowly as he went on, turning to quiet alarm. The innkeeper leaned more and more forward until he was perched on the edge of his chair the same as Rand was. Loial listened impassively, except that every so often he rubbed his broad nose and the tufts on his ears gave a little twitch.

Rand told everything that had happened, everything except what Elaida had whispered to him. And what Gawyn had said at the Palace gate. One he did not want to think about; the other had nothing to do with anything. *I'm Tam al'Thor's son, even if I wasn't born in the Two Rivers. I am! I'm Two Rivers blood, and Tam is my father.*

Abruptly he realized he had stopped talking, caught up in his thoughts, and they were looking at him. For one panicky moment he wondered if he had said too much.

"Well," Master Gill said, "there's no more waiting for your friends for you. You will have to leave the city, and fast. Two days at the most. Can you get Mat on his feet in that time, or should I send for Mother Grubb?"

Rand gave him a perplexed look. "Two days?"

"Elaida is Queen Morgase's advisor, right next to Captain-General Gareth Bryne himself. Maybe ahead of him. If she sets the Queen's Guards looking for you—Lord Gareth won't stop her unless she interferes with their other duties—well, the Guards can search every inn in Caemlyn in two days. And that's saying some ill chance doesn't bring them here the first day, or the first hour. Maybe there's a little time if they start over at the Crown and Lion, but none for dawdling."

Rand nodded slowly. "If I can't get Mat out of that bed, you send for Mother Grubb. I have a little money left. Maybe enough."

"I'll take care of Mother Grubb," the innkeeper said gruffly. "And I suppose I can lend you a couple of horses. You try walking to Tar Valon and you'll wear through what's left of your boots halfway there."

"You're a good friend," Rand said. "It seems like we've brought you nothing but trouble, but you're still willing to help. A good friend."

Master Gill seemed embarrassed. He shrugged his shoulders and cleared his throat and looked down. That brought his eyes to the stones board, and he jerked them away again. Loial was definitely winning. "Aye, well, Thom's always been a good friend to me. If he's willing to go out of his way for you, I can do a little bit, too."

"I would like to go with you when you leave, Rand," Loial said suddenly.

"I thought that was settled, Loial." He hesitated—Master

Gill still did not know the whole of the danger—then added, "You know what waits for Mat and me, what's chasing us."

"Darkfriends," the Ogier replied in a placid rumble, "and Aes Sedai, and the Light knows what else. Or the Dark One. You are going to Tar Valon, and there is a very fine grove there, which I have heard the Aes Sedai tend well. In any case, there is more to see in the world than the groves. You truly are *ta'veren*, Rand. The Pattern weaves itself around you, and you stand in the heart of it."

This man stands at the heart of it. Rand felt a chill. "I don't stand at the heart of anything," he said harshly.

Master Gill blinked, and even Loial seemed taken aback at his anger. The innkeeper and the Ogier looked at each other, and then at the floor. Rand forced his expression smooth, drawing deep breaths. For a wonder he found the void that had eluded him so often of late, and calmness. They did not deserve his anger.

"You can come, Loial," he said. "I don't know why you would want to, but I'd be grateful for the company. You . . . you know how Mat is."

"I know," Loial said. "I still cannot go into the streets without raising a mob shouting 'Trolloc' after me. But Mat, at least, only uses words. He has not tried to kill me."

"Of course not," Rand said. "Not Mat." *He wouldn't go that far. Not Mat.*

A tap came at the door, and one of the serving maids, Gilda, stuck her head into the room. Her mouth was tight, and her eyes worried. "Master Gill, come quickly, please. There's Whitecloaks in the common room."

Master Gill leaped up with an oath, sending the cat jumping from the table to stalk out of the room, tail stiff and offended. "I'll come. Run tell them I'm coming, then stay out of their way. You hear me, girl? Keep away from them." Gilda bobbed her head and vanished. "You had best stay here," he told Loial.

The Ogier snorted, a sound like sheets ripping. "I have no desire for any more meetings with the Children of the Light."

Master Gill's eye fell on the stones board and his mood seemed to lighten. "It looks as if we'll have to start the game over later."

"No need for that." Loial stretched an arm to the shelves and took down a book; his hands dwarfed the clothbound volume. "We can take up from where the board lies. It is your turn."

Master Gill grimaced. "If it isn't one thing, it's another," he muttered as he hurried from the room.

Rand followed him, but slowly. He had no more desire than Loial to become involved with the Children. *This man stands at the heart of it*. He stopped at the door to the common room, where he could see what went on, but far enough back that he hoped he would not be noticed.

Dead silence filled the room. Five Whitecloaks stood in the middle of the floor, studiously being ignored by the folk at the tables. One of them had the silver lightning-flash of an under-officer beneath the sunburst on his cloak. Lamgwin was lounging against the wall by the front door, intently cleaning his fingernails with a splinter. Four more of the guards Master Gill had hired were spaced across the wall from him, all industriously paying no attention at all to the Whitecloaks. If the Children of the Light noticed anything, they gàve no sign. Only the under-officer showed any emotion at all, impàtiently tapping his steel-backed gauntlets against his palm as he waited for the innkeeper.

Master Gill crossed the room to him quickly, a cautiously neutral look on his face. "The Light illumine you," he said with a careful bow, not too deep, but not slight enough to actually be insulting, either, "and our good Queen Morgase. How may I help—"

"I've no time for your drivel, innkeeper," the under-officer snapped. "I've been to twenty inns already today, each a worse pigsty than the last, and I'll see twenty more before the sun sets. I'm looking for Darkfriends, a boy from the Two Rivers—"

Master Gill's face grew darker with every word. He puffed up as if he would explode, and finally he did, cutting the Whitecloak off in turn. "There are no Darkfriends in my establishment! Every man here is a good Queen's man!"

"Yes, and we all know where Morgase stands," the under-officer twisted the Queen's name into a sneer, "and her Tar Valon witch, don't we?"

The scrape of chair legs was loud. Suddenly every man in the room was on his feet. They stood still as statues, but every one staring grimly at the Whitecloaks. The under-officer did not appear to notice, but the four behind him looked around uneasily.

"It will go easier with you, innkeeper," the under-officer said, "if you cooperate. The temper of the times goes hard with those who shelter Darkfriends. I wouldn't think an inn with the Dragon's Fang on its door would get much custom. Might have trouble with fire, with that on your door."

"You get out of here now," Master Gill said quietly, "or I'll send for the Queen's Guards to cart what's left of you to the middens."

Lamgwin's sword rasped out of its sheath, and the coarse scrape of steel on leather was repeated throughout the room as swords and daggers filled hands. Serving maids scurried for the doors.

The under-officer looked around in scornful disbelief. "The Dragon's Fang—"

"Won't help you five," Master Gill finished for him. He held up a clenched fist and raised his forefinger. "One."

"You must be mad, innkeeper, threatening the Children of the Light."

"Whitecloaks hold no writ in Caemlyn. Two."

"Can you really believe this will end here?"

"Three."

"We'll be back," the under-officer snapped, and then he was hastily turning his men around, trying to pretend he was leaving in good order and in his own time. He was hampered in this by the eagerness his men showed for the door, not running, but not making secret that they wanted to be outside.

Lamgwin stood across the door with his sword, only giving way in response to Master Gill's frantic waves. When the Whitecloaks were gone, the innkeeper dropped heavily onto a chair. He rubbed a hand across his forehead, then stared at it as if surprised that it was not covered with sweat. All over the room men seated themselves again, laughing over what they had done. Some went over to clap Master Gill on the shoulder.

When he saw Rand, the innkeeper tottered off the chair and over to him. "Who would have thought I had it in me to be a hero?" he said wonderingly. "The Light illumine me."

Abruptly he gave himself a shake, and his voice regained almost its normal tone. "You'll have to stay out of sight until I can get you out of the city." With a careful look back into the common room, he pushed Rand deeper into the hall. "That lot will be back, or else a few spies wearing red for the day. After that little show I put on, I doubt they'll care whether you're here or not, but they'll act as though you are."

"That's crazy," Rand protested. At the innkeeper's gesture he lowered his voice. "The Whitecloaks don't have any reason to be after me."

"I don't know about reasons, lad, but they're after you and Mat for certain sure. What *have* you been up to? Elaida *and* the Whitecloaks."

Rand raised his hands in protest, then let them fall. It made no sense, but he had heard the Whitecloak. "What about you? The Whitecloaks will make trouble for you even when they don't find us."

"No worries about that, lad. The Queen's Guards still uphold the law, even if they do let traitors strut around showing white. As for the night . . . well, Lamgwin and his friends might not get much sleep, but I could almost pity anybody who tries to put a mark on my door."

Gilda appeared beside them, dropping a curtsy to Master Gill. "Sir, there's . . . there's a lady. In the kitchens." She sounded scandalized at the combination. "She's asking for Master Rand, sir, and Master Mat, by name."

Rand exchanged a puzzled look with the innkeeper.

"Lad," Master Gill. said, "if you've actually managed to bring the Lady Elayne down from the Palace to my inn, we'll all end up facing the headsman." Gilda squeaked at the mention of the Daughter-Heir and gave Rand a round-eyed stare. "Off with you, girl," the innkeeper said sharply. "And keep quiet about what you've heard. It's nobody's business." Gilda bobbed again and darted down the hallway, flashing glances over her shoulder at Rand as she went. "In five minutes"— Master Gill sighed—"she will be telling the other women you're a prince in disguise. By nightfall it will be all over the New City."

"Master Gill," Rand said, "I never mentioned Mat to

Elayne. It can't be—" Suddenly a huge smile lit up his face, and he ran for the kitchens.

"Wait!" the innkeeper called behind him. "Wait until you know. Wait, you fool!"

Rand threw open the door to the kitchens, and there they were. Moiraine rested her serene eyes on him, unsurprised. Nynaeve and Egwene ran laughing to throw their arms around him, with Perrin crowding in behind them, all three patting his shoulders as if they had to be convinced that he was really there. In the doorway leading to the stableyard Lan lounged with one boot up on the doorframe, dividing his attention between the kitchen and the yard outside.

Rand tried to hug the two women and shake Perrin's hand, all at the same time, and it was a tangle of arms and laughter complicated by Nynaeve trying to feel his face for fever. They looked somewhat the worse for wear—bruises on Perrin's face, and he had a way of keeping his eyes downcast that he had never had before—but they were alive, and together again. His throat was so tight he could barely talk. "I was afraid I'd never see you again," he managed finally. "I was afraid you were all. . . ."

"I knew you were alive," Egwene said against his chest. "I always knew it. Always."

"I did not," Nynaeve said. Her voice was sharp for just that moment, but it softened in the next, and she smiled up at him. "You look well, Rand. Not overfed by any means, but well, thank the Light."

"Well," Master Gill said behind him, "I guess you know these people after all. Those friends you were looking for?"

Rand nodded. "Yes, my friends." He made introductions all around; it still felt odd to be giving Lan and Moiraine their right names. They both eyed him sharply when he did.

The innkeeper greeted everyone with an open smile, but he was properly impressed at meeting a Warder, and especially at Moiraine. At her he gaped openly—it was one thing knowing an Aes Sedai had been helping the boys, quite something else having her appear in the kitchen—then bowed deeply. "You are welcome to The Queen's Blessing, Aes Sedai, as my guest. Though I suppose you will be staying at the Palace with Elaida Sedai, and the Aes Sedai who came with the false Dragon."

Bowing again, he gave Rand a quick, worried look. It was all very well to say he did not speak ill of Aes Sedai, but that was not the same as saying he wanted one sleeping under his roof. Rand nodded encouragingly, trying to tell him silently that it was all right. Moiraine was not like Elaida, with a threat hidden behind every glance, under every word. *Are you sure? Even now, are you sure?*

"I believe I will stay here," Moiraine said, "for the short time I remain in Caemlyn. And you must allow me to pay."

A calico cat sauntered in from the hallway to strop the innkeeper's ankles. No sooner had the calico begun than a fuzzy gray sprang from under the table, arching its back and hissing. The calico crouched with a threatening growl, and the gray streaked past Lan into the stableyard.

Master Gill began apologizing for the cats at the same time he protested that Moiraine would honor him by being his guest, and was she sure she would not prefer the Palace, which he would quite understand, but he hoped she would accept his best room as a gift. It made a jumble to which Moiraine seemed to pay no attention at all. Instead she bent down to scratch the orange-and-white cat; it promptly left Master Gill's ankles for hers.

"I've seen four other cats here, so far," she said. "You have a problem with mice? Rats?"

"Rats, Moiraine Sedai." The innkeeper sighed. "A terrible problem. Not that I don't keep a clean place, you understand. It's all the people. The whole city is full of people and rats. But my cats take care of it. You'll not be troubled, I promise."

Rand exchanged a fleeting look with Perrin, who put his eyes down again right away. There was something odd about Perrin's eyes. And he was so silent; Perrin was almost always slow to speak, but now he was saying nothing at all. "It could be all the people," he said.

"With your permission, Master Gill," Moiraine said, as if she took it for granted. "It is a simple matter to keep rats away from this street. With luck, the rats will not even realize they are being kept away."

Master Gill frowned at that last, but he bowed, accepting her offer. "If you are sure you don't want to stay at the Palace, Aes Sedai."

"Where is Mat?" Nynaeve said suddenly. "*She* said he was here, too."

"Upstairs," Rand said. "He's . . . not feeling well."

Nynaeve's head came up. "He's sick? I'll leave the rats to *her,* and I'll attend to him. Take me to him now, Rand."

"All of you go up," Moiraine said. "I will join you in a few minutes. We are crowding Master Gill's kitchen, and it would be best if we could all be somewhere quiet for a time." There was an undercurrent in her voice. *Stay out of sight. The hiding is not done yet.*

"Come on," Rand said. "We'll go up the back way."

The Emond's Field folk crowded after him to the back staircase, leaving the Aes Sedai and the Warder in the kitchen with Master Gill. He could not get over being back together. It was nearly as if he were home again. He could not stop grinning.

The same relief, almost joyous, seemed to be affecting the others. They chuckled to themselves, and kept reaching out to grip his arm. Perrin's voice seemed subdued, and he still kept his head down, but he began to talk as they climbed.

"Moiraine said she could find you and Mat, and she did. When we rode into the city, the rest of us couldn't stop staring—well, all except Lan, of course—all the people, the buildings, everything." His thick curls swung as he shook his head in disbelief. "It's all so big. And so many people. Some of them kept staring at us, too, shouting 'Red or white?' like it made some kind of sense."

Egwene touched Rand's sword, fingering the red wrappings. "What does it mean?"

"Nothing," he said. "Nothing important. We're leaving for Tar Valon, remember?"

Egwene gave him a look, but she removed her hand from the sword and took up where Perrin had left off. "Moiraine didn't look at anything any more than Lan did. She led us back and forth through all those streets so many times, like a dog hunting a scent, that I thought you couldn't be here. Then, all of a sudden, she took off down a street, and the next thing I knew we were handing the horses to the stablemen and marching into the kitchen. She never even asked if you were here. Just told a woman who was mixing batter to go tell Rand al'Thor and Mat Cauthon that someone wanted to see them. And there you were"—she grinned—"like a ball popping into the gleeman's hand out of nowhere."

"Where is the gleeman?" Perrin asked. "Is he with you?"

Rand's stomach lurched and the good feeling of having friends around him dimmed. "Thom's dead. I think he's dead. There was a Fade. . . ." He could not say any more. Nynaeve shook her head, muttering under her breath.

The silence thickened around them, stifling the little chuckles, flattening the joy, until they reached the head of the stairs.

"Mat's not sick, exactly," he said then. "It's. . . . You'll see." He flung open the door to the room he shared with Mat. "Look who's here, Mat."

Mat was still curled up in a ball on the bed, just as Rand had left him. He raised his head to stare at them. "How do you know they're really who they look like?" he said hoarsely. His face was flushed, the skin tight and slick with sweat. "How do I know you're who you look like?"

"Not sick?" Nynaeve gave Rand a disdainful look as she pushed past him, already unslinging her bag from her shoulder.

"Everybody changes," Mat rasped. "How can I be sure? Perrin? Is that you? You've changed, haven't you?" His laugh sounded more like a cough. "Oh, yes, you've changed."

To Rand's surprise Perrin dropped onto the edge of the other bed with his head in hands, staring at the floor. Mat's hacking laughter seemed to pierce him.

Nynaeve knelt beside Mat's bed and put a hand to his face, pushing up his headcloth. He jerked back from her with a scornful look. His eyes were bright and glazed. "You're burning," she said, "but you should not be sweating with this much fever." She could not keep the worry out of her voice. "Rand, you and Perrin fetch some clean cloths and as much cool water as you can carry. I'll bring your temperature down first, Mat, and—"

"Pretty Nynaeve," Mat spat. "A Wisdom isn't supposed to think of herself as a woman, is she? Not a pretty woman. But you do, don't you? Now. You can't make yourself forget that you're a pretty woman, now, and it frightens you. Everybody changes." Nynaeve's face paled as he spoke—whether with anger or something else, Rand could not tell. Mat gave a sly

· laugh, and his feverish eyes slid to Egwene. "Pretty Egwene," he croaked. "Pretty as Nynaeve. And you share other things now, don't you? Other dreams. What do you dream about now?" Egwene took a step back from the bed.

"We are safe from the Dark One's eyes for the time being," Moiraine announced as she walked into the room with Lan at her heels. Her eyes fell on Mat as she stepped through the doorway, and she hissed as if she had touched a hot stove. "Get away from him!"

Nynaeve did not move except for turning to stare at the Aes Sedai in surprise. In two quick steps Moiraine seized the Wisdom by the shoulders, hauling her across the floor like a sack of grain. Nynaeve struggled and protested, but Moiraine did not release her until she was well away from the bed. The Wisdom continued her protests as she got to her feet, angrily straightening her clothes, but Moiraine ignored her completely. The Aes Sedai watched Mat to the exclusion of everything else, eyeing him the way she would a viper.

"All of you stay away from him," she said. "And be quiet."

Mat stared back as intently as she. He bared his teeth in a silent, snarling rictus, and pulled himself into an ever tighter knot, but he never took his eyes from hers. Slowly she put one hand on him, lightly, on a knee drawn up to his chest. A convulsion shook him at her touch, a shudder of revulsion spasming through his entire body, and abruptly he pulled one hand out, slashing at her face with the ruby-hilted dagger.

One minute Lan was in the doorway, the next he was at the bedside, as if he had not bothered with the intervening space. His hand caught Mat's wrist, stopping the slash as if it had struck stone. Still Mat held himself in that tight ball. Only the hand with the dagger tried to move, straining against the Warder's implacable grip. Mat's eyes never left Moiraine, and they burned with hate.

Moiraine also did not move. She did not flinch from the blade only inches from her face, as she had not when he first struck. "How did he come by this?" she asked in a steel voice. "I asked if Mordeth had given you anything. I asked, and I warned you, and you said he had not."

"He didn't," Rand said. "He. . . . Mat took it from the treasure room." Moiraine looked at him, her eyes seeming to burn

as much as Mat's. He almost stepped back before she turned
away again, back to the bed. "I didn't know until after we were
separated. I didn't know."

"You did not know." Moiraine studied Mat. He still lay with
his knees pulled up to his chest, still snarled soundlessly at her,
and his hand yet fought Lan to reach her with the dagger. "It is
a wonder you got this far, carrying this. I felt the evil of it when
I laid eyes on him, the touch of Mashadar, but a Fade could
sense it for miles. Even though he would not know exactly
where, he would know it was near, and Mashadar would draw
his spirit while his bones remembered that this same evil swallowed an army—Dreadlords, Fades, Trollocs, and all. Some
Darkfriends could probably feel it, too. Those who have truly
given away their souls. There could not help but be those who
would wonder at suddenly feeling this, as if the very air around
them itched. They would be compelled to seek it. It should
have drawn them to it as a magnet draws iron filings."

"There were Darkfriends," Rand said, "more than once, but
we got away from them. And a Fade, the night before we
reached Caemlyn, but he never saw us." He cleared his throat.
"There are rumors of strange things in the night outside the
city. It could be Trollocs."

"Oh, it's Trollocs, sheepherder," Lan said wryly. "And
where Trollocs are, there are Fades." Tendons stood out on the
back of his hand from the effort of holding Mat's wrist, but
there was no strain in his voice. "They've tried to hide their
passage, but I have seen sign for two days. And heard farmers
and villagers mutter about things in the night. The Myrddraal
managed to strike into the Two Rivers unseen, somehow,'but
every day they come closer to those who can send soldiers to
hunt them down. Even so, they won't stop now, sheepherder."

"But we're in Caemlyn," Egwene said. "They can't get to us
as long as—"

"They can't?" the Warder cut her off. "The Fades are building their numbers in the countryside. That's plain enough from
the sign, if you know what to look for. Already there are more
Trollocs than they need just to watch all the ways out of the
city, a dozen fists, at least. There can only be one reason; when
the Fades have enough numbers, they will come into the city
after you. That act may send half the armies of the south

marching to the Borderlands, but the evidence is that they're willing to take that risk. You three have escaped them too long. It looks as if you've brought a new Trolloc War to Caemlyn, sheepherder."

Egwene gave a gasping sob, and Perrin shook his head as though to deny it. Rand felt a sickness in his stomach at the thought of Trollocs in the streets of Caemlyn. All those people at one another's throats, never realizing the real threat waiting to come over the walls. What would they do when they suddenly found Trollocs and Fades in their midst, killing them? He could see the towers burning, flames breaking through the domes, Trollocs pillaging through the curving streets and vistas of the Inner City. The Palace itself in flames. Elayne, and Gawyn, and Morgase . . . dead.

"Not yet," Moiraine said absently. She was still intent on Mat. "If we can find a way out of Caemlyn, the Halfmen will have no more interest here. If. So many if's."

"Better we were all dead," Perrin said suddenly, and Rand jumped at the echo of his own thoughts. Perrin still sat staring at the floor—glaring at it now—and his voice was bitter. "Everywhere we go, we bring pain and suffering on our backs. It would be better for everyone if we were dead."

Nynaeve rounded on him, her face half fury and half worried fear, but Moiraine forestalled her.

"What do you think to gain, for yourself or anyone else, by dying?" the Aes Sedai asked. Her voice was level, yet sharp. "If the Lord of the Grave has gained as much freedom to touch the Pattern as I fear, he can reach you dead more easily than alive, now. Dead, you can help no one, not the people who have helped you, not your friends and family back in the Two Rivers. The Shadow is falling over the world, and none of you can stop it dead."

Perrin raised his head to look at her, and Rand gave a start. The irises of his friend's eyes were more yellow than brown. With his shaggy hair and the intensity of his gaze, there was something about him. . . . Rand could not grasp it enough to make it out.

Perrin spoke with a soft flatness that gave his words more weight than if he had shouted. "We can't stop it alive, either, now can we?"

"I will have time to argue with you later," Moiraine said, "but your friend needs me now." She stepped aside so they could all see Mat clearly. His eyes still on her with a rage-filled stare, he had not moved or changed his position on the bed. Sweat stood out on his face, and his lips were bloodless in an unchanging snarl. All of his strength seemed to be pouring into the effort to reach Moiraine with the dagger Lan held motionless. "Or had you forgotten?"

Perrin gave an embarrassed shrug and spread his hands wordlessly.

"What's wrong with him?" Egwene asked, and Nynaeve added, "Is it catching? I can still treat him. I don't seem to catch sick, no matter what it is."

"Oh, it is catching," Moiraine said, "and your . . . protection would not save you." She pointed to the ruby-hilted dagger, careful not to let her finger touch it. The blade trembled as Mat strained to reach her with it. "This is from Shadar Logoth. There is not a pebble of that city that is not tainted and dangerous to bring outside the walls, and this is far more than a pebble. The evil that killed Shadar Logoth is in it, and in Mat, too, now. Suspicion and hatred so strong that even those closest are seen as enemies, rooted so deep in the bone that eventually the only thought left is to kill. By carrying the dagger beyond the walls of Shadar Logoth he freed it, this seed of it, from what bound it to that place. It will have waxed and waned in him, what he is in the heart of him fighting what the contagion of Mashadar sought to make him, but now the battle inside him is almost done, and he almost defeated. Soon, if it does not kill him first, he will spread that evil like a plague wherever he goes. Just as one scratch from that blade is enough to infect and destroy, so, soon, a few minutes with Mat will be just as deadly."

Nynaeve's face had gone white. "Can you do anything?" she whispered.

"I hope so." Moiraine sighed. "For the sake of the world, I hope I am not too late." Her hand delved into the pouch at her belt and came out with the silk-shrouded *angreal*. "Leave me. Stay together, and find somewhere you will not be seen, but leave me. I will do what I can for him."

CHAPTER
42

Remembrance of Dreams

It was a subdued group that Rand led back down the stairs. None of them wanted to talk to him now, or to one another. He did not feel much like talking, either.

The sun was far enough across the sky to dim the back stairwell, but the lamps had not yet been lit. Sunlight and shadow striped the stairs. Perrin's face was as closed as the others, but where worry creased everyone else's brow, his was smooth. Rand thought the look Perrin wore was resignation. He wondered why, and wanted to ask, but whenever Perrin walked through a deeper patch of shadow, his eyes seemed to gather in what little light there was, glowing softly like polished amber.

Rand shivered and tried to concentrate on his surroundings, on the walnut paneled walls and the oak stair railing, on sturdy, everyday things. He wiped his hands on his coat several times, but each time sweat sprang out on his palms anew. *It'll all be all right, now. We're together again, and. . . . Light, Mat.*

He took them to the library by the back way that went by the kitchens, avoiding the common room. Not many travelers used the library; most of those who could read stayed at more elegant inns in the Inner City. Master Gill kept it more for his own enjoyment than for the handful of patrons who wanted a book now and then. Rand did not want to think why Moiraine wanted them to keep out of sight, but he kept remembering the Whitecloak under-officer saying he would be back, and Elaida's

eyes when she asked where he was staying. Those were reasons
enough, whatever Moiraine wanted.

He took five steps into the library before he realized that
everyone else had stopped, crowded together in the doorway,
openmouthed and goggling. A brisk blaze crackled in the fireplace, and Loial was sprawled on the long couch, reading, a
small black cat with white feet curled and half asleep on his
stomach. When they entered he closed the book with a huge
finger marking his place and gently set the cat on the floor, then
stood to bow formally.

Rand was so used to the Ogier that it took him a minute to
realize that Loial was the object of the others' stares. "These
are the friends I was waiting for, Loial," he said. "This is
Nynaeve, the Wisdom of my village. And Perrin. And this is
Egwene."

"Ah, yes," Loial boomed, "Egwene. Rand has spoken of
you a great deal. Yes. I am Loial."

"He's an Ogier," Rand explained, and watched their amazement change in kind. Even after Trollocs and Fades in the
flesh, it was still astonishing to meet a legend walking and
breathing. Remembering his own first reaction to Loial, he
grinned ruefully. They were doing better than he had.

Loial took their gaping in his stride. Rand supposed he
hardly noticed it compared with a mob shouting "Trolloc."
"And the Aes Sedai, Rand?" Loial asked.

"Upstairs with Mat."

The Ogier raised one bushy eyebrow thoughtfully. "Then he
is ill. I suggest we all be seated. She will be joining us? Yes.
Then there's nothing to do but wait."

The act of sitting seemed to loosen some catch inside the
Emond's Field folk, as if being in a well-stuffed chair with a fire
in the fireplace and a cat now curled up on the hearth made
them feel at home. As soon as they were settled they excitedly
began asking the Ogier questions. To Rand's surprise, Perrin
was the first to speak.

"The *stedding*, Loial. Are they really havens, the way the
stories say?" His voice was intent, as if he had a particular reason for asking.

Loial was glad to tell about the *stedding*, and how he came to be at The Queen's Blessing, and what he had seen in his travels. Rand soon leaned back, only partly listening. He had heard it all before, in detail. Loial liked to talk, and talk at length when he had the slightest chance, though he usually seemed to think a story needed two or three hundred years of background to make it understood. His sense of time was very strange; to him three hundred years seemed a reasonable length of time for a story or explanation to cover. He always talked about leaving the *stedding* as if it were just a few months before, but it had finally come out that he had been gone more than three years.

Rand's thoughts drifted to Mat. *A dagger. A bloody knife, and it might kill him just from carrying it. Light, I don't want any more adventure. If she can heal him, we should all go . . . not home. Can't go home. Somewhere. We'll all go somewhere they've never heard of Aes Sedai or the Dark One. Somewhere.*

The door opened, and for a moment Rand thought he was still imagining. Mat stood there, blinking, with his coat buttoned up and the dark scarf wrapped low around his forehead. Then Rand saw Moiraine, with her hand on Mat's shoulder, and Lan behind them. The Aes Sedai was watching Mat carefully, as one watches someone only lately out of a sickbed. As always, Lan was watching everything while appearing to watch nothing.

Mat looked as if he had never been sick a day. His first, hesitant smile included everyone, though it slipped into an openmouthed stare at the sight of Loial, as if he were seeing the Ogier for the first time. With a shrug and a shake, he turned his attention back to his friends. "I . . . ah . . . that is. . . ." He took a deep breath. "It . . . ah . . . it seems I've been acting . . . ah . . . sort of oddly. I don't remember much of it, really." He gave Moiraine an uneasy look. She smiled back confidently, and he went on. "Everything is hazy after Whitebridge. Thom, and the. . . ." He shivered and hurried on. "The further from Whitebridge, the hazier it gets. I don't really remember arriving in Caemlyn at all." He eyed Loial askance. "Not really. Moiraine Sedai says I . . . upstairs, I . . . ah. . . ." He grinned, and suddenly he truly was the old Mat. "You can't hold a man to blame for what he does when he's crazy, can you?"

"You always were crazy," Perrin said, and for a moment he, too, sounded as of old.

"No," Nynaeve said. Tears made her eyes bright, but she was smiling. "None of us blames you."

Rand and Egwene began talking at once then, telling Mat how happy they were to see him well and how well he looked, with a few laughing comments thrown in about hoping that he was done with tricks now that one so ugly had been played on him. Mat met banter with banter as he found a chair with all of his old swagger. As he sat down, still grinning, he absentmindedly touched his coat as if to make sure that something tucked behind his belt was still there, and Rand's breath caught.

"Yes," Moiraine said quietly, "he still has the dagger." The laughter and talk was still going on among the rest of the Emond's Field folk, but she had noticed his sudden intake of breath and had seen what had caused it. She moved closer to his chair, where she did not have to raise her voice for him to hear clearly. "I cannot take it away from him without killing him. The binding has lasted too long, and grown too strong. That must be unknotted in Tar Valon; it is beyond me, or any lone Aes Sedai, even with an *angreal*."

"But he doesn't look sick anymore." He had a thought and looked up at her. "As long as he has the dagger, the Fades will know where we are. Darkfriends, too, some of them. You said so."

"I have contained that, after a fashion. If they come close enough to sense it now, they will be on top of us anyway. I cleansed the taint from him, Rand, and did what I could to slow its return, but return it will, in time, unless he receives help in Tar Valon."

"A good thing that's where we're going, isn't it?" He thought maybe it was the resignation in his voice, and the hope for something else, that made her give him a sharp look before turning away.

Loial was on his feet, bowing to her. "I am Loial, son of Arent son of Halan, Aes Sedai. The *stedding* offers sanctuary to the Servants of the Light."

"Thank you, Loial, son of Arent," Moiraine answered dryly, "but I would not be too free with that greeting if I were you. There are perhaps twenty Aes Sedai in Caemlyn at this moment, and every one but I of the Red Ajah." Loial nodded sagely, as if he understood. Rand could only shake his head in confusion; he would be Lightblinded if *he* knew what she meant. "It is strange to find you here," the Aes Sedai went on. "Few Ogier leave the *stedding* in recent years."

"The old stories caught me, Aes Sedai. The old books filled my unworthy head with pictures. I want to see the groves. And the cities we built, too. There do not seem to be many of either still standing, but if buildings are a poor substitute for trees, they are still worth seeing. The Elders think I'm odd, wanting to travel. I always have, and they always have. None of them believe there is anything worth seeing outside the *stedding*. Perhaps when I return and tell them what I've seen, they will change their minds. I hope so. In time."

"Perhaps they will," Moiraine said smoothly. "Now, Loial, you must forgive me for being abrupt. It is a failing of human-kind, I know. My companions and I have urgent need to plan our journey. If you could excuse us?"

It was Loial's turn to look confused. Rand came to his rescue. "He's coming with us. I promised him he could."

Moiraine stood looking at the Ogier as if she had not heard, but finally she nodded. "The Wheel weaves as the Wheel wills," she murmured. "Lan, see that we are not taken un-aware." The Warder vanished from the room, silently but for the click of the door shutting behind him.

Lan's disappearance acted like a signal; all talk was cut off. Moiraine moved to the fireplace, and when she turned back to the room every eye was on her. Slight of build as she was, her presence dominated. "We cannot remain long in Caemlyn, nor are we safe here in The Queen's Blessing. The Dark One's eyes are already in the city. They have not found what they are searching for, or they would not still be looking. That we have to our advantage. I have set wards to keep them away, and by the time the Dark One realizes that there is a part of the city the rats no longer enter, we will be gone. Any ward that will turn a man aside, though, would be as good as a beacon fire for the Myrddraal, and there are Children of the Light in Caemlyn, also, looking for Perrin and Egwene." Rand made a sound, and Moiraine raised an eyebrow at him.

"I thought they were looking for Mat and me," he said.

The explanation made both the Aes Sedai's eyebrows lift. "Why would you think the Whitecloaks were looking for you?"

"I heard one say they were looking for someone from the Two Rivers. Darkfriends, he said. What else was I supposed to think? With everything that's been happening, I'm lucky I can think at all."

"It has been confusing, I know, Rand," Loial put in, "but you can think more clearly than that. The Children hate Aes Sedai. Elaida would not—"

"Elaida?" Moiraine cut in sharply. "What has Elaida Sedai to do with this?"

She was looking at Rand so hard that he wanted to lean back. "She wanted to throw me in prison," he said slowly. "All I wanted was a look at Logain, but she wouldn't believe I was in the Palace gardens with Elayne and Gawyn just by chance." They were all staring at him as if he had suddenly sprouted a third eye, all except Loial. "Queen Morgase let me go. She said there was no proof I meant any harm and she was going to uphold the law no matter what Elaida suspected." He shook his head, the memory of Morgase in all her radiance making him forget for a minute that anyone was looking at him. "Can you imagine me meeting a Queen? She's beautiful, like the queens in stories. So is Elayne. And Gawyn . . . you'd like Gawyn, Perrin. Perrin? Mat?" They were still staring. "Blood and ashes, I just climbed up on the wall for a look at the false Dragon. I didn't do anything wrong."

"That's what I always say," Mat said blandly, though he was suddenly grinning hard, and Egwene asked in a decidedly neutral voice, "Who's Elayne?"

Moiraine muttered something crossly.

"A Queen," Perrin said, shaking his head. "You really have had adventures. All we met were Tinkers and some Whitecloaks." He avoided looking at Moiraine so obviously that Rand saw the avoidance plain. Perrin touched the bruises on his face. "On the whole, singing with the Tinkers was more fun than the Whitecloaks."

"The Traveling People live for their songs," Loial said. "For all songs, for that matter. For the search for them, at least. I met some Tuatha'an a few years back, and they wanted to learn the songs we sing to trees. Actually, the trees won't listen to very many anymore, and so not many Ogier learn the songs. I have a scrap of that Talent, so Elder Arent insisted I learn. I taught the Tuatha'an what they could learn, but the trees never listen to humans. For the Traveling People they were only songs, and just as well received for that, since none was the song they seek. That's what they call the leader of each band, the Seeker. They come to Stedding Shangtai, sometimes. Few humans do."

"If you please, Loial," Moiraine said, but he cleared his throat suddenly and went on in a quick rumble as if afraid she might stop him.

"I've just remembered something, Aes Sedai, something I have always wanted to ask an Aes Sedai if ever I met one, since you know many things and have great libraries in Tar Valon, and now I have, of course, and . . . may I?"

"If you make it brief," she said curtly.

"Brief," he said as though wondering what it meant. "Yes. Well. Brief. There was a man came to Stedding Shangtai a little time back. This was not unusual in itself, at the time, since a great many refugees had come to the Spine of the World fleeing what you humans call the Aiel War." Rand grinned. A little time back; twenty years, near enough. "He was at the point of death, though there was no wound or mark on him. The Elders thought it might be something Aes Sedai had done"—Loial gave Moiraine an apologetic look—"since as soon as he was within the *stedding* he quickly got well. A few months. One night he left without a word to anyone, simply sneaked away when the moon was down." He looked at Moiraine's face and cleared his throat again. "Yes. Brief. Before he left, he told a curious tale which he said he meant to carry to Tar Valon. He said the Dark One intended to blind the Eye of the World, and slay the Great Serpent, kill time itself. The Elders said he was as sound in his mind as in his body, but that was what he said. What I have wanted to ask is, can the Dark One do such a thing? Kill time itself? And the Eye of the World? Can he blind the eye of the Great Serpent? What does it mean?"

Rand expected almost anything from Moiraine except what he saw. Instead of giving Loial an answer, or telling him she had no time for it now, she stood there staring right through the Ogier, frowning in thought.

"That's what the Tinkers told us," Perrin said.

"Yes," Egwene said, "the Aiel story."

Moiraine turned her head slowly. No other part of her moved. "What story?"

It was an expressionless look she gave them, but it made Perrin take a deep breath, though when he spoke he was as deliberate as ever. "Some Tinkers crossing the Waste—they said they could do that unharmed—found Aiel dying after a battle with Trollocs. Before the last Aiel died, she—they were all women, apparently—told the Tinkers what Loial just said. The Dark One—they called him Sightblinder—intends to blind the Eye of the World. This was only three years ago, not twenty. Does it mean something?"

"Perhaps everything," Moiraine said. Her face was still, but Rand had the feeling her mind raced behind those dark eyes.

"Ba'alzamon," Perrin said suddenly. The name cut off all sound in the room. No one appeared to breathe. Perrin looked at Rand, then at Mat, his eyes strangely calm and more yellow than ever. "At the time I wondered where I'd heard that name before . . . the Eye of the World. Now I remember. Don't you?"

"I don't want to remember anything," Mat said stiffly.

"We have to tell her," Perrin continued. "It's important now. We can't keep it secret any longer. You see it, don't you, Rand?"

"Tell me what?" Moiraine's voice was harsh, and she seemed to be bracing for a blow. Her gaze had settled on Rand.

He did not want to answer. He did not want to remember any more than Mat, but he did remember—and he knew Perrin was right. "I've. . . ." He looked at his friends. Mat nodded reluctantly, Perrin decisively, but at least they had done it. He did not have to face her alone. "We have had . . . dreams." He rubbed the spot on his finger where the thorn had stuck him once, remembering the blood when he woke. Queasily remembering the sunburned feel of his face another time. "Except maybe they weren't dreams, exactly. Ba'alzamon was in them." He knew why Perrin had used that name; it was easier than saying the Dark One had been in your dreams, inside your head. "He said . . . he said all sorts of things, but once he said the Eye of the World would never serve me." For a minute his mouth was as dry as dust.

"He told me the same thing," Perrin said, and Mat sighed heavily, then nodded. Rand found he had spit in his mouth again. "You aren't angry with us?" Perrin asked, sounding surprised, and Rand realized that Moiraine did not seem angry. She was studying them, but her eyes were clear and calm, if intent.

"More with myself than you. But I did ask you to tell me if you had strange dreams. In the beginning, I asked." Though her voice remained level, a flash of anger crossed her eyes, and was gone in an instant. "Had I known after the first such, I might have been able to. . . . There has not been a Dreamwalker in Tar Valon for nearly a thousand years, but I could have tried. Now it is too late. Each time the Dark One touches you, he makes the next touching easier for him. Perhaps my presence can still shield you somewhat, but even then. . . . Remember the stories of the Forsaken binding men to them? Strong men, men who had fought the Dark One from the start. Those stories are true, and none of the Forsaken had a tenth of the strength of their master, not Aginor or Lanfear, not Balthamel or Demandred, not even Ishamael, the Betrayer of Hope himself."

Nynaeve and Egwene were looking at him, Rand saw, him and Mat and Perrin all three. The women's faces were a blood-drained blend of fear and horror. *Are they afraid for us, or afraid of us?*

"What can we do?" he asked. "There has to be something."

"Staying close by me," Moiraine replied, "will help. Some. The protection from touching the True Source extends around me a little, remember. But you cannot always remain close to me. You can defend yourself, if you have the strength for it, but you must find the strength and will within yourself. I cannot give it to you."

"I think I've already found my protection," Perrin said, sounding resigned rather than happy.

"Yes," Moiraine said, "I suppose you have." She looked at him until he dropped his eyes, and even then she stood considering. Finally she turned to the others. "There are limits to the Dark One's power inside you. Yield even for an instant and he will have a string tied to your heart, a string you may never be able to cut. Surrender, and you will be his. Deny him, and his power fails. It is not easy when he touches your dreams, but it can be done. He can still send Halfmen against you, and Trollocs, and Draghkar, and other things, but he cannot make you his unless you let him."

"Fades are bad enough," Perrin said.

"I don't want him inside my head again," Mat growled. "Isn't there any way to keep him out?"

Moiraine shook her head. "Loial has nothing to fear, nor Egwene, nor Nynaeve. Out of the mass of humanity, the Dark One can touch an individual only by chance, unless that person seeks it. But for a time, at least, you three are central to the Pattern. A Web of Destiny is being woven, and every thread leads straight to you. What else did the Dark One say to you?"

"I don't remember it all that well," Perrin said. "There was something about one of us being chosen, something like that. I remember him laughing," he finished bleakly, "about who we were chosen by. He said I—we could serve him or die. And then we'd still serve him."

"He said the Amyrlin Seat would try to use us," Mat added, his voice fading as he remembered to whom he was speaking. He swallowed and went on. "He said just like Tar Valon used—he had some names. Davian, I think. I can't remember very well, either."

"Raolin Darksbane," Perrin said.

"Yes," Rand said, frowning. He had tried to forget everything about those dreams. It was unpleasant bringing them back. "Yurian Stonebow was another, and Guaire Amalasan." He stopped suddenly, hoping Moiraine had not noticed how suddenly. "I don't recognize any of them."

But he had recognized one, now that he dredged them from the depths of memory. The name he had barely stopped himself from saying. Logain. The false Dragon. *Light! Thom said they were dangerous names. Is that what Ba'alzamon meant? Moiraine wants to use one of us as a false Dragon? Aes Sedai hunt down false Dragons, they don't use them. Do they? Light help me, do they?*

Moiraine was looking at him, but he could not read her face.

"Do you know them?" he asked her. "Do they mean anything?"

"The Father of Lies is a good name for the Dark One," Moiraine replied. "It was always his way to seed the worm of doubt wherever he could. It eats at men's minds like a canker. When you believe the Father of Lies, it is the first step toward surrender. Remember, if you surrender to the Dark One, he will make you his."

An Aes Sedai never lies, but the truth she speaks may not be the truth you think you hear. That was what Tam had said, and she had not really answered his question. He kept his face expressionless and held his hands still on his knees, trying not to scrub the sweat off them on his breeches.

Egwene was crying softly. Nynaeve had her arms around her, but she looked as if she wanted to cry, too. Rand almost wished he could.

"They are *all* *ta'veren*," Loial said abruptly. He seemed brightened by the prospect, looking forward to watching from close by as the Pattern wove itself around them. Rand looked at him incredulously, and the Ogier gave an abashed shrug, but it was not enough to dim his eagerness.

"So they are," Moiraine said. "*Three* of them, when I expected one. A great many things have happened that I did not expect. This news concerning the Eye of the World changes much." She paused, frowning. "For a time the Pattern does seem to be swirling around all three of you, just as Loial says, and the swirl will grow greater before it becomes less. Sometimes being *ta'veren* means the Pattern is forced to bend to you, and sometimes it means the Pattern forces you to the needed path. The Web can still be woven many ways, and some of those designs would be disastrous. For you, for the world.

"We cannot remain in Caemlyn, but by any road, Myrddraal and Trollocs will be on us before we have gone ten miles. And just at this point we hear of a threat to the Eye of the World, not from one source, but three, each seeming independent of the others. The Pattern is forcing our path. The Pattern still weaves itself around you three, but what hand now sets the warp, and what hand controls the shuttle? Has the Dark One's prison weakened enough for him to exert that much control?"

"There's no need for that kind of talk!" Nynaeve said sharply. "You'll only frighten them."

"But not you?" Moiraine asked. "It frightens me. Well, perhaps you are right. Fear cannot be allowed to affect our course. Whether this is a trap or a timely warning, we must do what we must, and that is to reach the Eye of the World quickly. The Green Man must know of this threat."

Rand gave a start. *The Green Man?* The others stared, too, all but Loial, whose broad face looked worried.

"I cannot even risk stopping in Tar Valon for help," Moiraine continued. "Time traps us. Even if we could ride out of the city unhindered, it would take many weeks to reach the Blight, and I fear we no longer have weeks."

"The Blight!" Rand heard himself echoed in a chorus, but Moiraine ignored them all.

"The Pattern presents a crisis, and at the same time a way to surmount it. If I did not know it was impossible, I could almost believe the Creator is taking a hand. There is a way." She smiled as if at a private joke, and turned to Loial. "There was an Ogier grove here at Caemlyn, and a Waygate. The New City now spreads out over where the grove once stood, so the Waygate must be inside the walls. I know not many Ogier learn the Ways now, but one who has a Talent and learns the old Songs of Growing must be drawn to such knowledge, even if he believes it will never be used. Do you know the Ways, Loial?"

The Ogier shifted his feet uneasily. "I do, Aes Sedai, but—"

"Can you find the path to Fal Dara along the Ways?"

"I've never heard of Fal Dara," Loial said, sounding relieved.

"In the days of the Trolloc Wars it was known as Mafal Dadaranell. Do you know *that* name?"

"I know it," Loial said reluctantly, "but—"

"Then you can find the path for us," Moiraine said. "A curious turn, indeed. When we can neither stay nor leave by any ordinary means, I learn of a threat to the Eye, and in the same place there is one who can take us there in days. Whether it is the Creator, or fate, or even the Dark One, the Pattern has chosen our path for us."

"No!" Loial said, an emphatic rumble like thunder. Everyone turned to look at him and he blinked under the attention, but there was nothing hesitant about his words. "If we enter the Ways, we will all die—or be swallowed by the Shadow."

CHAPTER
43

Decisions and Apparitions

The Aes Sedai appeared to know what Loial meant, but she said nothing. Loial peered at the floor, rubbing under his nose with a thick finger, as if he was abashed by his outburst. No one wanted to speak.

"Why?" Rand asked at last. "Why would we die? What *are* the Ways?"

Loial glanced at Moiraine. She turned away to take a chair in front of the fireplace. The little cat stretched, its claws scratching on the hearthstone, and languidly walked over to butt its head against her ankles. She rubbed behind its ears with one finger. The cat's purring was a strange counterpoint to the Aes Sedai's level voice. "It is your knowledge, Loial. The Ways are the only path to safety for us, the only path to forestalling the Dark One, if only for a time, but the telling is yours."

The Ogier did not appear comforted by her speech. He shifted awkwardly on his chair before beginning. "During the Time of Madness, while the world was still being broken, the earth was in upheaval, and humankind was being scattered like dust on the wind. We Ogier were scattered, too, driven from the *stedding,* into the Exile and the Long Wandering, when the Longing was graven on our hearts." He gave Moiraine another sidelong look. His long eyebrows drew down into two points. "I will try to be brief, but this is not a thing that can be told too briefly. It is of the others I must speak, now, those few Ogier who held in their *stedding* while around them the world was

tearing apart. And of the Aes Sedai"—he avoided looking at
Moiraine, now—"the male Aes Sedai who were dying even as
they destroyed the world in their madness. It was to those Aes
Sedai—those who had so far managed to avoid the madness—
that the *stedding* first made the offer of sanctuary. Many accepted, for in the *stedding* they were protected from the taint of
the Dark One that was killing their kind. But they were cut off
from the True Source. It was not just that they could not wield
the One Power, or touch the Source; they could no longer even
sense that the Source existed. In the end, none could accept
that isolation, and one by one they left the *stedding,* hoping
that by that time the taint was gone. It never was."

"Some in Tar Valon," Moiraine said quietly, "claim that
Ogier sanctuary prolonged the Breaking and made it worse.
Others say that if all of those men had been allowed to go mad
at once, there would have been nothing left of the world. I am
of the Blue Ajah, Loial; unlike the Red Ajah, we hold to the
second view. Sanctuary helped to save what could be saved.
Continue, please."

Loial nodded gratefully. Relieved of a concern, Rand realized.

"As I was saying," the Ogier went on, "the Aes Sedai, the
male Sedai, left. But before they went, they gave a gift to the
Ogier in thanks for our sanctuary. The Ways. Enter a Waygate,
walk for a day, and you may depart through another Waygate a
hundred miles from where you started. Or five hundred. Time
and distance are strange in the Ways. Different paths, different
bridges, lead to different places, and how long it takes to get
there depends on which path you take. It was a marvelous gift,
made more so by the times, for the Ways are not part of the
world we see around us, nor perhaps of any world outside
themselves. Not only did the Ogier so gifted not have to travel
through the world, where even after the Breaking men fought
like animals to live, in order to reach another *stedding,* but
within the Ways there was no Breaking. The land between two
stedding might split open into deep canyons or rise in mountain
ranges, but in the Way between them there was no change.

"When the last Aes Sedai left the *stedding,* they gave to the
Elders a key, a talisman, that could be used for growing more.
They are a living thing in some fashion, the Ways and the Way-

gates. I do not understand it; no Ogier ever has, and even the Aes Sedai have forgotten, I am told. Over the years the Exile ended for us. As those Ogier who had been gifted by the Aes Sedai found a *stedding* where Ogier had returned from the Long Wandering, they grew a Way to it. With the stonework we learned during the Exile, we built cities for men, and planted the groves to comfort the Ogier who did the building, so the Longing would not overcome them. To those groves Ways were grown. There was a grove, and a Waygate, at Mafal Dadaranell, but that city was razed during the Trolloc Wars, no stone left standing on another, and the grove was chopped down and burned for Trolloc fires." He left no doubt which had been the greater crime.

"Waygates are all but impossible to destroy," Moiraine said, "and humankind not much less so. There are people at Fal Dara still, though not the great city the Ogier built, and the Waygate yet stands."

"How did they make them?" Egwene asked. Her puzzled look took in Moiraine and Loial both. "The Aes Sedai, the men. If they couldn't use the One Power in a *stedding*, how could they make the Ways? Or did they use the Power at all? Their part of the True Source was tainted. Is tainted. I don't know much about what Aes Sedai can do, yet. Maybe it's a silly question."

Loial explained. "Each *stedding* has a Waygate on its border, but outside. Your question is not silly. You've found the seed of why we do not dare travel the Ways. No Ogier has used the Ways in my lifetime, and before. By edict of the Elders, all the Elders of all the *stedding*, none may, human or Ogier.

"The Ways were made by men wielding Power fouled by the Dark One. About a thousand years ago, during what you humans call the War of the Hundred Years, the Ways began to change. So slowly in the beginning that none really noticed, they grew dank and dim. Then darkness fell along the bridges. Some who went in were never seen again. Travelers spoke of being watched from the dark. The numbers who vanished grew, and some who came out had gone mad, raving about *Machin Shin*, the Black Wind. Aes Sedai Healers could aid some, but even with Aes Sedai help they were never the same. And they never remembered anything of what had occurred. Yet it was as if the darkness had sunken into their bones. They never laughed again, and they feared the sound of the wind."

For a moment there was silence but for the cat purring beside Moiraine's chair, and the snap and crackle of the fire, popping out sparks. Then Nynaeve burst out angrily, "And you expect us to follow you into that? You must be mad!"

"Which would you choose instead?" Moiraine asked quietly. "The Whitecloaks within Caemlyn, or the Trollocs without? Remember that my presence in itself gives some protection from the Dark One's works."

Nynaeve settled back with an exasperated sigh.

"You still have not explained to me," Loial said, "why I should break the edict of the Elders. And I have no desire to enter the Ways. Muddy as they often are, the roads men make have served me well enough since I left Stedding Shangtai."

"Humankind and Ogier, everything that lives, we are at war with the Dark One," Moiraine said. "The greater part of the world does not even know it yet, and most of the few who do fight skirmishes and believe they are battles. While the world refuses to believe, the Dark One may be at the brink of victory. There is enough power in the Eye of the World to undo his prison. If the Dark One has found some way to bend the Eye of the World to his use. . . ."

Rand wished the lamps in the room were lit. Evening was creeping over Caemlyn, and the fire in the fireplace did not give enough light. He wanted no shadows in the room.

"What can we do?" Mat burst out. "Why are we so important? Why do we have to go to the Blight? The Blight!"

Moiraine did not raise her voice, but it filled the room, compelling. Her chair by the fire suddenly seemed like a throne. Suddenly even Morgase would have paled in her presence. "One thing we can do. We can try. What seems like chance is often the Pattern. Three threads have come together here, each giving a warning: the Eye. It cannot be chance; it is the Pattern. You three did not choose; you were chosen by the Pattern. And you are here, where the danger is known. You can step aside, and perhaps doom the world. Running, hiding, will not save you from the weaving of the Pattern. Or you can try. You can go to the Eye of the World, three *ta'veren*, three centerpoints of the Web, placed where the danger lies. Let the

Pattern be woven around you there, and you may save the world from the Shadow. The choice is yours. I cannot make you go."

"I'll go," Rand said, trying to sound resolute. However hard he sought the void, images kept flashing through his head. Tam, and the farmhouse, and the flock in the pasture. It had been a good life; he had never really wanted anything more. There was comfort—a small comfort—hearing Perrin and Mat add their agreement to his. They sounded as dry-mouthed as he.

"I suppose there isn't any choice for Egwene or me, either," Nynaeve said.

Moiraine nodded. "You are part of the Pattern, too, both of you, in some fashion. Perhaps not *ta'veren*—perhaps—but strong even so. I have known it since Baerlon. And no doubt by this time the Fades know it, too. And Ba'alzamon. Yet you have as much choice as the young men. You could remain here, proceed to Tar Valon once the rest of us have gone."

"Stay behind!" Egwene exclaimed. "Let the rest of you go off into danger while we hide under the covers? I won't do it!" She caught the Aes Sedai's eye and drew back a little, but not all of her defiance vanished. "I won't do it," she muttered stubbornly.

"I suppose that means both of us will accompany you." Nynaeve sounded resigned, but her eyes flashed when she added, "You still need my herbs, Aes Sedai, unless you've suddenly gained some ability I don't know about." Her voice held a challenge Rand did not understand, but Moiraine merely nodded and turned to the Ogier.

"Well, Loial, son of Arent son of Halan?"

Loial opened his mouth twice, his tufted ears twitching, before he spoke. "Yes, well. The Green Man. The Eye of the World. They're mentioned in the books, of course, but I don't think any Ogier has actually seen them in, oh, quite a long time. I suppose. . . . But must it be the Ways?" Moiraine nodded, and his long eyebrows sagged till the ends brushed his cheeks. "Very well, then. I suppose I must guide you. Elder Haman would say it's no less than I deserve for being so hasty all the time."

"Our choices are made, then," Moiraine said. "And now

that they are made, we must decide what to do about them, and how."

Long into the night they planned. Moiraine did most of it, with Loial's advice concerning the Ways, but she listened to questions and suggestions from everyone. Once dark fell Lan joined them, adding his comments in that iron-cored drawl. Nynaeve made a list of what supplies they needed, dipping her pen in the inkwell with a steady hand despite the way she kept muttering under her breath.

Rand wished he could be as matter-of-fact as the Wisdom. He could not stop pacing up and down, as if he had energy to burn or burst from it. He knew his decision was made, knew it was the only one he could make with the knowledge he had, but that did not make him like it. The Blight. Shayol Ghul was somewhere in the Blight, beyond the Blasted Lands.

He could see the same worry in Mat's eyes, the same fear he knew was in his own. Mat sat with his hands·clasped, knuckles white. If he let go, Rand thought, he would be clutching the dagger from Shadar Logoth instead.

There was no worry on Perrin's face at all, but what was there was worse: a mask of weary resignation. Perrin looked as though he had fought something until he could fight it no longer and was waiting for it to finish him. Yet sometimes. . . .

"We do what we must, Rand," he said. "The Blight. . . ." For an instant those yellow eyes lit with eagerness, flashing in the fixed tiredness of his face, as if they had a life of their own apart from the big blacksmith's apprentice. "There's good hunting along the Blight," he whispered. Then he shuddered, as if he had just heard what he had said, and once more his face was resigned.

And Egwene. Rand drew her apart at one point, over by the fireplace where those planning around the table could not hear. "Egwene, I. . . ." Her eyes, like big dark pools drawing him in, made him stop and swallow. "It's me the Dark One's after, Egwene. Me, and Mat, and Perrin. I don't care what Moiraine Sedai says. In the morning you and Nynaeve could start for home, or Tar Valon, or anywhere you want to go, and nobody will try to stop you. Not the Trollocs, not the Fades, not anybody. As long as you aren't with us. Go home, Egwene. Or go to Tar Valon. But go."

He waited for her to tell him she had as much right to go where she wanted as he did, that he had no right to tell her what to do. To his surprise, she smiled and touched his cheek. "Thank you, Rand," she said softly. He blinked, and closed his mouth as she went on. "You know I can't, though. Moiraine Sedai told us what Min saw, in Baerlon. You should have told me who Min was. I thought. . . . Well, Min says I am part of this, too. And Nynaeve. Maybe I'm not *ta'veren*," she stumbled over the word, "but the Pattern sends me to the Eye of the World, too, it seems. Whatever involves you, involves me."

"But, Egwene—"

"Who is Elayne?"

For a minute he stared at her, then told the simple truth. "She's the Daughter-Heir to the throne of Andor."

Her eyes seemed to catch fire. "If you can't be serious for more than a minute, Rand al'Thor, I do not want to talk to you."

Incredulous, he watched her stiff back return to the table, where she leaned on her elbows next to Moiraine to listen to what the Warder was saying. *I need to talk to Perrin,* he thought. *He knows how to deal with women.*

Master Gill entered several times, first to light the lamps, then to bring food with his own hands, and later to report on what was happening outside. Whitecloaks were watching the inn from down the street in both directions. There had been a riot at the gates to the Inner City, with the Queen's Guards arresting white cockades and red alike. Someone had tried to scratch the Dragon's Fang on the front door and been sent on his way by Lamgwin's boot.

If the innkeeper found it odd that Loial was with them, he gave no sign of it. He answered the few questions Moiraine put to him without trying to discover what they were planning, and each time he came he knocked at the door and waited till Lan opened it for him, just as if it were not his inn and his library. On his last visit, Moiraine gave him the sheet of parchment covered in Nynaeve's neat hand.

"It won't be easy this time of night," he said, shaking his head as he perused the list, "but I'll arrange it all."

Moiraine added a small wash-leather bag that clinked as she

handed it to him by the drawstrings. "Good. And see that we
are wakened before daybreak. The watchers will be at their
least alert, then."

"We'll leave them watching an empty box, Aes Sedai." Master Gill grinned.

Rand was yawning by the time he shuffled out of the room
with the rest in search of baths and beds. As he scrubbed himself, with a coarse cloth in one hand and a big yellow cake of
soap in the other, his eyes drifted to the stool beside Mat's tub.
The golden-sheathed tip of the dagger from Shadar Logoth
peeked from under the edge of Mat's neatly folded coat. Lan
glanced at it from time to time, too. Rand wondered if it was
really as safe to have around as Moiraine claimed.

"Do you think my da'll ever believe it?" Mat laughed, scrubbing his back with a long-handled brush. "Me, saving the
world? My sisters won't know whether to laugh or cry."

He sounded like the old Mat. Rand wished he could forget
the dagger.

It was pitch-black when he and Mat finally got up to their
room under the eaves, the stars obscured by clouds. For the
first time in a long while Mat undressed before getting into bed,
but he casually tucked the dagger under his pillow, too. Rand
blew out the candle and crawled into his own bed. He could
feel the wrongness from the other bed, not from Mat, but from
beneath his pillow. He was still worrying about it when sleep
came.

From the first he knew it was a dream, one of those dreams
that was not entirely dream. He stood staring at the wooden
door, its surface dark and cracked and rough with splinters.
The air was cold and dank, thick with the smell of decay. In the
distance water dripped, the splashes hollow echoes down stone
corridors.

Deny it. Deny him, and his power fails.

He closed his eyes and concentrated on The Queen's Blessing, on his bed, on himself asleep in his bed. When he opened
his eyes the door was still there. The echoing splashes came on
his heartbeat, as if his pulse counted time for them. He sought
the flame and the void, as Tam had taught him, and found inner calm, but nothing outside of him changed. Slowly he
opened the door and went in.

Everything was as he remembered it in the room that seemed burned out of the living rock. Tall, arched windows led onto an unrailed balcony, and beyond it the layered clouds streamed like a river in flood. The black metal lamps, their flames too bright to look at, gleamed, black yet somehow as bright as silver. The fire roared but gave no heat in the fearsome fireplace, each stone still vaguely like a face in torment.

All was the same, but one thing was different. On the polished tabletop stood three small figures, the rough, featureless shapes of men, as if the sculptor had been hasty with his clay. Beside one stood a wolf, its clear detail emphasized by the crudeness of the man-shape, and another clutched a tiny dagger, a point of red on the hilt glittering in the light. The last held a sword. The hair stirring on the back of his neck, he moved close enough to see the heron in exquisite detail on that small blade.

His head jerked up in panic, and he stared directly into the lone mirror. His reflection was still a blur, but not so misty as before. He could almost make out his own features. If he imagined he was squinting, he could nearly tell who it was.

"You've hidden from me too long."

He whirled from the table, breath rasping his throat. A moment before he had been alone, but now Ba'alzamon stood before the windows. When he spoke caverns of flame replaced his eyes and mouth.

"Too long, but not much longer."

"I deny you," Rand said hoarsely. "I deny that you hold any power over me. I deny that you are."

Ba'alzamon laughed, a rich sound rolling from fire. "Do you think it is that easy? But then, you always did. Each time we have stood like this, you have thought you could defy me."

"What do mean, each time? I deny you!"

"You always do. In the beginning. This contest between us has taken place countless times before. Each time your face is different, and your name, but each time it is you."

"I deny you." It was a desperate whisper.

"Each time you throw your puny strength against me, and each time, in the end, you know which of us is the master. Age after Age, you kneel to me, or die wishing you still had strength to kneel. Poor fool, you can never win against me."

"Liar!" he shouted. "Father of Lies. Father of Fools if you can't do better than that. Men found you in the last Age, in the Age of Legends, and bound you back where you belong."

Ba'alzamon laughed again, peal after mocking peal, until Rand wanted to cover his ears to shut it out. He forced his hands to stay at his sides. Void or no, they were trembling when the laughter finally stopped.

"You worm, you know nothing at all. As ignorant as a beetle under a rock, and as easily crushed. This struggle has gone on since the moment of creation. Always men think it a new war, but it is just the same war discovered anew. Only now change blows on the winds of time. Change. This time there will be no drifting back. Those proud Aes Sedai who think to stand you up against me. I will dress them in chains and send them running naked to do my bidding, or stuff their souls into the Pit of Doom to scream for eternity. All but those who already serve me. They will stand but a step beneath me. You can choose to stand with them, with the world groveling at your feet. I offer it one more time, one last time. You can stand above them, above every power and dominion but mine. There have been times when you made that choice, times when you lived long enough to know your power."

Deny him! Rand grabbed hold to what he could deny. "No Aes Sedai serve you. Another lie!"

"Is that what they told you? Two thousand years ago I took my Trollocs across the world, and even among Aes Sedai I found those who knew despair, who knew the world could not stand before Shai'tan. For two thousand years the Black Ajah has dwelt among the others, unseen in the shadows. Perhaps even those who claim to help you."

Rand shook his head, trying to shake away the doubts that came welling up in him, all the doubts he had had about Moiraine, about what the Aes Sedai wanted with him, about what she planned for him. "What do you want from me?" he cried. *Deny him! Light help me deny him!*

"Kneel!" Ba'alzamon pointed to the floor at his feet. "Kneel, and acknowledge me your master! In the end, you will. You will be my creature, or you will die."

The last word echoed through the room, reverberating back on itself, doubling and redoubling, till Rand threw up his arms as if to shield his head from a blow. Staggering back until he thumped into the table, he shouted, trying to drown the sound in his ears. "Noooooooooooo!"

As he cried out, he spun, sweeping the figures to the floor. Something stabbed his hand, but he ignored it, stomping the clay to shapeless smears underfoot. But when his shout failed, the echo was still there, and growing stronger:

die-die-die-die-die-DIE-DIE-DIE-DIE-DIE-DIE-DIE-DIE-DIE-DIE-DIE

The sound pulled on him like a whirlpool, drawing him in, ripping the void in his mind to shreds. The light dimmed, and his vision narrowed down to a tunnel with Ba'alzamon standing tall in the last spot of brightness at the end, dwindling until it was the size of his hand, a fingernail, nothing. Around and around the echo whirled him, down into blackness and death.

The thump as he hit the floor woke him, still struggling to swim up out of that darkness. The room was dark, but not so dark as that. Frantically he tried to center on the flame, to shovel fear into it, but the calm of the void eluded him. Tremors ran down his arms and legs, but he held the image of the single flame until the blood stopped pounding in his ears.

Mat was tossing and twisting on his bed, groaning in his sleep. ". . . deny you, deny you, deny you. . . ." It faded off into unintelligible moans.

Rand reached out to shake him awake, and at the first touch Mat sat up with a strangled grunt. For a minute Mat stared around wildly, then drew a long, shuddering breath and dropped his head into his hands. Abruptly he twisted around, digging under his pillow, then sank back clutching the ruby-hilted dagger in both hands on his chest. He turned his head to look at Rand, his face hidden in shadow. "He's back, Rand."

"I know."

Mat nodded. "There were these three figures. . . ."

"I saw them, too."

"He knows who I am, Rand. I picked up the one with the dagger, and he said, 'So that's who you are.' And when I looked again, the figure had my face. My face, Rand! It looked like flesh. It felt like flesh. Light help me, I could feel my own hand gripping me, like I was the figure."

Rand was silent for a moment. "You have to keep denying him, Mat."

"I did, and he laughed. He kept talking about some eternal war, and saying we'd met like that a thousand times before, and. . . . Light, Rand, the Dark One knows me."

"He said the same thing to me. I don't think he does," he added slowly. "I don't think he knows which of us. . . ." *Which of us what?*

As he levered himself up, pain stabbed his hand. Making his way to the table, he managed to get the candle lit after three tries, then spread his hand open in the light. Driven into his palm was a thick splinter of dark wood, smooth and polished on one side. He stared at it, not breathing. Abruptly he was panting, plucking at the splinter, fumbling with haste.

"What's the matter?" Mat asked.

"Nothing."

Finally he had it, and a sharp yank pulled it free. With a grunt of disgust he dropped it, but the grunt froze in his throat. As soon as the splinter left his fingers, it vanished.

The wound was still there in his hand, though, bleeding. There was water in the stoneware pitcher. He filled the basin, his hands shaking so that he splashed water onto the table. Hurriedly he washed his hands, kneading his palm till his thumb brought more blood, then washed them again. The thought of the smallest sliver remaining in his flesh terrified him.

"Light," Mat said, "he made me feel dirty, too." But he still lay where he was, holding the dagger in both hands.

"Yes," Rand said. "Dirty." He fumbled a towel from the stack beside the basin. There was a knock at the door, and he jumped. It came again. "Yes?" he said.

Moiraine put her head into the room. "You are awake already. Good. Dress quickly and come down. We must be away before first light."

"Now?" Mat groaned. "We haven't had an hour's sleep yet."

"An hour?" she said. "You have had four. Now hurry, we do not have much time."

Rand shared a confused look with Mat. He could remember

every second of the dream clearly. It had begun as soon as he closed his eyes, and lasted only minutes.

Something in that exchange must have communicated itself to Moiraine. She gave them a penetrating look and came all the way in. "What has happened? The dreams?"

"He knows who I am," Mat said. "The Dark One knows my face."

Rand held up his hand wordlessly, palm toward her. Even in the shadowed light from the one candle the blood was plain.

The Aes Sedai stepped forward and grasped his upheld hand, her thumb across his palm covering the wound. Cold pierced him to the bone, so chill that his fingers cramped and he had to fight to keep them open. When she took her fingers away, the chill went, too.

He turned his hand, then, stunned, scrubbed the thin smear of blood away. The wound was gone. Slowly he raised his eyes to meet those of the Aes Sedai.

"Hurry," she said softly. "Time grows very short."

He knew she was not speaking of the time for their leaving anymore.

CHAPTER
44

The Dark Along the Ways

In the darkness just before dawn Rand followed Moiraine down to the back hall, where Master Gill and the others were waiting, Nynaeve and Egwene as anxiously as Loial, Perrin almost as calm as the Warder. Mat stayed on Rand's heels as if he were afraid to be even a little alone now, even as much as a few feet away. The cook and her helpers straightened, staring as the party passed silently into the kitchen, already brightly lit and hot with preparations for breakfast. It was not usual for patrons of the inn to be up and out at that hour. At Master Gill's soothing words, the cook gave a loud sniff and slapped her dough down hard. They were all back to tending griddles and kneading dough before Rand reached the stableyard door.

Outside, the night was still pitch-black. To Rand, everyone else was only a darker shadow at best. He followed the innkeeper and Lan blindly, blind in truth, hoping Master Gill's knowledge of his own stableyard and the Warder's instincts would get them across it without someone breaking a leg. Loial stumbled more than once.

"I don't see why we can't have just one light," the Ogier grumbled. "We don't go running about in the dark in the *stedding*. I'm an Ogier, not a cat." Rand had a sudden image of Loial's tufted ears twitching irritably.

The stable loomed up suddenly out of the night, a threatening mass until the stable door creaked open, spilling a narrow stream of light into the yard. The innkeeper only opened it wide enough for them to go in one at a time, and hastily pulled it to behind Perrin, almost clipping his heels. Rand blinked in the sudden light inside.

The stablemen were not surprised by their appearance, as the cook had been. Their horses were saddled and waiting. Mandarb stood arrogantly, ignoring everyone but Lan, but Aldieb stretched her nose out to nuzzle Moiraine's hand. There was a packhorse, bulky with wicker panniers, and a huge animal with hairy fetlocks, taller even than the Warder's stallion, for Loial. It looked big enough to pull a loaded haywain by itself, but compared with the Ogier it seemed a pony.

Loial eyed the big horse and muttered doubtfully, "My own feet have always been good enough."

Master Gill motioned to Rand. The innkeeper was lending him a bay almost the color of his own hair, tall and deep of chest, but with none of the fire in his step that Cloud had had, Rand was glad to see. Master Gill said his name was Red.

Egwene went straight to Bela, and Nynaeve to her long-legged mare.

Mat brought his dun-colored horse over by Rand. "Perrin's making me nervous," he muttered. Rand looked at him sharply. "Well, he's acting strange. Don't you see it, too? I swear it's not my imagination, or . . . or. . . ."

Rand nodded. *Not the dagger taking hold of him again, thank the Light.* "He is, Mat, but just be easy. Moiraine knows about . . . whatever it is. Perrin's fine." He wished he could believe it, but it seemed to satisfy Mat, a little at least.

"Of course," Mat said hastily, still watching Perrin out of the corner of his eye. "I never said he wasn't."

Master Gill conferred with the head groom. That leathery-skinned man, with a face like one of the horses, knuckled his forehead and hurried to the back of the stable. The innkeeper turned to Moiraine with a satisfied smile on his round face. "Ramey says the way is clear, Aes Sedai."

The rear wall of the stable appeared solid and stout, lined with heavy racks of tools. Ramey and another stableman cleared away the hayforks, rakes, and shovels, then reached behind the racks to manipulate hidden latches. Abruptly a section of the wall swung inward on hinges so well concealed that

Rand was not sure he could find them even with the disguised door standing open. Light from the stable illuminated a brick wall only a few feet away.

"It's only a narrow run between buildings," the innkeeper said, "but nobody outside this stable knows there's a way into it from here. Whitecloaks or white cockades, there'll not be any watchers to see where you come out."

The Aes Sedai nodded. "Remember, good innkeeper, if you fear any trouble from this, write to Sheriam Sedai, of the Blue Ajah, in Tar Valon, and she will help. I fear my sisters and I have a good deal to put right already for those who have helped me."

Master Gill laughed; not the laugh of a worried man. "Why, Aes Sedai, you've already given me the only inn in all of Caemlyn without any rats. What more could I ask for? I can double my custom on that alone." His grin faded into seriousness. "Whatever you're up to, the Queen holds with Tar Valon, and I hold with the Queen, so I wish you well. The Light illumine you, Aes Sedai. The Light illumine you all."

"The Light illumine you, also, Master Gill," Moiraine replied with a bow of her head. "But if the Light is to shine on any of us, we must be quick." Briskly she turned to Loial. "Are you ready?"

With a wary look at its teeth, the Ogier took the reins of the big horse. Trying to keep that mouth the length of the reins from his hand, he led the animal to the opening at the back of the stable. Ramey hopped from one foot to the other, impatient to close it again. For a moment Loial paused with his head cocked as if feeling a breeze on his cheek. "This way," he said, and turned down the narrow alley.

Moiraine followed right behind Loial's horse, then Rand, and Mat. Rand had the first turn leading the packhorse. Nynaeve and Egwene made the middle of the column, with Perrin behind them, and Lan bringing up the rear. The hidden door swung hastily shut as soon as Mandarb stepped into the dirt alleyway. The *snick-snick* of latches locking, shutting them off, sounded unnaturally loud to Rand.

The run, as Master Gill had called it, was very narrow indeed, and even darker than the stableyard, if that was possible. Tall, blank walls of brick or wood lined both sides, with only a narrow strip of black sky overhead. The big, woven baskets slung on the packhorse scraped the buildings on both sides. The panniers bulged with supplies for the journey, most of it clay jars filled with oil. A bundle of poles was lashed lengthwise down the horse's back, and each had a lantern swinging at the end of it. In the Ways, Loial said, it was darker than the darkest night.

The partially-filled lanterns sloshed with the motion of the horse, and clinked against each other with a tinny sound. It was not a very loud noise, but in the hour before dawn Caemlyn was quiet. Silent. The dull metallic clinks sounded as if they could be heard a mile away.

When the run let out into a street, Loial chose his direction without a pause. He seemed to know exactly where he was going, now, as if the route he needed to follow was becoming clearer. Rand did not understand how the Ogier could find the Waygate, and Loial had not been able to explain very well. He just knew, he said; he could feel it. Loial claimed it was like trying to explain how to breathe.

As they hurried up the street Rand looked back toward the corner where The Queen's Blessing lay. According to Lamgwin, there were still half a dozen Whitecloaks not far down from that corner. Their interest was all on the inn, but a noise would surely bring them. No one was out at this hour for a reputable reason. The horseshoes seemed to ring on the paving stones like bells; the lanterns clattered as if the packhorse were shaking them deliberately. Not until they had rounded another corner did he stop looking over his shoulder. He heard relieved sighs from the other Emond's Fielders as they came round it, too.

Loial appeared to be following the most direct path to the Waygate, wherever it took them. Sometimes they trotted down broad avenues, empty save for an occasional dog skulking in the dark. Sometimes they hurried along alleys as narrow as the stable run, where things squished under an unwary step. Nynaeve complained softly about the resulting smells, but no one slowed down.

The darkness began to lessen, fading toward a dark gray. Faint glimmers of dawn pearled the sky above the eastern rooftops. A few people appeared on the streets, bundled up against

the early cold, heads down while they yet dreamed of their
beds. Most paid no mind to anyone else. Only a handful even
glanced at the line of people and horses with Loial at its head,
and only one of those truly saw them.

That one man flicked his eyes at them, just like the others,
already sinking back into his own thoughts when suddenly he
stumbled and almost fell, turning himself back around to stare.
There was only light enough to see shapes, but that was too
much. Seen at a distance by himself, the Ogier could have
passed for a tall man leading an ordinary horse, or for an ordinary man leading an under-sized horse. With the others in a
line behind him to give perspective, Loial looked exactly as big
as he was, half again as tall as any man should be. The man
took one look and, with a strangled cry, set off running, his
cloak flapping behind him.

There would be more people in the streets soon—very soon.
Rand eyed a woman hurrying past on the other side of the
street, seeing nothing but the pavement in front of her feet.
More people to notice soon. The eastern sky grew lighter.

"There," Loial announced at last. "It is under there." It was
a shop he pointed to, still closed for the night. The tables out
front were bare, the awnings over them rolled up tight, the
door stoutly shuttered. The windows above, where the shopkeeper lived, were still dark.

"Under?" Mat exclaimed incredulously. "How in the Light
can we—?"

Moiraine raised a hand that cut him off, and motioned for
them to follow her into the alley beside the shop. Horses and
people together, they crowded the opening between the two
buildings. Shaded by the walls, it was darker there than on the
street, near to full night again.

"There must be a cellar door," Moiraine muttered. "Ah,
yes."

Abruptly light blossomed. A coolly glowing ball the size of a
man's fist hung suspended over the Aes Sedai's palm, moving
as she moved her hand. Rand thought that it was a measure of
what they had been through that everyone seemed to take it as
a matter of course. She put it close to the doors she had found,
slanted almost flat to the ground, with a hasp held by thick

bolts and an iron lock bigger than Rand's hand and thick with old rust.

Loial gave the lock a tug. "I can pull it off, hasp and all, but it will make enough noise to wake the whole neighborhood."

"Let us not damage the goodman's property if we can avoid it." Moiraine studied the lock intently for a moment. Suddenly she gave the rusty iron a tap with her staff, and the lock fell open neatly.

Hastily Loial undid the lock and swung the doors up, propping them back. Moiraine went down the ramp thus revealed, lighting her way with the glowing ball. Aldieb stepped delicately behind her.

"Light the lanterns and come down," she called softly. "There is plenty of room. Hurry. It will be light out soon."

Rand hurriedly untied the poled lanterns off the packhorse, but even before the first was lit he realized he could see Mat's features. People would be filling the streets in minutes, and the shopkeeper would be coming down to open up for business, all wondering why the alleyway was crammed full of horses. Mat muttered something nervously about taking horses indoors, but Rand was glad to lead his down the ramp. Mat followed, grumbling but no less quickly.

Rand's lantern swung on the end of its pole, bumping the ceiling if he was not careful, and neither Red nor the packhorse liked the ramp. Then he was down and getting out of Mat's way. Moiraine let her floating light die, but as the rest joined them, the added lanterns lit the open space.

The cellar was as long and as wide as the building above, much of the space taken up by brick columns, flaring up from narrow bases to five times as big at the ceiling. The place seemed made up from a series of arches. There was plenty of room, but Rand still felt crowded. Loial's head brushed the ceiling. As the rusted lock had foretold, the cellar had not been used in a long time. The floor was bare except for a few broken barrels filled with odds and ends, and a thick layer of dust. Motes, stirred up by so many feet, sparkled in the lantern light.

Lan was last in, and as soon as he had Mandarb down the ramp he climbed back to pull the doors shut.

"Blood and ashes," Mat growled, "why would they build one of these gates in a place like this?"

"It was not always like this," Loial said. His rumbling voice echoed in the cavernous space. "Not always. No!" The Ogier was angry, Rand realized with a shock. "Once trees stood here. Every kind of tree that would grow in this place, every kind of tree that Ogier could coax to grow here. The Great Trees, a hundred spans high. Shade of branch, and cool breezes to catch the smell of leaf and flower and hold the memory of the peace of the *stedding*. All that, murdered for this!" His fist thumped a column.

The column seemed to shake under that blow. Rand was certain he heard bricks crack. Waterfalls of dry mortar slid down the column.

"What is already woven cannot be undone," Moiraine said gently. "It will not make the trees grow again for you to bring the building down on our heads." Loial's drooping eyebrows made him look more abashed than a human face could have managed. "With your help, Loial, perhaps we can keep the groves that still stand from falling under the Shadow. You have brought us to what we seek."

As she moved to one of the walls, Rand realized that that wall was different from the others. They were ordinary brick; this was intricately worked stone, fanciful swirls of leaves and vines, pale even under its coat of dust. The brick and mortar were old, but something about the stone said it had stood there long, long before the brick was fired. Later builders, themselves centuries gone, had incorporated what already stood, and still later men had made it part of a cellar.

One part of the carved stone wall, right in the center, was more elaborate than the rest. As well done as the rest was, it appeared a crude copy in comparison. Worked in hard stone, those leaves seemed soft, caught in one frozen moment as a gentle summer breeze stirred them. For all of that, they had the feel of age, as much greater than the rest of the stone as the rest was older than the brick. That old and more. Loial looked at them as if he would rather be anywhere else but there, even out in the streets with another mob.

"*Avendesora*," Moiraine murmured, resting her hand on a trefoil leaf in the stonework. Rand scanned the carving; that was the only leaf of its kind he could find. "The leaf of the Tree of Life is the key," the Aes Sedai said, and the leaf came away in her hand.

Rand blinked; from behind him he heard gasps. That leaf had seemed no less a part of the wall than any other. Just as simply, the Aes Sedai set it against the pattern a handspan lower. The three-pointed leaf fit there as if the space had been intended for it, and once more it was a part of the whole. As soon as it was in place the entire nature of the central stonework changed.

He was sure now that he could see the leaves ruffled by some unfelt breeze; he almost thought they were verdant under the dust, a tapestry of thick spring greenery there in the lantern-lit cellar. Almost imperceptibly at first, a split opened up in the middle of the ancient carving, widening as the two halves slowly swung into the cellar until they stood straight out. The backs of the gates were worked as the fronts, the same profusion of vines and leaves, almost alive. Behind, where should have been dirt or the cellar of the next building, a dull, reflective shimmering faintly caught their images.

"I have heard," Loial said, half mourning, half fearful, "that once the Waygates shone like mirrors. Once, who entered the Ways walked through the sun and the sky. Once."

"We have no time for waiting," Moiraine said.

Lan went past her, leading Mandarb, poled lantern in hand. His shadowy reflection approached him, leading a shadowy horse. Man and reflection seemed to step into each other at the shimmering surface, and both were gone. For a moment the black stallion balked, an apparently continuous rein connecting him to the dim shape of his own image. The rein tightened, and the warhorse, too, vanished.

For a minute everyone in the cellar stood staring at the Waygate.

"Hurry," Moiraine urged. "I must be the last through. We cannot leave this open for anyone to find by chance. Hurry."

With a heavy sigh Loial strode into the shimmer. Tossing its head, his big horse tried to hold back from the surface and was hauled through. They were gone as completely as the Warder and Mandarb.

Hesitantly, Rand poked his lantern at the Waygate. The lantern sank into its reflection, the two merging until both were gone. He made himself keep on walking forward, watching the pole disappear into itself inch by inch, and then he was stepping into himself, entering the gate. His mouth fell open. Something icy slid along his skin, as if he were passing through a wall of cold water. Time stretched out; the cold enveloped one hair at a time, shivered over his clothes thread by thread.

Abruptly the chill burst like a bubble, and he paused to catch his breath. He was inside the Ways. Just ahead Lan and Loial waited patiently by their horses. All around them was blackness that seemed to stretch on forever. Their lanterns made a small pool of light around them, too small, as if something pressed back the light, or ate it.

Of a sudden anxious, he jerked at his reins. Red and the packhorse came leaping through, nearly knocking him down. Stumbling, he caught himself and hurried to the Warder and the Ogier, pulling the nervous horses behind him. The animals whickered softly. Even Mandarb appeared to take some comfort from the presence of other horses.

"Go easy when you pass through a Waygate, Rand," Loial cautioned. "Things are . . . different inside the Ways than out. Look."

He looked back the way the Ogier pointed, thinking to see the same dull shimmer. Instead he could see into the cellar, as if through a large piece of smoked glass set in the blackness. Disturbingly the darkness around the window into the cellar gave a sense of depth, as though the opening stood alone with nothing around or behind it but the dark. He said as much with a shaky laugh, but Loial took him seriously.

"You could walk all the way around it, and you would not see a thing from the other side. I would not advise it, though. The books aren't very clear about what lies behind the Waygates. I think you could become lost there, and never find your way out."

Rand shook his head and tried to concentrate on the Waygate itself rather than what lay behind it, but that was just as disturbing in its own fashion. If there had been anything to look at in the darkness besides the Waygate, he would have looked at it. In the cellar, through the smoky dimness, Moiraine and the others were plain enough, but they moved as if in a dream. Every blink of an eye seemed a deliberate, exaggerated gesture. Mat was making his way to the Waygate as though walking through clear jelly, his legs seeming to swim forward.

"The Wheel turns faster in the Ways," Loial explained. He looked at the darkness surrounding them, and his head sunk in between his shoulders. "None alive know more than fragments. I fear what I don't know about the Ways, Rand."

"The Dark One," Lan said, "cannot be defeated without chancing risks. But we are alive at this moment, and before us is the hope of remaining alive. Do not surrender before you are beaten, Ogier."

"You would not speak so confidently if you had ever been in the Ways." The normal distant thunder of Loial's voice was muted. He stared at the blackness as if he saw things there. "I never have before, either, but I've seen Ogier who have been through a Waygate and come out again. You would not speak so if you had."

Mat stepped through the gate and regained normal speed. For an instant he stared at the seemingly endless darkness, then came running to join them, his lantern bobbing on its pole, his horse leaping behind him, almost sending him sprawling. One by one the others passed through, Perrin and Egwene and Nynaeve, each pausing in shocked silence before hurrying to join the rest. Each lantern enlarged the pool of light, but not as much as it should have. It was as if the dark became denser the more light there was, thickening as it fought against being diminished.

That was not a line of reasoning Rand wanted to follow. It was bad enough just being there without giving the darkness a will of its own. Everyone seemed to feel the oppressiveness, though. There were no wry comments from Mat here, and Egwene looked as if she wished she could rethink her decision to come. They all silently watched the Waygate, that last window into the world they knew.

Finally only Moiraine was left in the cellar, dimly lit by the lantern she had taken. The Aes Sedai still moved in that dreamlike way. Her hand crept as it found the leaf of *Avendesora*. It was located lower in the stonework on this side, Rand saw, just where she had placed it on the other. Plucking it free, she put it back in the original position. He wondered suddenly if the leaf on the other side had moved back, too.

The Aes Sedai came through, leading Aldieb, as the stone
gates slowly, slowly began closing behind her. She came to join
them, the light of her lantern leaving the gates before they were
shut. Blackness swallowed the narrowing view of the cellar. In
the constrained light of their lanterns, blackness surrounded
them totally.

Suddenly it seemed as if the lanterns were the only light left
in the world. Rand realized that he was jammed shoulder-to-
shoulder in between Perrin and Egwene. Egwene gave him a
wide-eyed look and pressed closer, and Perrin made no move
to give him room. There was something comforting about
touching another human being when the whole world had just
been swallowed up by dark. Even the horses seemed to feel the
Ways pushing them into a tighter and tighter knot.

Outwardly unconcerned, Moiraine and Lan swung into their
saddles, and the Aes Sedai leaned forward, arms resting on her
carved staff across the high pommel of her saddle. "We must be
on our way, Loial."

Loial gave a start, and nodded vigorously. "Yes. Yes, Aes
Sedai, you are right. Not a minute longer than need be." He
pointed to a broad strip of white running under their feet, and
Rand stepped away from it hastily. All the Two Rivers folk did.
Rand thought the floor had been smooth once, but the smooth-
ness was pitted now, as if the stone had the pox. The white line
was broken in several places. "This leads from the Waygate to
the first Guiding. From there. . . ." Loial looked around anxiously, then scrambled onto his horse with none of the reluctance he had shown earlier. The horse wore the biggest saddle
the head groom had been able to find, but Loial filled it from
pommel to cantle. His feet hung down on either side almost to
the animal's knees. "Not a minute longer than need be," he
muttered. Reluctantly the others mounted.

Moiraine and Lan rode on either side of the Ogier, following
the white line through the dark. Everyone else crowded in behind as close as they could get, the lanterns bobbing over their
heads. The lanterns should have given enough light to fill a
house, but ten feet away from them it stopped. The blackness
stopped it as if it had struck a wall. The creak of saddles and
click of horseshoes on stone seemed to travel only to the edge
of light.

Rand's hand kept drifting to his sword. It was not that he thought there was anything out there against which he could use the sword to defend himself; it did not seem as if there was anywhere for something to be. The bubble of light around them could as well have been a cave surrounded by stone, completely surrounded, with no way out. The horses might have been walking a treadmill for the change around them. He gripped the hilt as if the pressure of his hand there could press away the stone he felt weighing down on him. Touching the sword, he could remember Tam's teaching. For a little while he could find the calm of the void. But the weight always returned, compressing the void until it was only a cavern inside his mind, and he had to start over again, touching Tam's sword to remember.

It was a relief when something did change, even if it was only a tall slab of stone, standing on end, that appeared out of the dark before them, the broad white line stopping at its base. Sinuous curves of metal inlaid the wide surface, graceful lines that vaguely reminded Rand of vines and leaves. Discolored pocks marked stone and metal alike.

"The Guiding," Loial said, and leaned out of his saddle to frown at the cursive metal inlays.

"Ogier script," Moiraine said, "but so broken I can barely make out what it says."

"I hardly can, either," Loial said, "but enough to know we go this way." He turned his horse aside from the Guiding.

The edges of their light caught other stoneworks, what appeared to be stone-walled bridges arcing off into the darkness, and gently sloping ramps, without railings of any kind, leading up and down. Between the bridges and the ramps ran a chest-high balustrade, however, as though falling was a danger there at any rate. Plain white stone made the balustrade, in simple curves and rounds fitted together in complex patterns. Something about all of it seemed almost familiar to Rand, but he knew it had to be his imagination groping for anything familiar where everything was strange.

At the foot of one of the bridges Loial paused to read the single line on the narrow column stone there. Nodding, he rode up onto the bridge. "This is the first bridge of our path," he said over his shoulder.

Rand wondered what held the bridge up. The horses' hooves

made a gritty sound, as if bits of stone flaked off at every step. Everything he could see was covered with shallow holes, some tiny pinpricks, others shallow, rough-edged craters a stride across, as if there had been a rain of acid, or the stone was rotting. The guardwall showed cracks and holes, too. In places it was gone altogether for as much as a span. For all he knew the bridge could be solid stone all the way to the center of the earth, but what he saw made him hope it would stand long enough for them to reach the other end. *Wherever that is.*

The bridge did end, eventually, in a place that looked no different from its beginning. All Rand could see was what their little pool of light touched, but he had the impression that it was a large space, like a flat-topped hill, with bridges and ramps leaving all around it. An Island, Loial called it. There was another script-covered Guiding—Rand placed it in the middle of the Island, with no way of knowing if he was right or not. Loial read, then took them up one of the ramps, curving up and up.

After an interminable climb, curving continuously, the ramp let off onto another Island just like the one where it had begun. Rand tried to imagine the curve of the ramp and gave up. *This Island can't be right on top of the other one. It* can't *be.*

Loial consulted yet another slab filled with Ogier script, found another signpost column, led them onto another bridge. Rand no longer had any idea in what direction they were traveling.

In their huddle of light in the dark, one bridge was exactly like another, except that some had breaks in the guardwalls and some did not. Only the degree of damage to the Guidings gave any difference to the Islands. Rand lost track of time; he was not even sure how many bridges they had crossed or how many ramps they had traveled. The Warder must have had a clock in his head, though. Just when Rand felt the first stir of hunger, Lan announced quietly that it was midday and dismounted to parcel out bread and cheese and dried meat from the packhorse. Perrin was leading the animal by that time. They were on an Island, and Loial was busily deciphering the directions on the Guiding.

Mat started to climb down from his saddle, but Moiraine said, "Time is too valuable in the Ways to waste. For us, much too valuable. We will stop when it is time to sleep." Lan was already back on Mandarb.

Rand's appetite slipped at the thought of sleeping in the Ways. It was always night there, but not the kind of night for sleeping. He ate while he rode, though, like everyone else. It was an awkward affair, trying to juggle his food, the lantern pole, and his reins, but for all of his imagined lack of appetite he licked the last crumbs of bread and cheese off his hands when he was done, and thought fondly of more. He even began to think the Ways were not so bad, not nearly as bad as Loial made out. They might have the heavy feel of the hour before a storm, but nothing changed. Nothing happened. The Ways were almost boring.

Then the silence was broken by a startled grunt from Loial. Rand stood in his stirrups to peer past the Ogier, and swallowed hard at what he saw. They were in the middle of a bridge, and only a few feet ahead of Loial the bridge ended in a jagged gap.

CHAPTER
45

What Follows in Shadow

The light of their lanterns stretched just far enough to touch the other side, thrusting out of the dark like a giant's broken teeth. Loial's horse stamped a hoof nervously, and a loose stone fell away into the dead black below. If there was any sound of it striking bottom, Rand never heard it.

He edged Red closer to the gap. As far down as he could thrust his lantern on its pole, there was nothing. Blackness below as blackness above, shearing off the light. If there was a bottom, it could be a thousand feet down. Or never. But on the other side, he could see what was under the bridge, holding it up. Nothing. Less than a span in thickness, and absolutely nothing underneath.

Abruptly the stone under his feet seemed as thin as paper, and the endless drop over the edge pulled at him. The lantern and pole seemed suddenly heavy enough to pull him right out of the saddle. Head spinning, he backed the bay away from the abyss as cautiously as he had approached.

"Is it to this you've brought us, Aes Sedai?" Nynaeve said. "All this just to find out we have to go back to Caemlyn after all?"

"We do not have to go back," Moiraine said. "Not all the way to Caemlyn. There are many paths along the Ways to any place. We need only go back far enough for Loial to find another path that will lead to Fal Dara. Loial? Loial!"

The Ogier pulled himself away from staring at the gap with a visible effort. "What? Oh. Yes, Aes Sedai. I can find another path. I had. . . ." His eyes drifted back to the chasm, and his ears twitched. "I had not dreamed the decay had gone so far. If the bridges themselves are breaking, it may be that I cannot find the path you want. It may be that I cannot find a path back, either. The bridges could be falling behind us even now."

"There has to be a way," Perrin said, his voice flat. His eyes seemed to gather the light, to glow golden. *A wolf at bay,* Rand thought, startled. *That's what he looks like.*

"It will be as the Wheel weaves," Moiraine said, "but I do not believe the decay is as fast as you fear. Look at the stone, Loial. Even I can tell that this is an old break."

"Yes," Loial said slowly. "Yes, Aes Sedai. I can see it. There is no rain or wind here, but that stone has been in the air for ten years, at least." He nodded with a relieved grin, so happy with the discovery that for a moment he seemed to forget his fear. Then he looked around and shrugged uncomfortably. "I could find other paths more easily than Mafal Dadaranell. Tar Valon, for instance? Or Stedding Shangtai. It's only three bridges to Stedding Shangtai from the last Island. I suppose the Elders want to talk to me by this time."

"Fal Dara, Loial," Moiraine said firmly. "The Eye of the World lies beyond Fal Dara, and we must reach the Eye."

"Fal Dara," the Ogier agreed reluctantly.

Back at the Island Loial pored over the script-covered slab intently, drooping eyebrows drawn down as he muttered half to himself. Soon he was talking completely to himself, for he dropped into the Ogier language. That inflected tongue sounded like deep-voiced birds singing. It seemed odd to Rand that a people so big had such a musical language.

Finally the Ogier nodded. As he led them to the chosen bridge, he turned to peer forlornly at the signpost beside another. "Three crossings to Stedding Shangtai." He sighed. But he took them on past without stopping and turned onto the third bridge beyond. He looked back regretfully as they started across, though the bridge to his home was hidden in the dark.

Rand took the bay up beside the Ogier. "When this is over, Loial, you show me your *stedding,* and I'll show you Emond's

Field. No Ways,. though. We'll walk, or ride, if it takes all summer."

"You believe it will ever be over, Rand?"

He frowned at the Ogier. "You said it would take two days to reach Fal Dara."

"Not the Ways, Rand. All the rest." Loial looked over his shoulder at the Aes Sedai, talking softly with Lan as they rode side-by-side. "What makes you believe it will ever be over?"

The bridges and ramps led up and down and across. Sometimes a white line ran off into the dark from the Guiding, just like the line they had followed from the Waygate in Caemlyn. Rand saw that he was not the only one who eyed those lines curiously, and a little wistfully. Nynaeve, Perrin, Mat, and even Egwene left the lines reluctantly. There was a Waygate at the other end of each of them, a gate back into the world, where there was sky and sun and wind. Even the wind would have been welcome. Leave them they did, under the Aes Sedai's sharp eye. But Rand was not the only one to look back even after dark swallowed Island and Guiding and line.

Rand was yawning by the time Moiraine announced that they would stop for the night on one of the Islands. Mat looked at the blackness all around them and snickered loudly, but he got down as quickly as anyone else. Lan and the boys unsaddled and hobbled the horses while Nynaeve and Egwene set up a small oil stove to make tea. Looking like the base of a lantern, it was what Lan said Warders used in the Blight, where the wood could be dangerous to burn. The Warder produced tripod legs from the baskets they took off the packhorse, so the lantern poles could be set in a circle around their campsite.

Loial examined the Guiding for a moment, then dropped down cross-legged and rubbed a hand across the dusty, pockmarked stone. "Once things grew on the Islands," he said sadly. "All the books tell of it. There was green grass to sleep on, soft as any feather bed. Fruit trees to spice the food you'd brought with an apple or a pear or a bellfruit, sweet and crisp and juicy whatever the time of year outside."

"Nothing to hunt," Perrin growled, then looked surprised that he had spoken.

Egwene handed Loial a cup of tea. He held it without drinking, staring at it as if he could find the fruit trees in its depths.

"Aren't you going to set wards?" Nynaeve asked Moiraine. "Surely there must be worse than rats in this. Even if I haven't seen anything, I can still feel."

The Aes Sedai rubbed her fingers against her palms distastefully. "You feel the taint, the corruption of the Power that made the Ways. I will not use the One Power in the Ways unless I must. The taint is so strong that whatever I tried to do would surely be corrupted."

That made everyone as silent as Loial. Lan settled down to his meal methodically, as if he were stoking a fire, the food less important than fueling his body. Moiraine ate well, too, and as tidily as if they were not squatting on bare stone quite literally in the middle of nowhere, but Rand only picked at his food. The tiny flame of the oil stove gave just enough heat to boil water, but he crouched toward it as if he could soak up warmth. His shoulders brushed Mat and Perrin. They all made a tight circle around the stove. Mat held his bread and meat and cheese forgotten in his hands, and Perrin set his tin plate down after only a few bites. The mood became more and more glum, and everyone looked down, avoiding the dark around them.

Moiraine studied them as she ate. Finally she put her plate aside and patted her lips with a napkin. "I can tell you one cheerful thing. I do not think Thom Merrilin is dead."

Rand looked at her sharply. "But . . . the Fade. . . ."

"Mat told me what happened in Whitebridge," the Aes Sedai said. "People there mentioned a gleeman, but they said nothing of him dying. They would have, I think, if a gleeman had been killed. Whitebridge is not so big as for a gleeman to be a small thing. And Thom is a part of the Pattern that weaves itself around you three. Too important a part, I believe, to be cut off yet."

Too important? Rand thought. *How could Moiraine know . . . ?* "Min? She saw something about Thom?"

"She saw a great deal," Moiraine said wryly. "About all of you. I wish I could understand half of what she saw, but even she does not. Old barriers fail. But whether what Min does is old or new, she sees true. Your fates are bound together. Thom Merrilin's, too."

Nynaeve gave a dismissive sniff and poured herself another cup of tea.

"I don't see how she saw anything about any of us," Mat said with a grin. "As I remember it, she spent most of her time looking at Rand."

Egwene raised an eyebrow. "Oh? You didn't tell me that, Moiraine Sedai."

Rand glanced at her. She was not looking at him, but her tone had been too carefully neutral. "I talked to her once," he said. "She dresses like a boy, and her hair is as short as mine."

"You talked to her. Once." Egwene nodded slowly. Still not looking at him, she raised her cup to her lips.

"Min was just somebody who worked at the inn in Baerlon," Perrin said. "Not like Aram."

Egwene choked on her tea. "Too hot," she muttered.

"Who's Aram?" Rand asked. Perrin smiled, much like Mat's smile in the old days when he was up to mischief, and hid behind his cup.

"One of the Traveling People," Egwene said casually, but red spots bloomed in her cheeks.

"One of the Traveling People," Perrin said blandly. "He dances. Like a bird. Wasn't that what you said, Egwene? It was like flying with a bird?"

Egwene set her cup down deliberately. "I don't know if anyone else is tired, but I'm going to sleep."

As she rolled herself up in her blankets, Perrin reached over to nudge Rand in the ribs and winked. Rand found himself grinning back. *Burn me, if I didn't come out best for a change. I wish I knew as much about women as Perrin.*

"Maybe, Rand," Mat said slyly, "you ought to tell Egwene about Farmer Grinwell's daughter, Else." Egwene lifted her head to stare first at Mat, then at him.

He hastily got up to fetch his own blankets. "Sleep sounds good to me right now."

All the Emond's Field people began seeking their blankets then, and Loial, too. Moiraine sat sipping her tea. And Lan.

The Warder did not look as if he ever intended to sleep, or needed to.

Even rolled up for sleep, no one wanted to get very far from the others. They made a small circle of blanket-covered mounds right around the stove, almost touching one another.

"Rand," Mat whispered, "*was* there anything between you and Min? I barely got a look at her. She *was* pretty, but she must be nearly as old as Nynaeve."

"What about this Else?" Perrin added from the other side of him. "She pretty?"

"Blood and ashes," he mumbled, "can't I even talk to a girl? You two are as bad as Egwene."

"As the Wisdom would say," Mat chided mockingly, "watch your tongue. Well, if you won't talk about it, I'm going to get some sleep."

"Good," Rand grumbled. "That's the first decent thing you've said."

Sleep was not easily come by, though. The stone was hard, however Rand lay, and he could feel the pits through his blanket. There was no way to imagine he was anywhere but in the Ways, made by the men who had broken the world, tainted by the Dark One. He kept picturing the broken bridge, and the nothing under it.

When he turned one way he found Mat looking at him; looking through him, really. Mocking was forgotten when the dark around them was remembered. He rolled the other way, and Perrin had his eyes open, too. Perrin's face was less afraid than Mat's, but he had his hands on his chest, tapping his thumbs together worriedly.

Moiraine made a circuit of them, kneeling by each person's head and bending down to speak softly. Rand could not hear what she said to Perrin, but it made his thumbs stop. When she bent over Rand, her face almost touching his, she said in a low, comforting voice, "Even here, your destiny protects you. Not even the Dark One can change the Pattern completely. You are safe from him, so long as I am close. Your dreams are safe. For a time, yet, they are safe."

As she passed from him to Mat, he wondered if she thought it was that simple, that she could tell him he was safe and he would believe it. But somehow he did feel safe—safer, at least. Thinking that, he drifted into sleep and did not dream.

Lan woke them. Rand wondered if the Warder had slept; he did not look tired, not even as tired as those who had laid some hours on the hard stone. Moiraine allowed enough time to make tea, but only one cup apiece. They ate breakfast in the saddle, Loial and the Warder leading. It was the same meal as the others, bread and meat and cheese. Rand thought it would be easy to get tired of bread and meat and cheese.

Not long after the last crumb was licked off a finger, Lan said quietly, "Someone is following us. Or something." They were in the middle of a bridge, both ends of it hidden.

Mat jerked an arrow from his quiver and, before anyone could stop him, loosed it in the dark behind them.

"I knew I shouldn't have done this," Loial muttered. "Never deal with an Aes Sedai except in a *stedding*."

Lan pushed the bow down before Mat could nock another. "Stop that, you village idiot. There's no way to tell who it is."

"That's the only place they're safe," the Ogier went on.

"What else would be in a place like this besides something evil?" Mat demanded.

"That's what the Elders say, and I should have listened to them."

"We are, for one," the Warder said dryly.

"Maybe it's another traveler," Egwene said hopefully. "An Ogier, perhaps."

"Ogier have more sense than to use the Ways," Loial growled. "All but Loial, who has no sense at all. Elder Haman always said it, and it's true."

"What do you feel, Lan?" Moiraine asked. "Is it something that serves the Dark One?"

The Warder shook his head slowly. "I don't know," he said as if that surprised him. "I cannot tell. Perhaps it's the Ways, and the taint. It all feels wrong. But whoever it is, or whatever, he's not trying to catch us. He almost caught up at the last Island and scampered back across the bridge so as not to. If I fall behind, I might surprise him though, and see who, or what, he is."

"If you fall behind, Warder," Loial said firmly, "you'll spend the rest of your life in the Ways. Even if you can read Ogier, I have never heard or read of a human who could find his path off the first Island lacking an Ogier guide. *Can* you read Ogier?"

Lan shook his head again, and Moiraine said, "So long as he does not trouble us, we will not trouble him. We have no time. No time."

As they rode off the bridge onto the next Island, Loial said, "If I remember the last Guiding correctly, there is a path from here that leads toward Tar Valon. Half a day's journey at most. Not quite as long as it will take us to reach Mafal Dadaranell. I'm sure that—"

He cut off as the light of their lanterns reached the Guiding. Near the top of the slab, deeply chiseled lines, sharp and angular, made wounds in the stone. Suddenly Lan's alertness was no longer hidden. He remained easily erect in his saddle, but Rand had the sudden impression that the Warder could feel everything around him, even feel the rest of them breathing. Lan began circling his stallion around the Guiding, spiraling outward. He rode as if he were ready to be attacked, or to attack himself.

"This explains much," Moiraine said softly, "and it makes me afraid. So much. I should have guessed. The taint, the decay. I should have guessed."

"Guessed what?" Nynaeve demanded just as Loial asked, "What is it? Who did this? I've never seen or heard of anything like it."

The Aes Sedai faced them calmly. "Trollocs." She ignored their frightened gasps. "Or Fades. Those are Trolloc runes. The Trollocs have discovered how to enter the Ways. That must be how they got to the Two Rivers undiscovered; through the Waygate at Manetheren. There is at least one Waygate in the Blight." She glanced toward Lan before continuing; the Warder was far enough away that only the faint light of his lantern could be seen. "Manetheren was destroyed, but almost nothing can destroy a Waygate. That is how the Fades could gather a small army around Caemlyn without raising an alarm in every nation between the Blight and Andor." Pausing, she touched her lips thoughtfully. "But they cannot know all the paths yet, else they would have been pouring into Caemlyn through the gate we used. Yes."

Rand shivered. Walking through the Waygate to find Trollocs waiting in the dark, hundreds of them, perhaps thousands, twisted giants with half-animal faces snarling as they leaped forward in the blackness to kill. Or worse.

"They don't use the Ways easily," Lan called. His lantern was no more than twenty spans off, but the light of it was only a dim, fuzzy ball that seemed very distant to those around the Guiding. Moiraine led the way to him. Rand wished his stomach were empty when he saw what the Warder had found.

At the foot of one of the bridges the frozen shapes of Trollocs reared, caught flailing about them with hooked axes and scythe-like swords. Gray and pitted like the stone, the huge bodies were half sunken in the swollen, bubbled surface. Some of the bubbles had burst, revealing more snouted faces, forever snarling with fear. Rand heard someone retching behind him, and swallowed hard to keep from joining whoever it was. Even for Trollocs it had been a horrible way to die.

A few feet beyond the Trollocs the bridge ended. The signpost lay shattered into a thousand shards.

Loial got down from his horse gingerly, eyeing the Trollocs, as if he thought they might come back to life. He examined the remains of the signpost hurriedly, picking out the metal script that had been inlaid in the stone, then scrambled back into his saddle. "This was the first bridge of the path from here to Tar Valon," he said.

Mat was scrubbing the back of his hand across his mouth, with his head turned away from the Trollocs. Egwene hid her face in her hands. Rand moved his horse close to Bela and touched her shoulder. She twisted around and clutched him, shuddering. He wanted to shudder, too; her holding him was the only thing that kept him from it.

"As well we are not going to Tar Valon yet," Moiraine said.

Nynaeve rounded on the Aes Sedai. "How can you take it so calmly? The same could happen to us!"

"Perhaps," Moiraine said serenely, and Nynaeve ground her teeth so hard Rand could hear them grate. "It is more likely, though," Moiraine went on, unruffled, "that the men, the Aes

Sedai, who made the Ways protected them, building in traps for creatures of the Dark One. It is something they must have feared then, before the Halfmen and Trollocs had been driven into the Blight. In any case, we cannot tarry here, and whatever way we choose, back or ahead, is as likely to have a trap as any other. Loial, do you know the next bridge?"

"Yes. Yes, they did not ruin that part of the Guiding, thank the Light." For the first time Loial seemed as eager to go on as Moiraine did. He had his big horse moving before he finished speaking.

Egwene clung to Rand's arm for two more bridges. He regretted it when she finally let go with a murmured apology and a forced laugh, and not just because it had felt good having her hold onto him that way. It was easier to be brave, he discovered, when someone needed your protection.

Moiraine might not have believed a trap could be set for them, but for all the haste she spoke of, she made them travel more slowly than before, pausing before letting them onto any bridge, or off one onto an Island. She would step Aldieb forward, feeling the air in front of her with an outstretched hand, and not even Loial, or Lan, was allowed to go ahead until she gave permission.

Rand had to trust her judgment about traps, but he peered into the darkness around them as if he could actually see anything more than ten feet away, and strained his ears listening. If Trollocs could use the Ways, then whatever was following them could be another creature of the Dark One. Or more than one. Lan had said he could not tell in the Ways. But as they crossed bridge after bridge, ate a midday meal riding, and crossed still more bridges, all he could hear were their own saddles creaking, and the horses' hooves, and sometimes one of the others coughing, or muttering to himself. Later there was a distant wind, too, off in the black somewhere. He could not say in which direction. At first he thought it was his imagination, but with time he became sure.

It'll be good to feel the wind again, even if it's cold.

Suddenly he blinked. "Loial, didn't you say there isn't any wind in the Ways?"

Loial pulled his horse up just short of the next Island and cocked his head to listen. Slowly his face paled, and he licked his lips. *"Machin Shin,"* he whispered hoarsely. "The Black Wind. The Light illumine and protect us. It's the Black Wind."

"How many more bridges?" Moiraine asked sharply. "Loial, how many more bridges?"

"Two. I think, two."

"Quickly, then," she said, trotting Aldieb onto the Island. "Find it quickly!"

Loial talked to himself, or to anyone who was listening, while he read the Guiding. "They came out mad, screaming about *Machin Shin.* Light help us! Even those Aes Sedai could heal, they. . . ." He scanned the stone hastily, and galloped toward the chosen bridge with a shouted, "This way!"

This time Moiraine did not wait to check. She urged them on to a gallop, the bridge trembling beneath the horses, lanterns swinging wildly overhead. Loial ran his eyes over the next Guiding and wheeled his big mount around like a racer almost before it had stopped. The sound of the wind became louder. Rand could hear it even over the pounding of hooves on stone. Behind them, and gusting closer.

They did not bother with the last Guiding. As soon as the light of the lanterns caught the white line running from it, they swung in that direction, still galloping. The Island vanished behind, and there was only the pitted, gray stone underfoot and the white line. Rand was breathing so hard he was no longer sure if he could hear the wind.

Out of the darkness the gates appeared, vine-carved and standing alone in the black like a tiny piece of wall in the night. Moiraine leaned out of her saddle, reaching toward the carvings, and suddenly pulled back. "The *Avendesora* leaf is not here!" she said. "The key is gone!"

"Light!" Mat shouted. "Bloody Light!" Loial threw back his head and gave a mournful cry, like a howl of dying.

Egwene touched Rand's arm. Her lips trembled, but she only looked at him. He put his hand on top of hers, hoping he did not look more frightened than she did. He felt it. Back toward the Guiding, the wind howled. He almost thought he could hear voices in it, voices screaming vileness that, even half understood, brought bile up in his throat.

Moiraine raised her staff and flame lanced from the end of it. It was not the pure, white flame that Rand remembered from

Emond's Field, and the battle before Shadar Logoth. Sickly yellow streaked through the fire, and slow-drifting flecks of black, like soot. A thin, acrid smoke drifted from the flame, setting Loial coughing and the horses dancing nervously, but Moiraine thrust it at the gates. The smoke rasped Rand's throat and burned his nose.

Stone melted like butter, leaf and vine withering in the flame and vanishing. The Aes Sedai moved the fire as fast as she could, but cutting an opening big enough for everyone to get through was no quick task. To Rand, it seemed as if the line of melted stone crept along its arc at a snail's pace. His cloak stirred, as if caught by the edge of a breeze, and his heart froze.

"I can feel it," Mat said, his voice quavering. "Light, I can bloody feel it!"

The flame winked out, and Moiraine lowered her staff. "Done," she said. "Half done."

A thin line ran across the stone carving. Rand thought he could see light—dim, but still light—through the crack. But despite the cutting, the two big, curved wedges of stone still stood there, half an arc out of each door. The opening would be big enough for everyone to ride through, though Loial might have to lie flat on his horse's back. Once the two wedges of stone were gone, it would be big enough. He wondered how much each weighed. A thousand pounds? More? *Maybe if we all get down and push. Maybe we can push one of them over before the wind gets here.* A gust tugged at his cloak. He tried not to listen to what the voices cried.

As Moiraine stepped back, Mandarb leaped forward, straight toward the gates, Lan crouched in the saddle. At the last instant the warhorse twisted to catch the stone with his shoulder, just as he had been taught to catch other horses in battle. With a crash the stone toppled outward, and the Warder and his horse were carried by their momentum through the smoky shimmer of a Waygate. The light that came through was midmorning light, pale and thin, but it seemed to Rand as if the noonday summer sun blazed in his face.

On the far side of the gate Lan and Mandarb slowed to a crawl, stumbling in slow motion as the Warder reined back around toward the gate. Rand did not wait. Pushing Bela's head toward the opening, he slapped the shaggy mare hard on the croup. Egwene had just enough time to throw a startled look over her shoulder at him before Bela carried her out of the Ways.

"All of you, out!" Moiraine directed. "Quickly! Go!"

As she spoke, the Aes Sedai thrust her staff out at arm's length, pointed back toward the Guiding. Something leaped from the end of the staff, like liquid light rendered to a syrup of fire, a blazing spear of white and red and yellow, streaking into the black, exploding, coruscating like shattered diamonds. The wind shrieked in agony; it screamed in rage. The thousand murmurs that hid in the wind roared like thunder, roars of madness, half-heard voices cackling and howling promises that twisted Rand's stomach as much by the pleasure in them as by what he almost understood them to say.

He booted Red forward, crowding into the opening, squeezing after the others, all forcing through the smoky glistening at once. The icy chill ran through him again, the peculiar sensation of being slowly lowered facedown into a winter pond, the cold water crawling across his skin by infinitesimal increments. Just as before it seemed to go on forever, while his mind raced, wondering if the wind could catch them while they were held like that.

As suddenly as a pricked bubble the chill vanished, and he was outside. His horse, for one abrupt instant moving twice as fast as he had been, stumbled and almost pitched him over his head. He threw both arms around the bay's neck and hung on for dear life. While he got back into the saddle, Red shook himself, then trotted over to join the others as calmly as if nothing at all odd had happened. It was cold, not the chill of the Waygate, but welcome, natural winter-cold that slowly, steadily burrowed into flesh.

He pulled his cloak around him, his eyes on the dull glimmer of the Waygate. Beside him Lan leaned forward in his saddle, one hand on his sword; man and horse were tensed, as if on the point of charging back through if Moiraine did not appear.

The Waygate stood in a jumble of stones at the base of a hill, hidden by bushes except where the falling pieces had broken down the bare, brown branches. Alongside the carvings on the remains of the gates, the brush looked more lifeless than the stone.

Slowly the murky surface bulged like some strange, long bubble rising to the surface of a pond. Moiraine's back broke through the bubble. Inchmeal, the Aes Sedai and her dim reflection backed out of each other. She still held her staff out in front of her, and she kept it there as she drew Aldieb out of the Waygate after her, the white mare dancing with fear, eyes rolling. Still watching the Waygate, Moiraine backed away.

The Waygate darkened. The hazy shimmer became murkier, sinking through gray to charcoal, then to black as deep as the heart of the Ways. As if from a great distance the wind howled at them, hidden voices filled with an unquenchable thirst for living things, filled with a hunger for pain, filled with frustration.

The voices seemed to whisper in Rand's ears, right at the brink of understanding, and within it. *Flesh so fine, so fine to tear, to gash the skin; skin to strip, to plait, so nice to plait the strips, so nice, so red the drops that fall; blood so red, so red, so sweet; sweet screams, pretty screams, singing screams, scream your song, sing your screams. . . .*

The whispers drifted, the blackness lessened, faded, and the Waygate was again a murky shimmer seen through an arch of carved stone.

Rand let out a long, shuddering breath. He was not the only one; he heard other relieved exhalations. Egwene had Bela alongside Nynaeve's horse, and the two women had their arms around each other, their heads on each other's shoulders. Even Lan seemed relieved, though the hard planes of his face showed nothing; it was more in the way he sat Mandarb, a loosening of the shoulders as he looked at Moiraine, a tilt of the head.

"It could not pass," Moiraine said. "I thought it could not; I hoped it could not. Faugh!" She tossed her staff on the ground and scrubbed her hand on her cloak. Char, thick and black, marked the staff for over half its length. "The taint corrupts everything in that place."

"What was that?" Nynaeve demanded. "What was it?"

Loial appeared confused. "Why, *Machin Shin*, of course. The Black Wind that steals souls."

"But *what* is it?" Nynaeve persisted. "Even with a Trolloc, you can look at it, touch it if you have a strong stomach. But that. . . ." She gave a convulsive shiver.

"Something left from the Time of Madness, perhaps," Moiraine replied. "Or even from the War of the Shadow, the War of Power. Something hiding in the Ways so long it can no longer get out. No one, not even among the Ogier, knows how far the Ways run, or how deep. It could even be something of the Ways themselves. As Loial said, the Ways are living things, and all living things have parasites. Perhaps even a creature of the corruption itself, something born of the decay. Something that hates life and light."

"Stop!" Egwene cried. "I don't want to hear any more. I could hear *it*, saying. . . ." She cut off, shivering.

"There is worse to be faced yet," Moiraine said softly. Rand did not think she meant it to be heard.

The Aes Sedai climbed into her saddle wearily and settled there with a grateful sigh. "This is dangerous," she said, looking at the broken gates. Her charred staff received only a glance. "The thing cannot get out, but anyone could wander in. Agelmar must send men to wall it up, once we reach Fal Dara." She pointed to the north, to towers in the misty distance above the barren treetops.

CHAPTER
46

Fal Dara

The country around the Waygate was rolling, forested hills, but aside from the gates themselves there was no sign of any Ogier grove. Most of the trees were gray skeletons clawing at the sky. Fewer evergreens than Rand was used to dotted the forest, and of them, dead, brown needles and leaves covered many. Loial made no comment beyond a sad shaking of his head.

"As dead as the Blasted Lands," Nynaeve said, frowning. Egwene pulled her cloak around her and shivered.

"At least we're out," Perrin said, and Mat added, "Out where?"

"Shienar," Lan told them. "We're in the Borderlands." In his hard voice was a note that said home, almost.

Rand gathered his cloak against the cold. The Borderlands. Then the Blight was close by. The Blight. The Eye of the World. And what they had come to do.

"We are close to Fal Dara," Moiraine said. "Only a few miles." Across the treetops, towers rose to the north and east of them, dark against the morning sky. Between the hills and the woods, the towers often vanished as they rode, only to reappear again when they topped a particularly tall rise.

Rand noticed trees split open as if struck by lightning.

"The cold," Lan answered when he asked. "Sometimes the winter is so cold here the sap freezes, and trees burst. There are nights when you can hear them cracking like fireworks, and

the air is so sharp you think that might shatter, too. There are
more than usual, this winter past."

Rand shook his head. Trees *bursting*? And that was during
an ordinary winter. What must this winter have been like?
Surely like nothing he could imagine.

"Who says winter's past?" Mat said, his teeth chattering.

"Why this, a fine spring, sheepherder," Lan said. "A fine
spring to be alive. But if you want warm, well, it will be warm
in the Blight."

Softly Mat muttered, "Blood and ashes. Blood and bloody
ashes!" Rand barely heard him, but it sounded heartfelt.

They began to pass farms, but though it was the hour for
midday meals to be cooking, no smoke rose from the high
stone chimneys. The fields were empty of men and livestock
both, though sometimes a plow or a wagon stood abandoned as
if the owner meant to be back any minute.

At one farm close by the road a lone chicken scratched in the
yard. One barn door swung freely with the wind; the other had
broken off the bottom hinge and hung at an angle. The tall
house, odd to Rand's Two Rivers eyes, with its sharp-peaked
roof of big wooden shingles running almost to the ground, was
still and silent. No dog came out to bark at them. A scythe lay
in the middle of the barnyard; buckets were overturned in a
heap beside the well.

Moiraine frowned at the farmhouse as they rode by. She
lifted Aldieb's reins, and the white mare quickened her pace.

The Emond's Fielders were clustered with Loial a little behind the Aes Sedai and the Warder.

Rand shook his head. He could not imagine anything growing there ever. But then he could not really imagine the Ways,
either. Even now that he was past them, he could not.

"I don't think she expected this," Nynaeve said quietly, with
a gesture that took in all the empty farms they had seen.

"Where did they all go?" Egwene said. "Why? They can't
have been gone very long."

"What makes you say that?" Mat asked. "From the look of
that barn door, they could have been gone all winter."
Nynaeve and Egwene both looked at him as if he were slow-
witted.

"The curtains in the windows," Egwene said patiently.

"They look too light for winter curtains, even here. As cold as it is here, no woman would have had those up more than a week or two, maybe less." The Wisdom nodded.

"Curtains." Perrin chuckled. He immediately wiped the smile off his face when the two women raised their eyebrows at him. "Oh, I agree with you. There wasn't enough rust on that scythe for any more than a week in the open. You should have seen that, Mat. Even if you missed the curtains."

Rand glanced sideways at Perrin, trying not to stare. His eyes were sharper than Perrin's—or had been, when they used to hunt rabbits together—but he had not been able to see that scythe-blade well enough to make out any rust.

"I really don't care where they went," Mat grumbled. "I just want to find someplace with a fire. Soon."

"But why did they go?" Rand said under his breath. The Blight was not far off here. The Blight, where all the Fades and Trollocs were, those not down in Andor chasing them. The Blight, where they were going.

He raised his voice enough to be heard by those close to him. "Nynaeve, maybe you and Egwene don't have to go to the Eye with us." The two women looked at him as if he were speaking gibberish, but with the Blight so close he had to make one last try. "Maybe it's enough for you to be close. Moiraine didn't say you have to go. Or you, Loial. You could stay at Fal Dara. Until we come back. Or you could start for Tar Valon. Maybe there'll be a merchant train, or I'll bet Moiraine would even hire a coach. We will meet in Tar Valon, when it's all over."

"Ta'veren." Loial's sigh was a rumble like thunder on the horizon. "You swirl lives around you, Rand al'Thor, you and your friends. Your fate chooses ours." The Ogier shrugged, and suddenly a broad grin split his face. "Besides, it will be something to meet the Green Man. Elder Haman always talks about his meeting with the Green Man, and so does my father, and most of the Elders."

"So many?" Perrin said. "The stories say the Green Man is hard to find, and no one can find him twice."

"Not twice, no," Loial agreed. "But then, I have never met him, and neither have you. He doesn't seem to avoid Ogier quite the way he does you humans. He knows so much about trees. Even the Tree Songs."

Rand said, "The point I was trying to make is—"

The Wisdom cut him off. "*She* says Egwene and I are part of the Pattern, too. All woven in with you three. If she is to be believed, there's something about the way that piece of the Pattern is woven that might stop the Dark One. And I am afraid I do believe her; too much has happened not to. But if Egwene and I go away, what might we change about the Pattern?"

"I was only trying to—"

Again Nynaeve interrupted, sharply. "I know what you were trying to do." She looked at him until he shifted uneasily in his saddle, then her face softened. "I know what you were trying to do, Rand. I have little liking for any Aes Sedai, and this one least of all, I think. I have less for going into the Blight, but least of all is the liking I have for the Father of Lies. If you boys . . . you men, can do what has to be done when you'd rather do almost anything else, why do you think I will do less? Or Egwene?" She did not appear to expect an answer. Gathering her reins, she frowned toward the Aes Sedai up ahead. "I wonder if we're going to reach this Fal Dara place soon, or does she mean us to spend the night out in this?"

As she trotted toward Moiraine, Mat said, "She called us men. It seems like only yesterday she was saying we shouldn't be off leading strings, and now she calls us men."

"You still shouldn't be off your mother's apron strings," Egwene said, but Rand did not think her heart was in it. She moved Bela close to his bay, and lowered her voice so none of the others could hear although Mat, at least, tried. "I only danced with Aram, Rand," she said softly, not looking at him. "You wouldn't hold it against me, dancing with somebody I will never see again, would you?"

"No," he told her. *What had made her bring it up now?* "Of course not." But suddenly he remembered something Min had said in Baerlon, what seemed a hundred years ago. *She's not for you, nor you for her; at least, not in the way you both want.*

The town of Fal Dara was built on hills higher than the surrounding country. It was nowhere near as big as Caemlyn, but the wall around it was as high as Caemlyn's. For a full mile outside that wall in every direction the ground was clear of anything taller than grass, and that cut low. Nothing could come close without being seen from one of the many tall towers topped by wooden hoardings. Where the walls of Caemlyn had a beauty about them, the builders of Fal Dara seemed not to have cared if anyone found their wall beautiful. The gray stone was grimly implacable, proclaiming that it existed for one purpose alone: to hold. Pennants atop the hoardings whipped in the wind, making the stooping Black Hawk of Shienar seem to fly all along the walls.

Lan tossed back the hood of his cloak and, despite the cold, motioned for the others to do the same. Moiraine had already lowered hers. "It's the law in Shienar," the Warder said. "In all the Borderlands. No one may hide his face inside a town's walls."

"Are they all that good-looking?" Mat laughed.

"A Halfman can't hide with his face exposed," the Warder said in a flat voice.

Rand's grin slid off his face. Hastily Mat pushed back his hood.

The gates stood open, tall and covered with dark iron, but a dozen armored men stood guard in golden yellow surcoats bearing the Black Hawk. The hilts of long swords on their backs peeked over their shoulders, and broadsword or mace or axe hung at every waist. Their horses were tethered nearby, made grotesque by the steel bardings covering chests and necks and heads, with lances to stirrup, all ready to ride at an instant. The guards made no move to stop Lan and Moiraine and the others. Indeed, they waved and called out happily.

"Dai Shan!" one cried, shaking steel-gauntleted fists over his head as they rode past. "Dai Shan!"

A number of others shouted, "Glory to the Builders!" and, *"Kiserai ti Wansho!"* Loial looked surprised, then a broad smile split his face and he waved to the guards.

One man ran alongside Lan's horse a little way, unhampered by the armor he wore. "Will the Golden Crane fly again, Dai Shan?"

"Peace, Ragan," was all the Warder said, and the man fell away. He returned the guards' waves, but his face was suddenly even more grim.

As they rode through stone-paved streets crowded with people and wagons, Rand frowned worriedly. Fal Dara was bulging at the seams, but the people were neither the eager crowds of

Caemlyn, enjoying the grandeur of the city even as they squab-
bled, nor the milling throngs of Baerlon. Packed cheek by jowl,
these folk watched their party ride by with leaden eyes and
faces blanked of emotion. Carts and wagons jammed every
alleyway and half the streets, piled high with jumbled house-
hold furnishings, and carved chests packed so tight that clothes
spilled. On top sat the children. Adults kept the younglings up
where they could be seen and did not let them stray even to
play. The children were even more silent than their elders,
their eyes bigger, more haunting in their stares. The nooks and
crannies between the wagons were filled with shaggy cattle and
black-spotted pigs in makeshift pens. Crates of chickens and
ducks and geese fitfully made up for the silence of the people.
He knew now where all the farmers had gone.

Lan led the way to the fortress in the middle of the town, a
massive stone pile atop the highest hill. A dry moat, deep and
wide, its bottom a forest of sharp steel spikes, razor-edged and
as tall as a man, surrounded the towered walls of the keep. A
place for a last defense, if the rest of the town fell. From one of
the gate towers an armored man called down, "Welcome, Dai
Shan." Another shouted to the inside of the fortress, "The
Golden Crane! The Golden Crane!"

Their hooves drummed on the heavy timbers of the lowered
drawbridge as they crossed the moat and rode under the sharp
points of the stout portcullis. Once through the gates, Lan
swung down out of his saddle to lead Mandarb, signaling the
others to dismount.

The first courtyard was a huge square paved with big stone
blocks and surrounded by towers and battlements as fierce as
those on the outside of the walls. As big as it was, the courtyard appeared just as crowded as the streets, and as much in
turmoil, though there was an order to the crowding here. Everywhere were armored men and armored horses. At half a
dozen smithies around the court, hammers clanged, and big
bellows, tugged by two leather-aproned men apiece, made the
forge-fires roar. A steady stream of boys ran with new-made
horseshoes for the farriers. Fletchers sat making arrows, and
every time a basket was filled it was whisked away and replaced
with an empty one.

Liveried grooms appeared on the run, eager and smiling in

black-and-gold. Rand hastily untied his belongings from behind
the saddle and gave the bay up to one of the grooms as a man
in plate-and-mail and leather bowed formally. He wore a bright
yellow cloak edged in red over his armor, with the Black Hawk
on the breast, and a yellow surcoat bearing a gray owl. He
wore no helmet and was bareheaded, truly, for his hair had all
been shaved except for a topknot tied with a leather cord. "It
has been long, Moiraine Aes Sedai. It is good to see you, Dai
Shan. Very good." He bowed again, to Loial, and murmured,
"Glory to the Builders. *Kiserai ti Wansho.*"

"I am unworthy," Loial replied formally, "and the work
small. *Tsingu ma choba.*"

"You honor us, Builder," the man said. *"Kiserai ti Wansho."*
He turned back to Lan. "Word was sent to Lord Agelmar, Dai
Shan, as soon as you were seen coming. He is waiting for you.
This way, please."

As they followed him into the fortress, along drafty stone
corridors hung with colorful tapestries and long silk screens of
hunting scenes and battles, he continued. "I am glad the call
reached you, Dai Shan. Will you raise the Golden Crane banner once more?" The halls were stark except for the wall hangings, and even they used the fewest figures made with the
fewest lines necessary to convey meaning, though in bright colors.

"Are things really as bad as they appear, Ingtar?" Lan asked
quietly. Rand wondered if his own ears were twitching like
Loial's.

The man's topknot swayed as he shook his head, but he hesitated before putting on a grin. "Things are never as bad as they
appear, Dai Shan. A little worse than usual this year, that is all.
The raids continued through the winter, even in the hardest of
it. But the raiding was no worse than anywhere else along the
Border. They still come in the night, but what else can be expected in the spring, if this can be called spring. Scouts return
from the Blight—those who do come back—with news of Trolloc camps. Always fresh news of more camps. But we will meet
them at Tarwin's Gap, Dai Shan, and turn them back as we
always have."

"Of course," Lan said, but he did not sound certain.

Ingtar's grin slipped, but came back immediately. Silently he showed them into Lord Agelmar's study, then claimed the press of his duties and left.

It was a room as purpose-made as all the rest of the fortress, with arrowslits in the outer wall and a heavy bar for the thick door, which had its own arrowpiercings and was bound by iron straps. Only one tapestry hung here. It covered an entire wall and showed men, armored like the men of Fal Dara, fighting Myrddraal and Trollocs in a mountain pass.

A table, one chest, and a few chairs were the only furnishings except for two racks on the wall, and they caught Rand's eye as much as the tapestry. One held a two-handed sword, taller than a man, a more ordinary broadsword, and below them a studded mace and a long, kite-shaped shield bearing three foxes. From the other hung a suit of armor, complete and arranged as one would wear it. Crested helmet with its barred face-guard over a double-mail camail. Mail hauberk, split for riding, and leather undercoat, polished from wear. Breastplate, steel gauntlets, knee and elbow cops, and half-plate for shoulders and arms and legs. Even here in the heart of the Keep, weapons and armor seemed ready to be donned at any moment. Like the furniture, they were simply and severely decorated with gold.

Agelmar himself rose at their entrance and came around the table, littered with maps and sheafs of paper and pens standing in inkpots. He seemed at first glance too peaceful for the room in his blue velvet coat with its tall, wide collar, and soft leather boots, but a second look showed Rand differently. Like all the fighting men he had seen, Agelmar's head was shaved except for a topknot, and that pure white. His face was as hard as Lan's, the only lines creases at the corners of his eyes, and those eyes like brown stone, though they bore a smile now.

"Peace, but it is good to see you, Dai Shan," the Lord of Fal Dara said. "And you, Moiraine Aes Sedai, perhaps even more. Your presence warms me, Aes Sedai."

"*Ninte calichniye no domashita, Agelmar Dai Shan,*" Moiraine replied formally, but with a note in her voice that said they were old friends. "Your welcome warms me, Lord Agelmar."

"*Kodome calichniye ga ni Aes Sedai hei.* Here is always a welcome for Aes Sedai." He turned to Loial. "You are far from the *stedding*, Ogier, but you honor Fal Dara. Always glory to the Builders. *Kiserai ti Wansho hei.*"

"I am unworthy," Loial said, bowing. "It is you who do me honor." He glanced at the stark stone walls and seemed to struggle with himself. Rand was glad the Ogier managed to refrain from adding further comment.

Servants in black-and-gold appeared on silent, soft-slippered feet. Some brought folded cloths, damp and hot, on silver trays for wiping the dust from faces and hands. Others bore mulled wine and silver bowls of dried plums and apricots. Lord Agelmar gave orders for rooms to be prepared, and baths.

"A long journey from Tar Valon," he said. "You must be tired."

"A short journey the path we came," Lan told him, "but more tiring than the long way."

Agelmar looked puzzled when the Warder said no more, but he merely said, "A few days' rest will put you all in fine fettle."

"I ask one night's shelter, Lord Agelmar," Moiraine said, "for ourselves and our horses. And fresh supplies in the morning, if you can spare them. We must leave you early, I am afraid."

Agelmar frowned. "But I thought. . . . Moiraine Sedai, I have no right to ask it of you, but you would be worth a thousand lances in Tarwin's Gap. And you, Dai Shan. A thousand men *will* come when they hear the Golden Crane flies once more."

"The Seven Towers are broken," Lan said harshly, "and Malkier is dead; the few of her people left, scattered across the face of the earth. I am a Warder, Agelmar, sworn to the Flame of Tar Valon, and I am bound into the Blight."

"Of course, Dai Sh— Lan. Of course. But surely a few days' delay, a few weeks at most, will make no difference. You are needed. You, and Moiraine Sedai."

Moiraine took a silver goblet from one of the servants. "Ingtar seems to believe you will defeat this threat as you have defeated many others across the years."

"Aes Sedai," Agelmar said wryly, "if Ingtar had to ride alone to Tarwin's Gap, he would ride the whole way proclaiming that the Trollocs would be turned back once more. He has almost pride enough to believe he *could* do it alone."

"He is not as confident as you think, this time, Agelmar." The Warder held a cup, but he did not drink. "How bad is it?"

Agelmar hesitated, pulling a map from the tangle on the table. He stared unseeing at the map for a moment, then tossed it back. "When we ride to the Gap," he said quietly, "the people will be sent south to Fal Moran. Perhaps the capital can hold. Peace, it must. Something must hold."

"That bad?" Lan said, and Agelmar nodded wearily.

Rand exchanged worried looks with Mat and Perrin. It was easy to believe the Trollocs gathering in the Blight were after him, after them. Agelmar went on grimly.

"Kandor, Arafel, Saldaea—the Trollocs raided them all straight through the winter. Nothing like that has happened since the Trolloc Wars; the raids have never been so fierce, or so large, or pressed home so hard. Every king and council is sure a great thrust is coming out of the Blight, and every one of the Borderlands believes it is coming at them. None of their scouts, and none of the Warders, report Trolloc massing above their borders, as we have here, but they believe, and each is afraid to send fighting men elsewhere. People whisper that the world is ending, that the Dark One is loose again. Shienar will ride to Tarwin's Gap alone, and we will be outnumbered at least ten to one. At least. It may be the last Ingathering of the Lances.

"Lan—no!—Dai Shan, for you *are* a Diademed Battle Lord of Malkier whatever you say. Dai Shan, the Golden Crane banner in the van would put heart into men who know they are riding north to die. The word will spread like wildfire, and though their kings have told them to hold where they are, lances will come from Arafel and Kandor, and even from Saldaea. Though they cannot come in time to stand with us in the Gap, they may save Shienar."

Lan peered into his wine. His face did not change, but wine slopped over his hand; the silver goblet crumpled in his grip. A servant took the ruined cup and wiped the Warder's hand with a cloth; a second put a fresh goblet in his hand while the other was whisked away. Lan did not seem to notice. "I cannot!" he whispered hoarsely. When he raised his head his blue eyes burned with a fierce light, but his voice was calm again, and flat. "I am a Warder, Agelmar." His sharp gaze slid across Rand and Mat and Perrin to Moiraine. "At first light I ride to the Blight."

Agelmar sighed heavily. "Moiraine Sedai, will you not come, at least? An Aes Sedai could make the difference."

"I cannot, Lord Agelmar." Moiraine seemed troubled. "There is indeed a battle to be fought, and it is not chance that the Trollocs gather above Shienar, but our battle, the true battle with the Dark One, will take place in the Blight, at the Eye of the World. You must fight your battle, and we ours."

"You cannot be saying he is loose!" Rocklike Agelmar sounded shaken, and Moiraine quickly shook her head.

"Not yet. If we win at the Eye of the World, perhaps not ever again."

"Can you even find the Eye, Aes Sedai? If holding the Dark One depends on that, we might as well be dead. Many have tried and failed."

"I can find it, Lord Agelmar. Hope is not lost yet."

Agelmar studied her, and then the others. He appeared puzzled by Nynaeve and Egwene; their farmclothes contrasted sharply with Moiraine's silk dress, though all were travel-stained. "They are Aes Sedai, too?" he asked doubtfully. When Moiraine shook her head, he seemed even more confused. His gaze ran over the young men from Emond's Field, settling on Rand, brushing the red-wrapped sword at his waist. "A strange guard you take with you, Aes Sedai. Only one fighting man." He glanced at Perrin, and at the axe hanging from his belt. "Perhaps two. But both barely more than lads. Let me send men with you. A hundred lances more or less will make no difference in the Gap, but you will need more than one Warder and three youths. And two women will not help, unless they are Aiel in disguise. The Blight is worse than usual this year. It—stirs."

"A hundred lances would be too many," Lan said, "and a thousand not enough. The larger the party we take into the Blight, the more chance we will attract attention. We must reach the Eye without fighting, if we can. You know the outcome is all but foretold when Trollocs force battle inside the Blight."

Agelmar nodded grimly, but he refused to give up. "Fewer, then. Even ten good men would give you a better chance of escorting Moiraine Sedai and the other two women to the Green Man than will just these young fellows."

Rand abruptly realized the Lord of Fal Dara assumed it was Nynaeve and Egwene who with Moiraine would fight against the Dark One. It was natural. That sort of struggle meant using the One Power, and that meant women. *That sort of struggle means using the Power.* He tucked his thumbs behind his sword belt and gripped the buckle hard to keep his hands from shaking.

"No men," Moiraine said. Agelmar opened his mouth again, and she went on before he could speak. "It is the nature of the Eye, and the nature of the Green Man. How many from Fal Dara have ever found the Green Man and the Eye?"

"Ever?" Agelmar shrugged. "Since the War of the Hundred Years, you could count them on the fingers of one hand. No more than one in five years from all the Borderlands together."

"No one finds the Eye of the World," Moiraine said, "unless the Green Man wants them to find it. Need is the key, and intention. I know where to go—I have been there before." Rand's head whipped around in surprise; his was not the only one among the Emond's Fielders, but the Aes Sedai did not seem to notice. "But one among us seeking glory, seeking to add his name to those four, and we may never find it though I take us straight to the spot I remember."

"You have seen the Green Man, Moiraine Sedai?" The Lord of Fal Dara sounded impressed, but in the next breath he frowned. "But if you have already met him once: . . ."

"Need is the key," Moiraine said softly, "and there can be no greater need than mine. Than ours. And I have something those other seekers have not."

Her eyes barely stirred from Agelmar's face, but Rand was sure they had drifted toward Loial, just for an instant before the Aes Sedai pulled them back. Rand met the Ogier's eyes, and Loial shrugged.

"*Ta'veren,*" the Ogier said softly.

Agelmar threw up his hands. "It will be as you say, Aes Sedai. Peace, if the real battle is to be at the Eye of the World, I am tempted to take the Black Hawk banner after you instead of to the Gap. I could cut a path for you—"

"That would be disaster, Lord Agelmar. Both at Tarwin's Gap and at the Eye. You have your battle, and we ours."

"Peace! As you say, Aes Sedai."

Having reached a decision, however much he disliked it, the shaven-headed Lord of Fal Dara seemed to put it out of his mind. He invited them to table with him, all the while making conversation about hawks and horses and dogs, but with never a mention of Trollocs, or Tarwin's Gap, or the Eye of the World.

The chamber where they ate was as stark and plain as Lord Agelmar's study had been, with little more furnishing it than the table and chairs themselves, and they were severe in line and form. Beautiful, but severe. A big fireplace warmed the room, but not so much that a man called out hurriedly would be stunned by the cold outside. Liveried servants brought soup and bread and cheese, and the talk was of books and music until Lord Agelmar realized the Emond's Field folk we're not talking. Like a good host he asked gently probing questions designed to bring them out of their quiet.

Rand soon found himself competing to tell about Emond's Field and the Two Rivers. It was an effort not to say too much. He hoped the others were guarding their tongues, Mat especially. Nynaeve alone held herself back, eating and drinking silently.

"There's a song in the Two Rivers," Mat said. "'Coming Home From Tarwin's Gap.'" He finished hesitantly, as if suddenly realizing that he was bringing up what they had been avoiding, but Agelmar handled it smoothly.

"Little wonder. Few lands have not sent men to hold back the Blight over the years."

Rand looked at Mat and Perrin. Mat silently formed the word Manetheren.

Agelmar whispered to one of the servants, and while others cleared the table that man vanished and returned with a canister, and clay pipes for Lan, Loial, and Lord Agelmar. "Two Rivers tabac," the Lord of Fal Dara said as they filled their pipes. "Hard to come by, here, but worth the cost."

When Loial and the two older men were puffing contentedly, Agelmar glanced at the Ogier. "You seem troubled, Builder. Not beset by the Longing, I hope. How long have you been away from the *stedding*?"

"It is not the Longing; I have not been gone such a time as that." Loial shrugged, and the blue-gray streamer rising from his pipe made a spiral above the table as he gestured. "I expected—hoped—that the grove would still be here. Some remnant of Mafal Dadaranell, at least."

"*Kiserai ti Wansho*," Agelmar murmured. "The Trolloc Wars left nothing but memories, Loial, son of Arent, and people to build on them. They could not duplicate the Builders' work, any more than could I. Those intricate curves and patterns your people create are beyond human eyes and hands to make. Perhaps we wished to avoid a poor imitation that would only have been an ever-present reminder to us of what we had lost. There is a different beauty in simplicity, in a single line placed just so, a single flower among the rocks. The harshness of the stone makes the flower more precious. We try not to dwell too much on what is gone. The strongest heart will break under that strain."

"The rose petal floats on water," Lan recited softly. "The kingfisher flashes above the pond. Life and beauty swirl in the midst of death."

"Yes," Agelmar said. "Yes. That one has always symbolized the whole of it to me, too." The two men bowed their heads to one another.

Poetry out of Lan? The man was like an onion; every time Rand thought he knew something about the Warder, he discovered another layer underneath.

Loial nodded slowly. "Perhaps I also dwell too much on what is gone. And yet, the groves were beautiful." But he was looking at the stark room as if seeing it anew, and suddenly finding things worth seeing.

Ingtar appeared and bowed to Lord Agelmar. "Your pardon, Lord, but you wanted to know of anything out of the ordinary, however small."

"Yes, what is it?"

"A small thing, Lord. A stranger tried to enter the town. Not of Shienar. By his accent, a Lugarder. Sometimes, at least.

When the South Gate guards attempted to question him, he ran away. He was seen to enter the forest, but only a short time later he was found scaling the wall."

"A small thing!" Agelmar's chair scraped across the floor as he stood. "Peace! The tower watch is so negligent a man can reach the walls unseen, and you call it a small thing?"

"He is a madman, Lord." Awe touched Ingtar's voice. "The Light shields madmen. Perhaps the Light cloaked the tower watch's eyes and allowed him to reach the walls. Surely one poor madman can do no harm."

"Has he been brought to the keep yet? Good. Bring him to me here. Now." Ingtar bowed and left, and Agelmar turned to Moiraine. "Your pardon, Aes Sedai, but I must see to this. Perhaps he is only a pitiful wretch with his mind blinded by the Light, but. . . . Two days gone, five of our own people were found in the night trying to saw through the hinges of a horsegate. Small, but enough to let Trollocs in." He grimaced. "Darkfriends, I suppose, though I hate to think it of any Shienaran. They were torn to pieces by the people before the guards could take them, so I'll never know. If Shienarans can be Darkfriends, I must be especially careful of outlanders in these days. If you wish to withdraw, I will have you shown to your rooms."

"Darkfriends know neither border nor blood," Moiraine said. "They are found in every land, and are *of* none. I, too, am interested in seeing this man. The Pattern is forming a Web, Lord Agelmar, but the final shape of the Web is not yet set. It may yet entangle the world, or unravel and set the Wheel to a new weaving. At this point, even small things can change the shape of the Web. At this point I am wary of small things out of the ordinary."

Agelmar glanced at Nynaeve and Egwene. "As you wish, Aes Sedai."

Ingtar returned, with two guards carrying long bills, and escorting a man who looked like a ragbag turned inside out. Grime layered his face and matted his scraggly, uncut hair and beard. He hunched into the room, sunken eyes darting this way and that. A rancid smell wafted ahead of him.

Rand sat forward intently, trying to see through all the dirt.

"You've no cause to be holding me like this," the filthy man whined. "I'm only a poor destitute, abandoned by the Light and seeking a place, like everyone else, to shelter from the Shadow."

"The Borderlands are a strange place to seek—" Agelmar began, when Mat cut him off.

"The peddler!"

"Padan Fain," Perrin agreed, nodding.

"The beggar," Rand said, suddenly hoarse. He sat back at the sudden hatred that flared in Fain's eyes. "He's the man who was asking about us in Caemlyn. He has to be."

"So this concerns you after all, Moiraine Sedai," Agelmar said slowly.

Moiraine nodded. "I greatly fear that it does."

"I didn't want to." Fain began to cry. Fat tears cut runnels in the dirt on his cheeks, but they were unable to reach the bottom layer. "He made me! Him and his burning eyes." Rand flinched. Mat had his hand under his coat, no doubt clutching the dagger from Shadar Logoth again. "He made me his hound! His hound, to hunt and follow with never a bit of rest. Only his hound, even after he threw me away."

"It does concern us all," Moiraine said grimly. "Is there a place where I can talk with him alone, Lord Agelmar?" Her mouth tightened with distaste. "And wash him first. I may need to touch him." Agelmar nodded and spoke softly to Ingtar, who bowed and disappeared through the door.

"I will not be compelled!" The voice was Fain's, but he was no longer crying, and an arrogant snap had replaced the whine. He stood upright, not crouching at all. Throwing back his head, he shouted at the ceiling. "Never again! I—will—not!" He faced Agelmar as if the men flanking him were his own bodyguard and the Lord of Fal Dara his equal rather than his captor. His tone became sleek and oily. "There is a misunderstanding here, Great Lord. I am sometimes taken by spells, but that will pass soon. Yes, soon I will be rid of them." Contemptuously he flicked his fingers against the rags he wore. "Do not be misled by these, Great Lord. I have had to disguise myself against those who have tried to stop me, and my journey has been long and hard. But at last I have reached lands where men still know the dangers of Ba'alzamon, where men still fight the Dark One."

Rand stared, goggling. It *was* Fain's voice, but the words did not sound like the peddler at all.

"So you've come here because we fight Trollocs," Agelmar said. "And you are so important that someone wants to stop you. These people say you are a peddler called Padan Fain, and that you are following them."

Fain hesitated. He glanced at Moiraine and hurriedly pulled his eyes away from the Aes Sedai. His gaze ran across the Emond's Fielders, then jerked back to Agelmar. Rand felt the hate in that look, and the fear. When Fain spoke again, though, his voice was unruffled. "Padan Fain is simply one of the many disguises I have been forced to wear over the years. Friends of the Dark pursue me, for I have learned how to defeat the Shadow. I can show you how to defeat him, Great Lord."

"We do as well as men can," Agelmar said dryly. "The Wheel weaves as the Wheel wills, but we have fought the Dark One almost since the Breaking of the World without peddlers to teach us how."

"Great Lord, your might is unquestioned, but can it stand against the Dark One forever? Do you not often find yourself pressed to hold? Forgive my temerity, Great Lord; he will crush you in the end, as you are. I know; believe me, I do. But I can show you how to scour the Shadow from the land, Great Lord." His tone became even more unctuous, though still haughty. "If you but try what I advise, you will see, Great Lord. You will cleanse the land. You, Great Lord, can do it, if you direct your might in the right direction. Avoid letting Tar Valon entangle you in its snares, and you can save the world. Great Lord, you will be the man remembered through history for bringing final victory to the Light." The guards held their places, but their hands shifted on the long shafts of the bills as if they thought they might have to use them.

"He thinks a great deal of himself for a peddler," Agelmar said to Lan over his shoulder. "I think Ingtar is right. He is mad."

Fain's eyes tightened angrily, but his voice remained smooth. "Great Lord, I know my words must appear grandiose, but if you will only—" He cut off abruptly, stepping back, as Moiraine rose and started slowly around the table. Only the guards' lowered bills kept Fain from backing right out of the room.

Stopping behind Mat's chair, Moiraine put a hand on his shoulder and bent to whisper in his ear. Whatever she said, the tension went out of his face, and he took his hand from under his coat. The Aes Sedai went on until she stood beside Agelmar, confronting Fain. As she came to a halt, the peddler sank into a crouch once more.

"I hate him," he whimpered.. "I want to be free of him. I want to walk in the Light again." His shoulders began to shake, and tears streamed down his face even more heavily than before. "He made me do it."

"I am afraid he is more than a peddler, Lord Agelmar," Moiraine said. "Less than human, worse than vile, more dangerous than you can imagine. He can be bathed after I have spoken with him. I dare not waste a minute. Come, Lan."

Padan Fain

CHAPTER
47

More Tales of the Wheel

An itchy restlessness had Rand pacing beside the dining table. Twelve strides. The table was exactly twelve strides long no matter how many times he stepped it off. Irritably he made himself stop keeping tally. *Stupid thing to be doing. I don't care how long the bloody table is.* A few minutes later he discovered that he was counting the number of trips he made up the table and back. *What is he saying to Moiraine and Lan? Does he know why the Dark One is after us? Does he know which of us the Dark One wants?*

He glanced at his friends. Perrin had crumbled a piece of bread and was idly pushing the crumbs around on the table with one finger. His yellow eyes stared unblinking at the crumbs, but they seemed to see something far off. Mat slouched in his chair, eyes half closed and the beginnings of a grin on his face. It was a nervous grin, not amusement. Outwardly he looked like the old Mat, but from time to time he unconsciously touched the Shadar Logoth dagger through his coat. *What is Fain telling her? What does he know?*

Loial, at least, did not look worried. The Ogier was studying the walls. First he had stood in the middle of the room and stared, turning slowly in a circle; now he was almost pressing his broad nose against the stone while he gently traced a particular join with fingers thicker than most men's thumbs. Sometimes he closed his eyes, as if the feeling was more important than seeing. His ears gave an occasional twitch, and he muttered to himself in Ogier, appearing to have forgotten anyone else was in the room with him.

Lord Agelmar stood talking quietly with Nynaeve and Egwene in front of the long fireplace at the end of the room. He was a good host, adept at making people forget their troubles; several of his stories had Egwene in giggles. Once even Nynaeve threw back her head and roared with laughter. Rand gave a start at the unexpected sound, and jumped again when Mat's chair crashed to the floor.

"Blood and ashes!" Mat growled, ignoring the way Nynaeve's mouth tightened at his language. "What's taking her so long?" He righted his chair and sat back down without looking at anyone. His hand strayed to his coat.

The Lord of Fal Dara looked at Mat disapprovingly—his gaze took in Rand and Perrin without any improvement—then turned back to the women. Rand's pacing had taken him close to them.

"My Lord," Egwene was saying, as glibly as if she had been using titles all of her life, "I thought he was a Warder, but you call him Dai Shan, and talk about a Golden Crane banner, and so did those other men. Sometimes you sound almost as if he's a king. I remember once Moiraine called him the last Lord of the Seven Towers. Who is he?"

Nynaeve began studying her cup intently, but it was obvious to Rand that abruptly she was listening even more closely than was Egwene. Rand stopped and tried to overhear without seeming to eavesdrop.

"Lord of the Seven Towers," Agelmar said with a frown. "An ancient title, Lady Egwene. Not even the High Lords of Tear have older, though the Queen of Andor comes close." He heaved a sigh, and shook his head. "He will not speak of it, yet the story is well known along the Border. He is a king, or should have been, al'Lan Mandragoran, Lord of the Seven Towers, Lord of the Lakes, crownless King of the Malkieri." His shaven head lifted high, and there was a light in his eye as if he felt a father's pride. His voice grew stronger, filled with the force of his feeling. The whole room could hear without straining. "We of Shienar call ourselves Bordermen, but fewer than fifty years ago, Shienar was not truly of the Borderlands. North of us, and of Arafel, was Malkier. The lances of Shienar rode north, but it was Malkier that held back the Blight. Malkier, Peace favor her memory, and the Light illumine her name."

"Lan is from Malkier," the Wisdom said softly, looking up. She seemed troubled.

It was not a question, but Agelmar nodded. "Yes, Lady Nynaeve, he is the son of al'Akir Mandragoran, last crowned King of the Malkieri. How did he become as he is? The beginning, perhaps, was Lain. On a dare, Lain Mandragoran, the King's brother, led his lances through the Blight to the Blasted Lands, perhaps to Shayol Ghul itself. Lain's wife, Breyan, made that dare for the envy that burned her heart that al'Akir had been raised to the throne instead of Lain. The King and Lain were as close as brothers could be, as close as twins even after the royal 'al' was added to Akir's name, but jealousy wracked Breyan. Lain was acclaimed for his deeds, and rightfully so, but not even he could outshine al'Akir. He was, man and king, such as comes once in a hundred years, if that. Peace favor him, and el'Leanna.

"Lain died in the Blasted Lands with most of those who followed him, men Malkier could ill afford to lose, and Breyan blamed the King, saying that Shayol Ghul itself would have fallen if al'Akir had led the rest of the Malkieri north with her husband. For revenge, she plotted with Cowin Gemallan, called Cowin Fairheart, to seize the throne for her son, Isam. Now Fairheart was a hero almost as well loved as al'Akir himself, and one of the Great Lords, but when the Great Lords had cast the rods for king, only two separated him from Akir, and he never forgot that two men laying a different color on the Crowning Stone would have set him on the throne instead. Between them, Cowin and Breyan moved soldiers back from the Blight to seize the Seven Towers, stripping the Borderforts to bare garrisons.

"But Cowin's jealousy ran deeper." Disgust tinged Agelmar's voice. "Fairheart the hero, whose exploits in the Blight were sung throughout the Borderlands, was a Darkfriend. With the Borderforts weakened, Trollocs poured into Malkier like a flood. King al'Akir and Lain together might have rallied the land; they had done so before. But Lain's doom in the Blasted Lands had shaken the people, and the Trolloc invasion broke men's spirit and their will to resist. Too many men. Overwhelming numbers pushed the Malkieri back into the heartland.

"Breyan fled with her infant son Isam, and was run down by Trollocs as she rode south with him. No one knows their fate of a certainty, but it can be guessed. I can find pity only for the boy. When Cowin Fairheart's treachery was revealed and he was taken by young Jain Charin—already called Jain Farstrider—when Fairheart was brought to the Seven Towers in chains, the Great Lords called for his head on a pike. But because he had been second only to al'Akir and Lain in the hearts of the people, the King faced him in single combat and slew him. Al'Akir wept when he killed Cowin. Some say he wept for a friend who had given himself to the Shadow, and some say for Malkier." The Lord of Fal Dara shook his head sadly.

"The first peal of the doom of the Seven Towers had been struck. There was no time to gather aid from Shienar or Arafel, and no hope that Malkier could stand alone, with five thousand of her lances dead in the Blasted Lands, her Borderforts over-run.

"Al'Akir and his Queen, el'Leanna, had Lan brought to them in his cradle. Into his infant hands they placed the sword of Malkieri kings, the sword he wears today. A weapon made by Aes Sedai during the War of Power, the War of the Shadow that brought down the Age of Legends. They anointed his head with oil, naming him Dai Shan, a Diademed Battle Lord, and consecrated him as the next King of the Malkieri, and in his name they swore the ancient oath of Malkieri kings and queens." Agelmar's face hardened, and he spoke the words as if he, too, had sworn that oath, or one much similar. "To stand against the Shadow so long as iron is hard and stone abides. To defend the Malkieri while one drop of blood remains. To avenge what cannot be defended." The words rang in the chamber.

"El'Leanna placed a locket around her son's neck, for re-membrance, and the infant, wrapped in swaddling clothes by the Queen's own hand, was given over to twenty chosen from the King's Bodyguard, the best swordsmen, the most deadly fighters. Their command: to carry the child to Fal Moran.

"Then did al'Akir and el'Leanna lead the Malkieri out to face the Shadow one last time. There they died, at Herot's Crossing, and the Malkieri died, and the Seven Towers were broken. Shienar, and Arafel, and Kandor, met the Halfmen and the Trollocs at the Stair of Jehaan and threw them back, but not as far as they had been. Most of Malkier remained in Trolloc hands, and year by year, mile by mile, the Blight has swallowed it." Agelmar drew a heavyhearted breath. When he went on, there was a sad pride in his eyes and voice.

"Only five of the Bodyguards reached Fal Moran alive, every man wounded, but they had the child unharmed. From the cradle they taught him all they knew. He learned weapons as other children learn toys, and the Blight as other children their mother's garden. The oath sworn over his cradle is graven in his mind. There is nothing left to defend, but he can avenge. He denies his titles, yet in the Borderlands he is called the Uncrowned, and if ever he raised the Golden Crane of Malkier, an army would come to follow. But he will not lead men to their deaths. In the Blight he courts death as a suitor courts a maiden, but he will not lead others to it.

"If you must enter the Blight, and with only a few, there is no man better to take you there, nor to bring you safely out again. He is the best of the Warders, and that means the best of the best. You might as well leave these boys here, to gain a little seasoning, and put your entire trust in Lan. The Blight is no place for untried boys."

Mat opened his mouth, and shut it again at a look from Rand. *I wish he'd learn to keep it shut.*

Nynaeve had listened just as wide-eyed as Egwene, but now she was staring into her cup again, her face pale. Egwene put a hand on her arm and gave her a sympathetic look.

Moiraine appeared in the doorway, Lan at her heels. Nynaeve turned her back on them.

"What did he say?" Rand demanded. Mat rose, and Perrin, too.

"Country oaf," Agelmar muttered, then raised his voice to a normal tone. "Did you learn anything, Aes Sedai, or is he simply a madman?"

"He is mad," Moiraine said, "or close to it, but there is nothing simple about Padan Fain." One of the black-and-gold-liv-

eried servants bowed his way in with a blue washbasin and
pitcher, a bar of yellow soap, and a small towel on a silver tray;
he looked anxiously at Agelmar. Moiraine directed him to put
them on the table. "Your pardon for commanding your servants, Lord Agelmar," she said. "I took the liberty of asking
for this."

Agelmar nodded to the servant, who put the tray on the
table and left hurriedly. "My servants are yours to command,
Aes Sedai."

The water Moiraine poured into the basin steamed as if only
just off the boil. She pushed up her sleeves and began vigorously washing her hands without regard for the heat of the
water. "I said he was worse than vile, but I did not come close.
I do not believe I have ever met someone so abject and de-
based, yet at the same time so foul. I feel soiled from touching
him, and I do not mean for the filth on his skin. Soiled in
here." She touched her breast. "The degradation of his soul
almost makes me doubt he has one. There is something worse
to him than a Darkfriend."

"He looked so pitiful," Egwene murmured. "I remember
him arriving in Emond's Field each spring, always laughing and
full of news from outside. Surely there's some hope for him?
'No man can stand in the Shadow so long that he cannot find
the Light again,'" she quoted.

The Aes Sedai toweled her hands briskly. "I have always believed it so," she said. "Perhaps Padan Fain can be redeemed.
But he has been a Darkfriend more than forty years, and what
he has done for that, in blood and pain and death, would freeze
your heart to hear. Among the least of these—though not small
to you, I suspect—he brought the Trollocs to Emond's Field."

"Yes," Rand said softly. He heard Egwene gasp. *I should
have guessed. Burn me, I should have, as soon as I recognized
him.*

"Did he bring any here?" Mat asked. He looked at the stone
walls around them and shivered. Rand thought he was remembering the Myddraal more than Trollocs; walls had not stopped
the Fade at Baerlon, or at Whitebridge.

"If he did"—Agelmar laughed—"they'll break their teeth on
the walls of Fal Dara. Many others have before." He was
speaking to everyone, but obviously addressing his words to

Egwene and Nynaeve, from the glances he gave them. "And do not worry yourself about Halfmen, either." Mat's face reddened. "Every street and alley in Fal Dara is lit by night. And no man may hide his face inside the walls."

"Why would Master Fain do that?" Egwene asked.

"Three years ago. . . ." With a heavy sigh Moiraine sat down, folding up as if what she had done with Fain had drained her. "Three years, this summer. As far back as that. The Light surely favors us, else the Father of Lies would have triumphed while I still sat planning in Tar Valon. Three years, Fain has been hunting you for the Dark One."

"That's crazy!" Rand said. "He's come into the Two Rivers every spring as regular as a clock. Three years? We've been right there in front of him, and he never looked at any of us twice before last year." The Aes Sedai pointed a finger at him, fixing him.

"Fain told me everything, Rand. Or almost everything. I believe he managed to hold back something, something important, despite all I could do, but he said enough. Three years ago, a Halfman came for him in a town in Murandy. Fain was terrified, of course, but it is considered a very great honor among Darkfriends to be so summoned. Fain believed he had been chosen for great things, and he had, though not in the manner he believed. He was brought north to the Blight, to the Blasted Lands. To Shayol Ghul. Where he met a man with eyes of fire, who named himself Ba'alzamon."

Mat shifted uneasily, and Rand swallowed hard. It had to have been that way, of course, but that did not make it any easier to accept. Only Perrin looked at the Aes Sedai as if nothing could surprise him any longer.

"The Light protect us," Agelmar said fervently.

"Fain did not like what was done to him at Shayol Ghul," Moiraine continued calmly. "While we talked, he screamed often of fire and burning. It almost killed him, bringing it all out from where he had it hidden. Even with my Healing he is a shattered ruin. It will take much to make him whole again. I will make the effort, though, if for no other reason than to learn what more he still hides. He had been chosen because of where he did his peddling. No," she said quickly when they stirred, "not the Two Rivers only, not then. The Father of Lies

knew roughly where to find what he sought, but not much better than we in Tar Valon.

"Fain said he has been made the Dark One's hound, and in a
way he is right. The Father of Lies set Fain to hunt, first changing him so he could carry out that hunt. It is the things done to
bring about those changes that Fain fears to remember; he
hates his master for them as much as he fears him. So Fain was
sent sniffing and hunting through all the villages around
Baerlon, and all the way to the Mountains of Mist, and down to
the Taren and across into the Two Rivers."

"Three springs ago?" Perrin said slowly. "I remember that
spring. Fain came later than usual, but what was strange was
that he lingered on. A whole week he remained, idle and
gnashing his teeth about laying out money for a room at the
Winespring Inn. Fain likes his money."

"I remember, now," Mat said. "Everybody was wondering
was he sick, or had he fallen for a local woman? Not that any of
them would marry a peddler, of course. As well marry one of
the Traveling People." Egwene raised an eyebrow at him, and
he shut his mouth.

"After that, Fain was taken to Shayol Ghul again, and his
mind was—distilled." Rand's stomach turned over at the tone
in the Aes Sedai's voice; it told more of what she meant than
the grimace that flashed across her face. "What he had . . .
sensed . . . was concentrated and fed back. When he entered
the Two Rivers the next year, he was able to choose his targets
out more clearly. Indeed, more clearly even than the Dark One
had expected. Fain knew for a certainty that the one he sought
was one of three in Emond's Field."

Perrin grunted, and Mat began cursing in a soft monotone that
even Nynaeve's glare did not stop. Agelmar looked at them
curiously. Rand felt only the faintest chill, and wondered at it.
Three years the Dark One had been hunting him . . . hunting
them. He was sure it should have made his teeth chatter.

Moiraine did not allow Mat to interrupt her. She raised her
voice enough to be heard over him. "When Fain returned to
Lugard, Ba'alzamon came to him in a dream. Fain abased himself and performed rites that would strike you deaf to hear the
half of them, binding himself even more tightly to the Dark One.
What is done in dreams can be more dangerous than what is

done awake." Rand stirred at the sharp, warning look, but she did not pause. "He was promised great rewards, power over kingdoms after Ba'alzamon's victory, and told that when he returned to Emond's Field he was to mark the three he had found. A Halfman would be there, waiting for him with Trollocs. We know now how the Trollocs came to the Two Rivers. There must have been an Ogier grove and a Waygate at Manetheren."

"The most beautiful of all," Loial said, "except for Tar Valon." He had been listening as intently as everyone else. "Manetheren is remembered fondly by the Ogier." Agelmar formed the name silently, his eyebrows raised in wonder. Manetheren.

"Lord Agelmar," Moiraine said, "I will tell you how to find the Waygate of Mafal Dadaranell. It must be walled up and a guard set, and none allowed near. The Halfmen have not learned all of the Ways yet, but that Waygate is to the south and only hours from Fal Dara."

The Lord of Fal Dara gave himself a shake, as if he were coming out of a trance. "South? Peace! We don't need that, the Light shine on us. It shall be done."

"Did Fain follow us through the Ways?" Perrin asked. "He must have done."

Moiraine nodded. "Fain would follow you three into the grave, because he must. When the Myrddraal failed at Emond's Field, it brought Fain with the Trollocs on our trail. The Fade would not let Fain ride with him; although he thought he should have the best horse in the Two Rivers and ride at the head of the band, the Myrddraal forced him to run with the Trollocs, and the Trollocs to carry him when his feet gave out. They talked so that he could understand, arguing about the best way to cook him when his usefulness was done. Fain claims he turned against the Dark One before they reached the Taren. But sometimes his greed for his promised rewards seeps into the open.

"When we had escaped across the Taren the Myrddraal took the Trollocs back to the closest Waygate, in the Mountains of Mist, and sent Fain across alone. He thought he was free then, but before he reached Baerlon another Fade found him, and that one was not so kind. It made him sleep doubled up on himself in a Trolloc kettle at night, to remind him of the price of failure. That one used him as far as Shadar Logoth. By then Fain was willing to give the Myrddraal his mother if it would free him, but the Dark One never willingly loosens a hold he has gained.

"What I did there, sending an illusion of our tracks and smell off toward the mountains, fooled the Myrddraal, but not Fain. The Halfmen did not believe him; afterward, they dragged him behind them on a leash. Only when we seemed to keep always just ahead, no matter how hard they pressed, did some begin to credit him. Those were the four who returned to Shadar Logoth. Fain claims it was Ba'alzamon himself who drove the Myrddraal."

Agelmar shook his head contemptuously. "The Dark One? Pah! The man's lying or mad. If Heartsbane were loose, we'd all of us be dead by now, or worse."

"Fain spoke the truth as he saw it," Moiraine said. "He could not lie to me, though he hid much. His words. 'Ba'alzamon appeared like a flickering candle flame, vanishing and reappearing, never in the same place twice. His eyes seared the Myrddraal, and the fires of his mouth scourged us.'"

"Something," Lan said, "drove four Fades to where they feared to go—a place they fear almost as much as they fear the wrath of the Dark One."

Agelmar grunted as if he had been kicked; he looked sick.

"It was evil against evil in the ruins of Shadar Logoth," Moiraine continued, "foul fighting vile. When Fain spoke of it, his teeth chattered and he whimpered. Many Trollocs were slain, consumed by Mashadar and other things, including the Trolloc that held Fain's leash. He fled the city as if it were the Pit of Doom, at Shayol Ghul.

"Fain believed he was free at last. He intended to run until Ba'alzamon could never find him again, to the ends of the earth if necessary. Imagine his horror when he discovered that the compulsion to hunt did not lessen. Instead, it grew stronger and sharper with every day that passed. He could not eat, except what he could scavenge while he hunted you—beetles and lizards snatched while he ran, half-rotten refuse dug from midden heaps in the dark of night—nor could he stop until exhaustion collapsed him like an empty sack. And as soon as he had strength to stand again, he was driven on. By the time he reached Caemlyn he could *feel* his quarry even when it was a mile away. Here, in the cells below, he would sometimes look up without realizing what he was doing. He was looking in the direction of this room."

Rand had a sudden itch between his shoulder blades; it was as if he could feel Fain's eyes on him then, through the intervening stone. The Aes Sedai noticed his uneasy shrug, but she went on implacably.

"If Fain was half mad by the time he reached Caemlyn, he sank even further when he realized that only two of those he sought were there. He was compelled to find *all* of you, but he could do no other than follow the two who were there, either. He spoke of screaming when the Waygate opened in Caemlyn. The knowledge of how to do it was in his mind; he does not know how it came there; his hands moved of their own accord, burning with the fires of Ba'alzamon when he tried to stop them. The owner of the shop, who came to investigate the noise, Fain murdered. Not because he had to, but out of envy that the man could walk freely out of the cellar while his feet carried him inexorably into the Ways."

"Then Fain was the one you sensed following us," Egwene said. Lan nodded. "How did he escape the . . . the Black Wind?" Her voice shook; she stopped to swallow. "It was right behind us at the Waygate."

"He escaped, and he did not," Moiraine said. "The Black Wind caught him—and he claimed to understand the voices. Some greeted him as like to them; others feared him. No sooner did the Wind envelop Fain than it fled."

"The Light preserve us." Loial's whisper rumbled like a giant bumblebee.

"Pray that it does," Moiraine said. "There is much yet hidden about Padan Fain, much I must learn. The evil goes deeper in him, and stronger, than in any man I have yet seen. It may be that the Dark One, in doing what he did to Fain, impressed some part of himself on the man, perhaps even, unknowing, some part of his intent. When I mentioned the Eye of the World, Fain clamped his jaws shut, but I felt something knowing behind the silence. If only I had the time now. But we cannot wait."

"If this man knows something," Agelmar said, "I can get it out of him." His face held no mercy for Darkfriends; his voice promised no pity for Fain. "If you can learn even a part of what you will face in the Blight, it's worth an extra day. Battles have been lost for not knowing what the enemy intends."

Moiraine sighed and shook her head ruefully. "My lord, if we did not need at least one good night's sleep before facing the Blight, I would ride within the hour, though it meant the risk of meeting a Trolloc raid in the dark. Consider what I did learn from Fain. Three years ago the Dark One had to have Fain brought to Shayol Ghul to touch him, despite the fact that Fain is a Darkfriend dedicated to his marrow. One year ago, the Dark One could command Fain, the Darkfriend, through his dreams. This year, Ba'alzamon walks in the dreams of those who live in the Light, and actually appears, if with difficulty, at Shadar Logoth. Not in his own body, of course, but even a projection of the Dark One's mind, even a projection that flickers and cannot hold, is more deathly dangerous to the world than all the Trolloc hordes combined. The seals on Shayol Ghul are weakening desperately, Lord Agelmar. There is no time."

Agelmar bowed his head in acquiescence, but when he raised it again there was still a stubborn set to his mouth. "Aes Sedai, I can accept that when I lead the lances to Tarwin's Gap we will be no more than a diversion, or a skirmish on the outskirts of the real battle. Duty takes men where it will as surely as does the Pattern, and neither promises that what we do will have greatness. But our skirmish will be useless, even should we win, if you lose the battle. If you say your party must be small, I say well and good, but I beg you to make every effort to see that you *can* win. Leave these young men here, Aes Sedai. I swear to you that I can find three experienced men with no thought of glory in their heads to replace them, good swordsmen who are almost as handy in the Blight as Lan. Let me ride to the Gap knowing that I have done what I can to help you be victorious."

"I must take them and no others, Lord Agelmar," Moiraine said gently. "They are the ones who will fight the battle at the Eye of the World."

Agelmar's jaw dropped, and he stared at Rand and Mat and Perrin. Suddenly the Lord of Fal Dara took a step back, his hand groping unconsciously for the sword he never wore inside the fortress. "They aren't. . . . You are not Red Ajah,

Moiraine Sedai, but surely not even you would. . . ." Sudden sweat glistened on his shaven head.

"They are *ta'veren*," Moiraine said soothingly. "The Pattern weaves itself around them. Already the Dark One has tried to kill each of them more than once. Three *ta'veren* in one place are enough to change the life around them as surely as a whirlpool changes the path of a straw. When the place is the Eye of the World, the Pattern might weave even the Father of Lies into itself, and make him harmless again."

Agelmar stopped trying to find his sword, but he still looked at Rand and the others doubtfully. "Moiraine Sedai, if you say they are, then they are, but I cannot see it. Farmboys. Are you certain, Aes Sedai?"

"The old blood," Moiraine said, "split out like a river breaking into a thousand times a thousand streams, but sometimes streams join together to make a river again. The old blood of Manetheren is strong and pure in almost all these young men. Can you doubt the strength of Manetheren's blood, Lord Agelmar?"

Rand glanced sideways at the Aes Sedai. *Almost all.* He risked a look at Nynaeve; she had turned back to watch as well as listen, though she still avoided looking at Lan. He caught the Wisdom's eye. She shook her head; she had not told the Aes Sedai that he was not Two Rivers born. *What does Moiraine know?*

"Manetheren," Agelmar said slowly, nodding. "I would not doubt that blood." Then, more quickly, "The Wheel brings strange times. Farmboys carry the honor of Manetheren into the Blight, yet if any blood can strike a fell blow at the Dark One, it would be the blood of Manetheren. It shall be done as you wish, Aes Sedai."

"Then let us go to our rooms," Moiraine said. "We must leave with the sun, for time grows short. The young men must sleep close to me. Time is too short before the battle to allow the Dark One another strike at them. Too short."

Rand felt her eyes on him, studying him and his friends, weighing their strength, and he shivered. Too short.

CHAPTER
48

The Blight

T he wind whipped Lan's cloak, sometimes making him
hard to see even in the sunlight, and Ingtar and the
hundred lances Lord Agelmar had sent to escort them
to the Border, in case they met a Trolloc raid, made a brave
display in double column with their armor and their red pennants and their steel-clad horses led by Ingtar's Gray Owl banner. They were easily as grand as a hundred of the Queen's
Guards, but it was the towers just in sight ahead of them that
Rand studied. He had had all morning to watch the Shienaran
lances.

Each tower stood tall and solid atop a hill, half a mile from
its neighbor. East and west others rose, and more beyond
those. A broad, walled ramp spiraled around each stone shaft,
winding all the way around by the time it reached the heavy
gates halfway to the crenellated top. A sortie from the garrison
would be protected by the wall until it reached the ground, but
enemies striving to reach the gate would climb under a hail of
arrows and stones and hot oil from the big kettles poised on the
outward flaring ramparts above. A large steel mirror, carefully
turned down, away from the sun, now, glittered atop each
tower below the high iron cup where signal fires could be lit
when the sun did not shine. The signal would be flashed, to
towers further from the Border, and by those to still others,
and so relayed to the heartland fortresses, from where the

lances would ride to turn back the·raid. Were times normal, they would.

From the two nearest tower tops men watched them approach. Just a few men on each, peering curiously through the crenels. In the best of times the towers were only manned enough for self-defense, depending more on stone walls than strong arms to survive, but every man who could be spared, and more, was riding to Tarwin's Gap. The fall of the towers would not matter if the lances failed to hold the Gap.

Rand shivered as they rode between the towers. It was almost as if he had ridden through a wall of colder air. This was the Border. The land beyond looked no different from Shienar, but out there, somewhere beyond the leafless trees, was the Blight.

Ingtar lifted a steel fist to halt the lances short of a plain stone post in sight of the towers. A borderpost, marking the boundary between Shienar and what once was Malkier. "Your pardon, Moiraine Aes Sedai. Pardon, Dai Shan. Pardon, Builder. Lord Agelmar commanded me to go no further." He sounded unhappy about it, disgruntled at life in general.

"That is as we planned, Lord Agelmar and I," Moiraine said.

Ingtar grunted sourly. "Pardon, Aes Sedai," he apologized, not sounding as if he meant it. "To escort you here means we may not reach the Gap before the fighting is done. I am robbed of the chance to stand with the rest, and at the same time I am commanded not to ride one step beyond the borderpost, as if I had never before been in the Blight. And My Lord Agelmar will not tell me why." Behind the bars of his face-guard, his eyes turned the last word into a question to the Aes Sedai. He scorned to look at Rand and the others; he had learned they would accompany Lan into the Blight.

"He can have my place," Mat muttered to Rand. Lan gave them both a sharp look. Mat dropped his eyes, his face turning red.

"Each of us has his part in the Pattern, Ingtar," Moiraine said firmly. "From here we must thread ours alone."

Ingtar's bow was stiffer than his armor made it. "As you wish it, Aes Sedai. I must leave you, now, and ride hard in order to reach Tarwin's Gap. At least I will be . . . *allowed* . . . to face Trollocs there."

"Are you truly that eager?" Nynaeve asked. "To fight Trollocs?"

Ingtar gave her a puzzled look, then glanced at Lan as if the Warder might explain. "That is what I do, Lady," he said slowly. "That is why I am." He raised a gauntleted hand to Lan, open palm toward the warder. "*Suravye ninto manshima taishite, Dai Shan.* Peace favor your sword." Pulling his horse around, Ingtar rode east with his bannerman and his hundred lances. They went at a walk, but a steady pace, as fast as armored horses could manage with a far distance yet to go.

"What a strange thing to say," Egwene said. "Why do they use it like that? Peace."

"When you have never known a thing except to dream," Lan replied, heeling Mandarb forward, "it becomes more than a talisman."

As Rand followed the Warder past the stone borderpost, he turned in his saddle to look back, watching Ingtar and the lances disappear behind barren trees, and the borderpost vanish, and last of all the towers on their hilltops, looking over the trees. All too soon they were alone, riding north under the leafless canopy of the forest. Rand sank into watchful silence, and for once even Mat had nothing to say.

That morning the gates of Fal Dara had opened with the dawn. Lord Agelmar, armored and helmeted now like his soldiers, rode with the Black Hawk banner and the Three Foxes from the East Gate toward the sun, still only a red sliver above the trees. Like a steel snake undulating to mounted kettledrums, the column wound its way out of the town four abreast, Agelmar at its head hidden in the forest before its tail left Fal Dara keep. There were no cheers in the streets to speed them on their way, only their own drums and their pennants' cracking in the wind, but their eyes looked toward the rising sun with purpose. Eastward they would join other steel serpents, from Fal Moran, behind King Easar himself with his sons at his side, and from Ankor Dail, that held the Eastern Marches and guarded the Spine of the World; from Mos Shirare and Fal Sion and Camron Caan, and all the other fortresses in Shienar, great and small. Joined into a greater serpent, they would turn north to Tarwin's Gap.

Another exodus had begun at the same time, using the King's Gate that led out on the way to Fal Moran. Carts and wagons, people mounted and people afoot, driving their livestock, carrying children on their backs, faces as long as the morning shadows. Reluctance to leave their homes, perhaps forever, slowed their feet, yet fear of what was coming spurred them, so that they went in bursts, feet dragging, then breaking into a run for a dozen paces only to fall back, once more, to shuffling through the dust. A few paused outside the town to watch the soldiers' armored line winding into the forest. Hope blossomed in some eyes, and prayers were muttered, prayers for the soldiers, prayers for themselves, before they turned south again, trudging.

The smallest column went out of the Malkier Gate. Left behind were a few who would remain, soldiers and a sprinkling of older men, their wives dead and their grown children making the slow way south. A last handful so that whatever happened in Tarwin's Gap, Fal Dara would not fall undefended. Ingtar's Gray Owl led the way, but it was Moiraine who took them north. The most important column of all, and the most desperate.

For at least an hour after they passed the borderpost there was no change in land or forest. The Warder kept them at a hard pace, as fast a walk as the horses could maintain, but Rand kept wondering when they would reach the Blight. The hills became a little higher, but the trees, and the creepers, and the underbrush were no different than what he had seen in Shienar, gray and all but leafless. He began to feel warmer, warm enough to sling his cloak across the pommel of his saddle.

"This is the best weather we've seen all year," Egwene said, shrugging out of her own cloak.

Nynaeve shook her head, frowning as if listening to the wind. "It feels wrong."

Rand nodded. He could feel it, too, though he could not say what it was exactly he was feeling. The wrongness went beyond the first warmth he could remember out of doors this year; it was more than the simple fact that it should not be so warm this far north. It must be the Blight, but the land was the same.

The sun climbed high, a red ball that could not give so much warmth despite the cloudless sky. A little while later he unbuttoned his coat. Sweat trickled down his face.

He was not the only one. Mat took his coat off, openly displaying the gold-and-ruby dagger, and wiped his face with the end of his scarf. Blinking, he rewound the scarf into a narrow band low over his eyes. Nynaeve and Egwene fanned themselves; they rode slumped as if they were wilting. Loial undid his high-collared tunic all the way down, and his shirt as well; the Ogier had a narrow strip of hair up the middle of his chest, as thick as fur. He muttered apologies all around.

"You must forgive me. Stedding Shangtai is in the mountains, and cool." His broad nostrils flared, drawing in air that was becoming warmer by the minute. "I don't like this heat, and damp."

It *was* damp, Rand realized. It felt like the Mire in the depths of summer, back in the Two Rivers. In that boggy swamp every breath came as if through a wool blanket soaked in hot water. There was no soggy ground here—only a few ponds and streams, trickles to someone used to the Waterwood—but the air was like that in the Mire. Only Perrin, still in his coat, was breathing easily. Perrin and the Warder.

There were a few leaves now, on trees that were not evergreen. Rand reached out to touch a branch, and stopped with his hand short of the leaves. Sickly yellow mottled the red of the new growth, and black flecks like disease.

"I told you not to touch anything." The Warder's voice was flat. He still wore his shifting cloak, as if heat made no more impression on him than cold; it almost made his angular face seem to float unsupported above Mandarb's back. "Flowers can kill in the Blight, and leaves maim. There's a little thing called a Stick that likes to hide where the leaves are thickest, looking like its name, waiting for something to touch it. When something does, it bites. Not poison. The juice begins to digest the Stick's prey for it. The only thing that can save you is to cut off the arm or leg that was bitten. But a Stick won't bite unless you touch it. Other things in the Blight will."

Rand jerked his hand back, leaves untouched, and wiped it on his pants leg.

"Then we're in the Blight?" Perrin said. Strangely, he did not sound frightened.

"Just the fringe,". Lan said grimly. His stallion kept moving forward, and he spoke over his shoulder. "The real Blight still lies ahead. There are things in the Blight that hunt by sound, and some may have wandered this far south. Sometimes they cross the Mountains of Dhoom. Much worse than Sticks. Keep quiet and keep up, if you want to stay alive." He continued to set a hard pace, not waiting for an answer.

Mile by mile the corruption of the Blight became more apparent. Leaves covered the trees in ever greater profusion, but stained and spotted with yellow and black, with livid red streaks like blood poisoning. Every leaf and creeper seemed bloated, ready to burst at a touch. Flowers hung on trees and weeds in a parody of spring, sickly pale and pulpy, waxen things that appeared to be rotting while Rand watched. When he breathed through his nose, the sweet stench of decay, heavy and thick, sickened him; when he tried breathing through his mouth, he almost gagged. The air tasted like a mouthful of spoiled meat. The horses' hooves made a soft squishing as rotten-ripe things broke open under them.

Mat leaned out of his saddle and spewed until his stomach was empty. Rand sought the void, but calmness was little help against the burning bile that kept creeping up his throat. Empty or not, Mat heaved again a mile later, bringing up nothing, and yet again after that. Egwene looked as if she wanted to be sick, too, swallowing constantly, and Nynaeve's face was a white mask of determination, her jaw set and her eyes fixed on Moiraine's back. The Wisdom would not admit to feeling ill unless the Aes Sedai did, first, but Rand did not think she would have to wait long. Moiraine's eyes were tight, and her lips pale.

Despite the heat and damp, Loial wrapped a scarf around his nose and mouth. When he met Rand's gaze, the Ogier's outrage and disgust were plain in his eyes. "I had heard—" he began, his voice muffled by the wool, then stopped to clear his throat with a grimace. "Faugh! It tastes like. . . . Faugh! I had

heard and read about the Blight, but nothing could describe. . . ." His gesture somehow took in the smell as well as
the eye-sickening growth. "That even the Dark One should do
this to trees! Faugh!"

The Warder was not affected, of course, at least not that
Rand could see, but to his surprise neither was Perrin. Or
rather, not in the way the rest of them were. The big youth
glared at the obscene forest through which they rode as he
might have at an enemy, or the banner of an enemy. He ca-
ressed the axe at his belt as if unaware of what he was doing,
and muttered to himself, half growling in a way that made the
hair on Rand's neck stir. Even in full sunlight his eyes glowed,
golden and fierce.

The heat did not abate as the bloody sun fell toward the horizon. In the distance to the north, mountains rose, higher than
the Mountains of Mist, black against the sky. Sometimes an icy
wind from the sharp peaks gusted far enough to reach them.
The torrid humidity leached away most of the mountain chill,
but what remained was winter-cold compared to the swelter it
replaced, if just for a moment. The sweat on Rand's face
seemed to flash into beads of ice; as the wind died, the beads
melted again, running angry lines down his cheeks, and the
thick heat returned harder than before by comparison. For the
instant the wind surrounded them, it swept away the fetor, yet
he would have done without that, too, if he could have. The
cold was the chill of the grave, and it carried the dusty must of
an old tomb newly opened.

"We cannot reach the mountains by nightfall," Lan said,
"and it is dangerous to move at night, even for a Warder
alone."

"There is a place not far off," Moiraine said. "It will be a
good omen for us to camp there."

The Warder gave her a flat look, then nodded reluctantly.
"Yes. We must camp somewhere. It might as well be there."

"The Eye of the World was beyond the high passes when I
found it," Moiraine said. "Better to cross the Mountains of
Dhoom in full daylight, at noon, when the Dark One's powers
in this world are weakest."

"You talk as if the Eye isn't always in the same place." Egwene spoke to the Aes Sedai, but it was Loial who answered.

"No two among the Ogier have found it in exactly the same place. The Green Man seems to be found where he is needed. But it has always been beyond the high passes. They are treacherous, the high passes, and haunted by creatures of the Dark One."

"We must reach the passes before we need worry about them," Lan said. "Tomorrow we will be truly into the Blight."

Rand looked at the forest around him, every leaf and flower diseased, every creeper decaying as it grew, and he could not repress a shudder. *If this isn't truly the Blight, what is?*

Lan turned them westward, at an angle to the sinking sun. The Warder maintained the pace he had set before, but there was reluctance in the set of his shoulders.

The sun was a sullen red ball just touching the treetops when they crested a hill and the Warder drew rein. Beyond them to the west lay a network of lakes, the waters glittering darkly in the slanting sunlight, like beads of random size on a necklace of many strings. In the distance, circled by the lakes, stood jagged-topped hills, thick in the creeping shadows of evening. For one brief instant the sun's rays caught the shattered tops, and Rand's breath stilled. Not hills. The broken remnants of seven towers. He was not sure if anyone else had seen it; the sight was gone as quickly as it came. The Warder was dismounting, his face as lacking in emotion as a stone.

"Couldn't we camp down by the lakes?" Nynaeve asked, patting her face with her kerchief. "It must be cooler down by the water."

"Light," Mat said, "I'd just like to stick my head in one of them. I might never take it out."

Just then something roiled the waters of the nearest lake, the dark water phosphorescing as a huge body rolled beneath the surface. Length on man-thick length sent ripples spreading, rolling on and on until at last a tail rose, waving a point like a wasp's stinger for an instant in the twilight, at least five spans into the air. All along that length fat tentacles writhed like monstrous worms, as many as a centipede's legs. It slid slowly beneath the surface and was gone, only the fading ripples to say it had ever been.

Rand closed his mouth and exchanged a look with Perrin. Perrin's yellow eyes were as disbelieving as he knew his own must be. Nothing that big could live in a lake that size. *Those couldn't have been* hands *on those tentacles. They couldn't have been.*

"On second thought," Mat said faintly, "I like it right here just fine."

"I will set guarding wards around this hill," Moiraine said. She had already dismounted from Aldieb. "A true barrier would draw the attention we do not want like flies to honey, but if any creation of the Dark One or anything that serves the Shadow comes within a mile of us, I will know."

"I'd be happier with the barrier," Mat said as his boots touched the ground, "just as long as it kept that, that . . . thing on the other side."

"Oh, do be quiet, Mat," Egwene said curtly, at the same time as Nynaeve spoke. "And have them waiting for us when we leave in the morning? You *are* a fool, Matrim Cauthon." Mat glowered at the two women as they climbed down, but he kept his mouth shut.

As he took Bela's reins, Rand shared a grin with Perrin. For a moment it was almost like being home, having Mat saying what he should not at the worst possible time. Then the smile faded from Perrin's face; in the twilight his eyes *did* glow, as if they had a yellow light behind them. Rand's grin slipped away, too. *It isn't like home at all.*

Rand and Mat and Perrin helped Lan unsaddle and hobble the horses while the others began setting up the camp. Loial muttered to himself as he set up the Warder's tiny stove, but his thick fingers moved deftly. Egwene was humming as she filled the tea kettle from a bulging waterbag. Rand no longer wondered why the Warder had insisted on bringing so many full waterskins.

Setting the bay's saddle in line with the others, he unfastened his saddlebags and blanketroll from the cantle, turned, and stopped with a tingle of fear. The Ogier and the women were gone. So was the stove and all the wicker panniers from the packhorse. The hilltop was empty except for evening shadows.

With a numb hand he fumbled for his sword, dimly hearing Mat curse. Perrin had his axe out, his shaggy head swiveling to find the danger.

"Sheepherders," Lan muttered. Unconcernedly the Warder strode across the hilltop, and at his third step, he vanished.

Rand exchanged wide-eyed looks with Mat and Perrin, and then they were all darting for where the Warder had disappeared. Abruptly Rand skidded to a halt, taking another step when Mat ran into his back. Egwene looked up from setting the kettle atop the tiny stove. Nynaeve was closing the mantle on a second lit lantern. They were all there, Moiraine sitting crosslegged, Lan lounging on an elbow, Loial taking a book out of his pack.

Cautiously Rand looked behind him. The hillside was there as it had been, the shadowed trees, the lakes beyond sinking into darkness. He was afraid to step back, afraid they would all disappear again and perhaps this time he would not be able to find them. Edging carefully around him, Perrin let out a long breath.

Moiraine noticed the three of them standing there, gaping. Perrin looked abashed, and slipped his axe back into the heavy belt loop as if he thought no one might notice. A smile touched her lips. "It is a simple thing," she said, "a bending, so any eye looking at us sees around us, instead. We cannot have the eyes that will be out there seeing our lights tonight, and the Blight is no place to be in the dark."

"Moiraine Sedai says I might be able to do it." Egwene's eyes were bright. "She says I can handle enough of the One Power right now."

"Not without training, child," Moiraine cautioned. "The simplest matter concerning the One Power can be dangerous to the untrained, and to those around them." Perrin snorted, and Egwene looked so uncomfortable that Rand wondered if she had already been trying her abilities.

Nynaeve set down the lantern. Together with the tiny flame of the stove, the pair of lanterns gave a generous light. "When you go to Tar Valon, Egwene," she said carefully, "perhaps I'll go with you." The look she gave Moiraine was strangely defensive. "It will do her good to see a familiar face among strangers. She'll need someone to advise her besides Aes Sedai."

"Perhaps that would be for the best, Wisdom," Moiraine said simply.

Egwene laughed and clapped her hands. "Oh, that *will* be wonderful. And you, Rand. You'll come, too, won't you?" He paused in the act of sitting across the stove from her, then slowly lowered himself. He thought her eyes had never been bigger, or brighter, or more like pools that he could lose himself in. Spots of color appeared in her cheeks, and she gave a smaller laugh. "Perrin, Mat, you two will come, won't you? We'll all be together." Mat gave a grunt that could have signified anything, and Perrin only shrugged, but she took it for assent. "You see, Rand. We'll all be together."

Light, but a man could drown in those eyes and be happy doing it. Embarrassed, he cleared his throat. "Do they have sheep in Tar Valon? That's all I know, herding sheep and growing tabac."

"I believe," Moiraine said, "that I can find something for you to do in Tar Valon. For all of you. Not herding sheep, perhaps, but something you will find interesting."

"There," Egwene said as if it were settled. "I know. I will make you my Warder, when I'm an Aes Sedai. You would like being a Warder, wouldn't you? My Warder?" She sounded sure, but he saw the question in her eyes. She wanted an answer, needed it.

"I'd like being your Warder," he said. *She's not for you, nor you for her. Why did Min have to tell me that?*

Darkness came down heavily, and everyone was tired. Loial was the first to roll over and ready himself for sleep, but others followed soon after. No one used their blankets, except for a pillow. Moiraine had put something in the oil of the lamps that dispelled the stench of the Blight from the hilltop, but nothing diminished the heat. The moon gave a wavering, watery light, but the sun might have been at its zenith for all the cool the night had.

Rand found sleep impossible, even with the Aes Sedai stretched out not a span away to shield his dreams. It was the thick air that kept him awake. Loial's soft snores were a rumble that made Perrin's seem nonexistent, but they did not stop weariness from claiming the others. The Warder was still awake, seated not far from him with his sword across his knees, watching the night. To Rand's surprise, so was Nynaeve.

The Wisdom looked at Lan silently for a long time, then

poured a cup of tea and brought it to him. When he reached out with a murmur of thanks, she did not let go right away. "I should have known you would be a king," she said quietly. Her eyes were steady on the Warder's face, but her voice trembled slightly.

Lan looked back at her just as intently. It seemed to Rand that the Warder's face actually softened. "I am not a king, Nynaeve. Just a man. A man without as much to his name as even the meanest farmer's croft."

Nynaeve's voice steadied. "Some women don't ask for land, or gold. Just the man."

"And the man who would ask her to accept so little would not be worthy of her. You are a remarkable woman, as beautiful as the sunrise, as fierce as a warrior. You are a lioness, Wisdom."

"A Wisdom seldom weds." She paused to take a deep breath, as if steeling herself. "But if I go to Tar Valon, it may be that I will be something other than a Wisdom."

"Aes Sedai marry as seldom as Wisdoms. Few men can live with so much power in a wife, dimming them by her radiance whether she wishes to or not."

"Some men are strong enough. I know one such." If there could have been any doubt, her look left none as to whom she meant.

"All I have is a sword, and a war I cannot win, but can never stop fighting."

"I've told you I care nothing for that. Light, you've made me say more than is proper already. Will you shame me to the point of asking you?"

"I will never shame you." The gentle tone, like a caress, sounded odd to Rand's ears in the Warder's voice, but it made Nynaeve's eyes brighten. "I will hate the man you choose because he is not me, and love him if he makes you smile. No woman deserves the sure knowledge of widow's black as her brideprice, you least of all." He set the untouched cup on the ground and rose. "I must check the horses."

Nynaeve remained there, kneeling, after he had gone.

Sleep or no, Rand closed his eyes. He did not think the Wisdom would like it if he watched her cry.

CHAPTER
49

The Dark One Stirs

awn woke Rand with a start, the sullen sun pricking his eyelids as it peeked reluctantly over the treetops of the Blight. Even so early, heat covered the spoiled lands in a heavy blanket. He lay on his back with his head pillowed on his blanketroll, staring at the sky. It was still blue, the sky. Even here, that, at least, was untouched.

He was surprised to realize that he had slept. For a minute the dim memory of a conversation overheard seemed like part of some dream. Then he saw Nynaeve's red-rimmed eyes; she had not slept, obviously. Lan's face was harder than ever, as if he had resumed a mask and did not intend to let it slip again.

Egwene went over and crouched beside the Wisdom, her face concerned. He could not make out what they said. Egwene spoke, and Nynaeve shook her head. Egwene said something else, and the Wisdom waved her away dismissively. Instead of going, Egwene bent her head closer, and for a few minutes the two women talked even more softly, with Nynaeve still shaking her head. The Wisdom ended it with a laugh, hugging Egwene and, by her expression, making soothing talk. When Egwene stood, though, she glared at the Warder. Lan did not seem to notice; he did not look in Nynaeve's direction at all.

Shaking his head, Rand gathered his things, and gave his hands and face and teeth a hasty wash with the little water Lan allowed for such things. He wondered if women had a way of reading men's minds. It was an unsettling thought. *All women are Aes Sedai.* Telling himself he was letting the Blight get to him, he rinsed out his mouth and hurried to get the bay saddled.

It was more than a little disconcerting, having the campsite disappear before he reached the horses, but by the time his saddle girth was tight everything on the hill winked back into view. Everyone was hurrying.

The seven towers stood plain in the morning light, distant broken stumps, like huge, rough hills that merely hinted at grandeur gone. The hundred lakes were a smooth, unruffled blue. Nothing broke the surface this morning. When he looked at the lakes and the ruined towers, he could almost ignore the sickly things growing around the hill. Lan did not seem to be avoiding looking at the towers, any more than he seemed to be avoiding Nynaeve, but somehow he never did as he concentrated on getting them ready to go.

After the wicker panniers were fastened on the packhorse, after every scrap and smudge and track were gone and everyone else was mounted, the Aes Sedai stood in the middle of the hilltop with her eyes closed, not even seeming to breathe. Nothing happened that Rand could see, except that Nynaeve and Egwene shivered despite the heat and rubbed their arms briskly. Egwene's hands suddenly froze on her arms, and she opened her mouth, staring at the Wisdom. Before she could speak, Nynaeve also ceased her rubbing and gave her a sharp look. The two women looked at one another, then Egwene nodded and grinned, and after a moment Nynaeve did, too, though her smile was only halfhearted.

Rand scrubbed his fingers through his hair, already more damp with sweat than with the water he had splashed in his face. He was sure there was something in the silent exchange that he should understand, but that feather-light brush across his mind vanished before he could grasp it.

"What are we waiting for?" Mat demanded, the low band of his scarf across his forehead. He had his bow across the pommel of his saddle with an arrow nocked, and his quiver pulled around on his belt for an easy reach.

Moiraine opened her eyes and started down the hill. "For me to remove the last vestige of what I did here last night. The residues would have dissipated on their own in a day, but I will not take any risk I can avoid now. We are too close, and the Shadow is too strong here. Lan?"

The Warder only waited for her to settle in Aldieb's saddle before he led them north, toward the Mountains of Dhoom, looming in the near distance. Even under the sunrise the peaks rose black and lifeless, like jagged teeth. In a wall they stretched, east and west as far as the eye could see.

"Will we reach the Eye today, Moiraine Sedai?" Egwene asked.

The Aes Sedai gave Loial a sidelong look. "I hope that we will. When I found it before, it was just the other side of the mountains, at the foot of the high passes."

"He says it moves," Mat said, nodding at Loial. "What if it isn't where you expect?"

"Then we will continue to hunt until we do find it. The Green Man senses need, and there can be no need greater than ours. Our need is the hope of the world."

As the mountains drew closer, so did the true Blight. Where a leaf had been spotted black and mottled yellow before, now foliage fell wetly while he watched, breaking apart from the weight of its own corruption. The trees themselves were tortured, crippled things, twisted branches clawing at the sky as if begging mercy from some power that refused to hear. Ooze slid like pus from bark cracked and split. As if nothing truly solid was left to them, the trees seemed to tremble from the passage of the horses over the ground.

"Look as if they want to grab us," Mat said nervously. Nynaeve gave him an exasperated, scornful look, and he added fiercely, "Well, they do look it."

"And some of them do want it," the Aes Sedai said. Her eyes over her shoulder were harder than Lan's for an instant. "But they want no part of what I am, and my presence protects you."

Mat laughed uneasily, as if he thought it a joke on her part.

Rand was not so sure. This *was* the Blight, after all. *But trees don't move. Why would a tree grab a man, even if it could? We're imagining things, and she's just trying to keep us alert.*

Abruptly he stared off to his left, into the forest. That tree, not twenty paces away, *had* trembled, and it was none of his imagination. He could not say what kind it was, or had been, so gnarled and tormented was its shape. As he watched, the tree suddenly whipped back and forth again, then bent down, flailing at the ground. Something screamed, shrill and piercing. The tree sprang back straight; its limbs entwined around a dark mass that writhed and spat and screamed.

He swallowed hard and tried to edge Red away, but trees stood on every side, and trembled. The bay rolled his eyes, whites showing all the way around. Rand found himself in a solid knot of horseflesh as everyone else tried to do the same as he.

"Keep moving," Lan commanded, drawing his sword. The Warder wore steel-backed gauntlets now, and his gray-green scale tunic. "Stay with Moiraine Sedai." He pulled Mandarb around, not toward the tree and its prey, but in the other direction. With his color-shifting cloak, he was swallowed by the Blight before the black stallion was out of sight.

"Close," Moiraine urged. She did not slow her white mare, but she motioned the others to huddle nearer to her. "Stay as close as you can."

A roar sprang up from the direction the Warder had gone. It beat at the air, and the trees quivered from it, and when it faded away, it seemed to echo still. Again the roar came, filled with rage and death.

"Lan," Nynaeve said. "He—"

The awful sound cut her off, but there was a new note in it. Fear. Abruptly it was gone.

"Lan can look after himself," Moiraine said. "Ride, Wisdom."

From out of the trees the Warder appeared, holding his sword well clear of himself and his mount. Black blood stained the blade, and steam rose from it. Carefully, Lan wiped the blade clean with a cloth he took from his saddlebags, examining the steel to make sure he had gotten every spot. When he dropped the cloth, it fell apart before it reached the ground, even the fragments dissolving.

Silently a massive body leaped out of the trees at them. The Warder spun Mandarb, but even as the warhorse reared, ready to strike with steel-shod hooves, Mat's arrow flashed, piercing the one eye in a head that seemed mostly mouth and teeth. Kicking and screaming, the thing fell, one bound short of them.

Rand stared as they hurried past. Stiff hair like long bristles covered it, and it had too many legs, joining a body as big as a bear at odd angles. Some of them at least, those coming out of its back, had to be useless for walking, but the finger-long claws at their ends tore the earth in its death agony.

"Good shooting, sheepherder." Lan's eyes had already forgotten what was dying behind them, and were searching the forest.

Moiraine shook her head. "It should not have been willing to come so close to one who touches the True Source."

"Agelmar said the Blight stirs," Lan said. "Perhaps the Blight also knows a Web is forming in the Pattern."

"Hurry." Moiraine dug her heels into Aldieb's flanks. "We must get over the high passes quickly."

But even as she spoke the Blight rose against them. Trees whipped in, reaching for them, not caring if Moiraine touched the True Source or not.

Rand's sword was in his hand; he did not remember unsheathing it. He struck out again and again, the heron-mark blade slicing through corrupted limbs. Hungry branches jerked back severed, writhing stumps—he almost thought he heard them scream—but always more came, wriggling like snakes, attempting to snare his arms, his waist, his neck. Teeth bared in a rictus snarl, he sought the void, and found it in the stony, stubborn soil of the Two Rivers. "Manetheren!" He screamed back at the trees till his throat ached. The heron-mark steel flashed in the strengthless sunlight. "Manetheren! Manetheren!"

Standing in his stirrups, Mat sent arrow after arrow flashing into the forest, striking at deformed shapes that snarled and gnashed uncounted teeth on the shafts that killed them, bit at the clawed forms fighting to get over them, to reach the mounted figures. Mat, too, was lost to the present. *"Carai an Caldazar!"* he shouted as he drew fletchings to cheek and loosed. *"Carai an Ellisande! Al Ellisande! Mordero daghain pas duente cuebiyar! Al Ellisande!"*

Perrin also stood in his stirrups, silent and grim. He had taken the lead, and his axe hewed a path through forest and foul flesh alike, whichever came before him. Flailing trees and howling things shied from the stocky axeman, shying as much from the fierce golden eyes as from the whistling axe. He forced his horse forward, step by determined step.

Fireballs streaked from Moiraine's hands, and where they struck, a writhing tree became a torch, a toothed shape shrieked and beat with human hands, rent its own flaming flesh with fierce claws until it died.

Again and again the Warder took Mandarb into the trees, his blade and gauntlets dripping with blood that bubbled and steamed. When he came back now, more often than not there were gashes in his armor, bleeding gashes in his flesh, and his warhorse stumbled and bled, too. Each time the Aes Sedai paused to lay her hands on the wounds, and when she took them away, only the blood was left on unmarked flesh.

"I light signal fires for the Halfmen," she said bitterly. "Press on. Press on!" They made their way one slow pace at a time.

If the trees had not struck into the mass of attacking flesh as much as at the humans, if the creatures, no two alike, had not fought the trees and one another as much as to reach them, Rand was sure they would have been overwhelmed. He was not certain it would not happen still. Then a fluting cry arose behind them. Distant and thin, it cut through the snarling from the denizens of the Blight around them.

In an instant the snarling ceased, as if it had been sliced off with a knife. The attacking shapes froze; the trees went still. As suddenly as the things with legs had appeared, they melted away, vanishing into the twisted forest.

The reedy shrill came again, like a cracked shepherd's pipes, and was answered in kind by a chorus. Half a dozen, singing among themselves, far behind.

"Worms," Lan said grimly, bringing a moan from Loial. "They've given us a respite, if we have time to use it." His eyes were measuring the distance yet to the mountains. "Few things in the Blight will face a Worm, can it be avoided." He dug his heels into Mandarb's flanks. "Ride!" The whole party plunged after him, through a Blight that suddenly seemed truly dead, except for the piping behind.

"They were scared off by worms?" Mat said incredulously. He was bouncing in his saddle, trying to sling his bow across his back.

TO THE BLIGHT

"A Worm"—there was a sharp difference in the way the Warder said it from the way Mat had—"can kill a Fade, if the Fade hasn't the Dark One's own luck with it. We have an entire pack on our trail. Ride! Ride!" The dark peaks were closer now. An hour, Rand estimated, at the pace the Warder was setting.

"Won't the Worms follow us into the mountains?" Egwene asked breathlessly, and Lan gave a sharp laugh.

"They won't. Worms are afraid of what lives in the high passes." Loial moaned again.

Rand wished the Ogier would stop doing that. He was well aware that Loial knew more about the Blight than any of them except Lan, even if it was from reading books in the safety of a *stedding. But why does he have to keep reminding me that there's worse yet than we've seen?*

The Blight flowed past, weeds and grasses splashing rotten under galloping hooves. Trees of the kinds that had earlier attacked did not so much as twitch even when they rode directly under the twisted branches. The Mountains of Dhoom filled the sky ahead, black and bleak, and almost near enough to touch, it seemed. The piping came both sharp and clear, and there were squishing sounds behind them, louder than the things crushed under hooves. Too loud, as if half-decayed trees were being crushed by huge bodies slithering over them. Too near. Rand looked over his shoulder. Back there treetops whipped and went down like grass. The land began sloping upward, toward the mountains, tilting enough so that he knew they were climbing.

"We are not going to make it," Lan announced. He did not slow Mandarb's gallop, but his sword was suddenly in his hand again. "Watch yourself in the high passes, Moiraine, and you'll get through."

"No, Lan!" Nynaeve called.

"Be quiet, girl! Lan, even you cannot stop a Wormpack. I will not have it. I will need you for the Eye."

"Arrows," Mat called breathlessly.

"The Worms wouldn't even feel them," the Warder shouted. "They must be cut to pieces. Don't feel much but hunger. Sometimes fear."

Clinging to his saddle with a deathgrip, Rand shrugged, try-

ing to loosen the tightness in his shoulders. His whole chest felt
tight, until he could hardly breathe, and his skin stung in hot
pinpricks. The Blight had turned to foothills. He could see the
route they must climb once they reached the mountains, the
twisting path and the high pass beyond, like an axe blow cleav-
ing into the black stone. *Light, what's up ahead that can scare*
what's behind? Light help me, I've never been so afraid. I don't
want to go any further. No further! Seeking the flame and the
void, he railed at himself. *Fool! You frightened, cowardly fool!*
You can't stay here, and you can't go back. Are you going to
leave Egwene to face it alone? The void eluded him, forming,
then shivering into a thousand points of light, re-forming and
shattering again, each point burning into his bones until he
quivered with the pain and thought he must burst open. *Light*
help me, I can't go on. Light help me!

He was gathering the bay's reins to turn back, to face the
Worms or anything rather than what lay ahead, when the
nature of the land changed. Between one slope of a hill and the
next, between crest and peak, the Blight was gone.

Green leaves covered peacefully spreading branches. Wildflowers made a carpet of bright patches in grasses stirred by a
sweet spring breeze. Butterflies fluttered from blossom to blossom, with buzzing bees, and birds trilled their songs.

Gaping, he galloped on, until he suddenly realized that
Moiraine and Lan and Loial had stopped, the others, too.
Slowly he drew rein, his face frozen in astonishment. Egwene's
eyes were about to come out of her head, and Nynaeve's jaw
had dropped.

"We have reached safety," Moiraine said. "This is the Green
Man's place, and the Eye of the World is here. Nothing of the
Blight can enter here."

"I thought it was on the other side of the mountains," Rand
mumbled. He could still see the peaks filling the northern horizon, and the high passes. "You said it was always beyond the
passes."

"This place," said a deep voice from the trees, "is always
where it is. All that changes is where those who need it are."

A figure stepped out of the foliage, a man-shape as much
bigger than Loial as the Ogier was bigger than Rand. A man-
shape of woven vines and leaves, green and growing. His hair

was grass, flowing to his shoulders; his eyes, huge hazelnuts; his
fingernails, acorns. Green leaves made his tunic and trousers;
seamless bark, his boots. Butterflies swirled around him, lighting on his fingers, his shoulders, his face. Only one thing
spoiled the verdant perfection. A deep fissure ran up his cheek
and temple across the top of his head, and in that the vines
were brown and withered.

"The Green Man," Egwene whispered, and the scarred face
smiled. For a moment it seemed as if the birds sang louder.

"Of course I am. Who else would be here?" The hazelnut
eyes regarded Loial. "It is good to see you, little brother. In
the past, many of you came to visit me, but few of recent
days."

Loial scrambled down from his big horse and bowed formally. "You honor me, Treebrother. *Tsingu ma choshih, T'ing-
shen.*"

Smiling, the Green Man put an arm around the Ogier's
shoulders. Alongside Loial, he looked like a man beside a boy.
"There is no honoring, little brother. We will sing Tree Songs
together, and remember the Great Trees, and the *stedding,* and
hold the Longing at bay." He studied the others, just now getting down from their horses, and his eyes lit on Perrin. "A
Wolfbrother! Do the old times truly walk again then?"

Rand stared at Perrin. For his part, Perrin turned his horse
so it was between him and the Green Man, and bent to check
the girth. Rand was sure he just wanted to avoid the Green
Man's searching gaze. Suddenly the Green Man spoke to Rand.

"Strange clothes you wear, Child of the Dragon. Has the
Wheel turned so far? Do the People of the Dragon return to
the first Covenant? But you wear a sword. That is neither now
nor then."

Rand had to work moisture in his mouth before he could
speak. "I don't know what you're talking about. What do you
mean?"

The Green Man touched the brown scar across his head. For
a moment he seemed confused. "I . . . cannot say. My memories are torn and often fleeting, and much of what remains is
like leaves visited by caterpillars. Yet, I am sure. . . . No, it is
gone. But you are welcome here. You, Moiraine Sedai, are

more than a surprise. When this place was made, it was made
so that none could find it twice. How have you come here?"

"Need," Moiraine replied. "My need, the world's need.
Most of all is the world's need. We have come to see the Eye of
the World."

The Green Man sighed, the wind sighing through thick-
leafed branches. "Then it has come again. That memory remains whole. The Dark One stirs. I have feared it. Every turning of years, the Blight strives harder to come inside, and this
turn the struggle to keep it out has been greater than ever since
the beginning. Come, I will take you."

The Green Man

CHAPTER
50

Meetings at the Eye

Leading the bay, Rand followed the Green Man with the other Emond's Fielders, all staring as if they could not decide whether to look at the Green Man or the forest. The Green Man was a legend, of course, with stories told about him, and the Tree of Life, in front of every fireplace in the Two Rivers, and not just for the children. But after the Blight, the trees and flowers would have been a wonder of normality even if the rest of the world was not still trapped in winter.

Perrin hung a little to the rear. When Rand glanced back, the big, curly-haired youth looked as if he did not want to hear anything else the Green Man had to say. He could understand that. *Child of the Dragon.* Warily he watched the Green Man, walking ahead with Moiraine and Lan, butterflies surrounding him in a cloud of yellows and reds. *What did he mean? No. I don't want to know.*

Even so, his step felt lighter, his legs springier. The uneasiness still lay in his gut, churning his stomach, but the fear had become so diffuse it might as well be gone. He did not think he could expect more, not with the Blight half a mile away, even if Moiraine was right about nothing from the Blight being able to enter here. The thousands of burning points piercing his bones had winked out; at the very moment he came within the Green Man's domain, he was sure. *It's him that winked them out,* he thought, *the Green Man, and this place.*

Egwene felt it, and Nynaeve, too, the soothing peace, the

calm of beauty. He could tell. They wore small, serene smiles, and brushed flowers with their fingers, pausing to smell, and breathing deep.

When the Green Man noticed, he said, "Flowers are meant to adorn. The plants or humans, it is much the same. None mind, so long as you don't take too many." And he began plucking one from this plant and one from that, never more than two from any. Soon Nynaeve and Egwene wore caps of blossoms in their hair, pink wildrose and yellowbell and white morningstar. The Wisdom's braid seemed a garden of pink and white to her waist. Even Moiraine received a pale garland of morningstar on her brow, woven so deftly that the flowers still seemed to be growing.

Rand was not sure they were not growing. The Green Man tended his forest garden as he walked, while he talked softly to Moiraine, taking care of whatever needed care without really thinking about it. His hazelnut eyes caught a crooked limb on a climbing wildrose, forced into an awkward angle by the blossom-covered limb of an apple tree, and he paused, still talking, to run his hand along the bend. Rand was not sure if his eyes were playing tricks, or if thorns actually did bend out of the way so as not to prick those green fingers. When the towering shape of the Green Man moved on, the limb ran straight and true, spreading red petals among the white of apple blossoms. He bent to cup one huge hand around a tiny seed lying on a patch of pebbles, and when he straightened, a small shoot had roots through the rocks to good soil.

"All things must grow where they are, according to the Pattern," he explained over his shoulder, as if apologizing, "and face the turning of the Wheel, but the Creator will not mind if I give just a little help."

Rand led Red around the shoot, careful not to let the bay's hooves crush it. It did not seem right to destroy what the Green Man had done just to avoid an extra step. Egwene smiled at him, one of her secret smiles, and touched his arm. She was so pretty, with her unbound hair full of flowers, that he smiled back at her until she blushed and lowered her eyes. *I will protect you,* he thought. *Whatever else happens, I will see you safe, I swear it.*

Into the heart of the spring forest the Green Man took them, to an arched opening in the side of a hill. It was a simple stone arch, tall and white, and on the keystone was a circle halved by a sinuous line, one half rough, the other smooth. The ancient symbol of Aes Sedai. The opening itself was shadowed.

For a moment everyone simply looked in silence. Then Moiraine removed the garland from her hair and gently hung it on the limb of a sweetberry bush beside the arch. It was as if her movement restored speech.

"It's in there?" Nynaeve asked. "What we've come for?"

"I'd really like to see the Tree of Life," Mat said, not taking his eyes off the halved circle above them. "We can wait that long, can't we?"

The Green Man gave Rand an odd look, then shook his head. "*Avendesora* is not here. I have not rested beneath its ungentle branches in two thousand years."

"The Tree of Life is not why we came," Moiraine said firmly. She gestured to the arch. "In there, is."

"I will not go in with you," the Green Man said. The butterflies around him swirled as if they shared some agitation. "I was set to guard it long, long ago, but it makes me uneasy to come too close. I feel myself being unmade; my end is linked with it, somehow. I remember the making of it. Some of the making. Some." His hazelnut eyes stared, lost in memory, and he fingered his scar. "It was the first days of the Breaking of the World, when the joy of victory over the Dark One turned bitter with the knowledge that all might yet be shattered by the weight of the Shadow. A hundred of them made it, men and women together. The greatest Aes Sedai works were always done so, joining *saidin* and *saidar,* as the True Source is joined. They died, all, to make it pure, while the world was torn around them. Knowing they would die, they charged me to guard it against the need to come. It was not what I was made for, but all was breaking apart, and they were alone, and I was all they had. It was not what I was made for, but I have kept the faith." He looked down at Moiraine, nodding to himself. "I have kept faith, until it was needed. And now it ends."

"You have kept the faith better than most of us who gave you the charge," the Aes Sedai said. "Perhaps it will not come as badly as you fear."

The scarred, leafy head shook slowly from side to side. "I

know an ending when it comes, Aes Sedai. I will find another
place to make things grow." Nutbrown eyes swept sadly over
the green forest. "Another place, perhaps. When you come
out, I will see you again, if there is time." With that he strode
away, trailing butterflies, becoming one with the forest more
completely than Lan's cloak ever could.

"What did he mean?" Mat demanded. "If there's time?"

"Come," Moiraine said. And she stepped through the arch.
Lan went at her heels.

Rand was not sure what he expected when he followed. The
hair stirred uneasily on his arms, and rose on the back of his
neck. But it was only a corridor, its polished walls rounded
overhead like the arch, winding gently downward. There was
headroom enough and to spare for Loial; there would have
been room enough for the Green Man. The smooth floor, slick
to the eye like oiled slate, yet somehow gave a sure footing.
Seamless, white walls glittered with uncounted flecks in untold
colors, giving a low, soft light even after the sunlit archway
vanished around a curve behind. He was sure the light was no
natural thing, but he sensed it was benign, too. *Then why is
your skin still crawling?* Down they went, and down.

"There," Moiraine said at last, pointing. "Ahead."

And the corridor opened into a vast, domed space, the
rough, living rock of its ceiling dotted with clumps of glowing
crystals. Below it, a pool took up the entire cavern, except for
the walkway around it, perhaps five paces wide. In the oval
shape of an eye, the pool was lined about its rim with a low, flat
edging of crystals that glowed with a duller, yet fiercer, light
than those above. Its surface was as smooth as glass and as
clear as the Winespring Water. Rand felt as if his eyes could
penetrate it forever, but he could not see any bottom to it.

"The Eye of the World," Moiraine said softly beside him.

As he looked around in wonder, he realized that the long
years since the making—three thousand of them—had worked
their way while no one came. Not all the crystals in the dome
glowed with the same intensity. Some were stronger, some
weaker; some flickered, and others were only faceted lumps to
sparkle in a captured light. Had all shone, the dome would
have been as bright as noonday, but they made it only late
afternoon, now. Dust coated the walkway, and bits of stone

and even crystal. Long years waiting, while the Wheel turned
and ground.

"But *what* is it?" Mat asked uneasily. "That doesn't look like
any water I ever saw." He kicked a lump of dark stone the size
of his fist over the edge. "It—"

The stone struck the glassy surface and slid into the pool
without a splash, or so much as a ripple. As it sank, the rock
began to swell, growing ever larger, larger and more attenu-
ated, a blob the size of his head that Rand could almost see
through, a faint blur as wide as his arm was long. Then it was
gone. He thought his skin would creep right off his body.

"What is it?" he demanded, and was shocked at the hoarse
harshness of his own voice.

"It might be called the essence of *saidin*." The Aes Sedai's
words echoed round the dome. "The essence of the male half
of the True Source, the pure essence of the Power wielded by
men before the Time of Madness. The Power to mend the seal
on the Dark One's prison, or to break it open completely."

"The Light shine on us and protect us," Nynaeve whispered.
Egwene clutched her as if she wanted to hide behind the
Wisdom. Even Lan stirred uneasily, though there was no sur-
prise in his eyes.

Stone thudded into Rand's shoulders, and he realized he had
backed as far as the wall, as far from the Eye of the World as
he could get. He would have pushed himself right through the
wall, if he could have. Mat, too, was splayed out against the
stone as flat as he could make himself. Perrin was staring at the
pool with his axe half drawn. His eyes shone, yellow and fierce.

"I always wondered," Loial said uneasily. "When I read
about it, I always wondered what it was. Why? Why did they
do it? And how?"

"No one living knows." Moiraine no longer looked at the
pool. She was watching Rand and his two friends, studying
them, her eyes weighing. "Neither the how, nor more of the
why than that it would be needed one day, and that that need
would be the greatest and most desperate the world had faced
to that time. Perhaps ever would face.

"Many in Tar Valon have attempted to find a way to use this
Power, but it is as untouchable for any woman as the moon is
for a cat. Only a man could channel it, but the last male Aes

Sedai is nearly three thousand years gone. Yet the need they
saw was a desperate one. They worked through the taint of the
Dark One on *saidin* to make it, and make it pure, knowing that
doing so would kill them all. Male Aes Sedai and female together. The Green Man spoke true. The greatest wonders of
the Age of Legends were done in that way, *saidin* and *saidar*
together. All the women in Tar Valon, all the Aes Sedai in all
the courts and cities, even with those in the lands beyond the
Waste, even counting those who may still live beyond the Aryth
Ocean, could not fill a spoon with the Power, lacking men to
work with them."

Rand's throat rasped as if he had been screaming. "Why did
you bring us here?"

"Because you are *ta'veren*." The Aes Sedai's face was unreadable. Her eyes shimmered, and seemed to pull at him.
"Because the Dark One's power will strike here, and because it
must be confronted and stopped, or the Shadow will cover the
world. There is no need greater than that. Let us go out into
the sunlight again, while there is yet time." Without waiting to
see if they would follow, she started back up the corridor with
Lan, who stepped perhaps a bit more quickly than usual for
him. Egwene and Nynaeve hurried behind her.

Rand edged along the wall—he could not make himself get
even one step closer to what the pool was—and scrambled into
the corridor in a tangle with Mat and Perrin. He would have
run if it had not meant trampling Egwene and Nynaeve,
Moiraine and Lan. He could not stop shaking even when he
was back outside.

"I do not like this, Moiraine," Nynaeve said angrily when the
sun shone on them again. "I believe the danger is as great as
you say or I would not be here, but this is—"

"I have found you at last."

Rand jerked as if a rope had tightened around his neck. The
words, the voice . . . for a moment he believed it was Ba'alzamon. But the two men who walked out of the trees, faces
hidden by their cowls, did not wear cloaks the color of dried
blood. One cloak was a dark gray, the other almost as dark a
green, and they seemed musty even in the open air. And the
men were not Fades; the breeze stirred their cloaks.

"Who are you?" Lan's stance was cautious, his hand on his

sword hilt. "How did you come here? If you are seeking the Green Man—"

"He guided us." The hand that pointed to Mat was old and shriveled to scarcely human, lacking a fingernail and with knuckles gnarled like knots in a piece of rope. Mat took a step back, eyes widening. "An old thing, an old friend, an old enemy. But he is not the one we seek," the green-cloaked man finished. The other man stood as if he would never speak.

Moiraine straightened to her full height, no more than shoulder high to any man there, but suddenly seeming as tall as the hills. Her voice rang like a bell, demanding, "Who are you?"

Hands pushed back hoods, and Rand goggled. The old man was older than old; he made Cenn Buie look like a child in the bloom of health. The skin of his face was like crazed parchment drawn tight over a skull, then pulled tighter still. Wispy tufts of brittle hair stood at odd places on his scabrous scalp. His ears were withered bits like scraps of ancient leather; his eyes sunken, peering out of his head as if from the ends of tunnels. Yet the other was worse. A tight, black leather carapace covered that one's head and face completely, but the front of it was worked into a perfect face, a young man's face, laughing wildly, laughing insanely, frozen forever. *What is he hiding if the other shows what he shows?* Then even thought froze in his head, shattered to dust and blew away.

"I am called Aginor," the old one said. "And he is Balthamel. He no longer speaks with his tongue. The Wheel grinds exceedingly fine over three thousand years imprisoned." His sunken eyes slid to the arch; Balthamel leaned forward, his mask's eyes on the white stone opening, as if he wanted to go straight in. "So long without," Aginor said softly. "So long."

"The Light protect—" Loial began, his voice shaking, and cut off abruptly when Aginor looked at him.

"The Forsaken," Mat said hoarsely, "are bound in Shayol Ghul—"

"Were bound." Aginor smiled; his yellowed teeth had the look of fangs. "Some of us are bound no longer. The seals weaken, Aes Sedai. Like Ishamael, we walk the world again, and soon the rest of us will come. I was too close to this world in my captivity, I and Balthamel, too close to the grinding of the Wheel, but soon the Great Lord of the Dark will be free, and give us new flesh, and the world will be ours once more. You will have no Lews Therin Kinslayer, this time. No Lord of the Morning to save you. We know the one we seek now, and there is no more need for the rest of you."

Lan's sword sprang from its scabbard too fast for Rand's eye to follow. Yet the Warder hesitated, eyes flickering to Moiraine, to Nynaeve. The two women stood well apart; to put himself between either of them and the Forsaken would put him further from the other. Only for a heartbeat the hesitation lasted, but as the Warder's feet moved, Aginor raised his hand. It was a scornful gesture, a flipping of his gnarled fingers as if to shoo away a fly. The Warder flew backwards through the air as though a huge fist had caught him. With a dull thud Lan struck the stone arch, hanging there for an instant before dropping in a flaccid heap, his sword lying near his outstretched hand.

"NO!" Nynaeve screamed.

"Be still!" Moiraine commanded, but before anyone else could move the Wisdom's knife had left her belt, and she was running toward the Forsaken, her small blade upraised.

"The Light blind you," she cried, striking at Aginor's chest.

The other Forsaken moved like a viper. While her blow still fell, Balthamel's leather-cased hand darted out to seize her chin, fingers sinking into one cheek while thumb dug into the other, driving the blood out with their pressure and raising the flesh in pale ridges. A convulsion wracked Nynaeve from head to toe, as if she had been cracked like a whip. Her knife dropped uselessly from dangling fingers as Balthamel lifted her by his grip, brought her up to where the leather mask stared into her still-quivering face. Her toes spasmed a foot above the ground; flowers rained from her hair.

"I have almost forgotten the pleasures of the flesh." Aginor's tongue crossed his withered lips, sounding like stone on rough leather. "But Balthamel remembers much." The laughter of the mask seemed to grow wilder, and the wail that left Nynaeve burned Rand's ears like despair ripped from her living heart.

Suddenly Egwene moved, and Rand saw that she was going to help Nynaeve. "Egwene, no!" he shouted, but she did not stop. His hand had gone to his sword at Nynaeve's cry, but now he abandoned it and threw himself at Egwene. He thudded into her before she took her third step, carrying them both to the

ground. Egwene landed under him with a gasp, immediately
thrashing to get free.

Others were moving, too, he realized. Perrin's axe whirled
into his hands, and his eyes glowed golden and fierce.
"Wisdom!" Mat howled, the dagger from Shadar Logoth in his
fist.

"No!" Rand called. "You can't fight the Forsaken!" But they
ran past him as if they had not heard, their eyes on Nynaeve
and the two Forsaken.

Aginor glanced at them, unconcernedly . . . and smiled.

Rand felt the air stir above him like the crack of a giant's
whip. Mat and Perrin, not even halfway to the Forsaken,
stopped as if they had run into a wall, bounced back to sprawl
on the ground.

"Good," Aginor said. "A fitting place for you. If you learn
to abase yourself properly in worship of us, I might let you
live."

Hastily Rand scrambled to his feet. Perhaps he could not
fight the Forsaken—no ordinary human could—but he would
not let them believe for a minute that he was groveling before
them. He tried to help Egwene up, but she slapped his hands
away and stood by herself, angrily brushing off her dress. Mat
and Perrin had also stubbornly pushed themselves unsteadily
erect.

"You will learn," Aginor said, "if you want to live. Now that
I have found what I need"—his eyes went to the stone archway—"I may take the time to teach you."

"This shall not be!" The Green Man strode out of the trees
with a voice like lightning striking an ancient oak. "You do not
belong here!"

Aginor spared him a brief, contemptuous glance. "Begone!
Your time is ended, all your kind but you long since dust. Live
what life is left to you and be glad you are beneath our notice."

"This is my place," the Green Man said, "and you shall hurt
no living thing here."

Balthamel tossed Nynaeve aside like a rag, and like a
crumpled rag she fell, eyes staring, limp as if all her bones had
melted. One leather-clad hand lifted, and the Green Man
roared as smoke rose from the vines that wove him. The wind
in the trees echoed his pain.

Aginor turned back to Rand and the others, as if the Green
Man had been dealt with, but one long stride and massive,
leafy arms wrapped themselves around Balthamel, raising him
high, crushing him against a chest of thick creepers, black
leather mask laughing into hazelnut eyes dark with anger. Like
serpents Balthamel's arms writhed free, his gloved hands grasp-
ing the Green Man's head as though he would wrench it off.
Flames shot up where those hands touched, vines withering,
leaves falling. The Green Man bellowed as thick, dark smoke
poured out between the vines of his body. On and on he
roared, as if all of him were coming out of his mouth with the
smoke that billowed between his lips.

Suddenly Balthamel jerked in the Green Man's grasp. The
Forsaken's hands tried to push him away instead of clutching
him. One gloved hand flung wide . . . and a tiny creeper burst
through the black leather. A fungus, such as rings trees in the
deep shadows of the forest, ringed his arm, sprang from nowhere to full-grown, swelling to cover the length of it. Balthamel thrashed, and a shoot of stinkweed ripped open his
carapace, lichens dug in their roots and split tiny cracks across
the leather of his face, nettles broke the eyes of his mask,
deathshead mushrooms tore open the mouth.

The Green Man threw the Forsaken down. Balthamel
twisted and jerked as all the things that grew in the dark places,
all the things with spores, all the things that loved the dank,
swelled and grew, tore cloth and leather and flesh—Was it
flesh, seen in that brief moment of verdant rage?—to tattered
shreds and covered him until only a mound remained, indistin-
guishable from many in the shaded depths of the green forest,
and the mound moved no more than they.

With a groan like a limb breaking under too great a weight,
the Green Man crashed to the ground. Half his head was
charred black. Tendrils of smoke still rose from him, like gray
creepers. Burned leaves fell from his arm as he painfully
stretched out his blackened hand to gently cup an acorn.

The earth rumbled as an oak seedling pushed up between his
fingers. The Green Man's head fell, but the seedling reached
for the sun, straining. Roots shot out and thickened, delved
beneath the ground and rose again, thickened more as they
sank. The trunk broadened and stretched upward, bark turning

gray and fissured and ancient. Limbs spread and grew heavy, as big as arms, as big as men, and lifted to caress the sky, thick with green leaves, dense with acorns. The massive web of roots turned the earth like plows as it spread; the already huge trunk shivered, grew wider, round as a house. Stillness came. And an oak that could have stood five hundred years covered the spot where the Green Man had been, marking the tomb of a legend. Nynaeve lay on the gnarled roots, grown curved to her shape, to make a bed for her to rest upon. The wind sighed through the oak's branches; it seemed to murmur farewell.

Even Aginor seemed stunned. Then his head lifted, cavernous eyes burning with hate. "Enough! It is past time to end this!"

"Yes, Forsaken," Moiraine said, her voice as cold as deepwinter ice. "Past time!"

The Aes Sedai's hand rose, and the ground fell away beneath Aginor's feet. Flame roared from the chasm, whipped to a frenzy by wind howling in from every direction, sucking a maelstrom of leaves into the fire, which seemed to solidify into a red-streaked yellow jelly of pure heat. In the middle of it Aginor stood, his feet supported only by air. The Forsaken looked startled, but then he smiled and took a step forward. It was a slow step, as if the fire tried to root him to the spot, but he took it, and then another.

"Run!" Moiraine commanded. Her face was white with strain. "All of you run!" Aginor stepped across the air, toward the edge of the flames.

Rand was aware of others moving, Mat and Perrin dashing away at the edge of his vision, Loial's long legs carrying him into the trees, but all he could really see was Egwene. She stood there rigid, face pale and eyes closed. It was not fear that held her, he realized. She was trying to throw her puny, untrained wielding of the Power against the Forsaken.

Roughly he grabbed her arm and pulled her around to face him. "Run!" he shouted at her. Her eyes opened, staring at him, angry with him for interfering, liquid with hate for Aginor, with fear of the Forsaken. "Run," he said, pushing her toward the trees hard enough to start her. "Run!" Once started, she did run.

But Aginor's withered face turned toward him, toward the

running Egwene behind him, as the Forsaken walked through
the flames, as if what the Aes Sedai was doing did not concern
Aginor at all. Toward Egwene.

"Not her!" Rand shouted. "The Light burn you, not her!"
He snatched up a rock and threw it, meaning to draw Aginor's
attention. Halfway to the Forsaken's face, the stone turned to a
handful of dust.

He hesitated only a moment, long enough to glance over his
shoulder and see that Egwene was hidden in the trees. The
flames still surrounded Aginor, patches of his cloak smoldering,
but he walked as if he had all the time in the world, and the
fire's rim was near. Rand turned and ran. Behind him he heard
Moiraine begin to scream.

Aginor

CHAPTER
51

Against the Shadow

The land tended upward the way Rand went, but fear lent his legs strength and they ate ground in long strides, tearing his way through flowering bushes and tangles of wildrose, scattering petals, not caring if thorns ripped his clothes or even his flesh. Moiraine had stopped screaming. It seemed as if the shrieks had gone on forever, each one more throat-wrenching than the last, but he knew they had lasted only moments altogether. Moments before Aginor would be on his trail. He knew it would be him that Aginor followed. He had seen the certainty in the Forsaken's hollow eyes, in that last second before terror whipped his feet to run.

The land grew ever steeper, but he scrambled on, pulling himself forward by handfuls of undergrowth, rocks and dirt and leaves spilling down the slope from under his feet, finally crawling on hands and knees when the slant became too great. Ahead, above, it leveled out a little. Panting, he scrabbled his way the last few spans, got to his feet, and stopped, wanting to howl aloud.

Ten paces in front of him, the hilltop dropped away sharply. He knew what he would see before he reached it, but he took the steps anyway, each heavier than the one before, hoping there might be some track, a goat path, anything. At the edge he looked down a sheer hundred-foot drop, a stone wall as smooth as planed timber.

*There has to be some way. I'll go back and find a way around.
Go back and—*

When he turned, Aginor was there, just reaching the crest.
The Forsaken topped the hill without any difficulty, walking up
the steep slope as if it were level ground. Deep-sunken eyes
burned at him from that drawn parchment face; somehow, it
seemed less withered than before, more fleshed, as if Aginor
had fed well on something. Those eyes were fixed on him, yet
when Aginor spoke, it was almost to himself.

"Ba'alzamon will give rewards beyond mortal dreaming for
the one who brings you to Shayol Ghul. Yet my dreams have
always been beyond those of other men, and I left mortality
behind millennia ago. What difference if you serve the Great
Lord of the Dark alive or dead? None, to the spread of the
Shadow. Why should I share power with you? Why should I
bend knee to you? I, who faced Lews Therin Telamon in the
Hall of the Servants itself. I, who threw my might against the
Lord of the Morning and met him stroke for stroke. I think
not."

Rand's mouth dried like dust; his tongue felt as shriveled as
Aginor. The edge of the precipice grated under his heels, stone
falling away. He did not dare look back, but he heard the rocks
bounding and rebounding from the sheer wall, just as his body
would if he moved another inch. It was the first he knew that
he had been backing up, away from the Forsaken. His skin
crawled until he thought he must see it writhing if he looked, if
he could only take his eyes off the Forsaken. *There has to be
some way to get away from him. Some way to escape! There has
to be! Some way!*

Suddenly he felt something, saw it, though he knew it was
not there to see. A glowing rope ran off from Aginor, behind
him, white like sunlight seen through the purest cloud, heavier
than a blacksmith's arm, lighter than air, connecting the Forsaken to something distant beyond knowing, something within
the touch of Rand's hand. The rope pulsed, and with every
throb Aginor grew stronger, more fully fleshed, a man as tall
and strong as himself, a man harder than the Warder, more
deadly than the Blight. Yet beside that shining cord, the Forsaken seemed almost not to exist. The cord was all. It hummed.

It sang. It called Rand's soul. One bright finger-strand lifted away, drifted, touched him, and he gasped. Light filled him, and heat that should have burned yet only warmed as if it took the chill of the grave from his bones. The strand thickened. *I have to get away!*

"No!" Aginor shouted. "You shall not have it! It is mine!"

Rand did not move, and neither did the Forsaken, yet they fought as surely as if they grappled in the dust. Sweat beaded on Aginor's face, no longer withered, no longer old, that of a strong man in his prime. Rand pulsed with the beating in the cord, like the heartbeat of the world. It filled his being. Light filled his mind, till only a corner was left for what was himself. He wrapped the void around that nook; sheltered in emptiness. *Away!*

"Mine!" Aginor cried. "Mine!"

Warmth built in Rand, the warmth of the sun, the radiance of the sun, bursting, the awful radiance of light, of the Light. *Away!*

"Mine!" Flame shot from Aginor's mouth, broke through his eyes like spears of fire, and he screamed.

Away!

And Rand was no longer on the hilltop. He quivered with the Light that suffused him. His mind would not work; light and heat blinded it. The Light. In the midst of the void, the Light blinded his mind, stunned him with awe.

He stood in a broad mountain pass, surrounded by jagged black peaks like the teeth of the Dark One. It was real; he was there. He felt the rocks under his boots, the icy breeze on his face.

Battle surrounded him, or the tail end of battle. Armored men on armored horses, shining steel dusty now, slashed and stabbed at snarling Trollocs wielding spiked axes and scythe-like swords. Some men fought afoot, their horses down, and barded horses galloped through the fight with empty saddles. Fades moved among them all, nightblack cloaks hanging still however their dark mounts galloped, and wherever their light-eating swords swung, men died. Sound beat at Rand, beat at him and bounced from the strangeness that had him by the throat. The clash of steel against steel, the panting and grunting of men and Trollocs striving, the screams of men and Trollocs dying. Over the din, banners waved in dust-filled air. The Black Hawk of Fal Dara, the White Hart of Shienar, others. And Trolloc banners. In just the little space around him he saw the horned skull of the Dha'vol, the blood-red trident of the Ko'bal, the iron fist of the Dhai'mon.

Yet it was indeed the tail end of battle, a pausing, as humans and Trollocs alike fell back to regroup. None seemed to notice Rand as they paid a few last strokes and broke away, galloping, or running in a stagger, to the ends of the pass.

Rand found himself facing the end of the pass where the humans were re-forming, pennants stirring beneath gleaming lancepoints. Wounded men wavered in their saddles. Riderless horses reared and galloped. Plainly they could not stand another meeting, yet just as plainly they readied themselves for one final charge. Some of them saw him now; men stood in their stirrups to point at him. Their shouts came to him as tiny piping.

Staggering, he turned. The forces of the Dark One filled the other end of the pass, bristling black pikes and spearpoints swelling up onto mountain slopes made blacker still by the great mass of Trollocs that dwarfed the army of Shienar. Fades in hundreds rode across the front of the horde, the fierce, muzzled faces of Trollocs turning away in fear as they passed, huge bodies pulling back to make way. Overhead, Draghkar wheeled on leathery pinions, shrieks challenging the wind. Halfmen saw him now, too, pointed, and Draghkar spun and dove. Two. Three. Six of them, crying shrilly as they plummeted toward him.

He stared at them. Heat filled him, the burning heat of the touched sun. He could see the Draghkar clearly, soulless eyes in pale men's faces on winged bodies that had nothing of humanity about them. Terrible heat. Crackling heat.

From the clear sky lightning came, each bolt crisp and sharp, searing his eyes, each bolt striking a winged black shape. Hunting cries became shrieks of death, and charred forms fell to leave the sky clean again.

The heat. The terrible heat of the Light.

He fell to his knees; he thought he could hear his tears sizzling on his cheeks. "No!" He clutched at tufts of wiry grass for some hold on reality; the grass burst in flame. "Please, nooooooo!"

The wind rose with his voice, howled with his voice, roared with his voice down the pass, whipping the flames to a wall of fire that sped away from him and toward the Trolloc host faster than a horse could run. Fire burned into the Trollocs, and the mountains trembled with their screams, screams almost as loud as the wind and his voice.

"It has to end!"

He beat at the ground with his fist, and the earth tolled like a gong. He bruised his hands on stony soil, and the earth trembled. Ripples ran through the ground ahead of him in ever-rising waves, waves of dirt and rock towering over Trollocs and Fades, breaking over them as the mountains shattered under their hooved feet. A boiling mass of flesh and rubble churned across the Trolloc army. What was left standing was still a mighty host, but now no more than twice the human army in numbers, and milling in fright and confusion.

The wind died. The screams died. The earth was still. Dust and smoke swirled back down the pass to surround him.

"The Light blind you, Ba'alzamon! This has to end!"

IT IS NOT HERE.

It was not Rand's thought, making his skull vibrate.

I WILL TAKE NO PART. ONLY THE CHOSEN ONE CAN DO WHAT MUST BE DONE, IF HE WILL.

"Where?" He did not want to say it, but he could not stop himself. "Where?"

The haze surrounding him parted, leaving a dome of clear, clean air ten spans high, walled by billowing smoke and dust. Steps rose before him, each standing alone and unsupported, stretching up into the murk that obscured the sun.

NOT HERE.

Through the mist, as from the far end of the earth, came a cry. "The Light wills it!" The ground rumbled with the thunder of hooves as the forces of humankind launched their last charge.

Within the void, his mind knew a moment of panic. The charging horsemen could not see him in the dust; their charge would trample right over him. The greater part of him ignored the shaking ground as a petty thing beneath concern. Dull anger driving his feet, he mounted the first steps. *It has to be ended!*

Darkness surrounded him, the utter blackness of total nothing. The steps were still there, hanging in the black, under his feet and ahead. When he looked back, those behind were gone, faded away to nothing, into the nothingness around him. But the cord was yet there, stretching behind him, the glowing line dwindling and vanishing into the distance. It was not so thick as before, but it still pulsed, pumping strength into him, pumping life, filling him with the Light. He climbed.

It seemed forever that he climbed. Forever, and minutes. Time stood still in nothingness. Time ran faster. He climbed until suddenly a door stood before him, its surface rough and splintered and old, a door well-remembered. He touched it, and it burst to fragments. While they still fell, he stepped through, bits of shattered wood falling from his shoulders.

The chamber, too, was as he remembered, the mad, striated sky beyond the balcony, the melted walls, the polished table, the terrible fireplace with its roaring, heatless flames. Some of those faces that made the fireplace, writhing in torment, shrieking in silence, tugged at his memory as if he knew them, but he held the void close, floated within himself in emptiness. He was alone. When he looked at the mirror on the wall, his face was there as clear as if it *was* him. *There is calm in the void.*

"Yes," Ba'alzamon said from in front of the fireplace, "I thought Aginor's greed would overcome him. But it makes no difference in the end. A long search, but ended now. You are here, and I know you."

In the midst of the Light the void drifted, and in the midst of the void floated Rand. He reached for the soil of his home, and felt hard rock, unyielding and dry, stone without pity, where only the strong could survive, only those as hard as the mountains. "I am tired of running." He could not believe his voice was so calm. "Tired of you threatening my friends. I will run no more." Ba'alzamon had a cord, too, he saw. A black cord, thicker by far than his own, so wide it should have dwarfed the human body, yet dwarfed by Ba'alzamon, instead. Each pulse along that black vein ate light.

"You think it makes any difference, whether you run or stay?" The flames of Ba'alzamon's mouth laughed. The faces in the hearth wept at their master's mirth. "You have fled from me many times, and each time I run you down and make you eat your pride with sniveling tears for spice. Many times you have stood and fought, then groveled in defeat, begging mercy. You have this choice, worm, and this choice only: kneel at my feet and serve me well, and I will give you power above thrones; or be Tar Valon's puppet fool and scream while you are ground into the dust of time."

Rand shifted, glancing back through the door as if seeking a way to escape. Let the Dark One think that. Beyond the doorway was still the black of nothing, split by the shining thread that ran from his body. And out there Ba'alzamon's heavier cord ran as well, so black that it stood out in the dark as if against snow. The two cords beat like heartveins in countertime, against each other, the light barely resisting the waves of dark.

"There are other choices," Rand said. "The Wheel weaves the Pattern, not you. Every trap you've laid for me, I have escaped. I've escaped your Fades and Trollocs, escaped your Darkfriends. I tracked you here, and destroyed your army on the way. You do not weave the Pattern."

Ba'alzamon's eyes roared like two furnaces. His lips did not move, but Rand thought he heard a curse screamed at Aginor. Then the fires died, and that ordinary human face smiled at him in a way that chilled even through the warmth of the Light.

"Other armies can be raised, fool. Armies you have not dreamed of will yet come. And you tracked me? You slug under a rock, track me? I began the setting of your path the day you were born, a path to lead you to your grave, or here. Aiel allowed to flee, and one to live, to speak the words that would echo down the years. Jain Farstrider, a hero," he twisted the word to a sneer, "whom I painted like a fool and sent to the Ogier thinking he was free of me. The Black Ajah, wriggling like worms on their bellies across the world to search you out. I pull the strings and the Amyrlin Seat dances and thinks she controls events."

The void trembled; hastily Rand firmed it again. *He knows it all. He could have done. It could be the way he says.* The Light warmed the void. Doubt cried out and was stilled, till only the seed remained. He struggled, not knowing whether he wanted to bury the seed or make it grow. The void steadied, smaller than before, and he floated in calm.

Ba'alzamon seemed to notice nothing. "It matters little if I have you alive or dead, except to you, and to what power you might have. You will serve me, or your soul will. But I would rather have you kneel to me alive than dead. A single fist of Trollocs sent to your village when I could have sent a thousand. One Darkfriend to face you where a hundred could come on you asleep. And you, fool, you don't even know them all, neither those ahead, nor those behind, nor those by your side. You are mine, have always been mine, my dog on a leash, and I brought you here to kneel to your master or die and let your soul kneel."

"I deny you. You have no power over me, and I will not kneel to you, alive or dead."

"Look," Ba'alzamon said. "Look." Unwilling, Rand yet turned his head.

Egwene stood there, and Nynaeve, pale and frightened, with flowers in their hair. And another woman, little older than the Wisdom, gray-eyed and beautiful, clothed in a Two Rivers dress, bright blossoms embroidered round the neck.

"Mother?" he breathed, and she smiled, a hopeless smile. His mother's smile. "No! My mother is dead, and the other two are safe away from here. I deny you!" Egwene and Nynaeve blurred, became wafting mist, dissipated. Kari al'Thor still stood there, her eyes big with fear.

"She, at least," Ba'alzamon said, "is mine to do with as I will."

Rand shook his head. "I deny you." He had to force the words out. "She is dead, and safe from you in the Light."

His mother's lips trembled. Tears trickled down her cheeks; each one burned him like acid. "The Lord of the Grave is stronger than he once was, my son," she said. "His reach is longer. The Father of Lies has a honeyed tongue for unwary souls. My son. My only, darling son. I would spare you if I could, but he is my master, now, his whim, the law of my existence. I can but obey him, and grovel for his favor. Only you can free me. Please, my son. Please help me. Help me. Help me! PLEASE!"

The wail ripped out of her as barefaced Fades, pale and eyeless, closed round. Her clothes ripped away in their bloodless hands, hands that wielded pincers and clamps and things that stung and burned and whipped against her naked flesh. Her scream would not end.

Rand's scream echoed hers. The void boiled in his mind. His sword was in his hand. Not the heron-mark blade, but a blade of light, a blade of the Light. Even as he raised it, a fiery white bolt shot from the point, as if the blade itself had reached out. It touched the nearest Fade, and blinding canescence filled the chamber, shining through the Halfmen like a candle through paper, burning through them, blinding his eyes to the scene.

From the midst of the brilliance, he heard a whisper. "Thank you, my son. The Light. The blessed Light."

The flash faded, and he was alone in the chamber with Ba'alzamon. Ba'alzamon's eyes burned like the Pit of Doom, but he shied back from the sword as if it truly were the Light itself. "Fool! You will destroy yourself! You cannot wield it so, not yet! Not until I teach you!"

"It is ended," Rand said, and he swung the sword at Ba'alzamon's black cord.

Ba'alzamon screamed as the sword fell, screamed till the stone walls trembled, and the endless howl redoubled as the blade of Light severed the cord. The cut ends rebounded apart as if they had been under tension. The end stretching into the nothingness outside began to shrivel as it sprang away; the other whipped back into Ba'alzamon, hurling him against the fireplace. There was silent laughter in the soundless shrieks of the tortured faces. The walls shivered and cracked; the floor heaved, and chunks of stone crashed to the floor from the ceiling.

As all broke apart around him, Rand pointed the sword at Ba'alzamon's heart. "It is ended!"

Light lanced from the blade, coruscating in a shower of fiery sparks like droplets of molten, white metal. Wailing, Ba'alzamon threw up his arms in a vain effort to shield himself. Flames shrieked in his eyes, joining with other flames as the stone ignited, the stone of the cracking walls, the stone of the pitching floor, the stone showering from the ceiling. Rand felt the bright thread attached to him thinning, till only the glow itself remained, but he strained harder, not knowing what he did, or how, only that this had to be ended. *It* has *to be ended!*

Fire filled the chamber, a solid flame. He could see Ba'al-zamon withering like a leaf, hear him howling, feel the shrieks grating on his bones. The flame became pure, white light, brighter than the sun. Then the last flicker of the thread was gone, and he was falling through endless black and Ba'al-zamon's fading howl.

Something struck him with tremendous force, turning him to jelly, and the jelly shook and screamed from the fire raging inside, the hungry cold burning without end.

CHAPTER
52

There Is Neither Beginning Nor End

H e became aware of the sun, first, moving across a cloudless sky, filling his unblinking eyes. It seemed to go by fits and starts, standing still for days, then darting ahead in a streak of light, jerking toward the far horizon, day falling with it. Light. *That should mean something.* Thought was a new thing. *I can think. I means me.* Pain came next, the memory of raging fever, the bruises where shaking chills had thrown him around like a rag doll. And a stink. A greasy, burned smell, filling his nostrils, and his head.

With aching muscles, he heaved himself over, pushed up to hands and knees. Uncomprehending, he stared at the oily ashes in which he had been lying, ashes scattered and smeared over the stone of the hilltop. Bits of dark green cloth lay mixed in the char, edge-blackened scraps that had escaped the flames. *Aginor.*

His stomach heaved and twisted. Trying to brush black streaks of ash from his clothes, he lurched away from the remains of the Forsaken. His hands flapped feebly, not making much headway. He tried to use both hands and fell forward. A sheer drop loomed under his face, a smooth rock wall spinning in his eyes, depth pulling him. His head swam, and he vomited over the edge of the cliff.

Trembling, he crawled backwards on his belly until there was solid stone under his eyes, then flopped over onto his back, panting for breath. With an effort he fumbled his sword from its scabbard. Only a few ashes remained from the red cloth. His hands shook when he held it up in front of his face; it took both hands. It was a heron-mark blade— *Heron-mark? Yes. Tam. My father* —but only steel for that. He needed three wavering tries to sheathe it again. *It had been something else. Or there was another sword.*

"My name," he said after a while, "is Rand al'Thor." More memory crashed back into his head like a lead ball, and he groaned. "The Dark One," he whispered to himself. "The Dark One is dead." There was no more need for caution. "Shai'tan is dead." The world seemed to lurch. He shook in silent mirth until tears poured from his eyes. "Shai'tan is dead!" He laughed at the sky. Other memories. "Egwene!" That name meant something important.

Painfully he got to his feet, wavering like a willow in a high wind, and staggered past Aginor's ashes without looking at them. *Not important anymore.* He fell more than climbed down that first, steep part of the slope, tumbling and sliding from bush to bush. By the time he reached more level ground, his bruises ached twice as much, but he found strength enough to stand, barely. *Egwene.* He broke into a shambling run. Leaves and flower petals showered around him as he blundered through the undergrowth. *Have to find her. Who is she?*

His arms and legs seemed to flail about more like long blades of grass than go as he wanted them to. Tottering, he fell against a tree, slamming against the trunk so hard that he grunted. Foliage rained on his head while he pressed his face to the rough bark, clutching to keep from falling. *Egwene.* He pushed himself away from the tree and hurried on. Almost immediately he tilted again, falling, but he forced his legs to work faster, to run into the fall so that he was staggering along at a good clip, all the while one step from falling flat on his face. Moving made his legs begin to obey him more. Slowly, he found himself running upright, arms pumping, long legs pulling him down the slope in leaps. He bounded into the clearing, half-filled now by the great oak marking the Green Man's grave. There was the white stone arch marked with the ancient symbol of the Aes Sedai, and the blackened, gaping pit where fire and wind had tried to trap Aginor and failed.

"Egwene! Egwene, where are you?" A pretty girl looked up

with big eyes from where she knelt beneath the spreading branches, flowers in her hair, and brown oak leaves. She was slender and young, and frightened. *Yes, that's who she is. Of course.* "Egwene, thank the Light you're all right."

There were two other women with her, one with haunted eyes and a long braid, still decorated with a few white morningstars. The other lay outstretched, her head pillowed on folded cloaks, her own sky-blue cloak not quite hiding her tattered dress. Charred spots and tears in the rich cloth showed, and her face was pale, but her eyes were open. *Moiraine. Yes, the Aes Sedai. And the Wisdom, Nynaeve.* All three women looked at him, unblinking and intent.

"You *are* all right, aren't you? Egwene? He didn't harm you." He could walk without stumbling, now—the sight of her made him feel like dancing, bruises and all—but it still felt good to drop down cross-legged beside them.

"I never even saw him after you pushed—" Her eyes were uncertain on his face. "What about you, Rand?"

"I'm fine." He laughed. He touched her cheek, and wondered if he had imagined a slight pulling away. "A little rest, and I'll be newmade. Nynaeve? Moiraine Sedai?" The names felt new in his mouth.

The Wisdom's eyes were old, ancient in her young face, but she shook her head. "A little bruised," she said, still watching him. "Moiraine is the only . . . the only one of us who was really hurt."

"I suffered more injury to my pride than anything else," the Aes Sedai said irritably, plucking at her cloak blanket. She looked as if she had been a long time ill, or hard used, but despite the dark circles under them her eyes were sharp and full of power. "Aginor was surprised and angry that I held him as long as I did, but fortunately, he had no time to spare for me. I am surprised myself that I held him so long. In the Age of Legends, Aginor was close behind the Kinslayer and Ishamael in power."

"'The Dark One and all the Forsaken,'" Egwene quoted in a faint, unsteady voice, "'are bound in Shayol Ghul, bound by the Creator. . . .'" She drew a shuddering breath.

"Aginor and Balthamel must have been trapped near the surface." Moiraine sounded as if she had already explained this, impatient at doing so again. "The patch on the Dark One's prison weakened enough to free them. Let us be thankful no more of the Forsaken were freed. If they had been, we would have seen them."

"It doesn't matter," Rand said. "Aginor and Balthamel are dead, and so is Shai'—"

"The Dark One," the Aes Sedai cut him off. Ill or not, her voice was firm, and her dark eyes commanding. "Best we still call him the Dark One. Or Ba'alzamon, at least."

He shrugged. "As you wish. But he's dead. The Dark One's dead. I killed him. I burned him with. . . ." The rest of memory flooded back then, leaving his mouth hanging open. *The One Power. I wielded the One Power. No man can. . . .* He licked lips that were suddenly dry. A gust of wind swirled fallen and falling leaves around them, but it was no colder than his heart. They were looking at him, the three of them. Watching. Not even blinking. He reached out to Egwene, and there was no imagination in her drawing back this time. "Egwene?" She turned her face away, and he let his hand drop.

Abruptly she flung her arms around him, burying her face in his chest. "I'm sorry, Rand. I'm sorry. I don't care. Truly, I don't." Her shoulders shook. He thought she was crying. Awkwardly patting her hair, he looked at the other two women over the top of her head.

"The Wheel weaves as the Wheel wills," Nynaeve said slowly, "but you are still Rand al'Thor of Emond's Field. But, the Light help me, the Light help us all, you are too dangerous, Rand." He flinched from the Wisdom's eyes, sad, regretting, and already accepting loss.

"What happened?" Moiraine said. "Tell me *everything!*"

And with her eyes on him, compelling, he did. He wanted to turn away, to make it short, leave things out, but the Aes Sedai's eyes drew everything from him. Tears ran down his face when he came to Kari al'Thor. His mother. He emphasized that. "He had my mother. My mother!" There was sympathy and pain on Nynaeve's face, but the Aes Sedai's eyes drove him on, to the sword of Light, to severing the black cord, and the flames consuming Ba'alzamon. Egwene's arms tightened around him as if she would pull him back from what had happened. "But it wasn't me," he finished. "The Light . . . pulled me along. It wasn't really me. Doesn't that make any difference?"

"I had suspicions from the first," Moiraine said. "Suspicions are not proof, though. After I gave you the token, the coin, and made that bonding, you should have been willing to fall in with whatever I wanted, but you resisted, questioned. That told me something, but not enough. Manetheren blood was always stubborn, and more so after Aemon died and Eldrene's heart was shattered. Then there was Bela."

"Bela?" he said. *Nothing makes any difference.*

The Aes Sedai nodded. "At Watch Hill, Bela had no need of me to cleanse her of tiredness; someone had already done it. She could have outrun Mandarb, that night. I should have thought of who Bela carried. With Trollocs on our heels, a Draghkar overhead, and a Halfman the Light alone knew where, how you must have feared that Egwene would be left behind. You needed something more than you had ever needed anything before in your life, and you reached out to the one thing that could give it to you. *Saidin.*"

He shivered. He felt so cold his fingers hurt. "If I never do it again, if I never touch it again, I won't. . . ." He could not say it. Go mad. Turn the land and people around him to madness. Die, rotting while he still lived.

"Perhaps," Moiraine said. "It would be much easier if there was someone to teach you, but it might be done, with a supreme effort of will."

"You can teach me. Surely, you—" He stopped when the Aes Sedai shook her head.

"Can a cat teach a dog to climb trees, Rand? Can a fish teach a bird to swim? I know *saidar,* but I can teach you nothing of *saidin.* Those who could are three thousand years dead. Perhaps you are stubborn enough, though. Perhaps your will is strong enough."

Egwene straightened, wiping reddened eyes with the back of her hand. She looked as if she wanted to say something, but when she opened her mouth, nothing came out. *At least she isn't pulling away. At least she can look at me without screaming.*

"The others?" he said.

"Lan took them into the cavern," Nynaeve said. "The Eye is

gone, but there's something in the middle of the pool, a crystal column, and steps to reach it. Mat and Perrin wanted to look for you first—Loial did, too—but Moiraine said. . . ." She glanced at the Aes Sedai, troubled. Moiraine returned her look calmly. "She said we mustn't disturb you while you were. . . ."

His throat constricted until he could hardly breathe. *Will they turn their faces the way Egwene did? Will they scream and run away like I'm a Fade?* Moiraine spoke as if she did not notice the blood draining from his face.

"There was a vast amount of the One Power in the Eye. Even in the Age of Legends, few could have channeled so much unaided without being destroyed. Very few."

"You told them?" he said hoarsely. "If everybody knows. . . ."

"Only Lan," Moiraine said gently. "He must know. And Nynaeve and Egwene, for what they are and what they will become. The others have no need, yet."

"Why not?" The rasp in his throat made his voice harsh. "You will be wanting to gentle me, won't you? Isn't that what Aes Sedai do to men who can wield the Power? Change them so they can't? Make them safe? Thom said men who have been gentled die because they stop wanting to live. Why aren't you talking about taking me to Tar Valon to be gentled?"

"You are *ta'veren*," Moiraine replied. "Perhaps the Pattern has not finished with you."

Rand sat up straight. "In the dreams Ba'alzamon said Tar Valon and the Amyrlin Seat would try to use me. He named names, and I remember them, now. Raolin Darksbane and Guaire Amalasan. Yurian Stonebow. Davian. Logain." The last was the hardest of all to say. Nynaeve went pale and Egwene gasped, but he pressed on angrily. "Every one a false Dragon. Don't try to deny it. Well, I won't be used. I am not a tool you can throw on the midden heap when it's worn out."

"A tool made for a purpose is not demeaned by being used for that purpose," Moiraine's voice was as harsh as his own, "but a man who believes the Father of Lies demeans himself. You say you will not be used, and then you let the Dark One set your path like a hound sent after a rabbit by his master."

His fists clenched; and he turned his head away. It was too

close to the things Ba'alzamon had said. "I am no one's hound. Do you hear me? No one's!"

Loial and the others appeared in the arch, and Rand scrambled to his feet, looking at Moiraine.

"They will not know," the Aes Sedai said, "until the Pattern makes it so."

Then his friends were coming close. Lan led the way, looking as hard as ever but still somewhat the worse for wear. He had one of Nynaeve's bandages around his temples, and a stiff-backed way of walking. Behind him, Loial carried a large gold chest, ornately worked and chased with silver. No one but an Ogier could have lifted it unaided. Perrin had his arms wrapped around a big bundle of folded white cloth, and Mat was cupping what appeared to be fragments of pottery in his two hands.

"So you're alive after all." Mat laughed. His face darkened, and he jerked his head at Moiraine. "She wouldn't let us look for you. Said we had to find out what the Eye was hiding. I'd have gone anyway, but Nynaeve and Egwene sided with her and almost threw me through the arch."

"You're here, now," Perrin said, "and not too badly beaten about, by the look of you." His eyes did not glow, but the irises were all yellow, now. "That's the important thing. You're here, and we're done with what we came for, whatever it was. Moiraine Sedai says we're done, and we can go. Home, Rand. The Light burn me, but I want to go home."

"Good to see you alive, sheepherder," Lan said gruffly. "I see you hung onto your sword. Maybe you'll learn to use it, now." Rand felt a sudden burst of affection for the Warder; Lan knew, but on the surface at least, nothing had changed. He thought that perhaps, for Lan, nothing had changed inside either.

"I must say," Loial said, setting the chest down, "that traveling with ta'veren has turned out to be even more interesting than I expected." His ears twitched violently. "If it becomes any more interesting, I will go back to Stedding Shangtai immediately, confess everything to Elder Haman, and never leave my books again." Suddenly the Ogier grinned, that wide mouth splitting his face in two. "It is so good to see you, Rand al'Thor. The Warder is the only one of these three who cares

much at all for books, and he won't talk. What happened to
you? We all ran off and hid in the woods until Moiraine Sedai
sent Lan to find us, but she would not let us look for you. Why
were you gone so long, Rand?"

"I ran and ran," he said slowly, "until I fell down a hill and
hit my head on a rock. I think I hit every rock on the way
down." That should explain his bruises. He tried to watch the
Aes Sedai, and Nynaeve and Egwene, too, but their faces
never changed. "When I came to, I was lost, and finally I stumbled back here. I think Aginor is dead, burned. I found some
ashes, and pieces of his cloak."

The lies sounded hollow in his ears. He could not understand
why they did not laugh with scorn and demand the truth, but
his friends nodded, accepting, and made sympathetic sounds as
they gathered around the Aes Sedai to show her what they had
found.

"Help me up," Moiraine said. Nynaeve and Egwene lifted
her until she was sitting; they had to support her even then.

"How could these things be inside the Eye," Mat asked,
"without being destroyed like that rock?"

"They were not put there to be destroyed," the Aes Sedai
said curtly, and frowned away their questions while she took
the pottery fragments, black and white and shiny, from Mat.

They seemed like rubble to Rand, but she fitted them together deftly on the ground beside her, making a perfect circle
the size of a man's hand. The ancient symbol of the Aes Sedai,
the Flame of Tar Valon joined with the Dragon's Fang, black
siding white. For a moment Moiraine only looked at it, her face
unreadable, then she took the knife from her belt and handed it
to Lan, nodding to the circle.

The Warder separated out the largest piece, then raised the
knife high and brought it down with all his might. A spark flew,
the fragment leaped with the force of the blow, and the blade
snapped with a sharp crack. He examined the stump left attached to the hilt, then tossed it aside. "The best steel from
Tear," he said dryly.

Mat snatched the fragment up and grunted, then showed it
around. There was no mark on it.

"*Cuendillar,*" Moiraine said. "Heartstone. No one has been
able to make it since the Age of Legends, and even then it was

made only for the greatest purpose. Once made, nothing can break it. Not the One Power itself wielded by the greatest Aes Sedai who ever lived aided by the most powerful *sa'angreal* ever made. Any power directed against heartstone only makes it stronger."

"Then how . . . ?" Mat's gesture with the piece he held took in the other bits on the ground.

"This was one of the seven seals on the Dark One's prison," Moiraine said. Mat dropped the piece as if it had become white-hot. For a moment, Perrin's eyes seemed to glow again. The Aes Sedai calmly began gathering the fragments.

"It doesn't matter anymore," Rand said. His friends looked at him oddly, and he wished he had kept his mouth shut.

"Of course," Moiraine replied. But she carefully put all the pieces into her pouch. "Bring me the chest." Loial lifted it closer.

The flattened cube of gold and silver appeared to be solid, but the Aes Sedai's fingers felt across the intricate work, pressing, and with a sudden click a top flung back as if on springs. A curled, gold horn nestled within. Despite its gleam, it seemed plain beside the chest that held it. The only markings were a line of silver script inlaid around the mouth of the bell. Moiraine lifted the horn out as if lifting a babe. "This must be carried to Illian," she said softly.

"Illian!" Perrin growled. "That's almost to the Sea of Storms, nearly as far south of home as we are north now."

"Is it . . . ?" Loial stopped to catch his breath. "Can it be . . . ?"

"You can read the Old Tongue?" Moiraine asked, and when he nodded, she handed him the horn.

The Ogier took it as gently as she had, delicately tracing the script with one broad finger. His eyes went wider and wider, and his ears stood up straight. *"Tia mi aven Moridin isainde vadin,"* he whispered. "The grave is no bar to my call."

"The Horn of Valere." For once the Warder appeared truly shaken; there was a touch of awe in his voice.

At the same time Nynaeve said in a shaky voice, "To call the heroes of the Ages back from the dead to fight the Dark One."

"Burn me!" Mat breathed.

Loial reverently laid the horn back in its golden nest.

"I begin to wonder," Moiraine said. "The Eye of the World was made against the greatest need the world would ever face, but was it made for the use to which . . . we . . . put it, or to guard these things? Quickly, the last, show it to me."

After the first two, Rand could understand Perrin's reluctance. Lan and the Ogier took the bundle of white cloth from him when he hesitated, and unfolded it between them. A long, white banner spread out, lifting on the air. Rand could only stare. The whole thing seemed of a piece, neither woven, nor dyed, nor painted. A figure like a serpent, scaled in scarlet and gold, ran the entire length, but it had scaled legs, and feet with five long, golden claws on each, and a great head with a golden mane and eyes like the sun. The stirring of the banner made it seem to move, scales glittering like precious metals and gems, alive, and he almost thought he could hear it roar defiance.

"What is it?" he said.

Moiraine answered slowly. "The banner of the Lord of the Morning when he led the forces of Light against the Shadow. The banner of Lews Therin Telamon. The banner of the Dragon." Loial almost dropped his end.

"Burn me!" Mat said faintly.

"We will take these things with us when we go," Moiraine said. "They were not put here by chance, and I must know more." Her fingers brushed her pouch, where the pieces of the shattered seal were. "It is too late in the day for starting now. We will rest, and eat, but we will leave early. The Blight is all around here, not as along the Border, and strong. Without the Green Man, this place cannot hold long. Let me down," she told Nynaeve and Egwene. "I must rest."

Rand became aware of what he had been seeing all along, but not noticing. Dead, brown leaves falling from the great oak. Dead leaves rustling thick on the ground in the breeze, brown mixed with petals dropped from thousands of flowers. The Green Man had held back the Blight, but already the Blight was killing what he had made.

"It is done, isn't it?" he asked Moiraine. "It is finished."

The Aes Sedai turned her head on its pillow of cloaks. Her eyes seemed as deep as the Eye of the World. "We have done what we came here to do. From here you may live your life as the Pattern weaves. Eat, then sleep, Rand al'Thor. Sleep, and dream of home."

CHAPTER

53

The Wheel Turns

Dawn revealed devastation in the Green Man's garden. The ground was thick with fallen leaves, almost knee-deep in places. All the flowers were gone except a few clinging desperately to the edge of the clearing. Little could grow in the soil under an oak, but a thin circle of flowers and grass centered on the thick trunk above the Green Man's grave. The oak itself retained only half its leaves, and that was far more than any other tree had, as if some remnant of the Green Man still fought to hold there. The cool breezes had died, replaced by a growing sticky heat, the butterflies were gone, the birds silent. It was a silent group who prepared to leave.

Rand climbed into the bay's saddle with a sense of loss. *It shouldn't be this way. Blood and ashes, we won!*

"I wish he had found his other place," Egwene said as she mounted Bela. A litter, fashioned by Lan, was slung between the shaggy mare and Aldieb, to carry Moiraine; Nynaeve would ride beside with the white mare's reins. The Wisdom dropped her eyes whenever she saw Lan glance at her, avoiding his gaze; the Warder looked at her whenever her eyes were averted, but he would not speak to her. No one had to ask who Egwene meant.

"It is not right," Loial said, staring at the oak. The Ogier was the only one still not mounted. "It is not right that Treebrother should fall to the Blight." He handed the reins of his big horse to Rand. "Not right."

Lan opened his mouth as the Ogier walked to the great oak. Moiraine, lying on the litter, weakly raised her hand, and the Warder said nothing.

Before the oak, Loial knelt, closing his eyes and stretching out his arms. The tufts on his ears stood straight as he lifted his face to the sky. And he sang.

Rand could not say if there were words, or if it was pure song. In that rumbling voice it was as if the earth sang, yet he was sure he heard the birds trilling again, and spring breezes sighing softly, and the sound of butterfly wings. Lost in the song, he thought it lasted only minutes, but when Loial lowered his arms and opened his eyes, he was surprised to see the sun stood well above the horizon. It had been touching the trees when the Ogier began. The leaves still on the oak seemed greener, and more firmly attached than before. The flowers encircling it stood straighter, the morningstars white and fresh, the loversknots a strong crimson.

Mopping sweat from his broad face, Loial rose and took his reins from Rand. His long eyebrows drooped, abashed, as if they might think he had been showing off. "I've never sung so hard before. I could not have done it if something of Treebrother was not still there. My Tree Songs do not have his power." When he settled himself in his saddle, there was satisfaction in the look he gave the oak and the flowers. "This little space, at least, will not sink into the Blight. The Blight will not have Treebrother."

"You are a good man, Ogier," Lan said.

Loial grinned. "I will take that as a compliment, but I do not know what Elder Haman would say."

They rode in a single file, with Mat behind the Warder where he could use his bow to effect if needed, and Perrin bringing up the rear with his axe across the pommel of his saddle. They crested a hill, and in an eyeblink the Blight was all around them, twisted and rotted in virulent rainbow hues. Rand looked over his shoulder, but the Green Man's garden was nowhere to be seen. Only the Blight stretching behind them as before. Yet he thought, just for a moment, that he saw the towering top of the oak tree, green and lush, before it shimmered and was gone. Then there was only the Blight.

He half expected they would have to fight their way out as

they fought their way in, but the Blight was as quiet and still as death. Not a single branch trembled as if to lash at them, nothing screamed or howled, neither nearby nor in the distance. The Blight seemed to crouch, not to pounce, but as if it had been struck a great blow and waited for the next to fall. Even the sun was less red.

When they passed the necklace of lakes, the sun hung not far past its zenith. Lan kept them well away from the lakes and did not even look at them, but Rand thought the seven towers seemed taller than when he first saw them. He was sure the jagged tops were further from the ground, and above them something almost seen, seamless towers gleaming in the sun, and banners with Golden Cranes flying on the wind. He blinked and stared, but the towers refused to vanish completely. They were there at the edge of vision until the Blight hid the lakes once more.

Before sunset the Warder chose a campsite, and Moiraine had Nynaeve and Egwene help her up to set wards. The Aes Sedai whispered in the other women's ears before she began. Nynaeve hesitated, but when Moiraine closed her eyes, all three women did so together.

Rand saw Mat and Perrin staring, and wondered how they could be surprised. *Every woman is an Aes Sedai,* he thought mirthlessly. *The Light help me, so am I.* Bleakness held his tongue.

"Why is it so different?" Perrin asked as Egwene and the Wisdom helped Moiraine to her bed. "It feels. . . ." His thick shoulders shrugged as if he could not find the word.

"We struck a mighty blow at the Dark One," Moiraine replied, settling herself with a sigh. "The Shadow will be a long time recovering."

"How?" Mat demanded. "What did we do?"

"Sleep," Moiraine said. "We are not out of the Blight yet."

But the next morning, still nothing changed that Rand could see. The Blight faded as they rode south, of course. Twisted trees were replaced by straight. The stifling heat diminished. Rotting foliage gave way to the merely diseased. And then not diseased, he realized. The forest around them became red with new growth, thick on the branches. Buds sprouted on the undergrowth, creepers covered the rocks with green, and new wildflowers dotted the grass as thick and bright as where the Green Man walked. It was as if spring, so long held back by winter, now raced to catch up to where it should be.

He was not the only one who stared. "A mighty blow," Moiraine murmured, and would say no more.

Climbing wildrose entwined the stone column marking the Border. Men came out of the watchtowers to greet them. There was a stunned quality to their laughter, and their eyes shone with amaze, as if they could not believe the new grass under their steel-clad feet.

"The Light has conquered the Shadow!"

"A great victory in Tarwin's Gap! We have had the message! Victory!"

"The Light blesses us again!"

"King Easar is strong in the Light," Lan replied to all their shouts.

The watchmen wanted to tend Moiraine, or at least send an escort with them, but she refused it all. Even flat on her back on a litter, the Aes Sedai's presence was such that the armored men fell back, bowing and acceding to her wishes. Their laughter followed as Rand and the others rode on.

In the late afternoon they reached Fal Dara, to find the grim-walled city ringing with celebration. Ringing in truth. Rand doubted if there could be a bell in the city not clanging, from the tiniest silver harness chime to great bronze gongs in their tower tops. The gates stood wide open, and men ran laughing and singing in the streets, flowers stuck in their topknots and the crevices of their armor. The common people of the town had not yet returned from Fal Moran, but the soldiers were newly come from Tarwin's Gap, and their joy was enough to fill the streets.

"Victory in the Gap! We won!"

"A miracle in the Gap! The Age of Legends has come back!"

"Spring!" a grizzled old soldier laughed as he hung a garland of morningstars around Rand's neck. His own topknot was a white cluster of them. "The Light blesses us with spring once more!"

Learning they wanted to go to the keep, a circle of men clad in steel and flowers surrounded them, running to clear a way through the celebration.

Ingtar's was the first face Rand saw that was not smiling. "I was too late," Ingtar told Lan with a sour grimness. "Too late by an hour to see. Peace!" His teeth ground audibly, but then his expression became contrite. "Forgive me. Grief makes me forget my duties. Welcome, Builder. Welcome to you all. It is good to see you safely out of the Blight. I will bring the healer to Moiraine Sedai in her chambers, and inform Lord Agelmar—"

"Take me to Lord Agelmar," Moiraine commanded. "Take us all." Ingtar opened his mouth to protest, and bowed under the force of her eyes.

Agelmar was in his study, with his swords and armor back on their racks, and his was the second face that did not smile. He wore a troubled frown that deepened when he saw Moiraine carried in on her litter by liveried servants. Women in the black-and-gold fluttered over bringing the Aes Sedai to him without a chance to freshen herself or be brought the healer. Loial carried the gold chest. The pieces of the seal were still in Moiraine's pouch; Lews Therin Kinslayer's banner was wrapped in her blanketroll and still tied behind Aldieb's saddle. The groom who had led the white mare away had received the strictest orders to see the blanketroll was placed untouched in the chambers assigned to the Aes Sedai.

"Peace!" the Lord of Fal Dara muttered. "Are you injured, Moiraine Sedai? Ingtar, why have you not seen the Aes Sedai to her bed and brought the healer to her?"

"Be still, Lord Agelmar," Moiraine said. "Ingtar has done as I commanded him. I am not so frail as everyone here seems to think." She motioned two of the women to help her to a chair. For a moment they clasped their hands, exclaiming that she was too weak, that she should be in a warm bed, and the healer brought, and a hot bath. Moiraine's eyebrows lifted; the women shut their mouths abruptly and hurried to aid her into the chair. As soon as she was settled she waved them away irritably. "I would speak with you, Lord Agelmar."

Agelmar nodded, and Ingtar waved the servants from the room. The Lord of Fal Dara eyed those who remained expectantly; especially, Rand thought, Loial and the golden chest.

"We hear," Moiraine said as soon as the door shut behind Ingtar, "that you won a great victory in Tarwin's Gap."

"Yes," Agelmar said slowly, his troubled frown returning. "Yes, Aes Sedai, and no. The Halfmen and their Trollocs were destroyed to the last, but we barely fought. A miracle, my men call it. The earth swallowed them; the mountains buried them. Only a few Draghkar were left, too frightened to do else but fly north as fast as they could."

"A miracle indeed," Moiraine said. "And spring has come again."

"A miracle," Agelmar said, shaking his head, "but. . . . Moiraine Sedai, men say many things about what happened in the Gap. That the Light took on flesh and fought for us. That the Creator walked in the Gap to strike at the Shadow. But I saw a man, Moiraine Sedai. I saw a man, and what he did, cannot be, must not be."

"The Wheel weaves as the Wheel wills, Lord of Fal Dara."

"As you say, Moiraine Sedai."

"And Padan Fain? He is secure? I must speak with him when I am rested."

"He is held as you commanded, Aes Sedai, whining at his guards half the time and trying to command them the rest, but. . . . Peace, Moiraine Sedai, what of you, in the Blight? You found the Green Man? I see his hand in the new things growing."

"We found him," she said flatly. "The Green Man is dead, Lord Agelmar, and the Eye of the World is gone. There will be no more quests by young men seeking glory."

The Lord of Fal Dara frowned, shaking his head in confusion. "Dead? The Green Man? He cannot be. . . . Then you were defeated? But the flowers, and the growing things?"

"We won, Lord Agelmar. We won, and the land freed from winter is the proof, but I fear the last battle has not yet been fought." Rand stirred, but the Aes Sedai gave him a sharp look and he stood still again. "The Blight still stands, and the forges of Thakan'dar still work below Shayol Ghul. There are many Halfmen yet, and countless Trollocs. Never think the need for watchfulness in the Borderlands is gone."

"I did not think it so, Aes Sedai," he said stiffly.

Moiraine motioned for Loial to set the gold chest at her feet, and when he did, she opened it, revealing the horn. "The Horn of Valere," she said, and Agelmar gasped. Rand almost thought the man would kneel.

"With that, Moiraine Sedai, it matters not how many Halfmen or Trollocs remain. With the heroes of old come back from the tomb, we will march to the Blasted Lands and level Shayol Ghul."

"NO!" Agelmar's mouth fell open in surprise, but Moiraine continued calmly. "I did not show it to you to taunt you, but so that you will know that in whatever battles yet come, our might will be as great as that of the Shadow. Its place is not here. The Horn must be carried to Illian. It is there, if fresh battles threaten, that it must rally the forces of the Light. I will ask an escort of your best men to see that it reaches Illian safely. There are Darkfriends still, as well as Halfmen and Trollocs, and those who come to the horn will follow whoever winds it. It must reach Illian."

"It shall be as you say, Aes Sedai." But when the lid of the chest closed, the Lord of Fal Dara looked like a man being denied his last glimpse of the Light.

Seven days later, bells still rang in Fal Dara. The people had returned from Fal Moran, adding their celebration to that of the soldiers, and shouts and singing blended with the pealing of the bells on the long balcony where Rand stood. The balcony overlooked Agelmar's private gardens, green and flowering, but he did not give them a second look. Despite the sun high in the sky, spring in Shienar was cooler than he was used to, yet sweat glistened on his bare chest and shoulders as he swung the heron-mark blade, each move precise yet distant from where he floated in the void. Even there, he wondered how much joy there would be in the town if they knew of the banner Moiraine still kept hidden.

"Good, sheepherder." Leaning against the railing with his arms folded across his chest, the Warder watched him critically. "You are doing well, but don't push so hard. You can't become a blademaster in a few weeks."

The void vanished like a pricked bubble. "I don't care about being a blademaster."

"It's a blademaster's blade, sheepherder."

"I just want my father to be proud of me." His hand tightened on the rough leather of the hilt. *I just want Tam to be my father.* He slammed the sword into its scabbard. "Anyway, I don't have a few weeks."

"Then you've not changed your mind?"

"Would you?" Lan's expression had not altered; the flat planes of his face looked as if they could not change. "You won't try to stop me? Or Moiraine Sedai?"

"You can do as you will, sheepherder, or as the Pattern weaves for you." The Warder straightened. "I'll leave you now."

Rand turned to watch Lan go, and found Egwene standing there.

"Changed your mind about what, Rand?"

He snatched up his shirt and coat, suddenly feeling the cool. "I'm going away, Egwene."

"Where?"

"Somewhere. I don't know." He did not want to meet her eyes, but he could not stop looking at her. She wore red wild-roses twined in her hair, flowing about her shoulders. She held her cloak close, dark blue and embroidered along the edge with a thin line of white flowers in the Shienaran fashion, and the blossoms made a line straight up to her face. They were no paler than her cheeks; her eyes seemed so large and dark. "Away."

"I'm sure Moiraine Sedai will not like you just going off. After . . . after what you've done, you deserve some reward."

"Moiraine does not know I am alive. I have done what she wanted, and that's an end to it. She doesn't even speak to me when I go to her. Not that I've tried to stay close to her, but she's avoided me. She won't care if I go, and I don't care if she does."

"Moiraine is still not completely well, Rand." She hesitated. "I have to go to Tar Valon for my training. Nynaeve is coming, too. And Mat still needs to be Healed of whatever binds him to that dagger, and Perrin wants to see Tar Valon before he goes . . . wherever. You could come with us."

"And wait for some Aes Sedai besides Moiraine to find out what I am and gentle me?" His voice was rough, almost a sneer; he could not change it. "Is that what you want?"

"No."

He knew he would never be able to tell her how grateful he was that she had not hesitated before answering.

"Rand, you aren't afraid. . . ." They were alone, but she looked around and still lowered her voice. "Moiraine Sedai says you don't have to touch the True Source. If you don't touch *saidin*, if you don't try to wield the Power, you'll be safe."

"Oh, I won't ever touch it again. Not if I have to cut my hand off, first." *What if I can't stop? I never tried to wield it, not even at the Eye. What if I can't stop?*

"Will you go home, Rand? Your father must be dying to see you. Even Mat's father must be dying to see him by now. I'll be coming back to Emond's Field next year. For a little while, at least."

He rubbed his palm over the hilt of his sword, feeling the bronze heron. *My father. Home. Light, how I want to see. . . .* "Not home." *Someplace where there aren't any people to hurt if I can't stop myself. Somewhere alone.* Suddenly it felt as cold as snow on the balcony. "I'm going away, but not home." *Egwene, Egwene, why did you have to be one of those . . . ?* He put his arms around her, and whispered into her hair. "Not ever home."

In Agelmar's private garden, under a thick bower dotted with white blossoms, Moiraine shifted on her bedchair. The fragments of the seal lay on her lap, and the small gem she sometimes wore in her hair spun and glittered on its gold chain from the ends of her fingers. The faint blue glow faded from the stone, and a smile touched her lips. It had no power in itself, the stone, but the first use she had ever learned of the One Power, as a girl, in the Royal Palace in Cairhien, was using the stone to listen to people when they thought they were too far off to be overheard.

"The Prophecies will be fulfilled," the Aes Sedai whispered. "The Dragon is Reborn."

The End
of the First Book of
The Wheel of Time

GLOSSARY

A NOTE ON DATES IN THIS GLOSSARY. The Toman Calendar (devised by Toma dur Ahmid) was adopted approximately two centuries after the death of the last male Aes Sedai, recording years After the Breaking of the World (AB). So many records were destroyed in the Trolloc Wars that at their end there was argument about the exact year under the old system. A new calendar, proposed by Tiam of Gazar, celebrated freedom from the Trolloc threat and recorded each year as a Free Year (FY). The Gazaran Calendar gained wide acceptance within twenty years after the Wars' end. Artur Hawkwing attempted to establish a new calendar based on the founding of his empire (FF, From the Founding), but only historians now refer to it. After the death and destruction of the War of the Hundred Years, a third calendar was devised by Uren din Jubai Soaring Gull, a scholar of the Sea Folk, and promulgated by the Panarch Farede of Tarabon. The Farede Calendar, dating from the arbitrarily decided end of the War of the Hundred Years and recording years of the New Era (NE), is currently in use.

Adan, Heran *(ay-DAN, HEH-ran):* Governor of Baerlon.
Aes Sedai *(EYEZ seh-DEYE):* Wielders of the One Power. Since the Time of Madness, all are women. Widely distrusted and

feared, even hated. Blamed by many for the Breaking of the World, and thought to meddle in the affairs of nations. At the same time, few rulers will be without an Aes Sedai advisor, even in lands where the existence of such a connection must be secret. Used as an honorific, so: Sheriam Sedai, and as a high honorific, so: Sheriam Aes Sedai.

Age Lace: *see* Pattern of an Age.

Age of Legends: The Age ended by the War of the Shadow and the Breaking of the World. A time when Aes Sedai performed wonders we now can only dream of. *See also* Wheel of Time.

Agelmar; Lord Agelmar of House Jagad *(AGH-el-mar; JAH-gad):* Lord of Fal Dara. One of the Great Captains, the finest generals of his time. His sign is three running red foxes.

Aiel *(eye-EEL):* The people of the Aiel Waste. Fierce and hardy. Also called Aielmen. They veil their faces before they kill, giving rise to the saying "acting like a black-veiled Aiel" to describe someone who is being violent, which has become so wide-spread that it is used by people who have never seen an Aiel. Deadly warriors with weapons or with nothing but their bare hands, they will not touch a sword even if it means their death. Their pipers play them into battle with the music of dances, and Aielmen call battle "the Dance."

Aiel War, the: (976-78 NE) When King Laman of Cairhien cut down *Avendoraldera*, several clans of the Aiel crossed the Spine of the World. They looted and burned the capital city of Cairhien as well as many other cities and towns, and the conflict extended into Andor and Tear. The conventional view is that the Aiel were finally defeated at the Battle of the Shining Walls, before Tar Valon, but in fact, Laman was killed in that battle, and having done what they had come for, the Aiel recrossed the Spine. *See also Avendoraldera.*

Aiel Waste: The harsh, rugged and all-but-waterless land east of the Spine of the World. Few outsiders venture there, not only because water is almost impossible to find for one not born there, but because the Aiel consider themselves at war with all other peoples and do not welcome strangers.

Ajah *(AH-jah):* Societies among the Aes Sedai, to which all Aes Sedai belong. They are designated by colors: Blue Ajah, Red

Ajah, White Ajah, Green Ajah, Brown Ajah, Yellow Ajah, and Gray Ajah. Each follows a specific philosophy of the use of the One Power and purposes of the Aes Sedai. The Red Ajah bends all it energies to finding and gentling men who are attempting to wield the Power, and the Blue Ajah is known for becoming involved in causes. The Brown Ajah, on the other hand, forsakes involvement with the world and dedicates itself to seeking knowledge, both in the natural world and in history. The Yellow Ajah is dedicated to Healing, the White Ajah to logic and philosophy, and the Gray Ajah to mediation and negotiation, while the Green Ajah, known to some as the Battle Ajah, holds ready for the day when the Trollocs and Dreadlords appear once more and they will march to war. There are rumors (hotly denied and never safely mentioned in front of any Aes Sedai) of a Black Ajah, dedicated to serving the Dark One.

Al Ellisande! *(ahl ehl-lih-SAHN-dah):* In the Old Tongue, "For the Rose of the Sun!

Aldieb *(ahl-DEEB):* In the Old Tongue, "West Wind," the wind that brings the spring rains.

al'Meara, Nynaeve *(ahl-MEER-ah, NIGH-neev):* The Wisdom of Emond's Field.

al'Thor, Rand *(ahl-THOR, RAND):* A young farmer and sheepherder from the Two Rivers whose fate is intertwined with those of his friends, Mat Cauthon and Perrin Aybara, and with the fate of the world.

al'Vere, Egwene *(ahl-VEER, eh-GWAIN):* Youngest daughter of the innkeeper in Emond's Field who has a destiny of her own reaching as far as those of her friends from home.

Amadicia *(ah-man-DEE-see-ah):* A nation lying south of the Mountains of Mist. It's capital city is Amador (AH-mahdoor), where the headquarters of the Children of the Light is found. The sigil of Amadicia is a six-pointed silver star overlaid on a red thistle, both on a field of blue.

Amyrlin Seat *(AHM-ehr-lin):* (1) The title of the leader of the Aes Sedai. Elected for life by the Hall of the Tower, the highest council of the Aes Sedai, which consists of three representatives from each of the seven Ajahs. The Amyrlin Seat has, theoretically at least, almost supreme authority among the Aes Sedai. She ranks as the equal of a king or queen. (2) The throne upon which the leader of the Aes Sedai sits.

Andor *(AN-door):* The realm within which the Two Rivers lies. The sign of Andor is a rampant white lion on a field of red.

angreal *(ahn-gree-AHL):* A very rare object which allows anyone capable of channeling the One Power to handle a greater amount of the Power than would be safely possible unaided. Remnants of the Age of Legends, the means of their making is no longer known.

Aptarigine Cycle, the: a famous cycle of stories, which numbers in the hundreds, following the intrigues, loves and romances, both happy and doomed, that join and divide two dozen noble families over fifty generations. The stories of the *Aptarigine Cycle* are usually told by bards, and few gleemen know more than a handful of the stories.

Arafel *(AH-rah-fehl):* One of the Borderlands. The sign of Arafel is three white roses on a field of red, quartered with three red roses on a field of white.

Aram *(AY-ram):* A young man of the Tuatha'an.

Avendesora *(Ah-vehn-deh-SO-rah):* In the Old Tongue, "the Tree of Life." Mentioned in many stories and legends. Some people believe it just a myth, but they are wrong. Once there were many such trees. Now there is only one.

Avendoraldera *(ah-VEHN-dor-ahl-DEH-rah):* A tree grown in the city of Cairhien from a sapling of *Avendesora*. This sapling was a gift from the Aiel in 566 NE. *See also* Aiel War, the.

Aybara, Perrin *(ay-BAHR-ah, PEHR-rihn):* A young blacksmith's apprentice from Emond's Field. He has never wanted to be more than a good blacksmith, but fate holds a different future for him.

Ba'alzamon *(bah-AHL-zah-mon):* In the Trolloc tongue, "Heart of the Dark." Believed to be the Trolloc name for the Dark One.

Baerlon *(BAYR-lon):* A city in Andor on the road from Caemlyn to the mines in the Mountains of Mist.

Barran, Doral *(BAHR-rahn, DOOR-ahl):* The Wisdom in Emond's Field prior to Nynaeve al'Meara.

Bel Tine *(BEHL TINE):* Festival celebrating the end of winter and the reappearance of spring. Considered a celebration of renewal and of the spring planting soon to come. A good time for proposals of marriage and for weddings.

biteme (BITE-me): A small, almost invisible biting insect. Its bite is very sharp, like the stab of a needle.

Black Ajah: *See* Ajah

Blasted Lands: Desolated lands surrounding Shayol Ghul, beyond the Great Blight. Nothing grows in the Blasted Lands, and nothing can grow there. Even so, in the Blasted Lands, the land itself can kill.

Blight, the: *See* Great Blight, the.

Blue Ajah: *See* Ajah.

Borderlands, the: The four nations bordering the Great Blight: Saldaea, Arafel, Kandor and Shienar.

Bornhald, Dain *(BOHRN-hahld, DAY-in):* An officer of the Children of the Light, son of Lord Captain Geofram Bornhald. A young man eager to follow in his father's foot-steps.

Bornhald, Geofram: (BOHRN-hahld, JEHF-rahm): A Lord Captain of the Children of the Light. A man who holds duty above all else except honor.

Breaking of the World, the: When Lews Therin Telamon and the Hundred Companions resealed the Dark One's prison, the counterstroke tainted *saidin.* Eventually every male Aes Sedai went horribly insane. In their madness these men, who could wield the One Power to a degree now unknown, changed the face of the earth. They caused great earthquakes, leveled mountain ranges, raised new mountains, lifted dry land where seas had been, made the ocean rush in where dry land had been. Many parts of the world were completely depopulated, and the survivors were scattered like dust on the wind. This destruction is remembered in stories, legends and history as the Breaking of the World. *See also* Hundred Companions, the.

Bryne, Gareth *(BRIHN, GAH-rehth):* Captain-General of the Queen's Guard in Andor. Also serves as Morgase's First Prince of the Sword. A man of duty and honor, who loves his Queen as a man and not just as her subject. He is considered one of the Great Captains, one of the best generals of the Age. His sign is three golden stars, each of five rays.

Byar, Jaret *(BY-ahr, JAH-ret):* An officer of the Children of the Light who holds duty before all else, even honor.

Caemlyn *(KAYM-lihn):* The capital city of Andor. It consists of the Inner City and the surrounding New City. The Inner City was built by Ogier not long after the end of the Breaking of the World, though it was then known as Hai Caemlyn. The Inner City of Caemlyn is thought by many to be even more beautiful than Tar Valon itself.

Cairhien *(KEYE-ree-EHN):* Both a nation along the Spine of the world and the capital city of that nation. The capital is often called simply "the City" by Cairhienin. The city was burned and looted during the Aiel War (976-978 NE). The sign of Cairhien is a many-rayed golden sun rising from the bottom of a field of sky blue.

Carai an Caldazar! *(cah-REYE ahn cahl-dah-ZAHR):* In the Old Tongue, "For the honor of the Red Eagle!" The ancient battle cry of Manetheren.

Carai an Ellisande!: In the Old Tongue, "For the honor of the Rose of the Sun!" The battlecry of the last king of Manetheren.

Cauthon, Matrim *(CAW-thon, MAT-rihm):* a young farmer from the Two Rivers who delights in mischief and does not even dream of his destiny.

channel: (1) (verb) To control the flow of the One Power. (2) (noun) The act of controlling the flow of the One Power.

Charin, Jain *(CHAH-rihn, JAY-ihn): See* Farstrider, Jain.

Children of the Light: A society holding strict ascetic beliefs, dedicated to the defeat of the Dark One and the destruction of all Darkfriends. Founded during the War of the Hundred Years by Lothair Mantelar (LOH-thayr MAHN-tee-LAHR) to preach against increasing numbers of Darkfriends, they evolved during the war into a completely military organization, extremely rigid in their beliefs and completely certain that only they know the truth and the right. They hate Aes Sedai, considering them, and any who support or befriend them, Darkfriends. They are known disparagingly as Whitecloaks, a name they despise. Their sign is a golden sunburst on a field of white.

Covenant of the Ten Nations: A union formed in the centuries after the Breaking of the World (circa 200 AB) which was dedicated to the defeat of the Dark One. The nations that made the Covenant were Jaramide, Aramaelle, Almoren, Aridhol, Safer, Manetheren, Coremanda, Essenia, Eharon, and Aelgar. Few of the nations of the Covenant survived the Trolloc Wars, and none for long; all were replaced by new nations formed from the ruins of the old nations. *See* Trolloc Wars.

cuendillar (CWAIN-deh-yar): See heartstone.

currency: after many centuries of trade, the standard terms for coins are the same in every land: crowns (the largest coin in size), marks and pennies. Crowns and marks can be minted of gold or silver, while pennies can be silver or copper, the last often called simply a copper. In different lands, however, these coins can be of different sizes and weights. Even in one nation, coins of different sizes and weights have been minted by different rulers. Because of trade, the coins of many nations can be found almost anywhere. For that reason, bankers, moneylenders and merchants all use scales to determine the value of any given coin. Even large numbers of coins are weighed for this reason. The only paper currency are "letters-of-rights," which are issued by bankers, guaranteeing to present a certain amount of gold or silver when the letter of rights is presented. Because of the long distances between cities, the length of time needed to travel from one to another, and the difficulties of transactions at long distance, a letter-of-rights may be accepted at full value in a city near to the bank which issued it, but it may only be accepted at a lower value in a city further away. Generally, someone intending to be traveling for a long time will carry one or more letters-of-rights to exchange for coin when needed. Letters-of-rights are usually accepted only by bankers or merchants, and would never be used in shops.

Damodred, Lord Galadedrid (DAHM-oh-drehd, gah-LAHD-eh-drihd): Only son of Taringail Damodred and Tigraine; half-brother to Elayne and Gawyn. His sign is a winged silver sword, point down.

Damodred, Prince Taringail (DAHM-oh-drehd, TAH-rihn-gail): A Royal Prince of Cairhien, he married Tigraine and fathered Galadedrid. When Tigraine disappeared and was declared dead, he married Morgase and fathered Elayne and Gawyn. He vanished under mysterious circumstances and has been presumed dead for many years. His sign was a golden, double-bitted battle axe.

Dark One: Most common name, used in every land, for Shai'tan: the source of evil, antithesis of the Creator. Imprisoned by the Creator at the moment of Creation in a prison at Shayol Ghul; an attempt to free him from that prison brought about the War of the Shadow, the tainting of *saidin*, the Breaking of the World, and the end of the Age of Legends.

Dark One, naming the: Saying the true name of the Dark One (Shai'tan) draws his attention, inevitably bringing ill-fortune at best, disaster at worst. For that reason many euphemisms are used, among them the Dark One, Father of Lies, Sight-blinder, Lord of the Grave, Shepherd of the Night, Hearts-bane, Heartfang, Grassburner, and Leafblighter. In every land, someone who seems to be inviting ill fortune is often said to be "naming the Dark One."

Darkfriends: Those who follow the Dark One and believe they will gain great power and rewards when he is freed from his prison. Some even believe he will reward them by making them live forever. For that, they are willing to commit any crime and to murder even members of their families. Dark-friends are organized in a number of highly secretive groups which cooperate with one another at times but also compete with one another for power. Among Darkfriends, only rank within the Darkfriends is important. A beggar who is a Dark-friend and gave the proper signs would expect to be obeyed even by a king who is a Darkfriend.

Daughter-Heir: Title of the heir to the throne of Andor, where the eldest daughter of the Queen succeeds her mother on the throne. Without a surviving daughter, the throne goes to the woman who can show that she has the most lines of descent from the founding Queen of Andor. In the way of Andor, this woman would be considered the nearest female relation of the dead Queen, though among commoners they might not be considered related at all.

Dha'vol; Dhai'mon (DAH-vohl, DEYE-mon): See Trollocs.

Djevic K'Shar (DJEH-vihk KEH-SHAHR): In the Trolloc tongue, "The Dying Ground." The Trolloc name for the Aiel Waste. Trollocs live to kill, but even they know that going into the Waste means that they will die.

Domon, Bayle *(DOH-mon, BAIL):* The captain of the *Spray.* A collector, and a man so caught up in the Pattern of the Age that he might be almost the opposite of a *ta'veren.*

Draghkar *(DRAGH-kahr):* A creature of the Dark One, made originally during the War of the Shadow by twisting human stock. A Draghkar appears to be a large man with bat-like wings, whose skin is too pale and whose eyes are too large. The Draghkar's song can draw its prey to it, suppressing the victim's will. There is a saying: "The kiss of the Draghkar is death." It does not bite, but its kiss will consume first the soul of its victim, and then his or her life.

Dragon, the: The name by which Lews Therin Telamon was known during the War of the Shadow. In the madness which overtook all male Aes Sedai, Lews Therin killed every living person who carried any of his blood, as well as everyone he loved, thus earning the name Kinslayer. A saying is now used, "taken by the Dragon," or "possessed of the Dragon," to indicate that someone is endangering those around him or threatening them, especially if without cause. *See also* Dragon Reborn.

Dragon, false: Occasionally men claim to be the Dragon Reborn, and sometimes one of them gains following enough to require an army to put it down. Some have begun wars that involved many nations. Over the centuries most have been men unable to channel the One Power, but a few could. All, however, either disappeared, or were captured or killed, without fulfilling any of the Prophecies concerning the Rebirth of the Dragon. These men are called false Dragons. *See also* Dragon Reborn.

Dragon Reborn: According to prophecy and legend the Dragon will be born again at mankind's greatest hour of need to save the world. This is not something people look forward to, both because the prophecies say the Dragon Reborn will bring a new Breaking to the world, and because Lews Therin Kinslayer, the Dragon, is a name to make men shudder, even more than three thousand years after his death. *See also* Dragon, the; Dragon, false.

Dragon's Fang, the: A stylized mark, usually black, in the shape of a teardrop balanced on its point. Scrawled on the door of a house, it is an accusation of evil against the people inside.

Dragonwall, the: another name for the Spine of the World. *See also* Spine of the World, the.

Dreadlords: Those men and women who, able to channel the One Power, went over to the Shadow during the Trolloc Wars, acting as commanders of the Trolloc forces.

Easar; King Easar of House Togita *(EE-zar; toh-GHEE-tah):* King of Shienar. His sign is a white hart, which according to Shienaran custom is held also to be a sign of Shienar along with the Black Hawk.

Elaida *(eh-LY-dah):* An Aes Sedai of the Red Ajah who advises Queen Morgase of Andor. A woman of almost infinite desire for power, who believes that she knows the future.

Elayne *(ee-LAIN):* Queen Morgase's daughter, the Daughter-Heir to the Throne of Andor. Her sign is a golden lily.

Else; Else Grinwell *(EHLZ GRIHN-wehl):* A farmer's daughter met on the Caemlyn Road.

Eyeless, the: *See* Myrddraal.

Fade: *See* Myrddraal

Fain, Padan *(FAIN, PAHD-ahn):* A peddler who arrives in Emond's Field just before Winternight.

Far Dareis Mai *(FAHR DAH-rize MY):* Literally, in the Old Tongue, "Maidens of the Spear." One of a number of warrior societies of the Aiel; unlike any of the others, it admits women and only women. A Maiden may not marry and remain in the society, nor may she fight while carrying a child. Any child born to a Maiden is given to another woman to raise, in such a way that no one knows who the child's mother was. (Part of the ritual ceremony by which a woman becomes a Maiden goes as follows: "You may belong to no man, nor may any man belong to you, nor any child. The spear is your lover, your child, and your life.") These children are treasured, for it is prophesied that a child born of a Maiden will unite the clans and return the Aiel to the greatness they knew during the Age of Legends.

Farstrider, Jain *(JAY-ihn):* A hero of the northern lands who journeyed to many lands and had many adventures; the author of several books, as well as being the subject of books and stories. He vanished in 981 NE, after returning from a trip into the Great Blight which some say had taken him all the way to Shayol Ghul.

First Prince of the Sword: Title normally held by the eldest brother of the Queen of Andor, who has been trained since childhood to command the Queen's armies in time of war and to be her adviser in time of peace. If the Queen has no surviving brother, she will appoint someone to the title.

fist: The basic military unit of the Trollocs, varying in number; always more than one hundred, but never more than two hundred. A fist is usually, but not always, commanded by a Myrddraal.

Five Powers, the: There are threads to the One Power, and each person who can channel the One Power usually can grasp some threads better than others. These threads are named according to the sorts of things that can be done using them—Earth, Air (sometimes called Wind), Fire, Water, and Spirit—and are called the Five Powers. Any wielder of the One Power usually will have a greater degree of strength with one, or possibly two, of these, and lesser strength in the others. Some few may have great strength with three, but since the Age of Legends no one has had great strength with all five. Even then this was extremely rare. The degree of strength can vary greatly between individuals, so that some who can channel are much stronger than others. Performing specific acts with the One Power requires ability in one or more of the Five Powers. For example, starting or controlling a fire requires Fire, and affecting the weather requires Air and Water, while Healing requires Water and Spirit. While Spirit was found equally in men and in women, great ability with Earth and/or Fire was found much more often among men, with Water and/or Air among women. There were exceptions, but it was so often so that Earth and Fire came to be regarded as male Powers, Air and Water as female. Generally, no ability is considered stronger than any other, though there is a saying among Aes Sedai: "There is no rock so strong that water and wind cannot wear it away, no fire so fierce that water cannot quench it or wind snuff it out." It should be noted this saying came into use long after the last male Aes Sedai was dead. Any equivalent saying among male Aes Sedai is long lost.

Flame of Tar Valon: The symbol of Tar Valon and the Aes

Sedai. A stylized representation of a flame, a white teardrop with the point upward.

Forsaken, the: Name given to thirteen of the most powerful Aes Sedai ever known, who went over to the Dark One during the War of the Shadow in return for the promise of immortality. According to both legend and fragmentary records, they were imprisoned along with the Dark One when his prison was resealed. Their names were Aginor, Asmodean, Balthamel, Be'lal, Demandred, Graendal, Ishamael, Lanfear, Mesaana, Moghedien, Rahvin, Sammael and Semirhage. These names are still used to frighten children.

Foolday: a festival celebrated in the fall where people wear masks and play pranks, and everyone exchanges sweets and small pastries. Everyone's role is changed about, so that servants give orders and those whom the servants work for must themselves serve. The silliest and most foolish man and woman are crowned as King Fool and Queen Fool, and for that day everyone must do as they say.

Galad (gah-LAHD): See Damodred, Lord Galadedrid.

Gawyn (GAH-wihn): Queen Morgase's son, Elayne's brother, who will be First Prince of the Sword when Elayne ascends the throne. His sign is a white boar.

gentling: The act, performed by Aes Sedai, of shutting off a male who can channel from the One Power forever. This is necessary because any man who learns to channel will go insane from the taint upon *saidin* and will almost certainly do horrible things with the Power in his madness. A man who has been gentled can still sense the True Source, but he cannot touch it. Whatever madness has come before gentling is arrested by the act of gentling, but not cured by it, and if it is done soon enough death can be averted. Men who are gentled seldom want to live, though, and they seldom live long.

Ghealdan (GHEL-dahn): A small country east of the Mountains of Mists and south of Andor. Its capital city is Jehannah. The sign of Ghealdan is three silver stars, one above and two below, on a field of red.

gleeman: A traveling storyteller, musician, juggler, tumbler and all-around entertainer. Known by their trademark cloaks of many-colored patches, they perform mainly in the villages and smaller towns, since larger towns and cities have other entertainments available, though occasionally they may be hired by nobles or wealthy merchants to provide rustic amusement.

Great Blight, the: A region in the far north, entirely corrupted by the Dark One. A haunt of Trollocs, Myrddraal, and other creatures of the Dark One.

Great Hunt of the Horn, the: A cycle of stories concerning the legendary search for the Horn of Valere, in the years between the end of the Trolloc Wars and the beginning of the War of the Hundred Years. If told in their entirety, the cycle would take many days.

Great Lord of the Dark: The name by which Darkfriends refer to the Dark One, claiming that to use his true name would be blasphemous.

Great Pattern, the: The Wheel of Time weaves the Patterns of the Ages into the Great Pattern, which is the whole of existence and reality, past, present and future. Also known as the Lace of Ages. *See also* Pattern of an Age; Wheel of Time.

Great Serpent: A symbol for time and eternity, believed to have been ancient before the Age of Legends began, consisting of a serpent eating its own tail. A gold finger-ring made in the form of the Great Serpent is the sign of a woman who has trained in the White Tower.

Halfman: *See* Myrddraal.

Hall of the Servants: (1) In the Age of Legends, the guild that controlled and regulated all those who could channel. (2) The building that housed the guild. The main Hall of the Servants was in Paaran Disen, but all cities and most villages had branches.

Hawkwing, Artur: A legendary king who united all the lands west of the Spine of the World, forging the nations that had risen out of the ruins of the Trolloc Wars into one. He even sent armies across the Aryth Ocean, but all contact with these was lost at his death, which set off the War of the Hundred Years. Although loved and respected by the common people, every monument to him was destroyed during the War of a Hundred years. His sign was a golden hawk in flight. *See also* War of the Hundred Years.

Heartfang; Heartsbane: *See* Dark One.

heartstone: An indestructible substance created during the Age of Legends. Any known force used in an attempt to break it is absorbed, making heartstone stronger.

Horn of Valere *(vah-LEER):* The legendary object of the Great Hunt of the Horn. The Horn supposedly can call back dead heroes from the grave to fight against the Shadow.

Hundred Companions, the: According to legend, the hundred male Aes Sedai, among the most powerful of the Age of Legends, who, led by Lews Therin Telamon, launched the final stroke that ended the War of the Shadow by sealing the Dark One back into his prison. The Dark One's counterstroke tainted *saidin*; the Hundred Companions went mad and began the Breaking of the World.

Illian *(IHL-lee-ahn):* A great port on the Sea of Storms, capital city of the nation of the same name. The capital often is called simply "the City" by Illianers. The sign of the nation of Illian is nine golden bees on a field of dark green.

Ingtar; Lord Ingtar of House Shinowa *(IHNG-tahr; shih-NOH-wah):* A Shienaran warrior met at Fal Dara.

Kandor *(KANH-dohr):* One of the Borderlands. The sign of Kandor is a rearing red horse on a field of pale green.

Kinch, Hyam *(KIHNCH, HY-ahm):* A farmer met on the Caemlyn Road.

Ko'bal *(KOH-bahl):* See Trollocs.

Lace of Ages: See Great Pattern, the.

Laman *(LAY-mahn):* A king of Cairhien, of House Damodred, who lost his throne and life in the Aiel War.

Lan; al'Lan Mandragoran *(AHL-LAN man-DRAG-or-an):* A warrior from the north; Moiraine's companion and Warder. A man of many secrets and old pains.

Leafblighter: See Dark One.

league: A measure of distance equal to four miles. *See also* mile.

Luc; Lord Luc of House Mantear *(LUKE, MAN-tee-ahr):* Tigraine's brother, who would have been her First Prince of the Sword when she ascended the throne. His disappearance in the Great Blight is believed to be in some way connected to Tigraine's later disappearance. His sign was a golden acorn.

Lurk *(LUHRK):* See Myrddraal.

Machera, Elyas *(mah-CHEER-ah, ee-LY-ahs):* A man encountered by Perrin and Egwene in the forest.

***Mahdi** (MAH-dee):* In the Old Tongue, "Seeker." Title of the leader of a Tuatha'an caravan.

***Malkier** (mal-KEER):* A nation, once one of the Borderlands, now consumed by the Blight. The sign of Malkier was a golden crane in flight.

***Mandarb** (MAHN-dahrb):* In the Old Tongue, "Blade."

***Manetheren** (mahn-EHTH-ehr-ehn):* One of the Ten Nations that made the Second Covenant, and also the capital city of that nation. Both city and nation were utterly destroyed in the Trolloc Wars.

***Maradon** (MAH-rah-don):* The capital city of Saldaea.

***Merrilin, Thom** (MER-rih-lihn, TOM):* A gleeman who comes to Emond's Field to perform at Bel Tine. A man who is much more than he seems.

mile: A measure of distance equal to one thousand spans. Four miles make one league. *See also* span.

***Min** (MIN):* A young woman who can see things others cannot, encountered at the Stag and Lion in Baerlon.

***Moiraine** (mwah-RAIN):* A visitor to Emond's Field who arrives just before Winternight; an Aes Sedai of the Blue Ajah.

month: Under the Farede Calendar, a period consisting of twenty-eight days. There are thirteen months in a year. While the months have names—Taisham, Jumara, Saban, Aine, Adar, Saven, Amadaine, Tammaz, Maigdhal, Choren, Shaldine, Nesan, and Danu—these are seldom used except in official documents and by officials. For most people, using the seasons is good enough.

***Mordeth** (MOOR-death):* Councilor who turned the city of Aridhol to use Darkfriends' ways against the Darkfriends, thus bringing its destruction, and earning it a new name, Shadar Logoth. Only one thing survives in Shadar Logoth beside the hate that killed it, and that is Mordeth himself, bound in the ruins for two thousand years, waiting for someone to come whose soul he can consume and so take on new flesh.

***Morgase** (moor-GAYZ):* By Grace of the Light, Queen of Andor, High Seat of House Trakand (TRAHK-ahnd). Her sign is three golden keys. The sign of House Trakand is a silver keystone.

***Myrddraal** (MUHRD-draal):* Creatures of the Dark One, commanders of the Trollocs. Twisted offspring of Trollocs in

which the human stock used to create the Trollocs has re-
surfaced, but tainted by the evil that made the Trollocs. Phys-
ically they are like men except that they have no eyes, but
can see like eagles in light or dark. They have certain powers
stemming from the Dark One, including the ability to cause
paralyzing fear with a look and the ability to vanish wherever
there are shadows, traveling from one shadow to another far
away. One of their few known weaknesses is that they are
reluctant to cross running water. They do not give a clear
reflection in mirrors, almost appearing blurred. In different
lands they are known by many names, among them Halfmen,
the Eyeless, Shadowman, Lurk and Fade.

Ogier *(OH-gear):* (1) A non-human race, characterized by great
height (ten feet is average for adult males), broad, almost
snout-like noses, and long, tufted ears. They live in areas
called *stedding*. Their separation from these *stedding* after
the Breaking of the World (a time called the Exile by the
Ogier) resulted in what is called the Longing; an Ogier who
is too long out of the *stedding* sickens and dies. Widely
known as wondrous stone-masons who built the great human
cities after the Breaking, they consider stonework simply
something learned during the Exile and not as important as
tending the trees of the *stedding*, especially the towering
Great Trees. Except for stonework, they rarely leave their
stedding and typically have little contact with humankind.
Knowledge of them among humans is sparse, and many believe Ogier to be only legends. Although believed to be a
pacific people and extremely slow to anger, some old stories
say they fought alongside humans in the Trolloc Wars, and
call them implacable enemies. By and large, they are extremely fond of knowledge, and their books and stories often
contain information lost to humans. A typical Ogier life-span
is at least three to four times that of a human. (2) Any individual of that non-human race. *See also* Breaking of the
World; *stedding*.

One Power, the: The power drawn from the True Source. The
vast majority of people are completely unable to learn to
channel the One Power. A very small number can be taught
to channel, and an even tinier number have the ability inborn.
For these few, there is no need to be taught; they will touch

the True Source and channel the Power whether they want to or not, perhaps without even realizing what they are doing. This inborn ability usually manifests itself in late adolescence or early adulthood. If control is not taught, or self-learned (extremely difficult, with a success rate of only one in four), death is certain. Since the Time of Madness, no man has been able to channel the Power without eventually going completely, horribly mad; and then, even if he has learned some control, dying from a wasting sickness which causes the sufferer to rot alive, a sickness caused, as is the madness, by the Dark One's taint on *saidin*. For a woman the death that comes without control if the Power is less horrible, but it is death just the same. Aes Sedai search for girls with the inborn ability as much to save their lives as to increase Aes Sedai numbers, and for men with it in order to stop the terrible things they inevitably do with the Power in their madness. *See also* channel; Time of Madness; True Source.

Pattern of an Age: The Wheel of Time weaves the threads of human lives into the Pattern of an Age, which forms the substance of reality for that Age; also known as Age Lace.

Questioners, the: An order within the Children of the Light. Their avowed purposes are discovering the truth in disputations and uncovering Darkfriends. In the search for truth and the Light, as they see it, they are even more zealous than the Children of the Light as a whole. Their normal method of inquiry is by torture; their normal attitude that they know the truth already and must only make their victim confess to it. The Questioners refer to themselves as the Hand of the Light, and at times act as if they were entirely separate from the Children and the Council of the Anointed, which commands the Children. The head of the Questioners is the High Inquisitor, who sits on the Council of the Anointed.

Red Ajah: *See* Ajah.

Ring of Tamyrlin *(TAHM-ehr-lin):* a legendary ring, believed mythical by most people, worn by the leader of the Aes Sedai during the Age of Legends. Stories about the Ring of Tamyrlin include that it was an *angreal* or *sa'angreal* or *ter'angreal* of immense power. It supposedly was named after the first person to learn how to tap into the Source and channel the One Power, and in some tales, was actually made by that man or woman. Despite what many Aes Sedai say, no one knows whether it was a man or a woman who first learned to channel. Some believe that the present title of Amyrlin is a corruption of Tamyrlin.

sa'angreal (SAH-ahn-GREE-ahl): An extremely rare object which allows an individual to channel much more of the One Power than would otherwise be possible or safe. A *sa'angreal* is like unto, but much, much more powerful than, an *angreal*. Remnants of the Age of Legends, the means of their making is no longer known.

saidar; saidin (sah-ih-DAHR; sah-ih-DEEN): See True Source.

Saldaea (sahl-DAY-ee-ah): One of the Borderlands. The sign of Saldaea is three silver fish on a field of dark blue.

Sea Folk: An informal name for the Atha'an Miere (ah-thah-AHN mee-EHR), which translates from the Old Tongue as "People of the Sea," or "Sea Folk." Inhabitants of islands in the Aryth (AH-rihth) Ocean and the Sea of Storms, they spend little time on those islands, living most of their lives on their ships. Most seaborne trade is carried by the Sea Folk's ships.

Second Covenant: another name for the Covenant of the Ten Nations. Obviously there must have been a First Covenant for this to have been the Second, but the nature of the First and when it was made are unknown. *See* Covenant of the Ten Nations.

Shadar Logoth (SHAH-dahr LOH-goth): In the Old Tongue, "the Place Where the Shadow Waits." A city, once called Aridhol and capital of the nation of the same name, now abandoned and shunned since the Trolloc Wars. Also called "Shadow's Waiting."

Shadowman: See Myrddraal.

Shai'tan (SHAH-ih-TAN): See Dark One.

Shayol Ghul (SHAY-ol GHOOL): A mountain in the Blasted Lands, the site of the Dark One's prison.

Shepherd of the Night: See Dark One.

Sheriam (SHEER-ee-ahm): An Aes Sedai, of the Blue Ajah.

Shienar (shy-NAHR): One of the Borderlands. The sign of Shienar is a stooping black hawk.

shoufa (SHOO-fah): A garment of the Aiel, a cloth, usually of the color of sand or rock, that wraps around the head and neck, leaving only the face bare.

Sightburner: *See* Dark One.

Span: A measure of distance equal to two paces. A thousand spans make a mile.

Spine of the World, the: A towering mountain range, with only a few passes, which separates the Aiel Waste from the lands to the west. Also called the Dragonwall.

stedding *(STEHD-ding):* An Ogier homeland. Many *stedding* have been abandoned since the Breaking of the World. They are portrayed in story and legend as havens, and with reason. They are shielded in some way, no longer understood, so that within them no Aes Sedai can channel the One Power, nor even sense that the True Source exists. Attempts to wield the One Power from outside a *stedding* have no effect inside a *stedding* boundary. No Trolloc will enter a *stedding* unless driven, and even a Myrddraal will do so only at the greatest need and then with the greatest reluctance and distaste. Even Darkfriends, if truly dedicated, feel uncomfortable within a *stedding.*

Stone of Tear: The immense fortress guarding the city of Tear. Said to be the earliest fortress built after the Time of Madness, and said by some to have been built *during* the Time of Madness. *See also* Tear.

Sunday: A feast day and festival in midsummer, widely celebrated. Sunday is unusual in that, for those who actually refer to calendars, it does not count as a day of the month in which it occurs.

tabac *(tah-BAHK):* A noxious weed, widely cultivated. The leaves of it, when dried and cured, are burned in wooden holders called "pipes," the fumes being inhaled, which is a nasty habit

Tallanvor, Martyn *(TAHL-ahn-vohr, mahr-TEEN):* Guardsman-Lieutenant of the Queen's Guard; met in Caemlyn.

Ta'maral'ailen *(tah-MAHR-ahl-EYE-lehn):* in the Old Tongue, "Web of Destiny." *See ta'veren.*

Tanreall, Artur Paendrag *(tahn-REE-ahl, AHR-tuhr PAY-ehn-DRAG):* *See* Hawkwing, Artur.

Tar Valon *(TAHR VAH-lon):* A city on an island in the River

Erinin. The center of Aes Sedai power, and location of the
White Tower and the Amyrlin Seat.

ta'veren *(tah-VEER-ehn):* A person around whom the Wheel of
Time weaves all surrounding life-threads, to form a Web of
Destiny. *See also* Pattern of an Age.

Tear *(TEER):* (1) A nation on the Sea of Storms. (2) A great
seaport and the capital of the nation of the same name. The
city of Tear is often called simply "the City" by Tairens. The
sign of the nation of Tear is three white crescents on a field
of red and gold.

Telamon, Lews Therin *(TEHL-ah-mon, LOOZ THEH-rihn): See*
Dragon, the.

Thakan'dar *(thah-kahn-DAHR):* An eternally fog-shrouded val-
ley below the slopes of Shayol Ghul.

Tigraine *(tee-GRAIN):* As Daughter-Heir of Andor, she married
Taringail Damodred and bore his son Galadedrid. Her disappearance in 972 NE, shortly after her brother Luc vanished
in the Blight, led to the struggle in Andor called the Succession, and caused the events in Cairhien which eventually
brought on the Aiel War. Her sign was a woman's hand
gripping a thorny rose-stem with a white blossom.

Time of Madness: another name used for the Breaking of the
World. *See* Breaking of the World, the.

Tinkers: another name for the Tuatha'an. *See* Tuatha'an

Traveling People: another name for the Tuatha'an. *See* Tuatha'an

Tremalking *(treh-MAL-king):* largest of the Sea Folk islands. *See
also* Sea Folk.

Trolloc Wars: A series of wars, beginning about 1000 AB and
lasting more than three hundred years, during which Trolloc
armies ravaged the world. Eventually the Trollocs were slain
or driven back into the Great Blight, but some nations ceased
to exist, while others were almost depopulated. All records
of the time are fragmentary. *See also* Covenant of the Ten
Nations.

Trollocs *(TRAHL-lohks):* Creatures of the Dark One, created during the War of the Shadow. Huge in stature, vicious in the
extreme, they are a twisted blend of animal and human stock,
and kill for the pure pleasure of killing. Sly, deceitful and
treacherous, they can be trusted only by those they fear. They
are omnivorous and will eat any kind of meat, including hu-

man flesh and the flesh of other Trollocs. Largely of human origin, they are able to interbreed with humankind, but the offspring are usually stillborn, and those which are not often fail to survive. They are divided into tribe-like bands, chief among them being the Ahf'frait, Al'ghol, Bhan'sheen, Dha'vol, Dhai'mon, Dhjin'nen, Ghar'ghael, Ghob'lhin, Gho'hlem, Ghraem'lan, Ko'bal and the Kno'mon.

True Source: The driving force of the universe, which turns the Wheel of Time. It is divided into a male half (*saidin*) and a female half (*saidar*), which work at the same time with and against each other. Only a man can draw on *saidin* , only a woman on *saidar*. Since the beginning of the Time of Madness, *saidin* has been tainted by the Dark One's touch. *See also* One Power.

Tuatha'an (too-AH-thah-AHN): A wandering folk, also know as the Tinkers and as the Traveling People, who live in brightly painted wagons and follow a totally pacifist philosophy called the Way of the Leaf. A Tuatha'an will not do violence to another human being even to save his or her own life or the lives of loved ones. Things mended by Tinkers are often better than new, but the Tuatha'an are shunned by many villages because of stories that they steal children and try to convert young people to their beliefs.

Village Council: In most villages a group of men, elected by the townsmen and headed by a Mayor, who are responsible for making decisions which affect the village as a whole and for negotiating with the Councils of other villages over matters which affect the villages jointly. They are at odds with the Women's Circle in so many villages that this conflict is seen as almost traditional; it certainly appears in many stories, most humorous. *See also* Women's Circle.

War of the Hundred Years: A series of overlapping wars among constantly shifting alliances, precipitated by the death of Artur Hawkwing and the resulting struggle for his empire. It lasted from approximately FY 994 to FY 1117. The dates are uncertain because of the destruction of so many records, of which only fragments remain. The war depopulated large parts of the lands between the Aryth Ocean and the Aiel Waste, from the Sea of Storms to the Great Blight. The em-

pire of Artur Hawkwing was pulled apart, and the nations of
the present day were formed.

War of the Shadow: Also known as the War of Power, it ended
the Age of Legends. It began shortly after the attempt to free
the Dark One, and soon involved the whole world. In a world
where even the memory of war had been forgotten, every
facet of war was rediscovered, often twisted by the Dark
One's touch on the World, and the One Power was used as
a weapon. The war was ended by the resealing of the Dark
One into his prison.

Warder: A warrior bonded to an Aes Sedai. The bonding is a
thing of the One Power, and by it he gains such gifts as
quick healing, the ability to go long periods without food,
water or rest, and the ability to sense the taint of the Dark
One at a distance. So long as a Warder lives, the Aes Sedai
to whom he is bonded knows he is alive and in what direction
from her he is however far away, and when he dies she will
know the moment and manner of his death. The bond creates
a certain awareness in both Aes Sedai and Warder of the
physical and emotional condition of the other. While most
Ajahs believe an Aes Sedai may have one Warder bonded to
her at a time, the Red Ajah refuses to bond any Warders at
all, while the Green Ajah believes an Aes Sedai may bond
as many Warders as she wishes. Ethically the Warder must
accede to the bonding, but it has been known to be done
involuntarily. What the Aes Sedai gain from the bonding is
a closely-held secret. *See also* Aes Sedai.

Ways, the: Pathways from one *stedding* to another, grown from
the One Power during the Breaking of the World. A gift from
male Aes Sedai to the *stedding* in thanks for shelter from the
taint on *saidin*, they exist outside the normal confines of time
and space. A day's walking inside the Ways may carry the
traveler to a destination hundreds of miles away, but
strangely, sometimes a more distant place can be reached
more quickly than one that is nearer. The Ways appear to
consist of ramps, bridges and islands seemingly suspended
in the air unsupported. Each island has a stone, called a guiding, with directions in Ogier script for reaching various des-
tinations from that point. Once well-lit and beautiful, the
islands covered with grasses, flowers and fruit trees, the

Ways have deteriorated, growing dank and dim, and the islands are now only bare stone. It is believed that this is the result of the taint on *saidin,* which was used in the initial making of the Ways. The Ogier are said to possess a device, possibly a *ter'angreal,* which allowed them to make the Ways grow to other places, but this certainly has not been used since the Ways went dark.

Web of Destiny: A great change in the Pattern of an Age, centered around one or more people who are *ta'veren.*

week: Under the Farede Calendar, a period of time lasting ten days.

weight, units of: 10 ounces 1 pound; 10 pounds 1 stone; 10 stone 1 hundredweight; 10 hundredweight 1 ton.

Wheel of Time, the: Time is a wheel with seven spokes, each spoke an Age. As the Wheel turns, the Ages come and go, each leaving memories that fade to legend, then to myth, and are forgotten by the time that Age comes again. The Pattern of an Age is slightly different each time an Age comes, and each time it is subject to greater change, but each time it is the same Age. Not a repeat of exactly what went before, when that Age last came, but close enough in its general outline that it might seem the same at a glance.

White Ajah: *See* Ajah.

White Tower: (1) An immense tower of white stone, constructed with the One Power, which rises in the center of Tar Valon. It is the palace of the Amyrlin Seat and the center of Aes Sedai power, with parts of it belonging to the different Ajahs. (2) The extensive grounds surrounding the immense tower described in (1).

Wisdom: In villages of Andor, a woman chosen by the Women's Circle to sit in the Circle for her knowledge of such things as healing and foretelling the weather, as well as for common good sense. Usually a position of great responsibility and authority, both actual and implied. She is generally considered the equal of the Mayor, and in some villages his superior, and almost always is considered the leader of the Women's Circle. Unlike the Mayor, she is chosen for life, and it is very rare for a Wisdom to be removed from office before her death. Almost traditionally in conflict with the Mayor, to the extent that such conflicts often appear in hu-

morous stories. In lands other than Andor, Wisdoms are
known by other names, such as Wise Woman or Adviser or
Reader, but in one form or another, they exist everywhere.
See also Women's Circle.

Women's Circle: In Andor, a group of women elected by the
women of a village, responsible for deciding such matters as
are considered solely women's responsibility (for example,
when to plant the crops and when to harvest). Equal in authority to the Village council, with clearly delineated lines
and areas of responsibility. Frequently at odds with the Village Council; this conflict is often at the heart of humorous
stories. In lands other than Andor, the Women's Circle is
often known by another name, such as the Ring or the Gathering, but in one form or another, they exist everywhere. *See
also* Village Council.

year: Under the Farede Calendar, a period time consisting of thirteen months, each of twenty-eight days.

"BUT IT WAS *A* BEGINNING."
⌐ *Robert Jordan*

For the first time, fans can explore all that lies between the Aryth Ocean and the Spine of the World . . . and more. The ***Wheel of Time*** ™ ***Roleplaying Game,*** based on the d20 system, allows you to use information from every book to date and even takes you places you have yet to experience. Leave no stone unturned. Create your own plot twists. Most importantly, begin and end however and wherever you see fit.

Available at a book or game store near you.

www.wizards.com/wheeloftime

Wheel of Time is a trademark of Robert Jordan.
© Robert Jordan game mechanic.
Wizards of the Coast and d20 logos are trademarks
of Wizards of the Coast, Inc.
© 2001 Wizards

The Best in Fantasy

Robert Jordan • *The Wheel of Time*

Book One: *The Eye of the World*

0-812-51181-6 • $6.99 ($8.99 CAN) / in hardcover: 0-312-85009-3 • $27.95

"Jordan writes with the stark vision of light and darkness, and sometimes childish sense of wonder, that permeates J.R.R. Tolkien's works. His style is undebatably his own.

—*Pittsburgh Press*

Book Two: *The Great Hunt*

0-812-51772-5 • $7.99 ($9.99 CAN) / in hardcover: 0-312-85140-5 • $27.95

"Those who like fantasy can rejoice. This is the genuine article." —John Lee, author of *The Unicorn Solution*

Book Three: *The Dragon Reborn*

0-812-51371-1 • $7.99 ($9.99 CAN) / in hardcover: 0-312-85248-7 • $27.95

"One of *the* books to read this year."

—*Science Fiction Review*

Book Four: *The Shadow Rising*

0-812-51373-8 • $7.99 ($9.99 CAN) / in hardcover: 0-312-85431-5 • $27.95 ($39.95 CAN)

"Complex, exciting. One of the best yet."

—*The Post and Courier* (Charleston, SC)

Book Five: *The Fires of Heaven*
0-812-55030-7 • $7.99 ($9.99 CAN) / in hardcover: 0-312-85427-7 • $25.95 ($29.95 CAN)

"This volume, indeed the whole saga, surpasses all but a few of its peers." —*Booklist*

Book Six: *Lord of Chaos*
0-812-51375-4 • $7.99 ($9.99 CAN) / in hardcover: 0-312-85428-5 • $27.95 ($39.95 CAN)

"A great read....Some surprising new developments....I can't recommend starting anywhere but at the beginning, but the volumes only get richer as they go along." —*Locus*

Book Seven: *A Crown of Swords*
0-812-55028-5 • $7.99 ($9.99 CAN) / in hardcover: 0-312-85767-5 • $27.95 ($34.95 CAN)

"Jordan's preeminent saga [has] remained remarkably rich....Will not disappoint." —*Booklist*

Book Eight: *The Path of Daggers*
0-812-55029-3 • $7.99 ($9.99 CAN) / in hardcover: 0-312-85769-1 • $27.95 ($38.95 CAN)

"For sheer imagination and storytelling skill . . . *The Wheel of Time* rivals Tolkien's *The Lord of the Rings*."
              —*Publishers Weekly* (starred review)

Book Nine: *Winter's Heart*
0-812-57558-X • $7.99 ($9.99 CAN) / in hardcover: 0-312-86425-6 • $29.95 ($41.95 CAN)

"The plot continues to thicken and intrigue, as always, runs rampant." —*Booklist*

All these books are available in both hardcover and paperback. If you do not see them on display, ask your bookseller to order them for you.

A SOUNDTRACK FOR

THE WHEEL OF TIME™

PERFORMED, PRODUCED AND
WRITTEN BY ROBERT BERRY

Music Inspired by Robert Jordan's Best Selling Series "The Wheel Of Time"

MA-9052-2

"**M**USIC HAS ALWAYS BEEN AN INTEGRAL PART OF MY WRITING. NOT ONLY DO I WRITE TO MUSIC, BUT I THINK OF MY WRITING IN TERMS OF MUSIC. THE WORDS MUST FLOW IN CERTAIN RHYTHMS, AND THE STORY HAS ITS OWN RHYTHMS. IN A WAY, IT'S LIKE ORCHESTRATING THE CHARACTERS."

ROBERT JORDAN / AUTHOR ·
"THE WHEEL OF TIME" SERIES

COVER ARTWORK BY DARRELL K SWEET

magna carta

Available at Progressive CD stores. Or send $16.98 for each
CD to Magna Carta. Outside the USA add $5.00 per disc.
Magna Carta, PMB 1820, 208 E 51st St, New York, NY 10022-6500.
Credit card orders can be faxed to (716) 381-0658.
Email: magcart@aol.com
Visit the Magna Carta website at www.magnacarta.net